THE
SUMMER
BOOK CLUB

SUSAN MALLERY

THE
SUMMER
BOOK CLUB

CANARY STREET PRESS

CANARY
STREET
PRESS™

Recycling programs
for this product may
not exist in your area.

ISBN-13: 978-1-335-44866-8
ISBN-13: 978-1-335-45448-5 (International edition)

The Summer Book Club

For questions and comments about the quality of this book, please contact us
at CustomerService@Harlequin.com.

TM is a trademark of Harlequin Enterprises ULC.

Canary Street Press
22 Adelaide St. West, 41st Floor
Toronto, Ontario M5H 4E3, Canada
CanaryStPress.com

Printed in U.S.A.

Andrea and Jessica—a double thank-you for sharing delightful pictures and information on the adorable Mochi. She was the inspiration for Tinsel in *Home Sweet Christmas*. I hope you enjoyed her antics and her wardrobe! A sweetie like her needs to be fabulous. Due to a mix-up, instead of getting that book dedicated to you, you get this one. There's no Tinsel in this one, but thank you for lending me your last names!

one

"How is it I'm thirty-seven years old and I still get a knot in my stomach when I get a note from the teacher, asking me to stop by?" Laurel Richards held out her cell phone. "Or in this case, a text."

Paris grinned. "We never outgrow our fear of authority. We should, but we don't. Which teacher?"

"Jagger's homeroom teacher. I don't get it. Neither of the girls is a troublemaker and it's only three weeks until school's out."

She tried to ignore the unsettled feeling in her stomach. As far as she knew, her twelve-year-old was happy, had plenty of friends and was doing great in school. She was wrapping up seventh grade, had mostly As and Bs and, perhaps until today, had never been in trouble at school.

"Do you think it's really bad?" she asked.

Paris, a pretty brunette with hazel eyes and an easy smile, rolled her eyes. "I love you, but if I had psychic powers I would use them to win the lottery. Jagger's a sweetie. Maybe the teacher wants to give her an award. Don't assume the worst."

Laurel pressed a hand to her belly, wishing the yucky feeling would go away. "You're right." She quickly texted, confirming she would be at the school at 2:20. "Maybe it isn't bad at all. Maybe it's great. Maybe they've decided Jagger is gifted and should start college in the fall. Not that I've saved enough to pay for it. I was supposed to have five more years. Oh, wait. If she's that smart, she'll get a scholarship. Problem solved!"

Paris's humor returned. "I'm pretty sure it's not going to be about her skipping the next five years of school."

They both laughed before returning their attention to the crate of strawberries Paris had set on her battered desk. Each berry was a beautiful deep red and large, with that perfect shape. Next to the crate was an open box with scraps of fabric, glue, toothpicks, doll clothes and random pieces of doll furniture.

"I have the stage from when I did *Romeo and Juliet* with zucchini last summer," Paris said, digging through the box. "I think I saved the costumes."

"Zucchini costumes aren't going to fit strawberries." Laurel paused. "Weirdest thing I've ever said."

"Last time we brainstormed about my fruit of the month, we decided on dancing asparagus. That was pretty weird."

"But effective."

The Los Lobos Farm Stand, a fruit and vegetable stand by the highway in Los Lobos, had been in Paris's family for three generations and was popular with both locals and tourists. Laurel was helping her friend expand her presence on social media. Part of that was a featured fruit—or vegetable—of the month. Sometimes the item chosen was simply photographed but other times Paris went all out with props, costumes and staging. The first strawberries of the season seemed event worthy.

"So we're agreed," Paris said, motioning to the crate. "A strawberry concert."

Laurel nodded as she opened her backpack. She pulled out a sheet of paper printed with six tiny stand microphones. They would cut those out and glue them onto toothpicks. The stage Paris already had would be the backdrop. They would dress the strawberries, set them in front of the microphones and take pictures for all the fruit stand's accounts. Once that was done, the stage would be placed on a shelf by the fresh flowers. Customers liked seeing it in person and getting their pictures taken beside it.

Two hours later six strawberries had been dressed in bits of lace or covered in glitter. Three sported pipe cleaner headpieces. The little microphones were in place and they'd used miniature cactus and wisps of decorative grasses to fill in the back of the stage.

"'Strawberry Fields Forever,'" Paris said with a laugh.

"It's going to be a hit."

Laurel collected the halo lights she'd brought from her barn and set them up around the stage, then took about thirty pictures. They saved the dozen or so best ones.

"I'll write the backstory tonight," Paris said. "And post everything tomorrow. What are you going to do between now and 2:20?"

"Panic. Tell myself not to panic. I might also worry a little."

Paris hugged her. "Jagger isn't in trouble. It's not in her nature. Have a little faith."

"I have a text from her teacher. Panic is required. It's in the parent handbook."

"Then you need an updated version." Paris walked her to her minivan. "Let me know what happens."

"You'll be the first. We're still on for book club?"

"You know it. I'm reading and loving *Mackenzie's Mountain*."

"Me, too." Laurel grinned. "I mean, come on. Wolf Mackenzie? I have no interest in dating but there's something about that man."

Paris sighed. "He's sexy and powerful. I just know he has a really low, velvet-on-chocolate voice. The man makes me swoon and I think we can all agree I'm not the swooning type."

"It's the power of a good writer with a great story. Talk soon."

Laurel left and drove back to her place, bypassing the big Victorian where she lived with her daughters and heading for her oversize barn. The massive structure was solid enough with a good roof. It needed paint and possibly new windows, but her priorities this past year had been getting more shelving and upgrading her shipping area, while also refurbishing the mother-in-law apartment in her house so she could rent it out and get some income from the unused space. Windows and paint were on next year's list.

She spent the time until she had to leave for the middle school taking pictures of items she was ready to list on eBay, including several pieces of carnival glass she'd bought at an estate sale in Riverside. Three photo boxes sat on a counter on the west side of her barn. Two were large enough to hold a decent-sized lamp or piece of artwork. One had a white background, the other black. Her third photo box was smaller, for things like jewelry or glassybaby votive candle holders with the advantage of different colored backdrops.

She focused on getting the right shots, using a ruler to show the size. The largest carnival glass platter had a small chip on the bottom and she shot it from a foot away, as well as close-up. When she posted the pictures, she would add an arrow so no one missed the chip. Her customers should be delighted by what they bought, not disappointed.

She left in plenty of time for her appointment and, after signing in at the front desk, walked into Mrs. Krysty's empty homeroom class at exactly 2:19.

The fortysomething teacher with prematurely gray hair smiled as soon as she saw Laurel.

"You look panicked."

"I'm having some breathing issues," Laurel admitted lightly, shaking the other woman's hand before sitting in the chair next to her desk. "I don't usually get asked in for either of my girls."

"That's right. Jagger has a younger sister."

"Ariana. She's ten. She'll be in middle school next fall."

"We look forward to having her." Mrs. Krysty rested her

hands on the desk. "I want to start by saying that Jagger's doing well in all her classes. I spoke to her other teachers myself and they think she's an excellent student. She's friendly, cooperative, bright and well-liked."

The other woman smiled. "She seems to be a natural leader and has no trouble expressing her opinion."

Laurel told herself to relax, that so far nothing bad was being shared—only she was pretty sure there was a giant "but" in her future.

"There have been a few odd comments," Mrs. Krysty said slowly.

Odd comments? "About what?"

"It's more a who." She paused. "About men, actually."

"Men? What does that mean?"

"Last week, in her European history class, the teacher showed how the Cold War was linked to World War II and other events of the past hundred years. Jagger said wars were started by men and if they would mind their own business, the world would be a better place."

Mrs. Krysty offered a faint smile. "Conversation became heated and Jagger and another student got into a shouting match. Jagger told him that men have always subjugated women, that they only care about themselves and not their families, and for him to give her one example of a woman starting a war. Any war."

"She's not wrong," Laurel murmured. "Women haven't been in power until recently so they couldn't start wars, but I'm guessing that isn't your point."

"No. In her social studies class they were discussing different forms of courtship. How some customs are similar to what we're familiar with and some are not. The example was that even in modern India, many couples use matchmakers."

Mrs. Krysty put on her reading glasses and glanced at her notes. "Jagger said she was never getting married because men can't be trusted and always let you down. Women would be better off living together in groups and only letting in men so they can have babies, then locking them out."

She dropped her glasses to the desk. "I understand you and Jagger's father are recently divorced and that's always traumatic for the children, but this seems like more than that. Jagger seems to dislike and mistrust men."

"That can't be true," Laurel said automatically, as confused by what her daughter meant as by where she'd developed that attitude. "She's never said anything to me."

At least she didn't think she had. It wasn't as if they sat around discussing gender roles and whether or not men made good fathers in general. She knew Jagger was furious with her dad for leaving and that her oldest had become protective, but not to the point where she didn't like men.

"What about the male role models in her life?" Mrs. Krysty asked. "How is she getting along with them?"

"Male role models?"

"Yes. An uncle, or grandfather. A family friend. Perhaps someone you're seeing."

"You mean am I dating? God, no. Not only does love turn women into idiots, the last thing I need in my life is some man screwing up everything that I've…" Her voice trailed off as horror swept through her.

"I would never say that in front of her," she added quickly, then wondered if she was telling the truth. Because it was very possible that she had. Or that Jagger had overheard her complaining to Paris. She knew her daughters had heard her crying when Beau had walked out, even though she'd tried to keep her pain from them.

As for men in their lives, well, there was…

She searched her mind. There were no male relatives. Her dad was living the dream in Alaska and barely kept in touch with her or her daughters. Her mother, who'd moved to Ohio for her second husband, and to Vermont for her third, rarely visited and when she did, left husband number four behind.

Laurel was an only child, and both her parents had been onlies, so no cousins or uncles.

"All the people in my life are women," she said slowly, desperately searching for one lone male exception. "My employees are women, my best friend is a woman. In fact, all my friends are women." She looked at Mrs. Krysty. "There's Bandit, but he doesn't really count."

"A relative?"

"My friend's dog."

The teacher's expression of understanding shifted to disapproval. "No, a dog doesn't count."

"She likes her two male teachers," Laurel said, trying not to sound frantic.

Mrs. Krysty relaxed. "Yes, she does. And she usually gets along well with the boys in her class. I checked with her teachers and she's been fine in all her coed group projects."

The teacher offered a faint smile. "I wanted to let you know what has been happening. At this point, I don't think Jagger requires immediate intervention, but there does seem to be a trend and I thought you should be aware. Perhaps if she were around a few men in her life. Husbands of your friends, a pastor, a neighbor, fathers of her friends. Just seeing them doing ordinary things like cooking on a barbecue might go a long way to helping her see that we all have value in our society."

Laurel nodded, thinking none of her friends were married and at the nondenominational church they sporadically attended, the pastor was—wait for it—a woman. There simply weren't any men to hang around.

"You're right," Laurel said firmly. "It's a matter of expanding her social circle. In a safe way, of course." She offered a smile that felt a little fake, mostly because she was upset, embarrassed, concerned and trying to tell herself she hadn't screwed up her daughter.

"Now that you've made me aware of the problem, we can work on it together."

"Excellent." Mrs. Krysty offered a more sincere smile. "Jagger is a wonderful girl. Such a pleasure to have in class."

"That's what every mom wants to hear."

She said her goodbyes, signed out at the front desk, then walked to her bright red Pacifica minivan. Once inside, she leaned her head back, closed her eyes, and let the shame and horror wash over her.

This was her fault. Okay, hers and Beau's. Both girls had taken their father's abandonment hard, but while Ariana had cried for her daddy every day for three months, Jagger had gotten quiet and mad.

But it was more than that, Laurel thought. It was listening to her complain about Beau in particular and men in general. It was hearing sisters Marcy and Darcy Barnes, the two women who worked for her, trash all their ex-husbands, including Laurel's father—her daughters' grandfather—who had, yes, married each of them, one after the other. Both marriages had ended in divorce.

Mrs. Krysty was right. If Laurel didn't do something, her daughter would grow up hating men. It wasn't right, it wasn't healthy. Her relationship choices should come from a place of confidence and mental strength. Not from a twisted view of the world.

There were good guys out there, Laurel thought. She personally didn't know any, but there were rumors they existed. She just had to find a couple and...and...

"What?" she said out loud. "Ask them to be my friend?" There was no way she was interested in dating anyone.

She glanced at her watch and saw she was going to be late getting home. Not a problem as the girls went directly to the barn where they hung out with Marcy and Darcy, got spoiled a little before sitting down to do their homework. Still, she wanted to see her daughters and hold them tight.

Later, when they were in bed, she would come up with a plan to help them both see the world was filled with wonderful and diverse personalities, and that of course men could be good, kind and supportive. That there was no reason to hate them or think less of them. Men could be friends, they could be trusted.

The only problem, Laurel thought as she started the drive home, was first she had to convince herself.

two

"Come to Mama," Paris Zublena murmured, inspecting the crates of avocados. They were the right size—not too big, not too small. Good color. She would display them right out front.

She counted the crates before looking at Fred, her delivery guy. "All that's left are the heirloom tomatoes."

Fred shifted uneasily. "Yeah, well, I don't have those."

"I don't want to hear that. What happened?" She put her free hand on her hip. "Don't tell me someone bought them out from under me. I had an order."

"You did and the tomato guy said they weren't ready. Thursday for sure. They'll be ripe and here for weekend sales."

"They'd better be."

She'd saved space for the tomatoes. Now she would have to move things around.

"Thursday for sure," she said, noting her order form. "And I want thirty extra pounds."

"I can get you twenty."

"Sold."

Fred held out his tablet for her to sign. She scanned the screen, made sure he'd noted her twenty extra pounds of heirlooms, and scrawled her signature.

"See you Thursday," she said before calling for Bandit. The black-and-white border collie mix trotted over, his swishy tail wagging back and forth. He settled next to her as Fred pushed his now empty handcart toward his truck.

"No heirlooms for us," she told the dog. "We'll feature the sweet onions instead. I can put out recipe cards for onion jam."

Bandit tilted his head, as if considering the statement.

"I know," she said, walking toward the rear of the farm stand, her dog keeping pace with her. "We have more asparagus to move, but they've been up front for weeks now. We need something different."

The Los Lobos Farm Stand, otherwise known as LoLo's, sat on about an acre, just off Highway 1 on the feeder road. The main building was a long, low structure with plenty of display space. Parking was on the left and the garden section was on the right. Behind was a shaded picnic area and an open field. There were pony rides on summer weekends, a giant Christmas tree lot in December and community events in between.

The sign on top of the building featured dancing produce. Cold water was available for free and every Saturday afternoon amateur bakers sold their homemade wares out front.

Paris swung by the storage closet and dug out the box of printed recipe cards, along with the recipe card holder. As she headed for the main store, she passed Tim, her general manager and jack-of-all-trades.

"There weren't any heirlooms," she told him. "Let's move the sweet onions up front." She waved the recipe cards. "Onion jam is perfect for summer barbecues."

"Did one of those big organic stores buy out the supply?" he asked with a scowl. "They think they own the world."

"The tomato guy said they weren't ready. We'll get the order plus another twenty pounds on Thursday."

Tim grinned. "Just in time for the weekend rush."

"That's what I thought."

Together they began loading a rolling display with the sweet onions. Bandit kept watch, prepared to leap into action, should his help be needed. They'd just finished when a battered pickup followed by two equally patched-up sedans pulled into the parking lot. A flurry of grad students got out. Their professor, a tall, golden-haired god, who looked amazingly like a human version of the cartoon Hercules from the Disney movie, followed.

"Hey, Paris." He waved.

"Raphael." She managed to speak his name without sighing. Bandit raced over to get his pets.

"Heading back to the dig?" she asked.

Raphael nodded as he walked over. "Nearly every day this summer. This is my new crew. Five grad students and an overeager freshman."

Dr. Raphael Houston had started teaching at the university a year ago. He specialized in early American history and had been brought in to explore an ancient village discovered outside of town. Some old guy from back East owned the land. No one knew anything about him, but he'd given the university permission to excavate.

Paris wasn't interested in Raphael romantically. Not only didn't she trust herself in a relationship, there was zero chemistry between them. But she did enjoy the show. The man was unearthly gorgeous. Plus, seeing women act stupid around him was fun, too. Oh, and he was sweet to her dog, so she had to like him.

The seven of them loaded up on fresh fruit and juice from the cold case. Paris rang them up.

"See you tomorrow," Raphael called as he walked toward his truck.

A middle-age female customer dropped both potatoes she'd been holding as he strolled by. Paris held in a snort of laughter. Sometimes she really loved her job. She closed the cash register, ready to get on to the next task in her endless to-do list when she heard a familiar voice behind her.

"Hello, Paris."

Her heart stumbled on its next beat as panic raced through her. She wondered how Jonah could be here, while simultaneously hoping she was wrong about the speaker's identity or that she was having a mental breakdown and had only imagined the words.

She turned slowly. No breakdown, nor had she been mistaken. Standing right there—alive and well—was her ex-husband.

"Oh, um, hi."

She did her best to offer a happy-to-see-you smile with a touch of did-I-know-you-were-in-town and whisper of why-no-it-doesn't-bother-me-to-talk-to-you.

"Hi." He smiled back, looking much as he always had. Dark-haired with too-long bangs falling over his forehead. Glasses, a chiseled jaw and good shoulders. He was lean, unassuming and except for her friend Laurel, the one person on the planet who had seen her at her absolute worst. Unlike Laurel, he hadn't loved her anyway. Instead, he'd left her—walked out on their marriage and never looked back. Something for which, honest to God, she couldn't blame him.

"You must be here to visit your mom," she said brightly. "I haven't seen her in a couple of weeks." She frowned. "Or longer. How's she doing?"

Paris wasn't exactly friends with her ex–mother-in-law, but Los Lobos was a small town and they frequently ran into each other. Especially here at the farm stand. Once Paris had realized she alone was responsible for the end of her marriage, she'd made it a point to be friendly to the older woman. Jonah's mom had only been trying to help, even if it hadn't seemed like it at the time.

"Good. Well, she's having knee replacement surgery in two weeks. We're staying with her for a couple of months, until she's back to normal."

"I'm sure she appreciates that."

Paris spoke automatically, trying not to think about the "we" in question. They would include Jonah's son and his wife, aka the woman he'd fallen in love with after he'd left Paris. She'd never met her, but assumed she was lovely. Smart and funny. Sweet. No doubt she had a normal kind of personality. Sure she got mad, but she didn't scream or throw things or overturn a table at a restaurant because her order was wrong. She had probably never lost the man she'd loved because she couldn't control her vicious temper. She'd never once scared herself with fury that erupted without warning.

Paris deliberately took a mental step back from the images her thoughts had produced. She and Jonah had broken up ten-plus years ago. They'd both moved on and were different people now. At least she was. She'd gotten help, had worked hard and these days had the skills to deal with life's irritations. She was calm and in control. She wasn't who she had been.

At least that was what she told herself. She didn't always believe it.

"I thought I should stop by so you'd know I was here," he said. "In town."

Now her smile was genuine. "To lessen the shock?" she teased.

His mouth curved upward. "It's been a long time. Nearly eleven years." He looked around. "The farm stand looks great."

"Thanks. We did a big refurbish a couple of years ago. It made a difference. Business is good." She motioned to Bandit, who moved closer. "This is my guy. Bandit, this is Jonah. Say hi."

Her dog moved close and sniffed the outstretched hand, then sat politely as Jonah patted him.

"He's well trained."

Paris nodded. "I worked with him a lot when he was a puppy, plus being here with me all day keeps him socialized. He loves kids. Summer's his favorite time of year. There are a lot of family picnics out back. He gets all the love, plus scraps. It's doggie heaven."

"Sounds like it." Jonah glanced behind her. "Is that a strawberry concert?"

"It is. Strawberries are our fruit of the month."

He studied the display. "I like it. Last time it was dancing asparagus."

She frowned. "How would you know that?"

"I follow the stand on social media."

The obvious question was why would he bother, but she didn't want to go there.

"I'm not a natural with social media, but I'm getting better."

He returned his attention to her. "I won't keep you. I wanted to say hi so things wouldn't be strange. In this town, we're likely to run into each other."

"That's sweet. Thank you." She felt her mouth twist. "Given what happened the last time we were together, it's more than I deserve."

He waved away her comment. "Stuff happens."

"That wasn't just stuff and I am sorry for how I acted." She paused. "I mean that, Jonah. I was horrible." She held up a hand. "You don't have to say anything back. I want you to know that I was wrong. I apologize for what I did and said. You deserved better."

"Thank you."

"Tell your mom I wish her the best for her surgery."

"I will." He shoved his hands into his jeans front pockets. "I thought I'd bring Danny by in a couple of days to meet you." He smiled. "And Bandit."

His son? Why? "Ah, sure. I'm here all day. And if you want to bring your wife, that would be great."

He frowned. "My wife? Didn't Mom tell you? She passed away over a year ago."

Paris stared at him in disbelief. What? How was that possible?

"No. How did she— I mean, I didn't know. I'm so sorry. That must have been so hard on both of you." And shocking. From the pictures she'd seen, his wife had been his age. So young.

On the heels of shock, she felt a flash of irritation. Seriously, Jonah's mom stopped by LoLo's at least once a month and frequently chatted for a few minutes. She was forever showing off pictures of Jonah and his son. She could do all that and never mention Jonah's wife had *died*?

Except she had an excellent reason not to share that particular detail, Paris thought as her annoyance faded and shame took its place. Because when Jonah had left, she'd begged her mother-in-law to know where he was. She'd sobbed and screamed and threatened. She'd probably terrified the older woman.

"It's better now," he said, drawing her back to the present. "Danny had a rough few months, but he's more himself. I'm hoping time in Los Lobos will be good for him."

"I hope so, too."

He looked like he was going to say something else, but instead nodded at her before walking away.

She deliberately went in the opposite direction, Bandit at her heels.

Jonah was a good guy, she told herself. He'd taken the time to let her know he was back in town. He'd always been thoughtful that way—even when she hadn't deserved it. Even now, he had no way of knowing whether she'd changed. If she were him, she would give herself a wide berth. But he'd showed up.

She promised herself she would repay his kindness with one of her own. She would be casually friendly but nothing more. She'd killed whatever love they'd once had, and they'd both moved on. Her one job would be to show him he had nothing to fear from her. She owed him that.

three

Laurel collected food from the refrigerator. Thursday dinners were typically leftovers. The basis of the dinner was a big salad. As long as she added raisins, apples and pecans, her girls would happily eat the greens and veggies. The eclectic meal would also include small squares of lasagna, a cut-up sandwich, potato salad and strawberries from the farm stand.

She chopped and diced automatically, her mind still caught up in the talk with Jagger's teacher. Part of her simply couldn't accept that her daughter resented all men, but it was hard to deny.

She knew Beau's leaving was a big part of the problem. Ariana missed her father, cried for him, defended him and until recently had been constantly asking if he was coming back. Not Jagger. She'd reacted with anger and resentment rather than with tears, something Laurel had attributed to a difference in personality. But maybe it was more than that. Maybe Jagger was hiding behind easier and safer emotions rather than expressing her true feelings.

Laurel knew she would spend many a sleepless night trying to figure it out. She told herself that now that she knew there was a problem, she could get on with helping fix it. If only she

could escape the chant in her head that loudly proclaimed she
was a bad mother who had made her daughter hate men.

She finished the prep work and walked to the bottom of the
stairs, ready to call her daughters to set the table, but before she
could say anything, she heard shouts from the second floor.

"Why won't you tell me?"

"There's nothing to tell."

"I don't believe you."

Ariana sounded tearful, while Jagger's voice was sharp with
annoyance. Laurel held in a sigh as she climbed the stairs.

She found her daughters in the hallway, facing each other.
They were blue-eyed blondes, with fair skin, cheeks flushed
with emotion. Jagger was taller. Not only was she two years
older, she had her father's athletic build. Ariana was more wiry,
like her mother.

We're skinny but strong, their grandmother had always said. Laurel was twenty pounds less skinny than she had been a decade
ago, but she could lift boxes with the best of them.

"What?" she asked, keeping her voice soft to defuse the tension. "I could hear you two screaming all the way downstairs."

Ariana rushed to her, tears streaming down her cheeks. "Dad
said he would text. He *said*. But when I asked her, she wouldn't
tell me if he did." She wiped her cheeks with the back of her
hand. "She's supposed to tell me. It's the rules."

Laurel had decided that her daughters had to be eleven before
they got their own cell phone, something she now regretted, although there hadn't been a problem until Beau had left. Rather
than contacting Ariana on Laurel's phone, he texted Jagger and
asked her to pass on messages. Something she didn't always do.
Ariana was in a position of forever begging for a crumb of information. Given how little Beau was in touch with his kids,
that begging often went unanswered.

Only a couple more months, she reminded herself. Ariana

would turn eleven this summer and then she would get her own phone.

She looked at her oldest. "Did your father text?"

Jagger grimaced. "Of course not. He never does." She rolled her eyes. "Ariana is such a baby. We're never going to hear from him. He doesn't care. He never cared."

Before Laurel could say anything, Ariana pushed her sister. "You're *lying*. Our dad loves us."

Jagger shoved her back. "Dads who love their kids don't leave. He left. He doesn't care at all."

"Hey, enough."

Laurel moved between them, but the damage had been done. Ariana ran to her room and slammed the door, her sobs still audible. Jagger turned her back on her mother.

"I hate him."

Laurel hesitated, then pointed at Jagger's room. "Wait for me in there, please."

Her oldest spun to face her. "I didn't do anything wrong."

"We both know that's not true. Wait in your room."

Jagger stomped off, then slammed *her* door. Laurel thought briefly of her quiet, child-free days, then went into Ariana's room.

Her youngest was curled up on her bed, crying as if her heart was broken, which it probably was. Nothing about the divorce had been easy. Maybe if she and Beau could have presented themselves as a team, things would have gone better, but that had been impossible. Beau had taken off for Jamaica with little warning. Actually, he'd charged up the joint credit cards, emptied their bank accounts and *then* had taken off for Jamaica, but why go there?

Laurel sat on the bed and gently pulled her daughter into her arms. Ariana clung to her, crying harder, her whole body shaking with the strength of her sobs. Laurel rubbed her back and smoothed her hair off her face, waiting until the tears subsided and her youngest finally quieted.

"She's mean," Ariana said. "She doesn't have to be but she is."

"Sometimes, but sometimes she takes care of you."

"Maybe." She raised her head. "He said, Mom. He said he'd text by Friday."

Laurel didn't doubt that was true. Beau was forever making promises he might mean in the moment but rarely bothered to keep.

"It's not Friday yet," she said instead, telling herself that later she would text Beau herself and remind him he had two kids who needed to hear from him. Hopefully that would be enough.

"Do you think he'll text tomorrow?"

The hope in her daughter's voice nearly broke her heart. "He said he would, so let's wait and see. But no matter what happens, he's your dad and he loves you very much."

"I wish he didn't have to go away. I wish he was still here at home."

No way Laurel could lie her way through a "me, too." She hated what the divorce had done to her kids, but she didn't want Beau back.

"I know this has been hard," she said instead. "You're being really brave."

"I miss him so much."

"You do."

Ariana had always been his advocate. No matter the behavior, she sided with her dad. At times her attitude had been difficult for Laurel, but with Beau gone, she found it easier to accept her youngest's "yay, Dad" mindset.

"I'm hungry."

"Me, too. Let me go talk to your sister, then we can all set the table."

"Is she in trouble?"

Laurel touched her daughter's nose. "Maybe you could sound a little less gleeful when you ask the question."

"She was mean. I can't wait until I get my own phone. We

should have gotten them at the same time, Mom. Your decision made a lot of trouble for the family."

While Laurel agreed, saying that wasn't the best idea.

"Only a couple more months."

"I can't wait to be eleven. I wish I could be the oldest."

"Sorry. You're stuck being the youngest." Laurel kissed the top of her head.

She went down the hall to Jagger's room, knocked once, then let herself in. Jagger sat at her desk, her attention on her tablet. She didn't bother looking up.

Laurel silently counted to five, then lightly said, "You're already in trouble. Do you want to make it worse by being rude?"

The tablet hit the desk as Jagger turned toward her.

"She's ridiculous, Mom. Dad never remembers to text unless you tell him to. He's not coming back, but he's all she talks about. Dad this and Dad that. He's not worth it."

Laurel sat on the bed. "I don't get it. I know you love your sister, so why do you torture her?"

"Because she's being stupid!"

Laurel waited.

Jagger looked away, sighed heavily, then looked back. "Okay, she's not stupid, but she expected our dad to act like some actor in a movie on TV. He's never going to remember us or care. She thinks he is and he doesn't and then she cries. That's not my fault."

"You make the situation worse when you don't have to. I don't think you're a bully, but sometimes you act like one."

"Mom!" Jagger's blue eyes filled with tears. "That's not fair. I'm realistic."

"You're cruel."

"No! Don't say that. She's such a baby."

"She loves her dad, like you do. She just shows it differently."

"I don't love him." Jagger jumped to her feet, her hands curled into fists. "I hate him!"

The words were a kick to the gut. Laurel held open her arms. Jagger ignored her for about three heartbeats then rushed forward. Laurel pulled her close.

"I hate him," her oldest repeated.

"No, you don't. You're so angry, you don't know how to deal with how you feel because it's really big and sometimes it scares you, so you pretend not to care. I'm sorry he hurts you."

"He doesn't. He can't. I don't care about him."

"We both know you're lying."

"He should stay away and stop pretending he's our dad. It would be bad for a while, but then we could get over him."

Laurel drew back so she could see her daughter's face. "Life isn't that tidy, and despite what you say, I know you still want to see him."

"What I want doesn't matter. He only cares about himself."

"That's not true," she said, ignoring the voice in her head that asked who was lying now.

"Why do you take his side? He hurt you, too."

"It's different for me. He's not my father. The relationship between a parent and a child is special. Almost sacred. You may not like it, but you need him."

Jagger stepped back. "I don't need him for anything, which is a good thing because he's never here."

Laurel dropped that line of conversation in favor of the one that had started this all.

"You were mean to your sister. You're supposed to tell her if your dad texts. We've talked about this." She held out her hand. "You're losing phone privileges until Monday morning."

Jagger's eyes widened as her mouth fell open. "No! Not my phone. Anything else. I can go to bed without dinner and do all Ariana's chores and get up at five and work in the barn." The tears returned. "Not my phone."

Laurel's hand stayed steady. "Don't make me tell you again."

Jagger began to cry in earnest. She shook her head even as she moved toward her desk. "This isn't fair."

"It's very fair. I get you two are sisters and you're going to fight, but you know the texts make her crazy. You need to let her know whether you've heard from your dad. I warned you last time what the punishment would be."

Jagger placed the phone in her hand. "But not until Monday. Can't it be overnight?"

"No."

Jagger threw herself on the bed, crying as if her heart was broken. "You're so awful. None of the other mothers do this."

"I doubt that." Laurel patted her back, then stood. "I'm going to give you ten minutes to sulk, then you can join us downstairs for dinner."

"I'm not hungry."

"Ten minutes to sulk," Laurel repeated. "If you stay up here, you'll be breaking the attitude rule. Do you really want to give up TV for the weekend as well as your phone?"

"I don't care."

"It's totally up to you."

Laurel went out onto the landing. Honestly, parenting was the hardest job ever. Most of the time she thought she did okay, but now she was really questioning herself. The whole Beau thing was a nightmare and hearing about Jagger's "man hating" had rattled her. Later, when the kids were in bed, she would do some personal assessment. And text her ex to remind him to get in touch with his daughters. Oh, and figure out ways to get positive male role models into the family.

A full evening, she thought. But an important one. To her, Jagger and Ariana were everything. Whatever it took, she would get it right so they could live happy, productive lives, because she'd never, ever loved anyone more.

four

Cassie Hayden braked quickly to keep her small SUV from plowing into a group of tourists more interested in their phones than the traffic on the busy waterfront road. She waited while they crossed against the light. Her errands would wait. Cars behind her honked, but she clutched her steering wheel and thought about how it was only the beginning of June. The tourist situation in Bar Harbor was going to get a lot worse before it got better. Patience would be required or sanity would be lost. And Cassie was a big believer in staying sane. And sticky notes. More than once, a well-placed sticky note had reminded her of something very important.

Finally free of the elderly sightseers, no doubt brought to town by the cruise ship sitting about a mile past the harbor, Cassie headed for the intersection with Route 1 where the linen truck had blown a tire and half rolled, half slid into a ditch. No one was hurt, but it meant someone (Cassie) had to go pick up the linens.

She would take them to her lunch shift at her brother's bar then later swing by the high school to pick up her nieces. Their mom—Cassie's sister, Faith—claimed the girls were plenty capable of walking home, but Cassie couldn't help worrying. Some of the roads were busy and people didn't always look where they were going. After that, she would swing by the library to pick up a book she had on reserve, then cover the reception desk of her sister's B and B until seven.

Family, she thought, spotting the flashing lights of the tow truck up ahead. Can't live without them, can't stop rescuing them. With any luck, once she was done with work, she would be able to hang out with her boyfriend, Edmund. She hadn't seen him in the past couple of weeks—mostly because their schedules were so different. He went out early on the fishing boat and she was forever scrambling to do what needed doing at the bar or B and B, with a side job of being on call for whatever the current family emergency might be.

Cassie made it back to the bar in time to start serving the lunch crowd. In the summer—even in early June—they had a nice mix of locals and tourists. Come the high season of summer, when the very wealthy flocked to the little town, she would serve her share of celebrities and tycoons. Just for the record—the rich didn't necessarily tip any better than a little old lady from Kansas.

Cassie greeted her regulars, covering both the bar and the tables. The lunch menu was typical for the area. In addition to the usual burgers and sandwiches, there were crab or lobster rolls, crab or lobster grilled cheese panini, and an array of salads. The well drinks were poured right, the beer selection heavily favored local microbreweries and during playoff games of any sport, her brother made his famous lobster pizza—a dish so popular, you had to preorder a week in advance.

She worked efficiently, laughing when the customers joked with her and keeping away from a couple of handsy old-timers. By two, the bar was mostly empty. She finished cleaning up the tables and reviewing the liquor inventory before her replacement came on. Her brother, Garth, started closer to three and worked until the bar closed around midnight.

A few months ago, his regular lunch person had gotten pregnant and gone on leave. Cassie, who'd signed up for a couple
of classes at the local community college in the hopes of *finally*
getting started on her degree, had dropped the classes to fill in
at the bar.

One day, she thought, leaving Garth a note that he was low
on Jameson. One day her family would get its act together so
she didn't have to be responsible for everything. One day she
could think about what she wanted from her future rather than
what was expected or better yet—go somewhere fun rather
than just reading about fun places. She was the youngest of the
three, but most days she felt dozens of years older and a whole
lot more weary.

She glanced at the wall clock in the back kitchen, noting her
replacement would arrive any second. She was about to start
checking pantry inventory while she waited when she heard
Edmund calling her name.

She hurried to the front of the bar and smiled at her boyfriend.

"Was I expecting you?" she asked, moving toward him for a
hug and a kiss. "I haven't seen you in what feels like forever. I
thought we were getting together tonight."

He surprised her by stepping back and not returning her smile.

"Hey, Cassie." He looked at her, then away. "We need to talk."

The words sounded ominous. It was only after he said them
that she took in the tension in his body and the firm set of his
chin.

Edmund wasn't the best-looking guy in town, nor especially
smart or ambitious. But he was nice and a decent boyfriend most
of the time. They'd been dating for nearly a year. While Cassie
was willing to admit she didn't feel butterflies, she liked him. Just
as significant, he was a refuge from the demands of her family.

"What's wrong? Is it your mom?"

Edmund's mother had recently relocated to a nice retirement
community in South Carolina.

"It's not her. It's me."

Cassie stared at him, her chest tightening as fear raced through her. "What does that mean? Are you sick?"

"I'm fine." Once again his gaze didn't meet hers. "This is hard. I'm gonna say it."

Before Cassie could brace herself, he blurted, "I've been in Iowa. Checking out the area. I got a job and an apartment."

She couldn't process any of what he was saying. Iowa? As in Iowa? He was moving?

"You said you were busy." She stared at him. "You were out of town? You've been lying to me?"

Betrayal joined hurt, both getting smothered by confusion.

"I don't understand. You were gone and you didn't tell me? We text, like, every day."

Finally, he looked at her. "I hate working on the fishing boat. With my mom gone, there's nothing to keep me in town."

Nothing? What about her? Them? A horrifying truth occurred to her. "Are you breaking up with me?"

His eyes shifted again. "Face it, Cassie. We don't have that much together. You're okay. I mean you're really pretty, but you're not that interesting. You never want to do anything fun. You're always dealing with your family. A guy doesn't like to come in second all the time."

She took a step back, then another. His words slammed into her, each one an individual blow until she didn't think she was going to be able to keep from throwing up.

She wanted to say something that would emotionally rip out his heart, but she couldn't remember how to speak. She could only watch and listen as he added, "I met someone. I think she's the one. It was magical. You and I never had magic. Plus, you know, the sex wasn't great."

He said a few more things, but she honest to God couldn't hear them over the rushing sound in her ears. Her breathing got faster and faster and she wondered if she was going to faint.

She never had, but now seemed like a good time to try it. Only while the world spun it never got dark or shifted or anything and after a few seconds, she was able to catch her breath.

"When are you leaving?"

As soon as she asked the question, she wanted to slap herself. No! That wasn't what she should be saying. She should be telling him he was a jerk who didn't deserve her and that he was going to regret letting her go. She should be mentioning how lately it felt like she was going through the motions of a relationship, that she didn't love him and she hoped he got a flat tire every day of his life. Not the pathetic, needy, small-voiced "When are you leaving."

"In the morning. I'm all packed up. I sold most of my stuff when I got back."

He'd done all of that without telling her, she thought in disbelief. He had ended things a long time ago and hadn't bothered to mention it.

She heard a familiar voice calling out from the kitchen as her replacement arrived.

"It's me. Sorry I was a few minutes late, Cass. I got caught behind a tour bus."

Cassie looked at the man she'd spent a year with and wondered how she could have wasted so much time with him. The brief moment of strength allowed her to walk past him without another word and into the kitchen where she summoned what she hoped was a decent smile.

"No problem," she said, getting her bag and her current book out of her locker. "Have a good shift."

"Thanks."

She went out the back door to her small SUV. Seconds later, she was driving to her sister's B and B. Emotions swirled, but she ignored them all. She had things to do. Important things. People depended on her. Later she would think about what had just happened. She would cry and scream and wonder why she kept picking guys who left her.

No, she thought bitterly. It was worse than that. Why did she pick loser guys she helped get back on their feet who *then* left her? Because when she'd met Edmund, he'd been out of work and in debt. She'd been the one to help him get the job on the fishing boat. She'd been the one who'd come up with a payment plan for all he owed.

"I'm such a fool," she muttered, swiping a wayward tear. She'd given him over a thousand dollars to pay off a credit card. She'd covered the cost of nearly everything they did so he could focus on his bills. She'd bought him a TV the previous Christmas. A really good one, with great sound.

This for a man who said she wasn't interesting and complained he didn't always come in first with her?

"Asshole!" she yelled, about ten minutes too late. She should have said it to his face. She should have told him the reason their sex life wasn't very good was because he didn't know what he was doing down there.

She managed to work herself up into a really good mad, which helped hide the pain. She knew she was avoiding the inevitable suffering a breakup always brought on, but she was fine with that. Maybe she could simply ignore what had happened and never deal with it. Edmund didn't deserve her hurt or her introspection.

Her sister's B and B was in one of the more modest aging mansions, typical for the area, with enough character to entice guests and enough modern amenities to keep them coming back year after year. Faith had owned the place a year—buying it with an inheritance from their great-uncle Nelson. He'd left Faith and Garth a sizable amount of money while he'd left Cassie "land and everything on it, including the contents of the cave" somewhere in California.

She had no idea why her uncle hadn't left her cash, as well.

At least that was something she could use. Instead, she was stuck with land she would never see and knew nothing about.

"A problem for another time," she told herself as she parked. Although thinking about her inheritance was better than wondering how she'd been such a fool as to believe Edmund cared about her.

She grabbed her bag and her book, then found her sister standing by the registration desk. Faith, ten years older and two inches shorter, had the Hayden family red hair. Cassie and her siblings shared the deep auburn color, along with pale skin, green eyes and freckles. No one seeing them together could miss the fact that they were related.

"What?" Cassie demanded, taking in the straight set of her sister's mouth—a telltale sign there was a problem. "Is it the girls?"

Faith glanced at the clerk on duty, then faked a smile. "Let's go into my office."

So not the girls, Cassie thought, following her sister to the back of the house. If something had happened to one of them, her sister would tell her what it was and immediately be out the door.

"Is it bad?" She really couldn't handle another crisis. "I'm not having a good day."

"I'm sorry to hear that." Faith's voice was tight. "It's not anything about me."

She stepped into her small office. Cassie followed, only to come to a stop when she saw her brother already sitting there. Garth stood, looking both determined and faintly guilty.

"Hi, sis."

Faith took her seat behind her desk and motioned for Cassie to come in and sit down. She stayed where she was—in the doorway. She didn't know what the disaster was, but for once they were going to have to handle it on their own.

"No," she told them. "Whatever it is, no. Edmund broke up with me. I can't take one more thing."

Faith and Garth stared at each other, communicating in that

silent way they had—something they'd done since they were kids. It probably came from only being ten months apart. Their connection had always made Cassie feel left out.

After a second, Garth shrugged and Faith nodded.

"Please," she said, again pointing to the chair across from hers. "We need to talk."

Cassie reluctantly did as she asked. Garth closed the door and took the chair next to hers.

Faith drew in a breath and tried to smile. When that didn't work, she leaned forward, her expression earnest.

"Cassie, we love you."

Oh, no. Nothing good happened after "Cassie, we love you" started a conversation. She braced herself, thinking she'd made it really clear she didn't have the reserves for whatever they wanted.

"You're great," Garth added. "You help out with both our businesses. We can always depend on you."

Cassie looked between them. Okay, that sounded nice, so why were the hairs on the back of her neck tingling?

"You're always available, always doing things for us," Faith added. "In a way, we've taken advantage of you, which maybe makes it all our fault."

Garth frowned. "It's not our fault. She's the one who's stuck."

"And we're part of the problem."

"What problem?" Cassie demanded. "Stop talking about me like I'm not in the room. You know that makes me crazy."

Faith looked at her. "You're right." She cleared her throat. "Cassie, you need a life and you don't have one. Like Garth said, you're stuck."

"I don't understand." And why were they picking on her? "I have things to do. If that's all, I'll just—"

"No." Faith's tone sharpened. "That's not all. Look, we get that when Mom and Dad died it was really hard for you. Garth and I were in our twenties, but you were only fourteen. With us focused on our own grief, you had no one to turn to. You were left on your own and you buried your feelings so deep, I'm not sure you've ever felt them. You hid out in your room, reading. When you weren't doing that, you were trying to make everyone else feel better. I'm afraid the lesson you learned was to take care of everyone else rather than thinking about what you want."

Cassie didn't want to talk about that time in her life. "I'm fine. It was tragic and now it's done."

"It's not. We should have paid attention to you. Uncle Nelson moved in, but he didn't know how to help you recover any more than we did. You stopped dreaming, stopped planning your future." Her voice softened. "You deserve to have a life. At the very least, you deserve to have your own adventure, rather than just reading about one."

Cassie felt her throat tighten as tears burned. "I don't want to talk about this right now." Or ever. "You guys need me and I'm happy to help."

"We don't need you," Garth said bluntly. "That's a story you tell yourself."

"Garth," Faith said with a groan. "You weren't supposed to say that."

"Why not? It's the truth."

Cassie stared at him, hurt and furious. "What are you talking about? You don't need me? That's a laugh. I'm the glue that holds this family together. You'd be lost without me. I handle whatever crisis happens. The linen truck crashes, I go pick up the order. Your server takes a leave, I fill in. I do everything for both of you and you don't get to say I don't!"

He and Faith exchanged one of those looks again.

Garth turned to her. "The linen company was sending out another truck. The order was due to be delivered this afternoon, well before I needed it. I tried to tell you, but you hung up before I could finish my sentence. As for the lunch shift, I told you I had help, but you didn't listen. You never listen, sis.

You jump in and take action because you think you're the only one who can, but you're not."

"You never said," she began, knowing he wasn't telling the truth. "I gave up college to help out."

"I told you not to and you gave up college because you're scared."

Faith nodded slowly. "The same with me. Come on, Cass. Do you really need to pick up the girls every day from school? They're fourteen and fifteen. They can cross a street by themselves."

No. None of this was true. "Why are you being so awful?"

"We're being honest," Faith told her. "I love you so much. When J.J. died, I knew I couldn't make it on my own, but you were right there with me. All of eighteen, you stepped in. I think that's another place where I screwed up. You should have been dealing with your own future, but you were too busy helping me."

"You had two little kids. You couldn't manage on your own."

"A lot of people do. I depended on you and taught you the wrong lesson. You believe we can't make it without you. You think you're the strong one in the family when the truth is you're hiding from your own life. You're twenty-eight years old and you've never lived on your own. You have no career, no plans and you keep finding loser guys to help get their acts together just for them to dump you."

Tears filled her eyes as she tried to find an escape. Staying here wasn't safe.

"Stop attacking me."

Garth touched her arm. "We're saying this because we love you. It's time to go, kid. Uncle Nelson left you an inheritance a year ago. We've been waiting and hoping you'd want to at least go see it, but you won't leave, so we're kicking you out."

Cassie wiped her face and grabbed one of the tissues her sister offered. "You don't get to say," she told them, speaking past her shattered heart. "You can't tell me what to do."

Faith started to cry, as well. She sucked in a breath, then said, "You're fired."

Cassie flinched. "What? Fired? You can't fire me?"

"Call it what you like. You don't work for me anymore. Or Garth. No more filling in, taking shifts. No more picking up the girls from school."

The tears fell faster and harder. She shrank back in her chair. "You're supposed to be my family!"

"That's why we're doing this. Go to California. See what Uncle Nelson left you. Come back in six months." Faith's voice was shaking. "I'm sorry, but we don't know what else to do. We love you so much."

Cassie sprang to her feet. "You don't love me. You're throwing me out of the family. You're horrible. Both of you and I'll hate you forever." Her voice rose with every word. "I hate you and I'll never forgive you."

"We can live with that," Garth said quietly. "But we can't live with the guilt of what we've done to you. We're not backing down. Go to Los Lobos and figure out what to do with the rest of your life."

She glared at him. "You're throwing me out of my home, too, aren't you?" Because she lived in the apartment above the bar, in the same room she'd had since she was a child.

"I am."

They'd turned against her, she thought in disbelief. They'd schemed and planned, and kept it all from her. Just like Edmund, she thought bitterly. She couldn't trust anyone.

"Go to hell."

She walked out of the office. She was shaking and thought she might be sick. Nothing made sense. Everything she'd thought was safe wasn't. She hurt, she was afraid and as her family was officially dead to her, she had no one to turn to.

In her SUV, she sat there, staring unseeingly out the windshield. The tears returned and this time she didn't fight them.

She gave in to the pain and bewilderment. Her entire world had been ripped from her. How was a person supposed to recover from that?

The driver's door opened and Faith tugged on her arm until she stepped out of the vehicle.

"I'm sorry," her sister said, holding her tight. "I love you and I need you to be happy. It's six months. That's all I'm asking."

"You don't get to ask me anything. You're a hideous person and I meant what I said. I'll hate you forever."

Faith continued to hang on. Eventually, Cassie hugged her back because what else was she supposed to do?

"I'm not leaving," she said. "I'm not moving out of my bedroom. I own a third of the building and there's nothing you can do about it."

Faith stepped back. "You need to go. You need to stand on your own. You're too dependent on us."

Cassie glared at her. "You think you know everything, but you don't. You won't last a day without me."

"Maybe not, but don't you think it's time I tried?"

Cassie began to cry again. "I don't want to go. I hate California. It's a stupid place where they eat too many avocados."

"I'm sure that's true, but Uncle Nelson left you land and whatever's on it. Go see what it is. Meet new people. Figure out where you belong."

"I belong here! We're supposed to be family."

"I love you enough to let you go."

Cassie wanted to punch her sister in the face. "That's the stupidest thing you've ever said."

"That doesn't mean it's not true."

"I really will hate you."

"I know and that's okay. Text me when you stop for the night and let me know you're okay."

Cassie's shoulders slumped. "You really want me to go?"

Faith's gaze was direct and filled with equal parts love and determination. "Yes. For both our sakes."

"You're going to miss me."

"Every minute of every day." Faith hugged her again. "Go home and pack, then come back here. The five of us will have dinner and you can head out in the morning."

"I can't be ready that fast. I need a few weeks to—"

"No. You're leaving in the morning."

"I'm back to hating you."

"As long as hating me means the start of something better."

five

Laurel held up two different drawer pulls. One was an old-fashioned black quarter round and the other was a more modern, slim T-shape. "Thoughts?"

"What do you want the look to be?" Paris asked.

Laurel grinned. "If I could answer that, I wouldn't have asked you to come with me to pick out the kitchen hardware."

Paris laughed, then studied the two options. While her preference would be for the more traditional style, she wasn't sure they went with the house.

"Your place is Victorian," she said, pointing to the black ones. "These are more from what? The 1940s?"

"Maybe. I'm not sure."

"My point is they're not classically Victorian. So go with the simple, clean lines that are, in their own way, very classic. That's my vote."

Laurel nodded slowly. "Good point. The updated kitchen is modern, so the black pulls would look out of place." She grinned. "Plus, the stainless ones are cheaper."

"There's a win."

They loaded what Laurel's contractor would need into the

cart and pushed it toward the checkout. When they were in the minivan, Laurel eyed her.

"You're quiet. Something's on your mind." She paused. "I'm not leaving this parking lot until you tell me."

"So we'll starve to death in these seats? I don't think so. Plus, what about the girls? At some point you're going to want to see them again."

"You can't distract me with your attempts to be funny." Laurel's gaze was direct. "Talk."

"I was going to tell you," Paris said. "I've been dealing." Or not dealing.

Laurel shifted in her seat. "Getting comfortable. Not moving until you spill."

"Jonah's in town for the summer."

A concept that had caused her some restless nights, she thought, instantly gratified by Laurel's wide-eyed stare.

"How do you know? Tell me everything. He's back? As in back-back?"

"I doubt he's moving here permanently, but yes, in Los Lobos for the next couple of months. His mom's getting knee-replacement surgery and he's staying with her to help."

"How did you find out? Did Natalie tell you? Are you okay? How do you feel? I have a thousand questions."

"I can tell. And it wasn't Natalie. Jonah stopped by the stand."

"And you're just now saying something?" Her voice was filled with outrage.

"After you and I talked last night, I figured you had enough going on with the whole Jagger-hates-men thing. I knew I'd be seeing you today."

Laurel poked her in the arm. "You tell me everything. That's always been our deal."

"And I just told you. It's fine. Breathe."

Laurel started the minivan. "I hate when you're rational. Jonah. Wow. How did he look?"

"Good. A little older, but still him."

Laurel drove onto the main road. "Is he here by himself or did he bring his family?"

"It's him and his son."

Laurel turned west, toward the ocean and her place. "And the wife?"

"She died."

"What?" Her voice was a yelp. "Don't say that while I'm driving. I could have steered us off the road."

"You're a better driver than that."

Laurel gave her a quick glance. "That's new information, right? We didn't know the wife was dead."

"We did not."

"Do we know her name? Now that she's dead, I'm not comfortable calling her 'the wife.'"

"I'm sure other people know it, but you and I don't."

"Awkward," Laurel murmured. "You talk to Natalie every now and then. I wonder why she didn't say anything."

"She was afraid I'd freak out and beat her or something. I was pretty scary after Jonah left me."

"That was years ago. I doubt she remembers."

Paris thought of how she'd screamed at the older woman, demanding information. "Oh, she remembers."

"You okay? What are you feeling?"

"About Jonah?" A question Paris had been trying to answer all night. "I'm not sure. Surprised, I guess. I appreciate that he wanted to tell me he was back face-to-face. It's more than I deserve. It's a small town so we were likely to run into each other. He made the effort. That shows courage. I don't think if I were him, I'd be willing to face me."

"Stop making yourself sound so awful. You had good times in your marriage."

Paris shook her head. "Don't downplay what happened. Believe me, I don't love having to deal with my past, but being honest is the only way to stay healthy and in control. I was horrible to Jonah and I terrorized him. He's the person I was supposed to love more than anyone in the world and I made his life hell."

"You were abused as a child," Laurel said quietly.

"You always defend me."

"I always love you."

"Thank you."

Their friendship was an anchor in her life, Paris thought gratefully. Laurel had always been there. The first time Paris had gone off on her friend they'd both been seven. Paris had blown up, screaming and threatening Laurel, who had calmly punched her in the mouth.

The reaction—swift and, given their ages, appropriate—had taught Paris not to mess with her friend. She never had again. Oh, there had been arguments and disagreements, but all of the normal, everyday variety.

"You did what you were taught," Laurel continued. "You did what you had to in order to survive."

"I'm not saying my past doesn't affect how I acted, I'm saying it's not an excuse. My mother abused me and from that I learned to abuse other people. The cycle went on."

"Until you broke it. You're very quick to take the blame, but a lot more resistant to taking credit for the changes you've made."

Paris made a noncommittal noise. Laurel was right—Paris didn't fully trust herself to stay who she'd become. Lurking in the back of her mind was the possibility of losing control and destroying everything she'd worked so hard to rebuild.

"I don't want to hurt anyone," Paris admitted.

"You're not that person. What's it going to take for you to see that? I trust you completely. More important, I trust you with my children."

"That's different. I'd never do anything to threaten them."

"So you have selective worry."

"Yes."

She'd worked hard to learn the coping skills she should have been taught as a child. She understood conflict management and when it was better and easier to simply walk away. She knew the danger of wanting to be right, to take the win, more than anything. She trusted herself at work, with her friends, yes even with Jagger and Ariana, who were the most precious cargo she knew.

But romantically—that was different. She didn't want to show herself for who she was and she didn't want to take the chance of doing to another human being what she'd done to the man she'd married.

"I wish you'd start dating," Laurel said. "I hate that you're alone."

Paris grinned. "And the last time you went out with a guy was when?"

"I was married."

"So was I."

"My divorce is more recent. You have to admit being married to Beau would put anyone off a romantic relationship."

Paris gentled her tone. "And yet you married him."

"There is that."

They pulled onto the long driveway and stopped in front of the three-story Victorian house. Paris lived in the same house where she'd grown up—left to her after her mother's passing. By comparison to the grand, slightly run-down piece of history in front of them, her ranch house was small but worked for her. It had three bedrooms, two and a half bathrooms with a good-sized home office and family room, thanks to the down-to-the-studs remodel she'd endured about four years ago.

They collected the box of hardware and walked toward the side entrance of Laurel's Victorian.

"The floors are refinished and dry," Laurel said, fishing a key out of her jeans pocket. "But there's still the varnish smell, so brace yourself. I've been airing out the place every night, but it's determined to linger."

She pushed open the door and they walked inside. Paris sighed. "It's beautiful. This is so great, Laurel."

What had been a dark, grim mother-in-law suite was now a light and bright apartment. Walls had been removed to create an open-concept living room, kitchen and eating area. New windows allowed sunlight to fill the space. The walls were white, the floors more gray than brown. The ceilings were at least ten feet high.

They walked toward the refurbished kitchen. Laurel set the box on the island separating the cooking area from the eat-in section, then pointed to doors on either side of a hallway.

"We had to compromise," she said. "I really wanted a small pantry for the kitchen, but that ate into what would be the laundry room." She opened the second door to show a stacked washer and dryer.

"At least your renter won't have to go to the laundromat."

They walked down the short hallway. There was a full bath to the left and a decent-sized bedroom to the right. More big windows let in light and offered a view of the side yard. The bathroom had been updated with a new vanity and toilet, but Laurel had left in the big claw-foot tub. It had a shower curtain that pulled around and a rain shower fixture above the center of the tub. The fixtures were black, the countertop, toilet and tub were white, and the floor was done in a retro herringbone black-and-white pattern.

"I love it," Paris told her when they returned to the living room and began opening windows to continue airing out the place. "Have you decided? Short-term lease? Long-term lease? Furnished? Unfurnished?"

Laurel groaned. "I have no idea. I've never been a landlord before. I mean, I want the money, but someone living here? What if they're icky?"

"Put a don't-be-icky clause in the lease."

"Is that legal?"

"Probably not." Paris glanced around. "It's a great apartment. You're offering a lot, so you can afford to be picky. I have that HR service I contract with for the stand. I'll run any applicant through their background check. That will give us credit and criminal history. Ask for references and go with your gut."

Laurel nodded. "I know you're right—I worry because of the girls. It's not like the apartment has direct access into the house, but still, whoever lives here will be close."

"We'll do our best to avoid serial killers."

"Absolutely. No serial killers." Laurel brushed her fingers along the freshly painted windowsill. "Let's find a nice, older grandmother type. Someone quiet who likes to knit. If she wants the place furnished, I can move everything back."

"You're being very specific. What if she likes to do crossword puzzles instead?"

"That's fine. But she can't be in a band. Or selling meth or anything."

Paris laughed. "I agree on the no-meth clause. We should probably start writing these notes down."

Cassie set her e-reader next to her on the bench and looked out at what she assumed was the Pacific Ocean. Technically, it should have looked exactly like the one she'd left behind at home. Salt water was salt water. Only they weren't the same at all.

There was no harbor, no lobster boats, no little islands, no lighthouses, no anything. In this particular part of the West Coast, there was the shore and the water, with no other defining features.

Where were the trees, the Acadia National Park she'd grown up with? While she was sure there were tourists around, she didn't see any tour buses. There were no signs for lobster rolls, no marina, no anything. The only interesting detail was a long pier and what looked like a waterfront area beyond it. And while that was nice, it wasn't enough. Out here there was space—too much of it. Plus, there was something weird about the sky. It was too blue and too...something. Maybe it was too high, or maybe the lack of clouds kept it from feeling right.

The other possibility, she thought, was that six days alone had messed with her head. She had dealt with a lot in her life, but she didn't remember ever feeling so lonely or isolated. She could see other people—there was a family on the beach, not that far away—but she wasn't a part of them. She felt like the last person alive.

She'd left Bar Harbor the morning after Faith and Garth had fired her from the family. She'd packed up her small SUV, taking only clothes and toiletries, her e-reader, and a selection of print books she couldn't leave behind. After playing around with options on her phone, she'd chosen a more southern driving route because she hadn't wanted to risk seeing Edmund on the highway. So instead of taking I-90 across the northern half of the country and dropping down through Colorado and Utah, she'd gone south through Ohio, across Indiana and Missouri before joining I-40 in Oklahoma and heading west.

All states she'd heard about but had never seen. She'd stayed at modest highway hotels, eaten by herself at diners and fast-food places. She'd mentally railed against her brother and sister, promising herself she would never speak to them again, only to miss them so much she had to text.

After the first three hundred miles, her mad had subsided. At some point in New York state, she'd begun to wonder if maybe they were right. She really didn't have much of a life. She was twenty-eight years old and she didn't have a clue as to what she wanted to be when she grew up. While she was happy to help in the bar or the B and B, neither was her dream. She wasn't like Garth, who'd always been excited to take over the tavern one day. And she wasn't her sister, who had a degree in hotel management and had worked as an assistant manager at one of the big waterfront hotels before getting married and having kids.

Cassie had never had a plan. She'd only been fourteen when she'd lost her parents and back then the future had been so far away. Until the news of the accident came, her biggest concern had been keeping up her grades and whether or not Braydon Wilson had a crush on her.

After she'd lost her parents, she'd been so weighed down by grief that she'd simply gone through the motions of living. It had been years before she cared about anything and when she did resurface, it was with the knowledge that somehow she was responsible for everyone she cared about. She'd withdrawn from college to help Faith after her husband had been killed, leaving Faith with two little kids. Once her sister was better, it was easy to slip into helping Garth in the bar. When she needed an escape, there was always yet another book for her to read. Always enjoyable, but not exactly a life. Before she knew it, she was rudderless and being dumped by Edmund.

She stared out at the blue water and wondered how far it was to Hawaii. No, wait. Hawaii was south. So what was due west? China? Japan? She really should have paid attention to her geography in school.

She stood up and walked toward the pier, her bare feet digging into the sand. By the water, a family played in the waves. The youngest, a little boy who was maybe four or five, kept screaming he wanted to go in deeper. His older sister kept a grip on his hand and told him no.

She'd been like him once, she thought. The baby of the family, the one everyone doted on. She'd been pampered, watched out for, nearly always given what she wanted. Then one day everything had changed. In her heart of hearts, Cassie had to admit she hadn't felt safe since. Not really. There was always the sensation of impending doom.

Her phone rang. She answered without looking at the screen, because honestly, who else would be calling.

"I still hate you."

Faith laughed. "I'm sure that's true. Where are you?"

"Standing by the Pacific."

"Is it beautiful?"

"I guess. There aren't any trees and where are the cruise ships? Don't they stop here?"

"You're missing the cruise ships?"

"No, but I think they're a natural part of the skyline. California looks naked without them. It's naked and they eat too many avocados."

"What does that mean? Is everyone walking around with an avocado in their hand?"

"No, they do it in secret."

"Okay, now you're scaring me. Did you get a job?"

Cassie came to a stop. "I got here last night. When would I have time to start looking for a job?"

"Too busy eating avocados?"

"Very funny. I'm going to get an ice cream and then drive into town. The lady at the Los Lobos Highway Inn told me there's a cute main street. She was probably lying."

Faith laughed. "That's my little ray of sunshine. I'm glad you made it. Now I can stop worrying."

"You should worry. I could be kidnapped or run over by bikers." Cassie looked out at the water. "Is it weird I miss you more than Edmund?"

"No. He was never good enough for you. I hope he gets swept up in a tornado and thrown into a pile of cow manure."

"That's a very specific form of revenge."

"I've had time to work out the details." Her voice lowered. "Are you okay?"

"No. I'm lonely, scared and stuck in California. Under these circumstances, no one can be okay. I'm going to buy a calendar and start marking off the time until I can come home. And once I'm back, I'm never speaking to you again."

"I miss you."

"Good."

Faith laughed again. "You miss me, too."

"I don't. At all."

"You said you missed me more than Edmund."

"I was lying to make you feel better."

"And you did. Now go find a job and a place to stay. Make friends. Eat an avocado."

"I'm hanging up now."

"Love you."

"Love you, too."

Cassie shoved her phone back in her pocket. When she reached the pier, she slipped on her sandals, then bought an ice cream cone.

"This is my lunch, so there."

Not that there was anyone to hear her defiance, and she had a feeling that just eating ice cream for a meal could give her a stomachache, but she was determined.

Once she'd finished the cone, she walked back to her SUV. The trip to downtown Los Lobos took all of seven minutes. The main street was tree-lined with cute shops and several restaurants with outdoor seating. Cassie parked and grabbed her bag. She would make one pass, scouting a place to have dinner that evening, then go back to her room and go online to find a job.

She paused by the window of a cute boutique before glancing at the menu of a yummy-looking Chinese restaurant. Next to that was a—

"Oh, a bookstore."

As she reached for the handle of Books and Bottles, she saw a large *Help Wanted. Inquire Within* sign on the glass door. Cassie shook her head. No way it could be that easy. Finding a job her very first full day in Los Lobos would totally freak her out, like the fates had conspired or something.

She ignored the sign and went into the store. It was big and bright, with eye-catching displays. She browsed the selections, smiling when she saw one of her favorite authors had a new release. She'd always preferred physical books to the digital version, but had been forced to leave her personal library behind. Maybe she should buy something as a sort of welcome-to-California gift for herself.

She grabbed a copy, then began examining the shelves. Fifteen minutes later, she had three more books and knew she had to practice a little self-control. She was supposed to be looking for a job, not indulging herself. Once she had a job and an address, she could get a library card so she could feed her reading habit for free.

She continued to walk around the store. She turned a corner and saw a coffee area that was…

Cassie stared at the long bar and the glass shelves behind. Wait a second—they weren't selling coffee there. She studied the menu that was divided into *Wine, Food,* and *Not wine or food.*

There were nearly a dozen selections of red and white wines from California wineries, including single glasses or flights of wine, along with sodas and sparkling water. The food column was mostly finger food—like sandwiches and cheese plates.

"Way better than coffee," she murmured, continuing to browse in the store. After about ten minutes, she glided toward the customer service desk and smiled at the older woman standing there.

"Hi. I saw the help-wanted sign in the window. Can you tell me about the job?"

"We're looking for someone to take over at the wine bar. The hours are eleven to four, so not full-time, but you get to keep your tips." The other woman looked hopeful. "The owner wants someone with liquor experience. I don't suppose you have any."

Wait a second. What was happening here? Had she slipped into some *Everything Is Awesome* alternative universe? An easy job with easy hours and she just happened to have the perfect experience? What was the catch? Was there a hellmouth-like creature that stalked the town at night?

"I've worked in my brother's bar for years," she said.

"Oh, that's so great. I'm Alice by the way."

"Cassie."

"Nice to meet you. I'll give you the link for the application. If you want to fill it out now, you can meet with Marilyn, the owner, when she comes in at four. If this works out, you could start right away."

"Could I?" Cassie said, going for friendly, but fearing she'd landed on sarcastic.

Alice handed her a business card with a link on it. Cassie settled into one of the comfy chairs and used the store's free Wi-Fi to log in to the site.

Based on how her day was going, in a few hours, she would have the perfect job for her six-month stay. Now all she needed was a place to stay and a few friends. Oh, wait. While she was wishing for the moon, she would happily take an incredibly gorgeous guy who was totally into her. Someone the opposite of Edmund—funny, well-educated, faithful and dependable.

She laughed and started filling out the application.

six

"You don't have to do that," Laurel said, her tone mild.

Paris ignored her as she continued gently scrubbing the back of the Lenox Holiday Nouveau platter that had been part of a huge estate sale purchase. The trick to removing sticky labels from glass or porcelain was to soak the piece in really hot water for about fifteen minutes, then use a stiff sponge.

In this case the glue came from a stubborn name tag. The handwritten *Sally, this is mine* on the tag implied that the family had staked claims on grandma's treasures—possibly before she had passed.

People could get very possessive about what they saw as "theirs," Laurel thought. Ironically, often once the treasure was claimed, it lost its value. There had been dozens of instances where she'd expressed interest in something at an estate sale only to be told a granddaughter was desperate to have it. Laurel always left her card. Frequently, she got a call a few weeks later with an offer to sell.

One of those phone calls had netted her the serving pieces that went with the set she'd already purchased. Given that everything was trimmed in platinum rather than gold, she'd been thrilled. Once the "Sally" tags were removed, the pieces could be photographed, then listed. She was expecting a quick sale.

"I'm serious," Laurel told her friend. "I didn't bring you here to work."

"I find this relaxing. I don't do enough scrubbing in my life."

Laurel grinned. "What does that mean? You want to clean more?"

Paris laughed. "Not exactly."

"Because the girls' bathroom could use a good scrubbing."

"Sorry, no."

"You sure? That would make you the best friend ever."

Bandit trotted by, his tail swinging happily as he investigated new smells and searched for unwelcome visitors. When she and Beau had first bought the property, Bandit had been the one to discover the mouse family living in the northeast corner of the barn. Unfortunately both her daughters had been with him at the time, which meant the only solution for two softhearted girls was to relocate the rodent family to an unused shed at the very back of the property. Laurel was grateful the furry creatures hadn't found their way back. Should they try, Bandit was ready to out them.

"I'm glad Beau called," Paris said as she rinsed the tray.

"Me, too." It had been late Saturday afternoon, so a day late, but he'd talked to his daughters.

"I had to practically pry the phone out of Ariana's hands, but Jagger barely spoke to him."

Laurel grabbed a microfiber cloth and began to dry the tray as Paris went to work on a serving bowl.

"She's so angry at him."

"With good reason," Paris murmured.

"Yes, Beau is a dick. There, I've said it. I married a dick. Shame on me."

Her friend's lips twitched. "You mean he acts like a dick. You're not saying you married him for sex."

Laurel chuckled. "Yes, I married a man who acts dickish. I didn't marry to get dick. Just so we're clear."

"There are worse reasons to get married," Marcy said, walking into the barn. "I can list them if you'd like."

They both greeted the older woman. Marcy was Laurel's assistant-slash-lifesaver when it came to the business. She cleaned items, listed them, maintained inventory. Her sister, Darcy, handled shipping and returns. She was the quieter of the two, older by three years. Darcy was the pretty one, but Marcy's personality drew people to her.

Darcy had met and married Laurel's father first. They'd been together nearly five years. Obviously something had happened because one second he'd been with Darcy and the next, Marcy was on his arm. Their marriage had been as intense as it had been brief. They'd divorced less than a year later and Laurel's father had left the state. Laurel had been maybe nineteen at the time.

The sisters hadn't spoken for at least three years, living in houses across the street from each other, ignoring the other's presence at family events. Then one day they'd made up. Again, Laurel lacked any details. By the time she'd grown her business enough to need help, both sisters had offered to work for her. Part-time at first, then full-time.

Marcy leaned against the counter. "I assume we're talking about Beau." She pointed her finger at Laurel. "We have a rule. The next guy has to be nice."

"There's not going to be a next guy."

"Seems like there has to be," Paris reminded her.

"I meant not romantically."

Marcy, a five-foot-five-inch brunette with big brown eyes, raised her eyebrows. "Wouldn't it be easier to make it a twofer? Someone you want to date who could also be a role model for the girls? Because, let's face it, at some point, you're really going to want a little dick in your life."

"Maybe not a little one," Paris murmured, making all three of them laugh.

"No sexy man, regardless of the state of his equipment," Laurel said firmly, appreciating the support, but incredibly clear on her limitations. She'd grown up watching her parents first divorce each other then remarry other people at an alarming rate. Every time, she'd heard the same story.

But we're in love.

Ugh. From what she could tell, love made people act like fools or at the very least, clouded their judgement. Look at her and Beau. She'd known he was bad for her, but her heart and her girl parts had insisted, dragging her good sense along with them.

No more guys, she vowed. No more love. No more being stupid. As for the sex part, well, she hadn't figured that out yet. Hopefully, as she got older, she would want it less but until then, she would be strong. And celibate.

"I want my daughters to be okay," she said.

"Hire someone."

Both she and Paris stared at Marcy.

Paris managed to speak first. "You mean like an escort?"

"Sure. Aren't they supposed to be charming? Hire a man to hang out with your girls."

"No!" Laurel held up both hands. "Marcy, think about what you're saying. I'm not letting my daughters hang out with some sex worker. That's...that's... Okay, I don't know what, but no."

"It was just a suggestion."

"A bad one."

"You're so judgy."

Paris handed the serving bowl to Laurel to dry. "Yeah, I'm with her on this, Marcy. Ixnay on the male escort."

"Fine," Marcy huffed. "If you won't think out of the box, you're left with finding some guy to be friends with."

Laurel looked at Paris, who seemed just as confused.

"You mean like friend-friends?" she asked.

Marcy groaned. "You really are out of things. Yes. Go find a man to be friends with. Real friends. Do stuff together. You need a man in your life."

"I've been telling her that for months," Paris said cheerfully. "She won't listen."

"Tell me about it." Marcy grinned, then held up her hand for a high five.

Laurel put the dry bowl on a shelf. "A great idea in theory, but where exactly am I supposed to find a man to befriend? And how do I even do that? I haven't had a male friend since I was maybe six."

"What about that archeologist guy?" Marcy asked. "The one who's so good-looking, he's not human."

Paris sighed. "Raphael."

They both turned to her.

"Go on," Laurel encouraged. "I didn't know you had a crush on him."

"No crush. He and his team stop by LoLo's every morning to stock up on healthy fruits and juices. He walks around and smiles, I enjoy the show. That's it."

"What time does this happen?" Marcy asked eagerly. "I could take my break then."

Laurel knew there was no point in telling her former step-mother than the twenty-five-year age gap might be off-putting. Or maybe Raphael was into older women.

"Being friends with a guy that good-looking would be too weird," Laurel said.

Paris grinned. "So you can only be friends with an ugly guy?"

"I didn't say that."

"You kind of did."

Marcy patted her arm. "I've planted the seed, so my work is done here. I'm going to take pictures of the Lenox and get it up on eBay."

When she'd left, Paris eyed Laurel. "She's not wrong about

the whole friendship thing. It would solve a lot of problems if you could hang out together organically. Do stuff, have a few laughs. The girls would see what was happening and realize men are people, too."

"Do you hear yourself?" Laurel asked. "Hang out and do stuff with a guy? How does that happen? I don't know any men. Seriously, my UPS guy is a woman. There are no men in my life and there is absolutely no way in hell I'm going to date someone. Besides, that would send the wrong message."

Paris carefully lowered a stack of bowls into the sink. "I don't have any men in my life, either. Why is that?"

"You're afraid of who you used to be, so you hold yourself back from any relationship that isn't a hundred percent safe. You tell yourself you have a great life, but in truth, you're hiding and a little bit stunted emotionally." Laurel paused, thinking she might have sounded harsh. "I say that with love and adoration, because I'm stunted, too."

"Someone's been listening a little too well when I talk about all my years in therapy," Paris grumbled.

"We've both been hurt," Laurel continued, relieved her friend wasn't mad. "We're afraid to try something new, so we don't. You're only hurting yourself with that, but I've become a horrible mother."

"You're not allowed to say that about my friend," Paris told her forcefully. "You're a great mom. You love your girls and would do anything for them. This is a little hiccup and we're going to fix it."

"It's a hiccup with a penis."

They both laughed.

Paris leaned against the counter. "You need to make a friend."

"How? In theory I'm willing, but what do I do?"

Paris considered the question. "How do we make friends with other women?"

"I don't know. We start talking, we get along and tada— friends."

"So talk to a guy." Paris looked at her. "How hard can it be?"

"Won't he think I'm coming on to him? Won't he think I'm in it for the aforementioned penis?"

"Not if you..."

Laurel waited. "What? Tell him I only want to be friends? That's not going to go well."

"You don't know that. You haven't tried it."

"I just know."

Paris raised her eyebrows. "It's an attitude like that our founding fathers used to defeat the British."

Laurel groaned. "Fine. I'll do what you say. I'll walk up to a guy and start talking to him, all the while telling him I want to be friends and nothing more. Later, when I'm humiliated, I'm going to get right in your face and tell you that it's your fault."

"I accept the challenge."

"Easy for you to say. You're not the one being humiliated."

Paris shook her head. "Fear not, sweet friend. I, too, will have my awkward moments. We'll deal with them together."

Laurel hugged her. "Always."

Paris spent the rest of the week dreading having to face Jonah again yet oddly eager to meet his son. She found herself scanning the parking lot when customers arrived, not that she'd noticed what he drove. She was jumpy, anxious and faintly nauseous. Finally, she had a mental chitchat with herself, explaining she was acting like a crazy person. Her ex was back in town for the summer and he was gracious enough to tell her himself. He was a good guy. Yay, him. It wasn't as if he wanted to have anything to do with her, beyond a casual wave from a distance. She was putting way too much energy into the whole *I thought I'd bring Danny by to meet you.* It was the social equivalent to *We should get together sometime.* People said it, but didn't really mean it.

She'd nearly talked herself back to normal when she spotted Jonah with a maybe eight-year-old boy in the garden section.

Danny was a skinny kid with floppy hair like his dad's. He was smiling and seemed interested in their conversation.

She hesitated, not sure what to do. Hiding in her office seemed like the most obvious plan, but she ignored her trepidation, slapped a smile on her face and prepared to face her ex.

"Hey, Jonah," she called as she approached, Bandit at her heels.

"Paris." His smile was low and easy. "We were thinking about putting in some annuals in the flower box outside Mom's bedroom." He put his hands on his son's shoulders. "This is Danny. Danny, this is my friend Paris and her dog, Bandit."

Danny gave her a quick smile before turning his attention to the dog. "He's cool looking. What is he?"

"A border collie mix. He's really smart and friendly. Why don't you make a fist, then hold it out for him to sniff? Bandit, say hi."

Bandit obliged by sniffing the boy's hand, then up his arm.

"Good dog," she said. "Danny, start by petting him on the shoulder. Sometimes dogs don't want you reaching for their heads. It makes them feel attacked."

Danny stared at her. "Really? I didn't know that."

Jonah stuck out his hand, reaching for his son's head. "Pretend you don't know me."

Danny immediately stepped back, then grinned. "I get it. A hand coming at you *is* like an attack. And I don't have my sword or jewels with me."

He crouched down on one knee. "Hey, Bandit. Hi, buddy."

Bandit licked his cheek. Danny grinned.

"He likes me!"

"He does. You can pet him now."

Danny carefully stroked his shoulder and back. Bandit shifted, nudging his hand with his head, offering his face for pets, too.

"His sword and his jewels?" Paris asked, her voice teasing. "School's really changed. I had to leave my jewels at home."

Jonah grinned. "It's a video game thing."

"I figured."

She didn't play these days. Even so, she couldn't help remembering how terrible she'd been when she'd insisted Jonah play with her. A ridiculous request considering he was literally one of the best in the world. Of course she was going to lose—and back then Paris hadn't handled losing well at all. Even worse was when he let her win. That infuriated her as much as the loss. Either way, by the end of the game she was screaming at him, possibly throwing things, and he was walking out the door.

"Danny," Jonah said, bringing her back to the present. "Paris owns the farm stand."

The boy stood and looked around, his expression confused. "By yourself?"

"I have a lot of help, but yes, this is my business. My grandfather opened it seventy years ago."

"Wow! That's a long time." He scrunched up his nose. "You weren't alive back then, were you?"

She laughed. "No. Not even close."

Bandit barked, assuming the puppy play position.

"Someone's in the mood for a game of chase," she said. "You up for it, Danny? I'll warn you, Bandit's fast."

Danny's eyes brightened. "I can run fast, too."

She pointed to the picnic area and the field beyond. "You want to take him up there?" She glanced at Jonah. "It's completely fenced and this time of day, no one's around. They'll be safe."

"Sounds good." He nodded at his son. "Stay where I can see you."

Danny took off at a run, Bandit following along. When they reached the open area, Bandit found a yellow ball and nosed it toward Danny. The boy threw it to the back of the field. Bandit flew after it, nearly caught it in midair and immediately brought it back.

"That'll make him happy," Jonah said, looking at her.

"Danny or Bandit?"

He grinned. "Both."

"How's your mom doing? Excited and nervous about her surgery?"

"She's hoping for more mobility, but yeah, she's concerned about joint replacement. I've done a lot of research, and I think she's made the right decision."

Jonah had always been the guy to check things out, Paris thought, remembering the time he'd spent finding the right dishwasher when theirs had quit.

"I know she's happy to have you and Danny staying with her."

"She is." He glanced around at the farm stand. Families were piling out of three cars. "You're already getting busy."

"This is nothing. July is crazy."

"But you like it." His gaze was steady. "I thought you might go back to Hollywood."

Where she'd gone after college, she thought. She'd wanted to be a costume designer specializing in period movies. She'd been so determined, she thought, and that had been a long time ago.

"I belong here," she said lightly. "I didn't think so after my mom died or while we were together, but I do now."

She'd hated returning to Los Lobos to deal with the family business. The only bright spot had been being close to Laurel again. Then Jonah had showed up and they'd fallen in love and suddenly being in the small town had been magical. But over time, the walls had seemed to close in. Probably the result of her temper, she thought. She wouldn't have been happy anywhere—not back then.

He continued to study her, as if trying to solve a problem. She found herself admitting to an ugly truth.

"I was a mess when you left," she said quietly. "You know how people who drink go on a bender? I did the same thing, but it was an anger bender. I was furious with you in particular and the world in general. I terrorized nearly everyone I knew." Laurel had been the only one to escape her fury.

"Selling wasn't really an option. I came close to losing the business. I slapped one of my employees, fired most of the others, or they quit. I didn't know how to handle all I was feeling."

"I'm sorry," he began.

She held up her hand. "Not your fault or your rock. My inability to deal with my emotions is on me. I learned that anger was power and it was a hard lesson to unlearn. Unfortunately there was a lot of collateral damage, including you and our marriage. I'm sorry for that."

"I'm sorry for what you went through."

She tried to smile. "You're being too kind. I was horrible. You were smart to get out."

She looked around, seeing the fruit stand for what it was today. "Like I said, I got help. A lot of help. I worked hard to understand where I was messed up and where I was okay." This time she managed a real smile. "It turns out there are actual emotional skills the average toddler learns that I didn't. Let me just say, it's a bitch learning them at thirty. But I did. Then I started to build back my business, piece by piece, as they say. I apologized to the people I'd hurt, humiliated or both. I hired back the ones who were willing to give me a second chance. For a while I told myself when I got the farm stand up and running, I would finally be ready to leave, but by the time that happened, this was where I wanted to be."

She drew in a breath. "Whew. That was a lot to lay on you."

"I like knowing what happened to you. I'm glad you're okay."

"Thanks. So what about you? I heard you won a couple of tournaments. Congratulations. That's huge. Are you still playing?"

"Not professionally, but I'm still active in the gaming world."

He looked good, she thought with regret. More comfortable with himself. He'd always been a good guy, but now he was a good guy who knew stuff. From what she'd seen, he and Danny were tight.

Her heart clenched a little, making her wish, once again, that they'd stayed together and that she'd been able to learn all she knew now before he'd left. So much would have been different.

"You want to come over for dinner tomorrow night?" he asked, then smiled. "You and Bandit, of course. My mom's not having her surgery until next week, and when I mentioned I'd seen you, she suggested dinner. I'd like that, too."

"Why would you want to have dinner with me?" she asked before she could stop herself.

He chuckled. "We used to be married. I thought it would be interesting to catch up."

"You should hate me."

"I've never been very good at doing what I'm supposed to. Come on. It'll be fun."

Dinner with him, his son and his mother? An evening of talking about old times, most of which involved her acting like a jerk. She really didn't want a whole night of being the bad guy.

Only she knew facing her past was important. Accepting it meant recognizing how far she'd come, how much she'd learned, grown and changed. So while there was pain, there was also reward.

"I'm in," she said lightly. "And I'm pretty comfortable accepting on Bandit's behalf."

"I'll text you the time."

seven

Cassie studied the wine bottles in front of her. She closed her eyes, drew a breath, then opened her eyes.

"The Pinot Grigio has a lot of fruit with an outstanding finish, the Sauvignon Blanc is unexpectedly dry, so it doesn't have the sweetness some people don't enjoy. It's understated with a delicate nose, so we think you'll enjoy that one first."

She went through the rest of the wines in the flight, checked her notes, then mentally gave herself a little cheer for getting it right.

The job at Books and Bottles had come through. She'd sailed through her interview, had spent exactly one afternoon training and today was her first solo shift. The digital pay system was close enough to the one at the bar that she'd conquered it in minutes. The food was also a snap. It came prepacked from a local gourmet deli. Instructions were on every item. All she had to do was unwrap and plate, maybe slice a tomato or two, heat a savory pinwheel or grill a premade sandwich. Nothing she couldn't handle.

The bigger challenge came from the wines they served. They were all from the West Coast—mostly California, but also several from Oregon—mostly Pinot Noir—and a collection of Washington wines from a place called Painted Moon.

Amazingly, her boss had told her to take home any bottle that had less than a quarter in it so she could get to know what she was pouring. A generous offer.

She'd showed up at ten forty-five, fifteen minutes early for her shift. She'd spent the time prepping for the day, then quizzing herself on the wines. Now she looked around and wished for a few customers.

As if on command, two women walked into the bookstore and headed directly for the wine bar. She would guess they were in their early- to mid-thirties, both casually dressed in jeans and shirts. The taller of the two was a pretty brunette with a long ponytail, while the blonde was curvier, but just as attractive. They spotted her and smiled.

"You're open," the blonde said happily. "We tried to come here last week, but they said there was no one to work during the day. You are a welcome addition to the workforce."

They sat at the bar.

The blonde looked at Cassie's name badge. "Hi, Cassie. I'm Laurel and this is Paris." She pulled an old, battered paperback out of her bag and set it on the bar. "We're here for our summer book club meeting."

Paris shook her head. "You left out *sad*. Or *pathetic*." She sighed. "Everyone emailed to say they were passing."

Laurel leaned forward. "We have a big, rowdy town book club during the school year. In the past couple of years, Paris and I have continued it through the summer, reading lighter books. Last year we did classic mysteries. The year before was seriously old-timey science fiction." She held up her paperback. "This year it's romances from the 1980s. But apparently it's just going to be us."

"Is it the romance thing?" Cassie asked.

"No. It was just us last year, too." Paris tapped the book.

"Maybe we should take the hint and not have summer book club."

"But I love summer book club." Laurel shook her head. "We're doing this. We both have fun, so we'll be small but mighty."

"Like a miniature horse," Paris murmured.

Cassie did her best not to laugh. "There's a visual. All right, small but mighty summer book club. What can I get you?"

Both women looked at the chalkboard menu that listed wine flights and food offerings.

"The half flight of white wine for me," Paris said.

"Same," Laurel said.

Cassie pointed. "Want to get the lunch special?"

Paris nodded.

"It looks really good," Cassie told them. "There's a cheese plate, spinach artichoke squares, Italian deli pinwheels and a fruit tart."

"Sold!" Paris told her.

Cassie got the pastry items into the small oven before unwrapping two personal size cheese plates and putting them in front of the women. Once that was done, she carefully poured an ounce of four white wines into glasses. During her interview she'd been told the half flight was popular. Which made sense. Despite tasting four wines, volume wise, it added up to only a single glass.

"I love Wolf," Laurel said. "He's the perfect hero."

Paris grinned. "Too bad he's not real." She looked at Cassie. "Have you read this?" She held up her book.

Cassie looked at the cover. "*Mackenzie's Mountain.* I've never heard of it, so no. It looks old. Oh, wait. You said you were reading romances from the 1980s." She frowned. "I don't think I've ever read one that old. Are they different?"

"Some. The writing style and some of the circumstances." She grinned. "They don't have cell phones."

Cassie couldn't imagine life without her cell phone. Or her tablet. Or her e-reader. "I'd miss the technology."

She served the wine, then plated the pinwheels and squares. "Enjoy," she said with a smile.

Laurel picked up the first wineglass. "You're new in town, aren't you?"

"I am. How did you know?"

"You're not a familiar face." Laurel smiled. "Los Lobos is growing like crazy, but we've lived here all our lives. Even if we don't know everyone by name, we've seen them around."

Cassie could relate. It was the same back in Bar Harbor, she thought, trying to ignore the stab of homesickness. Tourists came and went but the locals—she knew them all.

"I moved here a few days ago," she admitted. "From Maine."

"Coast to coast," Paris said. "That's a long way. What brought you here?"

"I inherited some land from my great-uncle. It's land and caves. At least that's how it's described. I haven't seen it yet."

She heard her voice getting smaller and smaller as sadness overwhelmed her. She had no idea what Uncle Nelson had been thinking, leaving her brother and sister money but her land. She didn't want the land and she sure didn't want to live in stupid California. It was too far, too different and not home.

"Are you okay?" Paris asked kindly. "It's hard starting over."

"I'm not starting over!" Cassie said emphatically. "I'm only here for six months."

The women exchanged a glance, which reminded her so much of Garth and Faith. The silent communication and once again, she was the one left out.

Unexpected tears burned in her eyes. She blinked them away, but not fast enough.

"What's wrong?" Laurel asked, sounding concerned. "Do you want to talk? Should we change the subject? Do you hate us and so we should leave?"

"I don't hate you." Cassie cleared her throat. "Sorry. I'm not being very professional. I apologize."

Laurel waved her hand. "Oh, please. It's us. There's no one else here."

"I'm sorry I upset you," Paris said, watching her carefully. "But I don't know what happened."

"It's not you." Cassie looked away, then back at them. "Seriously, it's not you. Things have been tough lately. I just…" She paused to try to gather her thoughts.

"My boyfriend broke up with me. He said I was boring and that I cared more about my family than him, which might be true, but then he decided to move without telling me, which is awful." She sucked in a breath. "I'm the one who takes care of everything. I'm the one who manages it all. Edmund—"

"The boyfriend?" Paris clarified.

"Uh-huh. I helped him pay off his credit card."

Laurel winced. "You gave him money."

Cassie looked at the bar. "Not a lot."

She paused again. A thousand dollars was a lot, but she wasn't going to say that.

"On the same day he broke up with me, my sister and brother threw me out. They said I was doing too much for them and not living my life. They said I'm hiding behind what I think they need. So they said I had to come see my inheritance and live here for six months or I won't be allowed back in the family."

She swallowed. "So here I am." She tried to fake a smile. "I'm fine. It's been a lot."

"I so get the bad boyfriend," Laurel said, putting a piece of cheese on a cracker. "My ex is a total loser and I didn't have the strength or courage to dump him. He left me. It hurt, but I'm much happier without him." She frowned. "Does saying that help or make me seem insensitive?"

Cassie sighed. "It helps and I get what you're telling me. I miss my sister more than I miss Edmund. What does that say about our relationship? I know he wasn't good for me, but it was nice having someone, you know?" She leaned against the counter. "I had a lot of time to think on the drive here. Maybe I *have* been hiding from my life. I don't know. It felt like they always needed me."

"Like Miss Havisham in *Great Expectations*," Paris murmured.

"Oh, right. Stuck in a moment of time." Laurel turned back to Cassie. "So you're here for six months and then you're going home?"

"That's the plan."

"You've only been here a few days and you already have a job. So that's positive."

"You have kids, don't you?"

Laurel's eyes widened in surprise. "Yes. Why do you ask?"

"You were using a 'mom' voice. The one that encourages stuff that's not that impressive. I've heard my sister use it a lot."

Even on her, Cassie thought grimly. How many times had Faith praised her for something not very praiseworthy?

"I don't know what to think," she admitted. "I'm twenty-eight and what have I done? I never went to trade school or college, so my skills are limited. I help out my brother in his bar and my sister in her B and B. I fall for guys who always leave me. And now I'm in a strange place where I don't know anyone. I'm living at a crappy motel." She paused. "Okay, it's not that crappy, but still." And she was in California, but saying that to two natives and the only people she'd had a real conversation with since arriving seemed rude.

"I told my sister I'd hate her forever, but I don't. I miss her, and my nieces and my brother. I miss my life, but there's nothing *to* miss, so what's up with that? I'm a mess."

"You're in transition," Paris said. "That's a good thing."

"How?"

"You're not stuck anymore." She waved her book. "Want to join our book club?"

Cassie glanced at the cover. "But you've already read that one."

"We have." Laurel smiled at her. "We were just about to start a new one. It's *summer* book club so the rules are different." She counted off on her fingers. "We take turns picking the books. They have to be from the 1980s and none longer than five hundred pages."

She paused to smile. "We do have other commitments."

"I get that."

Laurel continued. "The meetings aren't formal. We text each other when we're done and then we arrange to meet and talk about the new book. So super simple. Oh, the next book is this one."

She pulled a copy of *A Knight in Shining Armor* by Jude Deveraux from her bag. "Marilyn, the store owner, got these for us. I think she ordered a couple of extra, so there might be one in stock."

Cassie looked from the book to the two women who had so graciously invited her to join their book club. "I'll get it today and read it over the next couple of days."

"Take your time."

Laurel tilted her head. "Do you want to rent an apartment?"

Cassie stared at her.

"I have a little apartment off my house. Private entrance, laundry. I fixed it up to rent it out, but now I'm not sure I want someone I don't know living so close to me and my two kids. But you seem nice and it's only for six months, so maybe we could see if it works out."

"Is it furnished?"

"It can be." She glanced at Paris. "I'd have to do a background check, right?"

"And a credit check." Paris smiled at Cassie.

Cassie was having trouble adapting to the shift in conversation. She wanted to say that Laurel couldn't rent to her—she didn't know her. Except as a rule landlords didn't know their tenants. And a furnished apartment with a six-month lease solved a lot of problems.

"I don't know what to say," she admitted. "You're both being so nice. I'd love to look at the place."

"How about tomorrow?" Laurel said.

"Does morning work?"

"It does." Laurel dug a piece of paper and a pen out of her bag. "Here's the address. It's not hard to find."

Cassie held the note tightly in her hand. "I'm looking forward to it."

"Me, too."

Laurel left her lunch-slash-small-but-mighty-book-club meeting feeling pretty good about the possibility of renting out the apartment. Cassie seemed nice. Hopefully the background check and credit report would be positive. The shorter lease would allow her to see if she liked being a landlord. Of course, figuring that out after spending all the money on the remodel seemed like a bad plan, but too late to change that now.

"One problem possibly solved, forty-seven to go," she murmured to herself as she pulled into the parking lot of the local UPS Store.

Normally, the delivery service came to her. Laurel's Happy Finds shipped on Tuesday and Thursday, with the big brown truck pulling up at about four in the afternoon to collect all the boxes Darcy had prepared that day. Most of her customers were happy with regular ground shipping, but every now and then, someone wanted something delivered overnight. And as it was neither Tuesday nor Thursday, she was dropping off the shipment herself.

She walked into the store with two packages and waved at Christian, the franchise owner. They'd gone to high school together, but had never been close.

"What is it today?" Christian asked with a grin. "A vintage toaster oven?"

"I've never bought a toaster oven for resale." She laughed.

"I'm not sure I'd make any money on that." She patted the box. "It's a cat figurine. Murano glass."

He scanned in the prelabeled package. "Yours is the strangest business in town. I know you do well, but it's hard for me to imagine that you can be successful buying stuff in thrift stores and then reselling it online."

She smiled. He wasn't the only one who couldn't grasp the concept. "I buy from estate sales, as well," she told him. "And online auctions. Sometimes people don't know the value of what they're giving away and sometimes they don't care. They want it gone."

Or a family did after someone had passed away. Having to deal with a house full of "treasures" could be overwhelming. Selling at a discount or giving it away was often the easiest and fastest solution.

He took the box. "I admire you, Laurel. You work hard and you're a good mom."

The unexpected words surprised her. "Thanks, Christian. I love my kids, so that part is easy. As for the working hard, I guess it's how I was raised."

"It's more than that. I have trouble getting help here, especially over the holidays. I pay top dollar, but a lot of people don't want to work." He shrugged. "You're a small business owner. You know what I'm talking about."

"I do, although I don't have your problem with hiring employees."

"That's right. You have your stepmother working for you." He frowned. "Or your ex-stepmother."

"Actually, I have two ex-stepmothers on the payroll. Dad married sisters."

"Brave man."

"Or foolish," she said with a grin.

"That, too."

Christian was easy to talk to. He was a nice, normal man. She thought maybe he'd been married and divorced, and she didn't think he had any kids. Still, she wasn't looking for a substitute dad—she wanted a guy to be friends with. Maybe he was a candidate.

"Would you like to get coffee sometime?"

Christian froze, his expression suddenly hunted. "Hey, I was being friendly. I'm seeing someone."

"What?" Laurel felt herself flush as she took a step back. "No. I wasn't asking you out. I was asking as friends. I don't have a lot of guy friends in my life."

"I really am seeing someone."

"I got that. And I really meant as friends." She was hot with embarrassment and didn't know how to undo what had been done.

"Men and women can't be friends," he told her.

Was it just her, or had this conversation gotten out of hand? "Of course they can." At least in theory.

"It's not a good idea."

"According to you. I happen to think it's a great idea." Okay, not really, but why was he being a jerk?

He frowned at her. "Has it occurred to you that the reason you're single is you're really pushy?"

She held in a shriek. "I take it back, Christian. I was never here and we never had this conversation."

With that, she walked toward the door. When she got there, another customer started to come in. She tried to get past him, but when she moved left, he moved right. As they were facing each other, that meant they ended up in the same spot. The same thing happened again. The whole time, she could feel Christian staring at her, making the situation worse.

"I have to get out of here," she said desperately. "Please."

The other customer, a man close to forty, with dark hair and eyes, gave her an easy smile.

"I'm going to stand right here to the side. Why don't you walk out? Not that I haven't enjoyed dancing with you."

He did as he said, stepping aside and holding open the door. Laurel rushed past him and practically dove into her minivan. Once the door was closed, she put her hands on the steering wheel, tried to shake it, then let loose a scream.

"I was not asking him out!"

The awkward encounter replayed in her mind like a bad movie on an endless loop. How was she supposed to ever face Christian again? Was she going to have to get a FedEx account now? All she wanted to do was help her daughters see that men were a welcome part of normal life. But apparently that wasn't going to be happening today.

eight

Paris had second, third and fourth thoughts on the short drive to her former mother-in-law's house. Why had she accepted an invitation to dinner? Why had Jonah invited her? And perhaps most significant, why was she so incredibly nervous? She and Jonah had been over more than a decade ago—they'd both moved on. He'd remarried and had a child. She'd gone into intensive therapy, had taken anger management classes, and reinvented her life into something satisfying and drama free. She'd even joined a book club at her therapist's suggestion because people had different opinions about books and it was a good place for her to practice disagreeing without throwing a lamp. She was normal these days. Calm, steady. There was no reason to feel nervous.

"I'm losing my mind," she said, glancing in the rearview mirror. Bandit, his head stuck out the window, enjoying the car ride, ignored her confession.

"Thanks for your concern and empathy."

Her dog, never one to understand sarcasm, wagged his tail.

They arrived right on time. Paris let out Bandit, then picked up the bouquet of flowers she'd brought from work. She told herself the evening would be fine and even if it wasn't, hard emotional work was good for her mental health.

The front door opened before she could knock, leaving her leaning forward and unexpectedly close to Jonah.

"Hi," he said, his smile welcoming. "We're all really excited to have you over for dinner."

Her breath caught and her heartbeat thundered. A visceral reaction that was more about the past than any connection they had now. He'd left with no warning, giving her no closure, no chance to say goodbye. Oh, she didn't blame him at all, but the circumstances had made getting over him doubly hard.

"We're happy to be here," she managed. "I fed Bandit before we came. He needs to stick to a familiar diet."

"You're here! You're here!

Danny surprised Paris by flinging his arms around her for a brief hug before dropping to his knees in front of her dog.

"Bandit! Do you remember me?"

Bandit answered the question by swiping his tongue across Danny's cheek. The boy laughed.

"We made a bed of blankets for you in the kitchen," he said before scrambling to his feet. "Can we play outside until dinner?"

"Bandit would like that." Paris pulled a medium-sized Frisbee from her bag and handed it to the boy. "Wait until you see how well he catches this."

Jonah raised his eyebrows. "You came prepared."

"I thought there might be a little energy to be burned off on both sides."

Danny ran through the house. Bandit hesitated, looking at her for direction.

"Go play," she said, making a forward motion with her hand.

Bandit bounded after the boy. Paris heard Danny yell, "Look, Grandma! This is Bandit. We'll be in the backyard."

Paris and Jonah followed at a more leisurely pace. She had time to look around and see that Natalie had made changes to the one-story house. The hall bath was updated and the paint was a different color. Vinyl plank flooring took the place of carpet.

She clutched the flowers, reminded herself Natalie had never been one to make a scene, then walked into the remodeled kitchen.

Natalie was by the sink, a stack of lettuce and vegetables on the counter. She smiled at Paris.

"You made it! I'm so glad."

Jonah's mother had his coloring, but was much more petite. She'd always been friendly and helpful, something Paris hadn't been able to see while she was married. Back then she'd seen Natalie's caring as interference.

"It's so good to see you," Paris said, holding in a wince as the other woman limped toward her. She closed the distance, wanting to save Natalie the steps. They hugged.

"How are you feeling?" Paris asked. "You must be ready for your surgery."

"I am, and I'm dreading it, as well." Natalie laughed. "It depends on when you ask me." She waved toward Jonah. "You should check on your son. Make sure he doesn't tire out Bandit."

Jonah glanced at Paris, as if making sure she was all right being left alone with his mother.

"Yes, go check on them," she said easily. "I'll help get dinner ready so your mom can get off her feet."

"Good luck with that," he told her. "She keeps telling me she's more than capable."

When he'd left, Paris walked to the table in the corner and pulled out a chair. "I'm capable, too. Tell me what you want done."

Natalie hesitated before sinking into the chair. "Thank you, Paris. Some days are worse than others and today is a bad one." She waved toward the kitchen. "There's not much to do. The casserole's in the oven. All that's left is the salad." She wrinkled her nose. "I'm sorry dinner isn't fancier. I wasn't up to anything else."

"I'm here for the company. The food is just a bonus. And from what I remember, it will be delicious."

Natalie smiled. "You were always such a sweet girl."

"I think we can both agree that the word *sweet* was never used to describe my behavior at any time in my marriage to your son."

"You loved him."

"With all my heart." But that hadn't stopped her from being a nightmare.

She walked to the sink and washed her hands, then listened while Natalie told her what to take out of the refrigerator.

"Jonah eats salad now," his mother said with a laugh. "Different kinds of lettuce, odd ingredients, nuts. Back when he lived with me, I could barely get him to eat a green bean."

"Maybe it's being a father," Paris said lightly. "He wants Danny to be healthy." Or possibly the influence of his second wife, she thought, before telling herself not to go there. What was the point in speculating about a woman she'd never met?

"I'm sure it's partly that. And Traci." Natalie looked at her. "I'm sorry, Paris. I should have told you she died. I didn't know how."

Traci. So that was her name. Paris turned it over in her mind, searching for meaning or an image, but there was neither.

She crossed to the table and sat across from her former mother-in-law. "Of course you didn't want to tell me about her. You had no idea how I'd react. You were afraid of me and I apologize for that."

Natalie shook her head. "I was never afraid. I knew you loved Jonah. Having him leave was so hard on you."

"And I took it out on you."

She'd done more than that. She'd showed up at Natalie's house, demanding to know what had happened. She'd screamed, threatened, shattering a couple of vases against the wall.

"I was horrible," she said, wishing she didn't have to remember what those days had been like. "You're right—I was devastated when Jonah walked out. But you weren't a part of that. In fact, you tried to warn me."

More than once, she thought sadly. Her mother-in-law had explained that Jonah didn't deal well with confrontation. The more Paris pushed, the more he retreated. Natalie had urged her to change her fighting style, to try quiet conversations where both sides got to express themselves. A sensible suggestion, but given who Paris was at the time, also a laughable one.

"Knowing what I know now, I should have listened," she said, her voice filled with regret. "But I couldn't back then. I thought I could bend him to my will, and I could, to a point. But that wasn't a relationship. That was me bullying him. I'm surprised he stayed as long as he did."

"He loved you." Natalie leaned toward her. "I'm sorry for what you went through."

"Thank you, but I've learned that I'm responsible for what happened. I created the circumstances and now I'll deal with the consequences." She changed the subject. "I'm sorry about Traci. That must have been so difficult for both of them, but especially Danny. No child should lose their mother at such a young age."

"He's doing better now. While I appreciate the help while I have my surgery, I'm also hoping a change in routine will be good for him." She glanced out the window where Jonah and Danny played with Bandit. "Maybe Jonah will think about getting him a dog."

"I'm very pro-dog, but it's a big responsibility. If Jonah's still traveling, a dog could be a complication."

"He takes a couple of big trips a year, but he's mostly home these days."

Missing his wife, Paris thought, getting up from the table to continue working on the salad. She chopped radishes and tomatoes, added fresh grilled corn that was cooling on the counter. The dressing was ranch with a bit of tang. She'd finished tossing the salad when the three of them came into the kitchen.

"Those two can run," Jonah said with a grin. "I'm tired, but I'm not sure I wore them out."

"I'm starved." Danny walked to the sink where he began to wash his hands. "I can't wait for dinner."

The timer dinged. Paris got the casserole out of the oven and set it on the table. The plates and flatware were already in place. She gave Bandit water before showing him the bed of old blankets. He scratched at the pile, circled a couple of times, then collapsed and gave a contented sigh.

Jonah carried over the salad, then got out milk for Danny and held up a bottle of Pinot Grigio.

"I'll take a glass," his mom said.

"Me, too." Paris hovered by the table. "Where should I sit?"

Danny pointed to the spot next to his, putting her across from Jonah. Once the drinks had been poured and set down, Jonah joined them.

"We say grace," he told her, holding out his hand to her.

That was new, she thought, bracing herself for the feel of his warm skin against hers. She offered her other hand to Danny.

Jonah offered a brief prayer of thanks for the meal, adding a special request that God look after his mom during her upcoming surgery. After a brief *Amen*, Danny released her hand and offered his bowl.

"Salad, please."

His casual assumption that she would do as he asked, warmed her. She was new in his life, yet he trusted her to act normally. He wasn't afraid or wary or hesitant. He was…confident, she thought, serving him salad. Healthy and loved. He moved through the world as if he belonged. He'd never had to huddle in a dark space, trying to get the lay of the land before venturing out. He didn't fear an unexpected, backhanded slap or worry that if he said the wrong thing, dinner would be flung against a wall and that he would, once again, go to bed hungry.

After Paris served him salad, his grandmother put casserole

on his plate, then he politely waited until everyone else had their food.

Paris tasted the chicken and rice casserole, then smiled at Natalie. "Delicious," she said. "As good as I remember."

"I'm glad you still like it."

Danny turned to her. "Paris, how do you know my dad?"

She looked at him, then at Jonah. He chuckled.

"I guess I never told him." Jonah smiled at his son. "Paris and I used to be married. Before I met your mom."

Danny frowned as he tried to grasp the concept. "I don't get it."

"Your friend Ben's parents are divorced. He has his mom and dad. They were married and they split up and now they're married to other people. I was married to Paris and when that ended, I met your mom."

"And fell in love." Danny speared a chunk of chicken. "Okay, now I understand." He looked at her. "So who did you marry?"

"I didn't."

She couldn't have. At first she'd missed Jonah too much to function. Later, when she'd realized she needed help—mostly because Laurel had cajoled and threatened until she admitted the truth—the thought of an intimate relationship terrified her. Alone she could keep control, but if another person came into the mix, she wasn't sure what would happen. It was easier to stay by herself. Lonelier, but easier.

"But Dad got married."

"He did and he had you." She smiled. "He's very lucky."

Danny frowned. "If you and my dad had stayed together, you could have been my mom. That's weird to think about."

Paris told herself to relax and smile. Danny was being a kid. As for being his (or anyone's) mom—that wasn't possible. Of course she'd always wanted children, but she couldn't take the chance. She never wanted her child to feel about her the way she felt about her mother. She never wanted her child to be terrified about what was coming next. It was safer to avoid the issue completely—not only for herself, but any child she might have.

"It *is* kind of strange," she said lightly. She turned her attention to Jonah. "You said you're staying in town for a couple of months?"

"That's the plan. I'm going to see if any summer camps have openings."

Danny sighed heavily. "Dad likes it when I play outside. He limited my video game time, even though I'm really, really good."

"Irony," Paris murmured with a smile.

Jonah grinned. "You're saying I spend too much time playing video games."

"I can't speak to what you're doing now, but you used to be in front of the TV or computer for hours and hours."

"I was in training."

"Is that what they're calling it these days?"

He chuckled. "I might have gotten carried away."

Their eyes locked. Paris told herself whatever she might be feeling—a low heat, anticipation, hope—was a reaction to a past she'd never gotten over. It wasn't real. Jonah was no more interested in her than he was in dating a dining room chair. She was his past. She would enjoy his kindness and remind herself that expecting more was just plain dumb.

"I can ask Laurel about summer camps. Her girls are in a few different programs."

"Girls? I remember Laurel and Beau having Jagger. She was just a baby when I…" He paused briefly. "How old is she now? Ten?"

"Twelve. Her sister, Ariana, is ten. Beau and Laurel split up over a year ago. He moved away, but Laurel's still here."

Danny had perked up at the talk of other kids, but when he heard their ages, his shoulders slumped. "They're never gonna want to play with me. They're too old."

"Oh, I don't know. They might want to hang out a little. I'll ask Laurel."

"I'd like to see her," Jonah said. "I remember when the four of us used to double-date. Beau was an interesting guy. A lot of personality."

But not much substance. Neither of them said the words she suspected they were both thinking.

"You said you weren't playing in tournaments anymore," she said.

"He's producing them," Natalie said proudly.

Paris looked at him. "Really?"

"Mom, I have a staff." He smiled at Paris. "They do the planning. I oversee it all and make sure the kids are taken care of. I saw a lot of exploitation when I was a player. Young teens driven too hard. Sure, everyone wants to win, but sometimes the cost is too high."

She understood. The elite teams were under a lot of pressure to succeed. They were often away from their families, practicing impossible hours, without a lot of oversight by advocates.

"A noble calling," she said.

The meal passed quickly, with all of them talking as if they'd known each other for years. Paris supposed in some ways, they had. She'd been in her early twenties when she'd met Jonah, and in her late twenties when he'd left her. Natalie had moved to town to be near the newlyweds, then had stayed.

After dinner the two of them cleaned the kitchen while Natalie retreated to her room to watch TV. Danny escaped for his lone hour of evening video game play, leaving Paris alone with Jonah. She wiped down the counters, then hung the towel before smiling at him.

"Dinner was great. Both the food and the company. Thank you for inviting me." She waved at Bandit. "Us."

"Thanks for coming."

He was watching her with a studied gaze. She had no idea what he was thinking. Maybe he was trying to reconcile the new calmer Paris with the ill-tempered woman he'd known before.

She got her bag and called for Bandit, then started for the door. Jonah went with her. When they stepped out onto the porch, he confirmed her suspicions by saying, "You're different."

"You mean I got through a whole meal without throwing anything at you?"

She'd meant the comment to be funny, but he didn't smile. "You're happier."

Okay, that was a safer topic. "I am. I know who I am and I'm proud of how I live my life. That feels good."

He shoved his hands into his pockets. "What happened to you wasn't your fault."

"You mean my mom abusing me? You're right—it's not. But what I did, repeating the pattern, that's totally on me. She was abusive, so that's what I learned. You were one of my main victims and I am sorry about that. There's so much I wish I hadn't put you through."

"Hey, stop apologizing. We're starting over where we are now."

She knew what he meant. He was back in town for his mom and they were old friends. Nothing more. She was very clear on that—she had to be. Because if she didn't keep herself in check, she would start reading too much into his words.

Maybe it was because he looked so good, she thought sadly. A little older, but still much the same as he had been. He needed a haircut, but the longer style suited him.

Her gaze dropped to his mouth. Involuntarily, she remembered what it was like to be kissed by him. Jonah was a slow kind of kisser. He took his time, as if he wanted to be sure he was getting it right. She loved his kisses, and the way he'd touched her. In her less volatile moments, she'd loved walking in the door and knowing he was in the house. Just seeing him had filled her heart so completely, she'd sometimes wondered if it would burst.

Bandit pressed his nose against her palm, as if reminding her they should go.

"Thanks again for dinner," she said, stepping off the porch. "It was fun."

"It was. Night, Paris."

She gave him a quick wave as she hurried to her truck. She opened the passenger door for her dog, then walked around to her side. She glanced back at the house, but Jonah had already gone inside. No trace of him lingered, except for the sense of loss and the knowledge that she'd destroyed everything good they'd ever had. He'd moved on so completely, he'd fallen for someone else. She could have all the regrets she wanted, but they weren't going to change a thing.

nine

Cassie followed the directions her phone called out, turning off a quiet street onto a long driveway. There was a big white Victorian toward the front of the lot and a huge, weathered barn in the back. A sign on the side of the driveway said *Laurel's Happy Finds* with an arrow pointing to the barn. When she'd texted Laurel to confirm her appointment to see the apartment, the other woman had told her to come to the barn.

Cassie parked and got out of her small SUV. The barn doors were open in the warm afternoon. In the yard was a green tractor, minus the motor and seat. A slightly battered but sturdy-looking playhouse stood beside a swing set.

Cassie walked to the open barn doors and peered inside. There was a long, low counter with a swinging half door and beyond that rows and rows of metal shelving units. From where she was standing, she couldn't figure out what Laurel's business was. She saw vases and stacks of dishes, tiny figurines and overflowing plastic bins.

"Hello? Laurel?"

"Oh, hi. You made it." Laurel stepped out from a row of shelves and smiled as she held open her arms. "Welcome to my mess."

Cassie looked around. "What is this place?"

"My workspace. I'm a thrifter. I buy things for as little as I can, then resell them. Most of my business is online. I have a booth at the big antique mall down the highway and once a year, at the end of August, I host a giant garage sale." She grinned. "It's my Christmas."

"Your what?"

"My Christmas. You know how retailers do about 25 or 30 percent of their business over the holidays?"

Cassie nodded.

"I do about that much of mine at the giant garage sale. The whole town participates. People come in from five states away. It's a thing. Anyway, that's what I do." She motioned to the shelves behind her. "Most of this is waiting to be listed on eBay, although I'm already collecting inventory for the garage sale."

"I'm overwhelmed," Cassie admitted, thinking she'd never known anyone who did what Laurel did. "Do you have employees?"

"Two. Marcy and Darcy. They're sisters. Marcy helps me catalog and price everything. She also gets things ready to be photographed so I can list them online. Darcy handles the shipping."

Laurel held open the swinging door, inviting her in. "Let's go back to my office and talk about the rental." Her smile returned. "You have excellent credit, by the way. And no history of a prison record. I hope you're still interested in the apartment."

"I am." Cassie was getting very tired of her small motel room and the noise from the highway. At first, eating out every meal had been kind of fun, but she was over it.

They walked through the maze of shelving units until they reached a small semi-open office area. There were three desks, lots of counter space and a half dozen file cabinets. A girl of about twelve sat at a laptop.

She was a cute blonde who looked enough like Laurel for Cassie to guess the relationship. But even as she smiled at the girl, she felt a tug of longing for her nieces. Texting wasn't the same as seeing them every day.

"Jagger, this is Cassie. She's interested in the apartment."

Cassie waved. "Nice to meet you."

Jagger frowned. "I've never seen you before. Are you from around here?"

"No. I grew up in Bar Harbor, Maine."

Jagger's eyes widened. "That's on the other side of the country. Is it nice? Do you miss it?"

"A lot, especially my family."

"So why are you here?"

"Jagger." Laurel's tone was warning. "Let's wait on the interrogation."

"But questions show I have an interest in people," her daughter protested. "It's a whole social thing, Mom."

Laurel's lips twitched, as if she were trying not to smile. "Thank you for explaining that. Now let's show Cassie the apartment." She turned to her. "Assuming you're still interested, because I actually have two kids. Ariana's ten. She's hanging out with her friends, but she lives here, too. It's preteen girls, just so you're warned."

"I can handle it." Maybe Laurel's daughters would help her feel less lonely.

The three of them walked to the house. The closer they got, the more worn the Victorian looked. No doubt the property was expensive to keep up, Cassie thought. After all, there was a reason Laurel was renting out the apartment.

"Are you married?" Jagger asked, then glanced at her mom. "Is it okay if I ask that?"

"Yes, asking if someone's married is fine."

"Rules." Jagger sighed. "Are you?"

"No. I, ah, no. I mean, my boyfriend and I broke up." Cassie didn't really miss Edmund, but she was still annoyed and hurt by what he'd said. "Actually, he dumped me."

"Men are horrible," Jagger muttered. "They find someone good and then they act stupid and ruin everything."

Cassie glanced at the girl. "I wouldn't say Edmund was horrible. And some men are great. My brother, Garth, is responsible and nice. He always treats his girlfriends like princesses. I miss him."

Jagger didn't look convinced. Laurel smiled tightly and pointed to the house. "Private entrance right around here."

Laurel fished a key out of her jeans front pocket and opened the pretty blue door. They all stepped inside.

Cassie hadn't known what to expect, but the completely renovated space stunned her. Everything was new and clean. The ceilings had to be at least ten feet high and the crown molding looked original. Tall windows let in plenty of light.

"As you can see, it's all been updated," Laurel said. "My contractor took out a couple of walls to make it more open concept."

"It's great," Cassie breathed, thinking it was so much more than she'd expected. She ran her hands across the small island. There was plenty of storage in the kitchen.

Laurel showed her the stacked washer and dryer. "There's just the one bathroom, but the bedroom is a good size."

Cassie glanced in the bedroom. Like the living room, the space had plenty of windows. The closet was a good size and she nearly swooned when she saw the claw-foot tub/shower in the bathroom.

She could see herself here, she thought happily. The apartment felt good.

"You'd said something about it being furnished." She glanced at Laurel. "I only have what I could fit in my car."

"I have everything that was in here." Laurel's voice was doubtful. "It's not new or especially in style, but it's good quality."

"It's grandma furniture," Jagger said bluntly. "Wait until you see the dresser. It's big and really fancy."

"I could do fancy."

She loved the apartment and could easily live with grandma

furniture. After all, she was only in Los Lobos for six months. At six months and one day, she was heading home.

"Let's talk terms," Cassie said.

They went back to the barn. Jagger took her laptop outside while Laurel printed out a copy of the lease she'd drawn up.

"It's pretty standard," she said. "I found it online and had Paris look at it."

"Is Paris a lawyer?"

Laurel laughed. "God, no! She owns the farm stand by the highway. But she's a terrific businesswoman." She motioned to the barn. "I can handle this, but she has to manage over a dozen employees, scores of vendors, the public and special events. She's my hero."

As far as Cassie was concerned, they were both impressive. Here she was, twenty-eight years old with virtually nothing to show for herself. Pathetic.

She pushed the thought away and scanned the lease. It was straightforward and the monthly rent was reasonable.

While Cassie was reading, Laurel made a couple of calls. When Cassie said, "I'll take it," Laurel waved her phone.

"I can have the furniture back in the apartment in two days. Does that work?"

"Absolutely. I mean, I'll miss my highway motel, but I'll recover."

Laurel grinned. "You're saying laundry and a kitchen will help with the pain."

"They will."

"I want you to be honest with me about the girls. If they're bugging you, tell them to go away. Or tell me. You're new and they're going to be very curious. I don't want them getting in the way."

"I don't think they'll be a problem, but I will let you know if I'm wrong."

They talked for a few more minutes, then Cassie signed the lease and paid the deposit. She would pay the first month's rent when she moved in.

She left Laurel's place and started back toward the motel. Now that she had somewhere to move to, she couldn't wait to get out of there. The apartment was perfect. The light, the cute kitchen, the tub.

A couple of miles before the motel, she spotted the sign for Los Lobos Farm Stand and impulsively turned into the parking lot. She'd seen the stand, but hadn't bothered to stop—she had nowhere to store produce. But now that she had a place, she could check it out.

She walked around the large, open displays. There were beautiful berries, asparagus, some pineapples from Hawaii and, of course, avocados. What was it with this state? She spotted Paris talking to a customer by the cash register and waited until she was done before walking over.

"Hi," she said. "I don't know if you remember me. I'm—"

"Cassie. Of course I know who you are. You promised to join our book club. How's it going?"

"Good. I'm nearly done with *A Knight in Shining Armor*, by the way."

Paris raised her eyebrows. "You read fast."

Cassie shrugged. "I don't have a whole lot to do with my day, except for my shift at work. I saw Laurel's apartment just now." She smiled. "Actually, I rented it."

"That's great. Welcome to town. Now you're a resident."

A border collie mix trotted over. Paris reached down to pet his head.

"This is the man in my life. Bandit, this is Cassie. Say hi."

Cassie let the handsome dog sniff her fingers before stroking his back. "He's so soft."

"He gets regular brushings. He lives a good life."

"Laurel told me you own this place and run it yourself. That's a lot."

"I've been working here since I was a kid. Except for a few

years down in LA while I was in college and right after, I've always been here." She smiled.

Cassie wasn't sure why she'd stopped by. She didn't know Paris and she didn't have anything specific to talk to her about. But instead of leaving, she felt herself wanting to *hover*.

After a couple of seconds, Paris said, "The first of the season raspberries are here. If you have a few minutes, we could sample them."

"Sure. That sounds great."

Paris took a pint container from the stack and led the way to a break room. There she washed the berries before dumping them back into their container. They went out back to a large open area with plenty of trees for shade and picnic benches. They took seats while Bandit stretched out on the grass and closed his eyes.

"You must be happy to have a real place to stay rather than the hotel," Paris said, taking a couple of the raspberries.

"I am. It's getting old."

"How do you like the town?"

"It's nice. I like that it's not huge. I'm not really a big city kind of person."

"Have you ever lived in one?"

"No, but sometimes you just know a thing."

Or were afraid to try, she thought grimly. Because this forced trip was the first time she'd ever been away from home on her own. It was also the longest she'd been gone.

"Have you been to see your inheritance?"

The unexpected question caught her off guard and made her squirm in her seat. "Not yet. I've been busy."

Paris looked at her without speaking.

"I have! I'm learning a new job and figuring out where stuff is in town and reading our book club book and…"

"What are you afraid of?" Paris asked the question gently, as if she really wanted to understand rather than accuse.

"I'm not afraid." Cassie paused. "Maybe I am a little. Or maybe I'm confused."

"And angry."

"I'm not angry."

"Really? So it's okay that your brother and your sister tossed you out with no warning? Weren't you the one asking why they get to decide about your life?"

Cassie's chest tightened as unexpected annoyance burned in her belly. "Why do I care what they think of me? I'm an adult. I can live my life however I want. And if they were so worried about me, why did they always accept my help? No one said anything before. It's not fair."

"You're right, it's not." Paris reached for more raspberries. "Are they wrong to worry about you?"

Cassie didn't like that question, but she made herself think about her answer. "Maybe. I know I was drifting and I wasn't really happy. I wasn't unhappy, either. Maybe that's the problem. I mean, it's my life. Shouldn't I have strong emotions?"

"Not all the time, but every now and then, sure. So I'm going to return to my original question. When it comes to your inheritance, what are you afraid of?"

"That it will be life-changing."

The words came from nowhere. Cassie wanted to claw them back, but she couldn't figure out how, so they just hung there.

"And that's bad?"

"It could be." Cassie groaned. "I know, I know. If I'm not happy or unhappy then maybe life-changing is exactly what I need. It's land and a cave and whatever is in it or on it. I can't remember which. I should probably go look at it."

"That's up to you."

"You're very reasonable."

"It's my preferred state of being."

"So like Spock from *Star Trek*?"

Paris laughed. "That's not how I see myself, but sure. It works."

"The young guy is really cute. The other one, the old one, I'm sure he's nice and all, but more like a grandfather." She paused. "I have the name of a lawyer who has all the paperwork on the land. I'll call her and then I'll go see it."

"Is that what you want?"

Cassie considered the question. "Before I talked to you I would have said no, but now I'm a little curious. What if it *is* life-changing? Maybe that's a good thing."

"It usually is."

Laurel dropped Jagger off at her friend's house, then continued to the farm stand. Her stomach churned with worry. Even if she'd been willing to brush off the teacher's concerns about her daughter, Jagger's response to Cassie would have convinced her there was a problem. She parked and went looking for her friend.

"My life sucks," she said when she found Paris opening crates of oranges, using a vicious-looking crowbar.

"In general or is it something specific? You just missed Cassie, by the way. I heard she rented the apartment."

"She did. I think I'm going to like having her around."

Paris handed her oranges to put into the display. "Talk," she said. "What happened?"

"It's Jagger. When Cassie came by to see the place, she mentioned her boyfriend had dumped her. Jagger said men were horrible and always ruin a good thing." She put the oranges into neat rows. "She hates men. And it's my fault."

"It's not and blaming yourself doesn't help the situation. You're a great mom."

"Apparently not. You know what's worse? I tried to make friends with a guy and I sucked at that, too."

"How do you make friends with a guy?"

"Don't ask me."

Laurel explained about asking Christian out for coffee. Her friend listened carefully, then burst out laughing.

"He thought you were hitting on him."

"It's not funny."

Paris continued to laugh. "Yes, it is. I can't believe he called you pushy."

"I was humiliated."

Her friend sobered. "I'm sorry about that. I agree it's awkward."

"What if I can't use UPS anymore?" She dropped her chin to her chest. "I need a man friend and don't know how to get one."

"I'm at a loss, too," Paris said. "This is one time when Amazon isn't going to help us."

Laurel pressed her lips together. "I need my girls to be okay."

"They are. This is a blip that we'll get fixed. You could be friends with Jonah."

"Your ex?"

"While he's in town for his mom's surgery. He has an eight-year-old son."

Laurel shook her head. "You're being weirder than usual. I'm not going to be friends with the man you used to be married to." There was an undefinable ick factor. "Not that I don't appreciate the offer," she added. "How did dinner at his mom's go?"

Paris looked away. "Good. Nice. Danny's a sweetie and Natalie has always been supportive."

Laurel studied her. "Tell me."

"It's nothing." Paris shifted uneasily. "I'm being silly."

"You still have a thing for him."

"No. But I still miss him."

"Isn't that the same thing?"

Paris tried to smile. "Hey, I'm the one with the years of therapy. Only I get to be insightful." She hesitated. "It's hard to be around him. I remember all the crap I put him through and feel awful."

"That was years ago and you're different now."

"I am, but I still did those things. I loved him and I drove him away. Danny found out we'd been married before and said I could have been his mom. If I hadn't messed up, Jonah and I could have stayed together. Who knows what would have happened. Only he couldn't stay because of who I was, so we were doomed."

Laurel understood that Paris had learned to face her past without trying to gloss over the ugly parts, but sometimes she took it too far. "You're being mean to my friend."

Paris looked at her. "I'm being honest about who I was."

"You're only focusing on the negative. You were difficult and now you're not. Be proud of that. Do you want to get back together with Jonah?"

"What?" Her voice was a yelp. "No. It's been over a decade. I barely know who he is now. I was missing what I lost."

Laurel wasn't sure if she believed her, but knew better than to push. It was very possible Paris had no idea what she was feeling. Jonah's arrival had been a surprise. She would need time to process.

They chatted for a few more minutes until all the oranges were unpacked. Laurel hugged her friend.

"I'm going to do a little produce shopping, then head back to the barn and go through some very large boxes I bought at an estate sale."

"Busy, busy. What's in the boxes?"

Laurel laughed. "I genuinely have no idea. But I only paid twenty bucks, so I'm fine if they're a bust."

Laurel grabbed one of the small grocery carts. She was thinking maybe she would fire up the barbecue and they could have kebabs for dinner tomorrow. She would need bell peppers and cherry tomatoes. Plus, they were low on fruit. She was so focused on her mental list that she wasn't watching where she was going and physically ran into another customer.

"Oh, no! I'm sorry. Did I hurt you?"

"I'm fine."

She looked at her victim and was surprised to find he seemed familiar. Only she couldn't place him. Dark hair, dark eyes and—

He smiled. "Hello, again. Did you want to dance?"

"The UPS Store," she said, trying not to think about her disastrous encounter with Christian. "At the door."

"That was me." He pointed at her cart. "Although this time you're armed."

"I really am sorry."

"I believe you." He held up a carton of strawberries. "This place gets the best berries in town. I've tried the local supermarkets and they can't touch what they have here."

"Paris gets most of her produce from local farmers. That's why it's better."

"You know the owner?"

"We've been friends since the first grade. We grew up here. But you're not a local."

He grinned. "I've been here nearly six months. How long do you think before I can be considered one?" He paused, as if thinking. "Small town rules, so maybe thirty years?"

"About that."

"Good to know, because I plan on sticking around."

"You should come here on Saturday afternoons. There's usually a bake sale."

"Sounds like a good time."

"It is. There are also pony rides, but I'm pretty sure you'd exceed the height requirement. Oh, and if you're here at midnight on the summer solstice, you'll see the local witch coven in action. Everyone is welcome, but no heckling."

His eyes widened. "There's a witch coven? Are you a member?"

"It's not my thing, but I have seen the ceremony. It's very fun." She smiled. "In high school, all the guys would come out to watch. I'm pretty sure they were hoping for nudity."

He chuckled. "I'm sure they were. Thanks for the information. This town gets more and more interesting."

"You're welcome." She pointed to the aisle. "You go first. I'm going to wait until you've rounded the corner before I move. I wouldn't want to run into you again."

Something flickered in his eyes. "That's a shame because I wouldn't mind if you did."

ten

Halfway through the third mystery box from the estate sale, Laurel had to admit she'd wasted twenty dollars. One box had been full of receipts from the 1970s, for everything from postage stamps to a toaster. The second had been filled with broken toys and old dishes that had no resale value. The third was worn clothes that she would sort into donate and toss piles.

She opened the fourth one and groaned. More crapola, she thought, pulling out a few golf trophies and a wool jacket that had been seriously attacked by moths. She put the trophies on the table. She would look up the name later. Maybe whoever it was who'd played golf so well in college had gone on to be someone. If not, she'd gotten a big fat nothing for her—

Her breath caught as she spied a record album still wrapped in plastic. She pulled it out and smiled. Miles Davis *Kind of Blue.*

"Oh, Mr. Davis, you're a favorite of mine."

Not only did she enjoy his music, his albums brought in really good money. Especially one that was in pristine condition, like this one. Assuming it wasn't a fake. She'd been fooled before.

She glanced at her watch—she had plenty of time before she had to go pick up her daughters. She could swing by the recording studio, talk to her friend Victoria about the album, then take a nice long walk on the beach to clear her head, pick up the girls and be home in time for dinner.

Laurel drove across town to the industrial area—such as it was. There were a few warehouses, a couple of auto repair shops. A few years ago one of the buildings had been converted into a large recording studio. Rumor had it famous songwriters and bands came and went at odd hours, doing whatever they did to make music.

Her friend Victoria worked at the front desk a few days a week. They weren't book club close, but knew each other well enough to grab a coffee every now and then. Victoria would take any album Laurel was curious about and have it assessed by one of the music geeks. In return, Victoria got first dibs on any Murano glass animal figurines Laurel picked up in her thrifting travels. It was a system that worked for both of them.

She parked and collected her treasure, smiling as she went. She always had a mild sense of anticipation as she walked into the building, wondering if maybe she would run into Justin Timberlake or one of her other high school music crushes. The closest she'd come was brushing past a drummer she'd never heard of but whom Victoria claimed was "really famous."

No one was at the reception desk, which wasn't unusual. When a session was going well, people tended to go watch and listen. She went down the main hallway, glancing left and right, searching for someone to talk to. She rounded the corner and ran smack into someone. Miles Davis went flying.

Laurel shrieked, knowing she had to save him. She lunged forward, only to realize she wouldn't get there in time.

"I got it."

The man she'd bumped into easily caught the album, then turned it face up. He glanced at the cover. "You have good taste. Oh, it's you."

His eyes widened in surprise as his mouth curved into a smile. "We keep bumping into each other. Are you stalking me?"

She blinked at the man she'd run into three times.

"No," she said, feeling herself flush. She took a step back. "Los Lobos is a small town. I run into people all the time." She paused as she realized how that sounded. "Not physically. Just, you know, we're in the same place at the same time."

"You don't have to explain," he said easily. "I was messing with you. I'm Colton Berger." He held out his free hand.

"Laurel Richards."

"Nice to meet you." He waved the album. "What are you doing with our friend here? Great album, by the way. Classic and yet it's hauntingly different every time I listen to it."

"You know music."

"I know some music. I'm a sound engineer here." He returned the album to her. "What brings you to our recording studio?"

"I wanted to ask Victoria to have someone verify the authenticity. I've been fooled before by someone shrink-wrapping an album."

"Victoria's out of town. But I'm probably the person she'd bring it to, so let's go into the studio and take a look."

He started down the hallway. Laurel hesitated a second before following. They went into a glassed-in room filled with computer monitors and rows and rows of complicated-looking equipment. Colton sat at a desk and flipped on an overhead light. He held the album carefully, only touching the corners.

"See how the plastic is loose? And the one seam is starting to split? If someone had shrink-wrapped it recently, the plastic would be tight." He turned the album over and studied the back. "No barcode. They started to appear in maybe the 1980s or 1990s. So a release after that would have a barcode. That's a good sign, too."

He pointed to the small price label. "There's a smudge there, from the ink in the pricing gun. A computer printed label wouldn't smudge like that. And the numbers themselves would be crisper."

He looked at her. "Of course they could fake all that and find a blurry font, so I could be wrong about this. But I think it's genuine. We could open it to check the actual LP, but that would hurt the value." His smile returned. "Let me guess. A very cool birthday present for your husband."

"What?" Husband? As if. "No. It's for my business. I'm a thrifter. I buy things at the Goodwill, estate sales and antique malls, then resell them online."

She sank down in one of the chairs. "I'll do some research on our friend here, then put him up for sale."

"You don't want to keep him?" Colton's voice sounded wistful. "I mean, it is Miles Davis."

"Sorry. I have two kids to feed." And a mortgage to pay and a savings account to refill. The latter was the most challenging. Beau had emptied it and their checking account when he'd taken off. Thankfully, she'd never put him on her business accounts, so he hadn't been able to touch those.

"Daughters, right?"

The question drew her back to the present. "How did you know?"

"I've seen you with them. Like you said, it's a small town. I only noticed because the three of you were laughing so hard, you could barely walk." He shrugged. "I'm from a small town, too. In Tennessee. The youngest of five and the only boy."

"You have four sisters?"

"I do and plenty of nieces and nephews. Anyway, the three of you laughing reminded me of my family. That's why I remembered. I wasn't being creepy."

She sensed he was telling her the truth. "According to you, I'm the one doing the stalking, so let's call it even."

"Done." He pointed at the album. "How do you sell something like that?"

"I put it up on eBay. I'll research whether it makes more sense to simply do a buy-it-now price or have an auction."

"Let me know what you decide. I might want that for my personal collection."

"Given how many times I've literally run into you, I should probably give you a discount."

"I don't need that. Just a fair price."

He was nice, she thought in surprise. If only Jagger was here, Laurel could point out that some men were nice. Some men were polite and honest. But her daughter wasn't here so the example wouldn't have value.

Had the problem started when Beau left? she wondered. Or had it been before that when they'd been fighting so much? Or had Laurel inadvertently been contemptuous of men before that? She didn't think she had been, but she also hadn't known that her daughter hated men, so relying on her memory seemed risky at best.

"You okay?"

She looked at Colton. "I'm fine."

"You sure?" He held up both hands. "I'm not pushing, but you have this look. Half determined, half defeated."

His accurate assessment caught her off guard. "You're really good at reading people."

"I remind you about the four sisters. Want to talk about it? I'm an excellent listener."

She managed a smile. "I'm fine. You're very nice for asking." She had more to say, but her throat suddenly got tight and she had the craziest sense that she was going to cry.

"Do you have kids?" she managed.

"No. Wish I did. I get an email from my mom nearly every day asking if I've gotten anyone pregnant. It's a fairly desperate situation."

His words made her laugh, but on the heels of that came a burning sensation in her eyes. She blinked it away and struggled for control, then found herself blurting, "Beau left. My husband, their father. It's been over a year and I'm fine, but the girls need their dad."

She looked at him. "He started a river rafting company in Jamaica. Surprisingly, it's been a success."

"Jamaica's far."

"Yes, so he doesn't get back to see them much at all. Or ever. He barely texts them. Ariana, my youngest, she's ten, loves her daddy and defends him. Whatever he does, she's totally understanding, but I know under that is a world of pain. Jagger's twelve and she has so much anger toward her father. The things she says about him—it breaks my heart."

She struggled to keep her breathing even. "It gets worse. A couple of weeks ago I was called in by Jagger's teacher."

She explained why the teacher was concerned. "I've been paying more attention to what Jagger says, and she really does believe men are bad." The burning increased until Laurel wasn't sure she could hold back the tears.

"I'm sorry. I don't mean to get emotional, but we're talking about my kids and I love them so much and what if I broke them? I want to be a good mother, but maybe I'm not and now what?"

The tears came fast, followed by sobs she couldn't control. This was neither the time nor the place for a breakdown, yet she couldn't seem to stop herself.

She felt a few tissues being pushed into her fingers and a comforting hand on her shoulder.

"It's okay," Colton said quietly. "You'll feel better if you let it all out. You feel how you feel. There's no judgment in it."

"There's plenty of judgment," she said, her voice shaking. "I judge myself all the time."

"Think about giving yourself a break."

She sucked in a few breaths. "I don't deserve one."

After a few more minutes, she managed to get herself under control. Colton returned to his seat and watched her with concern and what she thought might be compassion.

"You're a very nice man," she told him.

That made him laugh. "I'm not nice, I'm well trained and educated in the ways of being human."

"A subtle difference." She blew her nose. "This is not how you planned to spend your afternoon."

"I'm good. There's no one recording today, so I've been catching up on all the work that accumulates when we're busy. Nothing that can't wait. So the girls don't see their dad much?"

"No. Not since he moved to another country. I get he has his dreams, but what about his children? They should be a priority. Not that he would be the best male role model."

She tossed a couple of tissues into a nearby trash can and took two more from the box.

"Jagger's teacher suggested I find a male role model. You know, a family friend, an uncle or grandfather. It's good advice, right? Except I'm an only child, as were my parents. Beau doesn't have any family nearby. He's unavailable. So I looked around at my life and it is absolutely a male-free zone."

He chuckled. "For real?"

"If you don't count my best friend's dog, yes. I have two employees, both women. Paris, my BFF, is single. All my friends are single. I mean, I know married women but not well enough to say 'hey, can my girls and I hang out with you and your husband so they can see men aren't jerks?'"

"So what's your plan?"

She sighed. "I don't have one. I thought maybe I'd find a guy to be friends with." She felt herself flush. "My one attempt didn't go well."

"He thought you were hitting on him."

"Yes! Why? I just asked him out for coffee. It was so embarrassing and now I can never go back to the UPS Store."

"Have you seen you?" he asked casually. "If he wasn't sure you were hitting on him, he would be hoping you were."

"Why?"

"You're beautiful."

Laurel stared at him. Beautiful? Her? She was mildly pretty at best, she thought, and had never lost the twenty pounds she'd put on after Ariana had been born. She spent her life trying to make sure her size 14 clothes didn't get too tight. Her focus was her kids and her business. She barely had time to shower, let alone get fancy with makeup and coordinated clothing.

"You have me mistaken for someone else," she said flatly. "But yes, he did think I wanted to go out with him, which I totally didn't. I just wanted to be friends."

"I'll be friends with you."

She stared at him. "Why would you bother?"

The response, not exactly friendly, was honest and instinctive.

"Seriously," she continued. "I'm a mess, and this is about my girls, not me. I don't know you. What if you're yucky?"

Rather than being offended, he grinned at her. "Later you're going to replay this conversation in your head and wince."

"Probably, but I stand by what I said. It's a strange offer."

"But a genuine one. Look, I'm relatively new in town. I miss my family, especially my nieces and nephews. I'd like to be friends. I'm a decent guy, I'm great with emotional drama and I can teach your girls to throw a mean curve ball. I'm guessing it's a skill they don't have right now."

"Nor one they're going to need in life."

"You never know." He opened his desk drawer and pulled out a business card. "Investigate me. Talk to my boss, or better yet, talk to Quinn's wife, Courtney."

"Courtney Yates? I've known her forever. We were only a couple of years apart in high school."

"She's met me. I'm sure Quinn checked me out before he hired me."

She was having trouble taking it all in. "You're offering to be my friend and help me with my girls."

"I am."

"Because you're lonely."

"I'd like a reason that makes me sound less pathetic, but yes. And to help." His smile returned. "I'm a guy. I like to fix things. It's in my DNA. Plus, it's what my parents would expect me to do and I don't like to disappoint them, even from a distance."

Laurel wasn't sure her problem could be fixed, but she had to try. She wanted the best for her girls. Was Colton part of the solution?

She took the business card. "Thanks. I'll think about it."

"Good." He tapped the record. "You're going to get a good price for this."

"I think I will. Thank you for the information with that, too."

She collected her bag and the album and walked out to her minivan. Once she was behind the wheel, she looked back at the recording studio, not sure what to think. She'd had what had to be one of the strangest conversations ever with a man she didn't know.

After witnessing her meltdown, he'd offered to help. Weird, but assuming he wasn't some kind of scary, mentally deranged person, also very nice. On the surface, he seemed like a good guy. He was funny and kind and, okay, attractive. Not that his looks mattered when it came to her daughters. And he'd offered to be her friend. She didn't know what that meant, but given how dire the situation was, it seemed to be something she should consider.

She was sure Paris would help her run a background check and she could certainly talk to Courtney about him, although having to explain why she cared made her a little uncomfortable. But this wasn't about her or what she was feeling, it was about her girls and for them, she would do anything.

Cassie stood in the middle of what she was fairly sure was her inheritance. She hadn't known what to expect beyond the fact that it was land. According to the lawyer, it was over twenty-five acres and as she looked around, she had to admit the tract was huge and daunting.

There were trees for as far as the eye could see. Some looked tall and healthy, but some seemed sad and lifeless.

What she knew about trees could fit on a three-by-five card and leave room for a complicated recipe. She didn't know if they needed water, a tree doctor, fertilizer or to be cut down. Nor did she know what kind of trees they were. She thought there were at least two types, but wasn't sure.

She'd parked on a gravel road by a run-down house. According to the lawyer, that was hers, too, but it seemed closed up and forbidding, so there was no way she was going in by herself. As she walked through her property, she kept a close eye out for snakes because didn't they thrive in moderate temperatures? Were there poisonous snakes in the area? Not that she liked the nonpoisonous ones, either. At least if she saw one and screamed, there was no one around to point and laugh. Of course there wasn't anyone to help her if she was attacked by a snake. Life, as always, was complicated.

She continued through the orchard. The trees gradually thinned out, leaving the land covered with what she would guess were native plants and grasses. There was a gentle slope down. The lawyer had told her the property ended at the stone wall, wherever that was.

She kept walking, following what seemed to be a well-worn path and came to a stop when she saw the opening to a cave.

"The land, the cave and whatever is in it," she murmured to herself, eyeing the dark opening. What had Uncle Nelson been thinking when he left her this? So far none of it was life-changing in the least.

She started for the cave, telling herself she would be fine. There were probably spiders, but she was okay with that. Of course, if there was a nest of snakes, that was a whole other issue.

She got about ten feet into the cave before it took a turn. She hesitated, wanting to go on, but not sure she should do that by herself. Sunlight didn't spill in very far and she was a little nervous about the whole walking-in-the-dark-slash-snake thing.

She used the flashlight function on her phone to illuminate the way, then came to a stop when she saw drawings on the wall. She squinted at the images, trying to make sense of them.

There was a woman carrying a jug, with three children playing nearby. The animal next to them was difficult to make out.

"Is that a dog? A horse?"

Whatever it was, Uncle Nelson had obviously wanted to leave her a message.

She snapped a couple of pictures, then retreated toward the sunlight. Whatever had been left in the caves was going to have to wait until she had reinforcements.

Cassie continued her search for the stone wall that would delineate her property. The path got wider and more well-worn. She crested a small rise and heard voices. Lots of voices.

As she approached, the voices got louder. She stepped around a large boulder and found herself staring at what looked amazingly like an archeological dig.

Sticks and rope had been used to divide the area into a grid. The work went down at least three feet, with the excavation exposing part of a foundation. There were dozens of pieces of pottery and tools and at least five or six people diligently working while hip-hop music played on a portable speaker.

One of the workers, a woman a few years younger than Cassie, looked up and spotted her. She stood and smiled.

"Hi. We give tours on Wednesdays. We found a new section, so if you could come back, we'd really appreciate it."

Cassie had never seen a dig or whatever it was called in real life, although she had to say the site looked pretty much as it did in the movies—minus the large, expensive, fancy equipment. It was warm here, out in the open, and dusty. Note to

self—archeology probably wasn't going to make her final five
career choices.

"I don't need a tour," she said, looking around before spotting
a stone wall in the distance. She pointed at it. "I'm pretty sure
that's my property line. You're on my land."

The sunburned brunette immediately turned and shouted,
"Raphael, can you come here, please? There might be a problem."

"What? No. There's no problem. I was making a point, not..."

She had more to say, she was sure of it, but suddenly she found
it difficult to think. Or breathe. Or move.

A man moved toward them. No, she corrected herself. Not a
man. Calling him a man was like calling a perfect sunrise yellow. He was so much more than just a single color, or a regular,
you know, person. Instead, he reminded her of those romantic
heroes from the books she loved to read.

He was maybe six-two or -three, with broad shoulders and
all the muscles. He had on a worn T-shirt, cargo shorts and hiking boots. He was tanned, athletic and whatever word meant
more than handsome, gorgeous and holy-you-know-what all
rolled into one.

His eyes were blue, but dark blue, framed by the thick lashes
guys have, proving God was a man. He needed a shave, which
totally worked on his strong jaw. His stance was easy, his mouth
smiling and every single part of her knew that sex with him
would be the best day of her life.

His coworker pointed at her. "She says this is her land. I
thought it was that old guy."

"Nelson." Raphael looked at Cassie. "Your uncle?"

"Great-uncle." Whoa! She could speak in his presence. Amazing.

"Right. Great-uncle. He was a good guy. He'd been everywhere, knew everyone." He smiled. "He loved you very much."

She had no idea what they were talking about. Looking directly at him was too much like staring at the sun. She was getting dizzy.

Cassie forced herself to focus. Uncle Nelson. The inheritance. Her land.

"Oh, yes. He passed away about a year ago."

"I heard." Raphael's expression turned sympathetic. "It was a loss for everyone who knew him."

She nodded. "It was. He stayed with me after my parents died. My brother and sister were adults, but I was only fourteen. He showed up and stayed."

"That sounds like him." Raphael paused. "You know that he agreed to let the university excavate here, right? I have the paperwork back at my office. We're limited to this area, which was at our request."

The smile returned and for a second she thought she was going to faint. "Given the choice, we would dig up every inch of every bit of land, but people frown on that, so we've learned to keep our enthusiasm in check." He pointed to the west. "There's a village closer to the water. We think that was where the fishing happened and the catch was processed."

"They processed fish?"

"They mostly salted and dried it to preserve it. Up here is where the rest of the population lived. We think this village was mostly women and children, with the men living apart. It's unusual. Further north there's remnants of a powerful matriarchal tribe. Our theory is this is one of their offshoots. We'll figure it out."

"Sounds interesting." She looked around. "So that's what you do all day? Look for stuff in the ground?"

Raphael chuckled. The sound rubbed against her body like warm velvet on bare skin. She was aware of her breasts and how much she wanted to arch her back, thrusting them toward him. Or maybe flip her hair a couple of times.

Hormones, she told herself firmly. It was nothing but hormones. She was a rational, intelligent woman and she could act normal in the presence of an almost-god.

"It's summer," he said, putting his wide-brimmed hat on her head. "Be careful out in the sun. Redheads burn."

She told herself not to react to the kind gesture, or the weight of the hat on her head. *His* hat. The hat that had probably seen him naked. "I put on sunscreen."

"Your cheeks are getting flushed. You need to reapply regularly and if you're going to be out for a long time, wear a hat."

"Thanks for the advice."

"Anytime." The thigh-quivering smile returned. "Anyway, it's summer. I bring a team out here to work the site. Come September, it's only a sometime thing because I'll be back in the classroom teaching. A full-time team could excavate the site faster, but Nelson was never worried about the speed of our work." He looked at her. "Is that going to be a problem for you?"

She'd been so busy watching his mouth form words that she'd barely been listening. "Um, no. It's fine. Take as long as you like."

"I'm glad to hear that." He held out his hand. "I'm Raphael Houston."

"Cassie Hayden."

She put her smaller hand in his larger one and wasn't disappointed by the sparks zipping up her arm. He was incredible, she thought, and this was the most fun she'd had in forever. Not that any of it was real. Men like Raphael didn't notice women like her. Still, this was better than a free weekend of a streaming service.

She removed his hat and handed it back to him. "I'll let you get on with your work and I'll get myself out of the sun. Happy hunting."

"Thanks. You know your way back?"

She pointed to the path. "I follow that to the orchard."

She returned the way she'd come. Once she reached her car, she sank onto the driver's seat and immediately texted her sister.

I met the best-looking man I've ever seen in person.

Did he ask you out?

    Cassie laughed for several seconds. Of course not. But it was quite the show. They grow them pretty out here.

That could be fun. I gotta run. Guests are arriving. Love you.

Love you, too.

eleven

Paris pulled into the state park public parking lot. She tended to come here early enough to always find a spot, even in summer. As it was barely six, there were only a couple of other cars, but the sun was up and by the time she reached the top of the trail, the lingering mist would be gone.

She got out of the truck and zipped her key and phone into her leggings pocket. Bandit stood next to her, tail wagging, eyes bright with anticipation.

"Give me a couple of seconds," she told him, jogging in place for a slow count of fifty, then stretching her legs, using the wood bench by the trailhead. Next to her, Bandit did his downward dog, no doubt showing solidarity. She swung her arms a few times, tilted her head from shoulder to shoulder to loosen up her back and was about to start the familiar route when she saw Jonah getting out of his car, looking surprised.

"But you hate exercise," he said by way of greeting. "You said exercise kills. You mocked me for running."

"Good morning," she said with a laugh. "And none of that happened. I have no idea what you're talking about."

Which wasn't true. She remembered all of it. She could never reconcile Jonah's love of gaming with his willingness to run. On purpose. But he had, nearly every day.

He greeted Bandit. Her dog wagged his tail and gave a little dance of welcome, which was a nice distraction because she found herself noticing Jonah looked as fit as ever.

Let it go, she told herself. She'd always thought he was sexy and tempting. Old news.

He smiled at her. "Should I ask if you have a fever or something?"

"Exercise regulates emotion," she told him. "I've been a runner for about ten years."

"Impressive." He pointed to the trail. "This is your regular route?"

"It is. Five miles."

"Then let's see what you can do."

"Want to warm up first?"

"Naw. That's for sissies."

"I'll remind you of that when you get a leg cramp."

They moved toward the trailhead. Jonah let her set the pace, which was a slow jog for the first mile, with Bandit running ahead joyfully, circling back regularly.

She found herself wanting to pick up the pace, to impress Jonah with her speed and endurance. But that would be foolish and these days she did her very best to never act like a fool.

"How often do you run?" he asked.

"I aim for five to six days a week and usually make it four. If things are crazy at work or I can't face getting up early, Bandit and I take a long walk in the afternoon. He's got enough border collie in him that he needs the exercise. If he doesn't get it, he tends to be a chewer."

"So you have double motivation."

"I do. He's good out here. I let him run loose because he responds to a recall whistle." Something they practiced regularly.

The trail was wide enough for them to run side by side.

Around them birds called out morning greetings and the sun began to filter through the mist. The temperature was a comfortable sixty degrees, but the day was going to be a hot one later.

"How are you adjusting to life in Los Lobos?" she asked. "Is it familiar or are you counting the days until you can get back to the East Coast?"

"It's good." He glanced at her. "I like small towns. I feel less awkward than I do in big cities."

"You're not awkward," she told him. "Maybe as a kid, but that's what happens when you're supersmart and better at something than everyone else. Now you're just smooth."

He grinned. "Smooth, huh? I like that. But the truth is, I feel out of place in a big city. Like I'm never sure where I'm supposed to go next."

"But you lived in DC, or nearby."

"Yeah, so that took an adjustment. This is better. Quieter. Danny's doing well. I got him signed up for a couple of park programs, so I'm hoping he'll make some friends over the summer."

"He's a great kid."

"He is. He's been asking me when you're coming back for another dinner."

The kind words warmed her. "That's sweet. Tell him he's welcome to visit me and Bandit anytime he wants." She laughed. "Not that he can drive himself."

"Not yet anyway."

"I hope he has fun here and isn't wishing he was back home," she said.

"So far he's okay."

The trail wasn't steep but definitely sloped uphill. Paris reminded herself to keep her pace slow until she was fully warmed up. The scent of earth blended with hints of pine and a few mountain flowers she couldn't name.

"He must miss his mom," she said. "I mean both of you must miss her, but in different ways." She wanted to say more, but figured she should probably stop before putting her foot in her mouth.

"You're right," he said. "He tries to be brave. I tell him that it's okay to feel what he feels, but it's got to be hard. I'm thinking at the end of summer, when my mom's mobile, I'll leave him here for a couple of weeks, fly back and get the house ready to sell."

She moved from her warm-up pace to a steady run. "That's a big change."

"Yes, but one I've been planning for a while. It's time to find somewhere to make new memories."

"Do you have any idea where that will be? You can work from anywhere, can't you?"

Which meant he could move to Los Lobos, she thought, then told herself not to be silly. Jonah had no reason to move back and even if he did, she was in no way part of his plan. She was just the nightmare ex-wife.

"I *can* work from anywhere, which makes it hard to choose. I need a good school for Danny. He's in a private academy that focuses on STEM, so I'd need somewhere with a challenging curriculum."

She doubted their local public schools would qualify and although there were several private schools in the area, she didn't know anything about them. And again—what Jonah did or didn't do with his life had nothing to do with her.

"Was Traci a gamer, too?" she asked.

"No. She was a classical violinist."

The information was so surprising, Paris stumbled to a stop. "A what?"

"A classical—"

She held up a hand to stop him. "Never mind. I heard you. So she was in an orchestra?"

"She was."

Bandit raced back to check on her. She patted him, then started running again. Jonah fell in step beside her.

"Wow. That's unexpected."

"She loved music, sometimes more than conversation. She was gifted."

Of course she was. Paris told herself not to be bitter, that everyone was good at something, right? However running a farm stand on the edge of the highway wasn't exactly in the same category.

"Does Danny play?"

"Not anymore. Traci taught him to play before he could walk. He started formal lessons at three. He's good but doesn't have the passion for it. After she died, he asked to stop taking the lessons. I let him. I'm not sure if it was the right decision."

"It's been a year. Maybe he could try again, see how he feels. Maybe in his mind, music and his mom are linked."

"We've talked about that and he keeps explaining to me he really doesn't like to play violin. Maybe when we get settled I'll insist he give it another shot for six months, then reassess."

"How did you and Traci meet?"

He glanced at her. "At a fundraiser."

"Let me guess. You were seated next to her and swept her off her feet."

He laughed. "No. The buddy I was with had a thing for her and dragged me along to congratulate her after her solo. I stood back while he gushed. Later, she found me and we talked."

"So she chased you. Fun."

Paris spoke with a lightness she didn't feel. She wanted to ask how long this was after he'd left her. Had he missed her at all or had he been so grateful to be gone, that he'd never once thought about her? Had he mourned their marriage?

All answers she wouldn't get because she wouldn't voice the questions.

"She was different from you," he said. "Quiet and restful."

Paris ignored the stab of hurt and made herself smile as she said, "Nearly anyone would be in comparison."

"No," he said quickly, coming to a stop. "I'm sorry. That came out wrong."

She gave herself a couple of seconds to catch her breath before shrugging. "Jonah, don't worry. At the end of our marriage, I was out of control. I get that, so it's not a surprise that a beautiful, talented, classically trained violinist would be restful. You needed a break from my drama. She gave you that and I'm glad. You loved her, married her, had a child with her. There's no bad in that."

She paused. "No, I'm wrong. There is bad because you lost her and I'm so sorry you and Danny had to go through that."

She was pretty proud of herself for getting all that out. It was the right thing to say, it was what he deserved to hear and she mostly meant it. She *was* sorry he and his son had suffered a loss, and good for him for finding someone wonderful. She wished knowing all that didn't hurt quite so much.

"Thank you." He looked at her. "I want to stay at the hospital while my mom has her surgery. She says it's not a big deal and the doctor can call me at home, but I'd rather be close. Could I leave Danny with you that day? I know I'm asking a lot, but I'm afraid being at the hospital with me will remind him of when his mom was dying."

The air rushed out of her chest, and it had nothing to do with running. She stared at her ex-husband, not sure she'd truly understood what he was asking.

"You want me to take Danny."

"Yes."

"For the day?"

"Should I not have asked?"

"No, it's fine. Of course I'll take him. He's great."

It was just, how could he trust her with his kid? Didn't he remember how scary she'd been? She knew she was different now, but her knowing and him believing weren't the same thing.

"I'll keep him safe and I won't yell at him."

Jonah frowned. "I know that."

"I'm confirming."

He studied her for a second. "Is it just me or do you have trouble letting the past go with everyone?"

She instinctively folded her arms across her chest. "I don't know. I think it's mostly you, because you saw me at my worst. We haven't seen each other in a long time and now you're here. It's confusing."

He put his hands on her shoulders. "Paris, I trust you."

"Fool."

He laughed. "So yes on watching him."

She started running again. "You know it. Maybe I'll let him drive the forklift."

"That would be the highlight of his year."

Cassie's phone rang as she carried in the last box from her car. She pulled it out of her pocket and sank onto a chair in the small living room.

"Your timing is perfect," she said with a grin.

"You're unpacked?"

"It's been five minutes. No. I've brought my stuff in. The unpacking will take a bit."

"I'm excited," Faith told her. "I loved the pictures you texted. Tell me, tell me! How is it? Are you happy?"

Cassie glanced around at the remodeled space. The new shutters were opened to allow in bright California sunshine to spill onto the pretty floors. The old-fashioned furniture wasn't her style, but it was comfortable and she was grateful to have it. But this apartment, this town, this *state*, wasn't home.

"It never rains here."

"Excuse me?"

Cassie walked over to the window and looked out at a sad little side garden. "It never rains. There's fog and mist, but no actual rain. I have no idea how anything grows."

Faith laughed. "You haven't been there long. Give it a bit. You'll see rain."

"I don't think so. There's an unnatural amount of sun and everyone is very friendly."

"You say that like it's bad."

"I'm suspicious by nature."

Faith laughed again. "You're really not."

"They're so welcoming. It's freaking me out. Have a little reticence. Be wary. It's a more comfortable state of being."

"Since when?"

Since she'd been forced to leave everything she'd ever known and trek over three thousand miles to a strange place.

"Do you know I've only ever lived above the bar?"

"Yes. Mom and Dad brought you there when you came home from the hospital on that very special day when you were born."

"You've lived somewhere else. Garth has that year he took off to go find himself. But not me. This will be my first ever, on-my-own apartment. I'm twenty-eight. Shouldn't I have done this sooner?"

"That's on us. We held you back."

"But did you? Don't get me wrong. I'm still determined to hate you forever, but I've been thinking maybe I needed this push. I should have at least lived on my own. What if it turns out I'm afraid of the dark?"

"You're not afraid of the dark."

"I guess we'll find out. Gotta run, sis."

"Talk soon. Love you."

"Love you, too."

Cassie shoved her phone back in her jeans, then carried her suitcases into the bedroom. The closet was fairly big and it didn't take long to get all her clothes in place. She put family pictures in the bookcase by the window and filled the top shelf with the books she'd brought from home.

She set up her laptop on the small desk in the bedroom and

looked around. As she'd thought before, the energy of the apartment felt good, but even so, it felt strange to live alone.

When Garth had taken off, Uncle Nelson had still been living in the family apartment with her. She'd never cooked for just herself, or cleaned for just herself. Not having to think about when Garth would be home, or running to the B and B to help her sister, left her feeling a little lost. While she'd been in the motel, she could pretend it was temporary, but now she had an address and she was here for a full six months.

Cassie walked into the bright, modern kitchen. She checked out the fridge and saw Laurel had left her milk and eggs. There was bread and coffee in the pantry and a bouquet of flowers in a vase on the table.

The kind gesture surprised her. She touched a petal of one of the flowers and told herself not to cry.

She stood in the center of the room, not sure what to do next. At the same time, she realized the apartment was…quiet. As she'd reminded Faith, she'd always lived above the family bar. There she could hear the faint sound of music and laughter, late into the night. She'd grown used to falling asleep to the noise. There were the sounds from the street—always present. Even at her highway adjacent motel, she'd heard cars and trucks driving past, but here there was only the faint calls of birds.

"I'll get used to the quiet," she said aloud. Maybe she would find the difference restful.

She glanced at her watch. She had a couple of hours until work, but then what? Should she stop at the grocery store on her way home and get something for dinner? Or stock up so she wasn't shopping all the time? That made the most sense, so she should make a list. Only she wasn't used to only thinking about herself. She always had to take Garth's likes into account. He only wanted rye bread and he liked really green bananas. But in this small space, there was just her. She could get any bread she wanted and ripe bananas, or grapes, even.

She hugged herself tight, telling herself that freedom was good, that this was a growth experience, when in fact she felt small, lost and abandoned.

There was a knock at the door. Cassie flew across the room and flung it open.

"Hi!" she said loudly, grateful to whomever was there.

She recognized Jagger and a younger girl she would guess was Ariana.

Both girls stared at her, their expressions more wary than welcoming. Cassie stepped back and offered what she hoped was a friendly smile.

"Sorry that was so enthusiastic. You're my first visitors so I'm a little excited. Let's start over. Hi, Jagger." She turned to her sister. "You must be Ariana. I'm Cassie. Nice to meet you."

Ariana glanced at her sister, who nodded.

"We brought you cupcakes." Jagger held out a covered plate. "We made them ourselves and they're delicious."

"I bet they are. Thank you. Would you like to come in?"

Jagger looked past her, as if trying to get a glimpse of the place, but shook her head. "Mom said don't bother you. We're to deliver the cupcakes and *that's all*." She emphasized the last two words.

Cassie hesitated, not wanting to undermine Laurel. "Then I thank you for the delivery. We'll have to arrange a visit at another time when you can stay longer."

Ariana dimpled. "That would be very nice. Thank you. I read about having tea in a book. Could we have tea?"

"I could probably figure something out."

"Excellent!"

The girls waved before racing back around to the main house. Cassie left the cupcakes on the kitchen counter. Something to look forward to when she got home from work.

She ignored the sensation of the long, empty evening stretching out in front of her as she changed her clothes and put on makeup before leaving for her shift. On her way out, she stopped by the barn and found Laurel photographing a Miles Davis album.

Laurel put down her camera and smiled. "All moved in?"

"Yes, it didn't take long. Thank you for the homey touches. I appreciate the coffee and milk. I wouldn't have thought of that."

"You'll need to do grocery shopping." She named the best one in the neighborhood and offered easy directions.

"I'll head there later," Cassie said. "Oh, and thank you for the cupcakes. That was sweet." She smiled. "The girls were perfect. I invited them in and they said no, although we do have a date for tea at some point."

Laurel groaned. "Don't let them push you around. I'm not kidding. If they bug you, tell me. They're so excited to have someone in the apartment, I'm afraid they'll think of you as part of the family and have expectations."

Family and expectations actually sounded nice, Cassie thought. "You forget I have two nieces. I can stand up for myself."

"And yet you're serving them tea."

Cassie laughed. "Okay. Point taken. Anyway, I just wanted to thank you for making the move so easy."

"Of course." Laurel paused. "Tonight is pizza and game night. I limit screen time but we order in and the girls get to play games together for three hours. It's a big deal. Paris usually comes over. Jagger and Ariana eat in the family room and we hang out in the dining room, catching up. You're welcome to join us."

"Are you sure? I don't want to get in the way."

"We'd love to have you. You're off at four, right? Come over after work and we'll get the order in, then hang out. Oh, did you finish the book?"

Cassie wasn't sure what that had to do with anything, but okay. "I did. I really liked it."

Laurel smiled. "That's perfect. Paris and I did, as well. Let's talk about it tonight and figure out our next read. Is that good for you?"

"It is." An evening not on her own sounded like heaven. Plus, she liked both Laurel and Paris and she was always up for a bookcentric conversation. "What can I bring?"

"Wine. Anything red."

"You got it. See you around five thirty."

twelve

Cassie showed up right on time. After going to the wineshop across the street from the bookstore where she worked, she raced home and changed into jeans and a T-shirt. She replaced her black boots with sandals, grabbed her book and then went next door and knocked.

"I'll get it!" Ariana yelled, the sound of her running footsteps easily audible. She flung open the door and grinned up at Cassie. "You came! We're having pizza then playing games for hours and hours."

"Sounds like a good time."

"Are you going to play with us?" Her expression was hopeful.

"I was thinking I'd hang out with your mom and Paris. We're doing book club tonight."

"You'll be talking." Ariana sounded resigned. "Grown-ups talk all the time. Playing a game is so much more fun."

She stepped back to let Cassie in, then yelled, "Mom! She's here."

Laurel came into the foyer of the old Victorian. "Indoor voice," she said quietly.

Jagger ran down the stairs and slid to a stop at the bottom. "Hi, Cassie."

"Hi, Jagger."

Laurel waved her hand. "Our side of the house is not refurbished, as you can see."

"Now I feel guilty."

"Oh, good."

They both laughed.

Laurel showed her the formal living room with its high ceilings and original fireplace. The wallpaper was peeling a little in the corners, but the floors were original and gorgeous. The huge kitchen had been updated probably in the 1980s, and the formal dining room could seat twenty.

The furniture was an eclectic mixture of traditional and contemporary. She would guess that some of it had come with the house and the rest they'd brought from wherever they'd lived before. There was a sitting room off the kitchen and a library with floor-to-ceiling bookshelves.

"I love this!" Cassie said with a laugh. "It's gorgeous."

"The books are very old," Jagger told her. "We don't read a lot of them but we found a series called Little House on the Prairie and we're reading those."

Laurel nodded. "You're enjoying them, too. Pa is such a great character and he's a good man."

"He lived a long time ago, Mom. There's not going to be somebody like him around now."

"You never know." Laurel pointed to a painting on the wall of the dining room. "The owners left some artwork that I've sold. A couple of pieces helped with the mortgage." She gave Cassie a rueful smile. "Let's just say buying this place wasn't part of the plan. I wanted the barn and the land around it, but somehow we ended up with the whole lot."

"Dad loves the house," Ariana said. "He told us we could live here and be princesses."

"And then he left," Jagger muttered.

"Let's not talk about that." Laurel put her hands on both girls' shoulders. "Let's have a great evening."

There was a knock at the front door followed by Paris calling out, "It's me."

The girls ran to greet her and Bandit, who wagged his tail and gave everyone kisses.

Laurel grinned. "Paris always did have great timing."

Cassie wanted to ask why Laurel hadn't wanted to buy the house, but it was obviously a difficult topic.

In the kitchen, Paris handed Cassie a small crate of produce.

"Welcome to Los Lobos," she said with a grin. "I bring the freshest berries and vegetables in all the land."

"Thank you," Cassie said. Everything looked delicious, even the avocados. "Not traditional but very welcome."

"What did I miss?" Paris asked. "Did anyone win the lottery?"

"We don't play," Jagger said, hugging her. "I'm taking advanced math and I know the odds of winning. They're very small."

"That's true. So no on the lottery win."

They took turns washing their hands, then the girls set the table. Cassie collected the two bottles of wine she'd brought with her. Paris gave an approving nod.

"I like your style. Wine trumps berries."

The pizza arrived a few minutes later. Dinner was a loud, friendly affair with easy conversation. Cassie enjoyed hearing Jagger talk about her friends and Ariana discuss a craft project at her art camp. After dinner, the girls raced upstairs to play video games and the three women carried their wineglasses out to the comfortable, overstuffed chairs on the wide back porch. They each took one, with Bandit settling in the fourth and closing his eyes.

The sun was behind the house and the evening air was the perfect temperature. The birds had started settling for the night, leaving only the sounds of the crickets.

"Behold my kingdom," Laurel said, motioning to the barn and the small parking lot.

"It's a good kingdom," Paris told her.

"It is."

Cassie looked at her landlord. "You said something before about the house. You didn't want to buy it?"

"We couldn't afford it." Laurel sipped her wine. "I needed the barn for the business, but Beau wanted the house, too. It about broke us financially. After the divorce I thought about selling but by then, we'd all fallen in love with the place, so here I am, stuck with a crippling mortgage and too many projects."

"You're leaving out the part where Beau's an asshole," Paris murmured.

"Cassie's new in my life. I don't want to dump on her right away. She'll think less of me."

"I won't think less of you," Cassie told her. "How long were you and Beau married?"

"Over a decade, but we'd dated a while before that. He was the guy I couldn't quit. He kept dumping me and I kept telling myself it was the last time. Then, when it really was the last time for me, he proposed and like a fool, I said yes."

She paused and looked up at the sky. "I'm grateful for my girls, but he was such a mistake." She glanced at Paris. "Go ahead. You're dying to blurt it out."

"He's a jerk." Paris looked at Cassie. "He was forever coming up with get-rich-quick schemes. They never worked. Meanwhile, he was always too 'busy' to be a decent father and husband. He never helped with Laurel's business. Worse, he belittled her 'thrifting experiment.'"

Cassie tried not to wince. "I'm sorry you had to go through that."

"Me, too." Laurel picked up her wineglass. "When he took off, he emptied our bank accounts. It was community property so it's not like I could sue him. I literally didn't have five cents to my name."

Paris reached for her hand. Laurel squeezed it.

"You saved us."

"I gave you a loan."

"You fed my kids and kept me from killing Beau."

Paris grinned. "You were never going to actually kill him."

"No, but I wanted to at least hit him over the head with a shovel." She looked at Cassie. "Now he's in Jamaica, starting a river rafting company. Apparently it's doing well. He's even paid part of a single child support payment." She paused. "Did that sound bitter?"

"He's an asshole," Paris repeated.

Cassie had to agree. She understood a couple breaking up, but for Beau to disappear with all the money? No excuse.

"Does he see his daughters much?" she asked.

"No." Laurel sighed. "Ariana will forgive him anything, but Jagger is pissed. You probably got that when you were checking out the apartment." She looked at Paris. "Jagger went off on one of her crazy rants about men being awful."

Paris winced. "I'm sorry."

"Me, too. Okay, I've talked about Beau and my problems for too long. Let's talk about the book." She glanced at Cassie. "Did you love it?"

Cassie grinned. "I did. Dougless and Nicholas were both such great characters. And I could relate to Dougless—we both have a string of failed relationships. So when do I get my handsome knight?"

Paris sipped her wine. "I hate to break it to you, but I don't think time travel is real."

"Don't say that!"

They all laughed.

"Nicholas was my favorite," Laurel said. "I thought his reaction to indoor plumbing was hysterical. He was so well drawn." She paused, her humor fading. "But it was his honor that resonated with me. At the risk of sounding like my daughter, I haven't seen a whole lot of that in my life."

Paris reached out and squeezed her hand. "Good guys are out there."

"You promise?"

"I do."

Cassie knew her comment was as much about Beau messing up his kids with his actions as it was about the book. What kind of man did that? Not that she had a track record of picking winners, but she had to believe one day she would fall for someone amazing.

"I loved how Douglass evolved," Paris said. "She started out needing a rescue, but then got strong enough to rescue Nicholas."

"Just like you," Laurel said lightly.

"I haven't rescued anyone."

"But you could."

They talked about the book for a few more minutes, then discussed what to pick next.

"I believe it's my turn," Paris said. "And I want us to read *The Endearment* by LaVyrle Spencer. It's a historical set in Minnesota in the 1850s."

"Is there winter in the book?" Cassie asked with a grin. "I've lived through enough Maine winters to know I don't want to read about snow and freezing cold before people had central heat."

Paris laughed. "Oh, I don't know. Less central heat could mean more cuddling."

"I hadn't thought about the snow." Laurel waved her wineglass at Cassie. "That's something we have in our favor here in Los Lobos. No snow. In fact, we don't get below freezing. Okay, maybe once every thirty years."

"I'll agree that the lack of snow is a big plus. So *The Endearment*. Same rules? We meet when we've all read it?"

"That's the plan," Paris said. "And no rush. If you're busy, take your time."

"Busy with what?" Cassie asked, thinking of her beautiful but silent apartment. "It's not like I have a lot going on beyond my job and you guys."

"You should start dating," Laurel said.

Cassie stared at her. "Why?"

"I don't know. You're young, attractive and very likable. We could find you someone who isn't a loser."

She appreciated the thought, but wasn't looking for a guy right now. "Let's focus on finding you someone instead."

"I don't date."

"I meant to be a male influence."

"Oh, that."

"We do need to find you someone," Paris said. "I can't think of anyone. The girls know Tim at the fruit stand, but I wouldn't be comfortable asking him to hang out with them. Great guy, but it would be weird. I've offered Jonah. You should take me up on that."

Laurel groaned. "Tell Cassie who he is."

"My ex-husband." Paris smiled. "He's in town with his eight-year-old son from his second marriage. He's staying with his mom while she has knee-replacement surgery. So he is, by definition, a good man."

"He's your ex. I can't be friends with him." Laurel looked at Cassie. "Explain it to her, please."

"There's a really big weirdness factor for sure. If you don't want to date anyone, you need a male friend."

Paris nudged Laurel. "See. It's a good plan."

"Sometimes I wonder if men and women can *be* friends." Laurel pointed to Cassie. "Do you have any guy friends?"

"My brother."

"That doesn't count. Any nonrelatives?"

"No."

"Me, either. Nor does Paris and employees don't count, either." Laurel reached over to pet Bandit. "If only you were human, you could be my friend."

"I wish I knew a solution," Cassie said, feeling bad for Laurel. "There has to be someone you could hang out with in a way that would help Jagger."

Laurel shifted in her seat. "Okay, so I'm serious now. About the friendship thing. I met someone."

Paris's eyes widened. "Wait! What? You met someone? Like a guy?"

"Sort of."

Cassie and Paris looked at each other.

"You sort of met someone or he's sort of a guy?" Cassie asked.

Laurel grinned. "I sort of met someone. He works at the recording studio. Victoria was on vacation so Colton, the sound engineer, offered to look over a Miles Davis album. He was nice."

"Cute?" Paris asked.

"Does it matter?"

"Yes. Always."

Laurel rolled her eyes. "I don't care how he looks, I care if he's a decent human being who could show my daughters some men are good guys."

Paris continued to stare at her.

"Fine," Laurel grumbled. "Yes, he was cute. And very nice and he offered to be my friend."

"In a good way or a creepy way?" Paris asked.

"In a good way. I'm trying to decide what to do. He's from Tennessee, the youngest of five and they're all sisters. He seemed... nice. He gave me his business card and told me to check him out."

Cassie understood Laurel's problem, but the solution seemed strange. "So you'll make sure he's normal, then become his friend? How?"

"I don't know. Most relationships happen organically. I don't know how to start a friendship with a purpose."

"You get to know each other," Paris told her. "Go talk to him. Exchange stories about your childhood. That sort of thing. But first, we investigate. Give me his business card. I'll text him and get his social security number for a background check."

Laurel groaned. "Seriously? Hi, let's be friends. By the way, I want your social security number?"

"If he meant what he said about helping, he'll give it up. It'll be our first test." Paris glanced at Cassie. "While I'm being bossy, let's talk about you. Did you go see your land?"

Cassie grinned. "I did. It's big with many trees. I also have a cave and an archaeological dig."

Paris and Laurel looked at each other, then back at her.

"Did you meet Raphael?" Paris asked.

"Oh, yes." Cassie thought about the incredibly handsome man. "He's so attractive, he doesn't seem human."

"I know, right? He makes me swoon." Paris sagged back in her chair. "That butt."

"Those shoulders," Laurel said with a sigh. "Although it's probably wrong to objectify him like this. We'd be pissed if a man did it to us."

"I don't know," Paris said. "I think we could all use a little objectification in our lives."

By ten Saturday morning Laurel surrendered to the fact that she wasn't going to be able to work—not with so many thoughts swirling in her head. Thanks to the wonders of the internet and Paris's HR service, she knew a lot more about Colton Berger than she had the other day.

That report in hand, she'd spoken to Courtney about Colton. The other woman had assumed Laurel wanted to know for personal reasons and she'd gone along with that. Explaining the actual situation was a little too complicated. Courtney had said that Colton was gifted at his job and well-liked by all the musicians he worked with. Quinn said Colton was friendly, hard-working and honest. All excellent characteristics. From what Laurel could tell, there was absolutely no reason not to ask him to be friends. Well, excluding the awkwardness.

But the well-being of her daughters was at stake, which was why she found herself standing shuffling from foot to foot outside his house, unsure what to say, yet unable to walk away.

She pushed the doorbell, then immediately had the thought that she had no business showing up at his house, with no warning. What had she been thinking? Ack! Normal people texted first, or—

His door opened.

"Laurel."

He sounded more surprised than pleased, which made her want to slink away.

"Hi. Sorry. I wasn't thinking. I should have texted. Pretend I never showed up."

She turned to walk away but he called her back. "It's okay. Did you want to talk? Come on in."

She hesitated. "You're being very kind. Thank you. Yes, I did want to talk about what we discussed before."

"Being friends?" he asked with a smile.

"Yes, that."

His house was a typical one-story ranch. She followed him through an updated family room into an equally modern kitchen. She took in the stainless steel appliances, the quartz countertops and the bleached wood cabinets.

"I have kitchen envy," she admitted, taking a seat at the small table by the window. "It's so light and bright. I live in an old Victorian. I'm saving for a remodel, but it's gonna take a while."

He walked to a Nespresso machine. "I have coffee and coffee."

She grinned. "Coffee sounds great. Thank you. Black is fine."

He raised his eyebrows. "Unexpected. I take milk in mine."

"Then I can, too. I was trying to be easy."

In less time than she would have thought, they each had a freshly brewed cup of coffee. He sat across from her.

"You thought about my offer to be friends," he said.

"I did. You're being very generous and to be honest, the whole concept is strange. I've never gone looking for a friend before."

"A male friend."

She told herself not to wince. "Adding a gender to the sentence makes it even more uncomfortable."

"But my gender is the point."

"It is." She picked up her coffee. "I checked you out," she added, then immediately regretted the phrase. "In a paperwork kind of way."

He picked up his mug. "Then you know I'm not a felon."

"I do. I spoke to Courtney. Oh, she thinks I was asking about you for, um, other reasons."

"She thought you were interested in me romantically," he clarified. "You didn't want to tell her otherwise because it's about the girls and that's not anyone's business."

She nodded.

"I get that," he said. "You'd do anything for your kids, including asking a man you barely know to be your friend." He paused. "I assume that's where this is going."

"I guess." She groaned. "No, that's not right. I do want a male friend in my life and you're offering and you seem great, so yes, that's where this is going. But how we're doing it is so strange and confusing. I'm embarrassed."

"Nothing to be embarrassed about."

"You think I'm a bad mom. I'd have to be or I wouldn't be in this position."

"I don't judge people like that."

"How do you judge them?"

He grinned. "In other ways." His smiled faded. "Let's do this. We'll get to know each other. Hang out for a bit. When we're comfortable, I'll meet the girls."

"You're so nice."

"It's a flaw." His voice was teasing. "Always the nice guy. It keeps me from getting the girl."

Ha. He was way too good-looking for that to be true, she thought. "I doubt you lack for female companionship." Her eyes widened. "Oh, no. Are you seeing someone? Is she going to freak out?"

"I'm currently single. And you're divorced."

"Yes. Beau and I are officially not a couple and that's a relief. He was a mistake, but I was young and idealistic and crazy about him." She circled her mug on the table. "I wonder how much of his appeal was that he felt elusive. I could never pin him down, so he was always a temptation."

"The thrill of the bad boy."

"Possibly and I've learned my lesson. Next time, I want a nice, normal stable man." Not that she was ever getting married again. Or even involved.

"Sounds like a plan," he said lightly. "You told me you grew up here?"

"Yes. I've never lived anywhere else. My friend Paris went to LA for college and stayed a couple of years after, but I went to school locally." She frowned. "Maybe I should get out and see the world or something."

"Seems to me you have enough on your plate right now. Your kids, your regular life, your rotating stock on eBay."

She laughed. "What do you know about eBay? Are you a regular shopper?"

"No, but I did a little checking of my own and looked up your store. I watched a couple of auctions and a few things went for a lot of money."

"You sound surprised."

His expression turned sheepish. "I guess I am. None of what you sell is new."

"That's true. But that's part of what works. Say I buy a figurine for two dollars at a thrift store and I turn around and sell it for twenty-two plus shipping and handling. That's only a twenty-dollar profit, but if you multiply that by say a hundred, it starts to be real money. I've had some great finds. There's a candle votive—handblown, out of Seattle. They're about the size of a small stemless wineglass. They're called glassybabies and they're hugely popular right now. They cost anywhere from sixty to a hundred dollars new. I've seen them at estate sales for three dollars and the older ones that aren't available anymore can go for a couple of hundred online. Both my girls are experts at picking them out."

"You're training them early."

"I am."

She looked at him, at how at ease he was, talking with her. From all she'd heard, he was good at his job, decent, kind and handsome enough to get attention.

"Why aren't you married?"

One eyebrow rose. "Asking for a friend?"

"I'm curious."

"I was." His mouth straightened. "We're divorced. She left."

"Can I ask why?"

His expression turned rueful. "You can ask, but all I can tell you is one day she didn't want to be married anymore."

Laurel didn't know what to say. "It must be hard not to have closure." She was very clear on why Beau had left and her only regret was that she hadn't thought of ending things herself.

"It was at first, then I got over her and now it doesn't much matter."

"Is that why you moved here? To start over?"

"Some." His smile returned. "A lot of it was a very tempting job offer. The only downside is I miss my family."

"Makes sense. Before the divorce, did you like being married?"

His expression softened. "I did. I liked the routines, the little rituals that were just us."

He made it sound so nice, she thought sadly. She'd never felt that way about Beau. Nothing about being with him had been easy.

"You would have been a good dad," she said. "I'm sorry that didn't happen."

"Me, too." He studied her. "At the risk of blowing the mood, I don't get your ex. How does a man walk away from his own kids? They need him. Family is the most important thing. At the end of the day, the people we love are what matter most. The rest of it is just bullshit." He paused. "Ah, sorry for swearing."

His words had reduced her to a puddle. "Don't apologize. That's how I feel, too. I understand falling out of love with me. But Jagger and Ariana should be his world. I know they're mine. They're wonderful. Funny and sweet and smart. Jagger's so determined to take care of everything, and Ariana has the most forgiving heart."

"Here's what you're not saying," he told her, his gaze steady. "Beau's all flash and no substance. He's never showed up and done the work, which makes the fact that his business hasn't failed a surprise. While you're glad he finally has something he can be proud of, that only makes the situation with your daughters worse."

She nodded while fighting tears. "Sorry. I don't know why I'm so emotional."

"You're exhausted. You've had to deal with the divorce. You haven't said, but I can guess he crapped on you before leaving. You had your own pain, plus your daughters' shock and bewilderment. Dads aren't supposed to leave. Now you're worried about how they're adjusting, so even though you already have more to do than time in the day, you're making the effort to make friends with some guy because it's the right thing to do."

The tears fell faster. "How can you know all that?"

"I told you. I have four sisters."

He got up and walked into another room, then returned with a box of tissues. "Do you want more coffee?"

"Yes, please." She waved him into his seat. "I'll get it. I need to move around. Plus, your fancy coffeemaker intrigues me."

She wiped her face and rose. He walked to the counter and they bumped into each other. She moved right, he moved left, so they were still right in front of each other. He grinned.

"We have a problem coordinating." He put his hands on her shoulders. "You stay still. I'll move."

She looked at him, prepared to tease him. Only somehow when her gaze locked with his, she couldn't seem to speak. Or think. Or do anything but get lost in his dark eyes and think about how long it had been since she'd felt this good next to a man.

"Hey," he said gently, pulling her close. "It's going to be okay."

They barely knew each other, but somehow his hug was exactly what she needed. She leaned against him, letting herself relax against his strong, broad body. He felt good, she thought absently. Muscled without being too big. Safe, she thought, closing her eyes.

She told herself it was only for a second, that she had to let go or he would think she was coming on to him. But as soon as that thought formed, she realized that she liked the feel of his body on hers. More interesting, and okay, weird, was the sudden rush of arousal that boiled inside of her. She went from comforted to take-me-now in about two breaths. The realization startled her so much, she broke free.

They stared at each other. She had no idea what he could see on her face, but his expression changed from understanding to male awareness. Tension crackled between them.

She honest to God didn't know what to do. Part of her wanted to make a shrieky noise and run for safety. Part of her wanted to rip off her shirt and put his hands on her breasts. But mostly she wanted him to kiss her. A real kiss—the kiss of a man who wants the woman in front of him. No strings, no complications, skin on skin and—

He swore softly. "Tell me you mean it."

Because he knew what she was thinking and he wanted that, too? She wasn't sure and while asking seemed like the most sensible option, she couldn't find the words, so instead, she simply took a step toward him.

"Finally," he breathed as his mouth claimed hers.

thirteen

Laurel did her best to catch her breath. The aftershocks of her orgasm shimmied through her. She was relaxed, happy and oh, so content. Next to her, Colton exhaled slowly, then grinned at her.

"So, did you want that second cup of coffee?"

His low, teasing voice made her smile. She touched his face only to have reality slam into her hard, making her bolt upright in his bed.

"We had sex!"

"I know."

She glared at him. "Don't you dare sound smug. We had sex!"

"And it was great."

She waved that away. "Yes, it was amazing, but that's not why I'm here. I can't have sex with you. This isn't some man-woman-dating thing. We're supposed to be friends. I want to help my girls and look what happened."

No. No! What had she been thinking? Only she hadn't been, she thought grimly, scrambling out of his bed to search for her clothes. They were scattered everywhere. She thought maybe her sandals were back in the kitchen and her T-shirt was in the hallway. She retraced their steps, gradually dressing. When she had all her clothes on, she returned to the bedroom to find Colton wearing jeans and nothing else.

The sight of him caused her to stumble to a stop. The man was really sexy. She wasn't sure why she hadn't noticed that before, but he was. And he was a skilled lover. The things he'd done with his mouth and his hands... A shiver rippled through her belly as her muscles clenched in happy memory.

"No!" she said forcefully, more to herself than him. "I ruined everything."

"You didn't." He crossed to her. "Laurel, don't. We can still be friends."

"But we had sex."

"We did and yes, it was perfect, but what you're dealing with is more important. I still want to be friends."

He did? She stared at him. "You sure? Because we can't be doing this. They'd figure it out."

"I know. It was a onetime thing." He flashed her a grin. "I can't promise I won't think about it, but I meant what I said. I want to help."

That was good news. "I appreciate you saying that."

"I'm not just saying it. I mean it. Think about how you want to handle me meeting the girls. It might be easier to do a group thing where they can focus on other people rather than just me."

"Oh, that's a good idea." She considered her options. "Maybe a barbecue. I could invite my friends and you and it would be easy."

She impulsively hugged him. "Thank you for being such a good guy."

"Anytime."

She pressed her cheek to his bare chest. He felt good. Her fingers lingered on his back. Warmth crept through her making her want to...

"No!" She jumped back. "No sex. Just friends."

His eyes crinkled with humor. "Want to shake hands instead?"

"At this point, I don't think it's safe for me to touch you at all."

"Too bad because I really like your touch."

She pointed at him. "No tempting me, either. Think of England."

"Killjoy."

Paris parked in front of Laurel's barn but instead of heading inside, she walked back toward the house where she'd spotted Cassie reading out on the side porch.

"Hi," she said. "Getting settled?"

Cassie grinned. "I didn't have much to move, so yes." She waved her copy of *The Endearment*. "Anna's in such a difficult situation and I love Karl."

"Me, too." Paris pointed to her car. "I brought Danish. I was taking some to Laurel. Want to join us?"

Cassie was up instantly. "I'd love that."

They found Laurel in the barn photographing a small, slender vase.

"A Bohemian Moser handblown vase," she said. "Isn't it beautiful? The delicate lines, the way the color changes. I love it."

"Because it's gorgeous or because you're going to sell it for a lot?" Paris asked with a grin.

"Both!"

"I brought Danish."

Laurel instantly set down her camera. "I love you so much. I need sugar in my life. I didn't sleep. Let's go to the house for coffee."

"Where are the girls?" Cassie asked, falling into step with them. "I haven't seen them all morning."

"They both had sleepovers." Laurel sighed. "It was only Ariana's second, but the other mom texted me this morning and she did great. I'm picking them up at noon, then we're going out for Mexican food."

Once they reached the house, Laurel started the coffee while

Paris got plates and opened the box of Danish. When they were seated, Laurel looked at Paris.

"What's up?"

Paris reached for a bear claw. "Nothing. Everything." She licked her fingers. "I didn't tell you the other night, but I saw Jonah one day while I was out for a run. He wants me to look after Danny while Natalie's having her knee surgery so he can stay at the hospital."

Cassie smiled at her. "That's so romantic. It's like you're getting back together."

"We're not."

"But you could be."

Laurel got up and collected the now-full coffee carafe. "But that's not the problem, is it? You're worried about spending the day with Danny."

Cassie looked between them. "What's wrong with Danny?"

"Nothing," Laurel said, keeping her eyes on Paris.

"I don't get it," Cassie said. "You're good with Laurel's kids. You're a nice person. What's the problem?"

An excellent question, Paris thought. Laurel took a cheese Danish.

"There isn't a problem," her friend said. "I've said this before, but it's still true. You take care of the girls all the time."

"But I know them. I don't know Danny." And that scared her. Plus, she still didn't trust herself not to get mad and do something scary. "I want him to be okay."

"He will be."

Cassie leaned forward. "Why don't you plan out the day? If you have a bunch of stuff to do, he won't be worried about his grandmother and you won't panic about what to do next. You can have a whole list of things. Have so many you can't possibly get through them all."

"That's a good idea." Paris sipped her coffee. "He seems to like hanging out at the farm stand. We can take a walk with Bandit."

"Frisbee will tire them out."

They talked about other activities, including bringing Danny by the barn. Paris made notes on her phone.

"His mom was sick before she died, wasn't she?" Laurel asked. "Do you think his grandmother going into the hospital will be a problem? You might want to talk to Jonah about that ahead of time."

"I will." Paris didn't know where Danny was emotionally, but she wanted him to spend the day happy, not concerned. "I should bring dinner when I drop him off." She added another note. "Natalie will spend the night at the hospital and Jonah won't have time to make anything."

Cassie looked at her. "So no feelings for the ex?"

"It's not like that," she said, almost telling the truth. "He's a good guy and I like him, but it's not romantic."

"Too bad. I love a reunion story."

Laurel watched her carefully. "Paris, how much of your re-fusal to admit there might be something between you is about what's happening today and how much of it is about the past?"

"Jonah came home because his mom needs him. We've talked a few times and that's all. There's nothing here to dissect. I barely know the man." At least who he was today. She knew the old Jonah very well, and she still missed him.

"I'm with Cassie," Laurel said. "I love a reunion story, but we can change the subject. I made a friend."

Cassie grinned. "We're so proud. Was this on your first day of school? Did you play nice?"

"Very funny." Laurel looked at Paris. "It's Colton."

"The music guy."

"He's a sound engineer." Laurel frowned. "I think that's the technical term. He works the complicated board at the record-ing studio."

"You're not kidding," Cassie said. "This is a guy friend for the girls?"

"That's the plan. Paris ran him through her HR service and I talked to Courtney Yates, whose husband hired him. He totally checks out. I went to see him and we talked. He seems really sweet."

Paris watched her friend as she spoke and knew there was something Laurel wasn't saying. She could tell by her slightly guilty expression.

"Is he why you didn't sleep last night?" she asked.

"No," Laurel said quickly, only to squirm on her seat. "Maybe."

Cassie looked confused. "I thought he was a great guy. So why are you upset?"

"I'm not upset. Exactly."

Paris stared at her. "Then what are you?"

Laurel's mouth turned up in a smile. "Guilty. Confused. Satisfied."

Paris repeated the words in her brain, then felt her mouth drop open. "Holy crap! You had sex with him?"

"What?" Cassie yelped, spinning to face Laurel. "You're not supposed to sleep with your friends."

Paris could see Laurel trying to control her smile, but she couldn't do it. That must have been one great orgasm, she thought, only the tiniest bit envious.

"It just happened," Laurel said, sounding slightly defensive. "We were talking and I was upset about the girls and we hugged and then, you know."

"No, I don't know," Paris teased. "You hug and then you're naked?"

Laurel looked a little proud. "Sort of. But it was a onetime thing. His friendship is more important."

Cassie grinned. "Oh, no one believes that."

"It's true. We agreed."

Paris looked at Cassie and nodded. "Yeah, we'll see how long that lasts." She returned her attention to Laurel. "So what's the next step in this so-called friendship?"

"I want him to meet the girls, but casually. I was thinking of having a barbecue next weekend. I'd like you both to come. The more people, the better."

"I wouldn't miss it," Paris said, wondering how Laurel expected to make the whole friendship thing work now that she'd slept with Colton. Not that she judged the encounter. Laurel had been through hell. She deserved a sexy encounter with a good man. But then making it work as "just friends"? She wasn't sure that was possible.

"If I'm not working, you can count on me, too," Cassie said.

"Thanks. Like I said, casual." Laurel brightened. "Paris, bring Jonah and Danny."

"I'm not inviting my ex-husband to your barbecue."

"Chicken."

"I'm trying not to frighten him."

"Jonah doesn't scare that easily."

"Let's keep it that way."

fourteen

Cassie had to admit, if only to herself, she liked her new job. Once word had spread that there was a bartender at the wine bar, business had picked up. She was starting to get regulars and everyone was friendly. Plus, she got to browse the bookstore before and after her shift.

Getting her own apartment had made a huge difference in how she felt about Los Lobos. Having Laurel and her girls nearby helped her feel less alone.

She made quick work of checking inventory. So far nothing had ever been missing, but she always confirmed what she had. She wrote the day's offerings in both food and wine on the chalkboard. Starting at eleven, she had a steady flow of customers.

The food was always popular, as were the half-wine flights. She'd never heard of a place offering such small wine portions, but it kind of made sense. People got a taste of a new-to-them wine without worrying about driving back to work.

A little after one, when the lunch crowd had started to thin, she had a chance to take a breath. She glanced toward the entrance to see hunky Raphael walk into the bookstore.

The sunlight was behind him, so for just a second, he was in silhouette—like some scene from a movie. He was tall, he was built and the way he moved. Yummy, she thought happily. Just plain yummy. It was like lunch and a show.

He glanced around the store. Cassie told herself to look away. She didn't want to be caught staring. But the temptation was too great and when his gaze swung in her direction, their eyes locked.

For one brief heartbeat she would swear she felt tingles all the way down to her toes, which was ridiculous. Even more astounding was his immediate warm smile—as if he were pleased to see her. He started toward her with a purposeful stride. Wait, what? He couldn't be in the bookstore to visit her.

She actually turned to see if he was walking toward someone behind her, but there were only the mirrored shelves filled with wine. She faced front again and waited, confident he would explain himself.

Maybe he wanted her to sign some paperwork about the dig, or maybe he had a hot date and wanted a wine recommendation.

"Hi." He sat at the bar, his gorgeous come-take-me smile never wavering. "I heard you worked here."

Once again she wanted to turn around and see whom he was talking to, because it sure couldn't be her.

"Me?" she asked, her voice a breathless squeak. She cleared her throat and carefully repeated, "Me?" in a more normal tone.

"Yes, you." He glanced at the chalkboard menu. "What's good here?"

"You mean to eat?"

His blue eyes crinkled with amusement. "Yes, Cassie. I'm here for lunch."

"Why?" She immediately wanted to slap her mouth over her hand. "Sorry. That came out wrong. I only meant that you don't seem like the wine and cheese type."

"Maybe I'm not who you think."

Oh, if only that could be true, she thought desperately. If only he were the kind of man who had been looking for an out-of-place, confused person with no life direction and really bad taste in men. She could be his dream girl.

"The barbecue place down the road has a pulled pork sandwich to die for," she said before she could stop herself.

"I'm happy where I am." He pointed to the chalkboard. "Lunch, please. You can surprise me."

Could she? Or maybe the real question was could she surprise him in a good way? Raphael was a walking, breathing god and she was a mere mortal. Maybe she should simply enjoy the moment and let reality catch up with her later.

"We had a run on several options," she told him. "But I still have some sandwiches that are really good. Let me put something together." She glanced at the wine flight menu. "Did you want to try some wine?"

"Not today. I'll have water."

She offered him a quick smile, then got to work pulling together a Raphael-sized lunch. The man had to be at least six-two. She doubted finger food would satisfy him for long. She collected the last three caprese sandwiches and put them in the sandwich griller before combining two salads into one bowl and adding a side of kettle chips.

She slid the food in front of him and added a tall glass of ice water. "There you go."

"Looks great." The smile returned. "Can you keep me company?"

"Of course," she said, leaning against the bar and wondering how wrong it would be to ask him to take off his shirt while he ate. Just, you know, so she could look.

Bad her, she thought humorously. If she were a man thinking thoughts like that about a woman, she would be called all kinds of names. Something she should remember. Raphael was a human being and he deserved her respect.

"How long have you been in town?" he asked, before taking a bite of the sandwich.

"A couple of weeks."

"I'm trying to remember where Nelson said you were from."

"Nelson talked about me?" She couldn't imagine being interesting enough for that to happen.

"He mentioned he was leaving you the land." Raphael's breath-stealing smile returned. "He showed me your picture. I think it was from your senior year of high school."

She groaned. "The one with the purple streak? Not my best look. I was going through a phase." And not a particularly attractive one.

"That's what high school is for. Figuring out who we are and how we want our lives to look. Learning the rules of adulthood while navigating the surprisingly difficult teenager social terrain."

"Somehow I think you mastered that just fine," she murmured. "Where did you grow up?"

"I'm from a tiny farm town in the Midwest. You wouldn't have heard of it. I couldn't wait to leave. What about you?"

"Bar Harbor." Her tone turned wistful. "It's so beautiful and Acadia National Park was like my backyard."

"I've hiked the park a few times. There's nothing like standing on the summit, looking across the harbor and the Atlantic. Although the Pacific Ocean has its charms."

"I guess."

He chuckled. "You don't sound convinced."

"It's growing on me, but I miss home."

"So you're not a wanderer like your uncle."

"If I am, I haven't discovered that about myself yet. He went everywhere. He once told me that the longest he'd lived anywhere as an adult was when he stayed with my brother and me." She looked at him. "I was fourteen when my parents died. Nelson showed up two days later and didn't leave until I was eighteen."

"Did you know him very well?"

"Before he moved in? Not really." She smiled. "Poor man. I think teenage girls confused him."

"Plus your grief. I'm not sure he would have known how to deal with that."

"You're probably right." At least that had been Faith's theory. That she and Garth had been lost in their own pain, leaving Cassie to figure it out on her own. Maybe things would have been different for her if she'd gotten help to weather that time or develop coping skills. But there was no going back.

"How did you meet him?" she asked.

"I was exploring the area," Raphael said easily as he finished the third sandwich. "I found what became the site you saw the other day and contacted the owner. Nelson showed up a few weeks later and we agreed I could excavate there. We stayed in touch."

"You teach at the university?"

"I do. The study of our past helps us understand our present and future."

She grinned. "Lecture material?"

"Straight from the syllabus." He winked at her. "I study the ordinary world from the female point of view."

"What does that mean?"

"History is told by the victors. Those conquered often lose their heritage—through storytelling or artifact destruction. In most of history, women haven't had much of a voice. I like to look at what I find through the view of those who didn't go to war or hunting. Women kept the community running day-to-day. When the men are gone, who's in charge? Who makes decisions and rules?"

"But you're a man."

"Thank you for noticing."

She rolled her eyes. "I mean, isn't that an unusual interest for you to have?"

"I've gotten a little pushback from some of my colleagues, but I figure there's enough material for all of us."

"What does your family think?"

His humor faded. "There's just me. I was an only child. Never knew my dad. My mom stuck around until I got a scholarship to college. I haven't talked to her since."

"I'm sorry."

"It's okay. Her indifference is all I know. You, on the other hand, have a very involved family."

"Too involved. They basically forced me to come here and face my inheritance. I'm supposed to go back in six months."

Something flickered in his eyes. "Maybe you'll find you like it here."

"Maybe." Even she heard the doubt in her voice. "So you're an archeologist and a professor. I'm guessing you have more than one degree."

He finished the salad and started in on the fruit. "A couple."

"Uh-huh. How many?"

He paused. "Seven, I think. Yes, seven."

"Degrees?" As in seven? "I never completed a semester of community college. I work in a bar. Everyone's doing better than me."

He frowned. "Why would you say that? We each take a different path."

"Yeah. Yours is to know everything about everything and mine is to date a bunch of loser guys, then get kicked out by my family. I needed to pick a better path."

"Maybe you have now. You're here, you're happy."

She eyed him. "I'm not happy." She paused, considering the word. "I guess it's fair to say I'm happier than when I arrived. I'm starting to fit in."

"See. Progress."

She folded her arms across her chest. "Hey, is one of those degrees in psychology?"

"Not even close. I'm not into modern sciences."

So he was naturally insightful? There was a thought.

"Are you a good teacher?"

"I try to be."

"I'll bet all your students have a crush on you."

He winced. "I hope not. That's a line I don't cross."

"No sleeping with your students?"

"Are you asking about my sex life?"

"I'm suddenly curious."

She expected him to brush off the comment, but instead his expression turned oddly intense. "I don't sleep with my students. For me, it would violate my personal code of ethics. Plus, I'm not interested in casual sex."

"What does that mean?"

"I prefer sex in a relationship. I don't need a different woman every night. One woman, the right woman, makes me happy."

He was getting more perfect by the second, she thought, wondering who the lucky right woman was. No one like her, she thought with a sigh. Raphael had it all. Brains, a great body and a moral compass.

"What about you?" he asked. "What do you want from a man?" He paused. "Or any partner."

"I'd prefer a man," she said with a smile. "As for what I want? I don't know. Someone with a job who doesn't need to be rescued and won't dump me."

She paused, thinking how incredibly pathetic that list sounded. Raphael watched her without speaking.

"It's just I'm noticing a pattern. I think I'm attracted to men I can fix. I like helping them, I guess, or maybe I think that they'll only want me if I can fix them." Which had sounded a lot better in her head than out loud.

"I want someone nice, someone who cares about me. Someone I can depend on."

"That sounds reasonable."

"You'd be surprised how hard it is to find."

"Maybe you've been looking in the wrong places."

"Maybe." She waved to the wine bar, where he was the only customer. "I'm not sure I'm going to meet Mr. Right hanging out here. Or on my land."

"The land seems like a less likely spot for romance," Raphael admitted. "What did you think of it?"

"I have way more trees than I thought. I'm not even sure what they are. The cave freaked me out."

His gaze sharpened. "What did you say?"

"The cave freaked me out." She waved her hand. "I'm sure you could go prancing in with no problem, but I'm not a big fan of small dark spaces, or snakes. You know there have to be snakes."

"Nelson never mentioned a cave."

Okay, he suddenly seemed very obsessed. She wasn't sure what to say. "It's big. It's not far from your site. You didn't go exploring?"

He shook his head. "I've always respected the limits Nelson set."

"The land is mine now. I give you permission to go in the cave. Oh, you need a flashlight. It gets dark really fast." She pulled out her phone and flipped through pictures. "Ignore the messages from Nelson. I'm sure he was being funny."

"Messages?"

"He wrote on the cave wall. Drew, actually." She showed him the pictures. "I assume this is him telling me to get a life."

Raphael went very still. One of his large, warm, strong hands closed around her wrist.

"Nelson didn't draw these."

"How can you know?"

"They're about four thousand years old. They're cave paintings from the people who lived here before."

Excitement filled his voice and he looked at her as if she'd just given him a new Ferrari. She was dealing with her own shock. Four thousand years old? In her cave?

"I want to see them," he said.

"Sure. They'd be your thing." She glanced at her phone, then back at him. "So this is a find? That's exciting."

He looked at her. "Come with me."

"What?"

"Come see them with me, Cassie. I want to share them with you."

Excitement gripped her. "I'd like that." She wouldn't know what she was looking at, but he would explain it. It wasn't exactly time travel, but it was close.

He pulled out his phone and they exchanged numbers.

"I'll be in touch," he promised. "We'll look at them together and you'll see how we discover history."

"Blue first, then green," Jagger said.

"It's summer," Ariana insisted. "We need summer colors. The green one should be listed first, along with the pink one and the yellow one. The blue one is last."

"But everyone likes blue."

Ariana's tone rose. "We need a summer aesthetic."

Laurel was grateful she was several rows of shelving away so neither girl saw her grinning at their conversation. They were always fun to listen to. Jagger had the bigger personality, but Ariana was willing to stand her ground—especially when it came to her "aesthetic."

Laurel appreciated that both her girls enjoyed the business. They'd grown up with thrifting, joining her in their strollers pretty much from birth. By age six, Jagger could spot milk glass from across a room and Ariana had an innate ability to find the one designer handbag in a pile of used and battered purses.

Most summers the three of them had taken off in a U-Haul truck for different parts of the country to do thrifting while Marcy and Darcy ran the business. They'd stop for fun activities between new-to-them thrift stores and antique malls. But

this year, with more summer activities and friends, taking off
for five or six weeks didn't have the same appeal. While Laurel
would miss the travel time with the kids, the trip wasn't necessary for her business. Recently, she'd had great luck with a dozen
or so online auctions and the three estate sales she'd gone to in
the spring had netted huge amounts of inventory. She would
head down to Los Angeles for a day in the next few weeks and
replenish her stock. She knew the best Goodwills—those that
received donations from the wealthier neighborhoods. Santa
Monica was always a success, as were the western parts of the
San Fernando Valley. She would come home with a full minivan and a happy heart.

She continued to sort through the carnival glass she'd bought
at auction—always a crapshoot, but this gamble had paid off.
The pieces were as pristine as promised and the base color, a
deep amethyst, added a rich dimension. The glasses and pitcher
would sell well together, but she wasn't sure if she should sell the
small and large plates as a lot or break them up in two listings.

"Daddy! Daddy!"

Ariana's loud shriek had Laurel spinning, then jogging toward
the sound. Beau was here? But he'd never said he was coming.

She'd barely had time to think that when she saw her youngest launch herself at her father. Beau caught her and pulled her
close. Ariana hung on tight, sobbing loudly as she clung to him.
Beau turned and saw her.

"Hey," he said with a sheepish smile. "I thought I'd stop by."

She stared at him, trying to understand that he was really
here. "You didn't want to call and ask if this was a good time?"

His smile faded. "Happy to see you, too."

The derisive tone instantly made her feel defensive. She had to
stop herself from taking a step back. No, she told herself sharply.
She wasn't in the wrong. Beau had been gone for months. He
barely texted the girls, she never heard from him and the man
didn't bother paying his child support. She wasn't the bad guy.

Beau turned his attention back to Ariana. He spoke softly to her and tried to put her down, but she only held on tighter, refusing to let go. Laurel saw Jagger by one of the large sorting tables, hanging back and watching her father warily.

Finally, Beau disentangled himself from Ariana. He smiled at Jagger and held out his arms.

She deliberately turned away and pretended to study a small vase. Beau swung to glare at Laurel.

"What have you been telling them?"

The unfair slap caused her to approach him. "I haven't had to tell them anything, Beau." She looked at her daughters. "I need to talk to your dad. Please wait at the house."

Ariana immediately began to cry. "No. Daddy, no. I need to see you."

"Ten minutes." Laurel crouched in front of Ariana. "Just ten minutes, then I'll bring him to the house. I promise."

Jagger grabbed her sister's hand. "They need to talk, then you can spend the whole day with him."

Laurel wasn't sure how long Beau was staying but "the whole day" wasn't really his style. Still, she hoped he planned to make a little time for his kids.

The girls left. Laurel waited until they were out of earshot, then looked at Beau.

"Why are you here? It's been four, maybe five months since they've seen you. You don't call, you barely text. You certainly didn't give me any warning. You can't do that, Beau. You have to let me know so I can prepare them."

He shook his head. "Have you considered this kind of attitude is why I left?"

She thought briefly of finding something heavy and swinging it at his head. A fantasy, but a nice one. "Have you considered what you're doing to your children? You took off with no warning. One day you were their father and the next you were gone. They had no idea what was happening and I didn't know what to tell them. They miss you. Ariana cries herself to sleep nearly every night and Jagger's hiding her pain behind anger. They need you in their lives and when they ask me what's happening, I have no answer."

He walked away a few steps, then faced her. "You always do this," he told her. "You always ruin what's supposed to be a good thing. I'm here, aren't I? I was down in Los Angeles, meeting with some investors and I thought, hey, I should go visit the family. So here I am. But that's not good enough for you."

What on earth was she supposed to say to that? They should be thrilled he deemed to show up?

"Beau, your daughters love you. They need you and you walked out on them."

His expression turned defensive. "I couldn't stay. You were killing me with your ordinary life. This isn't what I was meant for, Laurel. I tried to tell you that, but you wouldn't listen. I had to take a chance on my dreams."

With *their* money, she thought bitterly.

He moved close and smiled. "I'm doing it. The rafting business is a success. I'm making it happen. We're popular with the tourists and we're growing. That's why I came to LA. To get money to expand."

She recognized the enthusiasm in his voice. Every time he'd discovered a new "dream," he'd been as enthused.

She tried to study him dispassionately. He was a good-looking man, she thought. Relaxed, tan, fit. There was an ease about him, a confidence that things would always go his way. The irony being, they often hadn't. At least not from her perspective.

"Do you miss them at all?" she asked quietly. "Do you ever think about them?"

He turned away. "Of course."

"Then why don't you reach out? They want so very little. Just some regular contact. It shouldn't be too much to ask."

"It's tough with the time difference."

"All of three hours? Seriously?"

He returned his attention to her. "You could never see the good in me. That's why I left you."

She wondered if he was being his version of honest or if he was trying to hurt her. There had been a time when Ariana hadn't been the only one to cry herself to sleep at night. But Laurel had known she didn't have the luxury of missing the man who had abandoned them and taken their money. Instead, she'd figured out how to make it on her own and within a month or two had realized she didn't miss Beau very much at all. Paris had been right—their marriage had ended long before he'd disappeared.

"I brought you this." He pulled a check out of his back pocket and handed it to her. "I know I'm a little behind in child support, so this is to help with that."

She unfolded the check. It was for three hundred dollars. He owed her nearly a thousand a month for both kids. They'd been divorced over a year and this was his second payment. Both fell short.

She tucked the check in her pocket without speaking. What was there to say? Sarcasm wouldn't make the situation better and threatening to have his rights revoked wasn't exactly realistic. Oh, she thought about it a lot. Especially when she couldn't sleep at two in the morning. But she wasn't sure she would ever do it. Knowing their father had signed away his children would destroy the girls.

"Why are you here?" she asked instead.

"I told you, I had a meeting, so I came to see my girls."

"You have to call me before you show up. We have lives."

"I'm their father." His expression hardened. "I have the right to see my daughters."

"With rights come responsibilities."

"I knew you'd be difficult."

"This isn't on me, Beau. You're the one not showing up."

He turned away again. "You don't get it. I'm successful." He spun back to face her. "I'm building an empire."

She tried not to let her disbelief show. Really? An empire, and of the thousands he owed in back child support, he paid her three hundred dollars?

"My schedule's better now," he continued. "That's what I wanted to talk about. I want to see the girls more regularly."

"I don't know what that means. You're in Jamaica. They live here." Frustration battled with the need to protect her children.

"They could come stay with me. I thought maybe later this summer. For a couple of weeks."

Every fiber of her being screamed that wasn't happening. Was he insane? No way she was trusting him with her daughters—not in another country.

"Beau, they don't know you anymore. You haven't lived here in, what? Eighteen months? You're more a concept than a person. If you want to see them regularly, that's great, but you have to start slow."

He glared at her. "That doesn't work for me. It's not like I live next door. I had to fly to Los Angeles, Laurel. Then drive up here. It takes a lot of time."

"You're the one who chose to move away. It's up to you to make accommodations."

His gaze narrowed. "Maybe we could talk to a lawyer about that."

The threat hit her like a fist. Beau was threatening her? Part of her didn't think he meant it, but the nearly feral rage born of a mother's love instantly sprang to life. But before she could tell him off, Jagger ran back into the barn.

"No!" she screamed, getting between Laurel and Beau. She glared at her father. "I'm not going anywhere with you. You're not my dad. You're no one! You left us. You left me and Ariana and Mom. You left and you never said why. You make promises and you break them. I hate you and I never want to see you again."

The room went silent. Laurel stared at her daughter, feeling the waves of pain pouring off her. She knew Beau would blame her for the outburst, but she was more concerned with all that Jagger had been holding inside. But even as she reached for her. Ariana flew in.

"No, Daddy, no! Stay. I love you. I love you, so much." She ran over and hugged Beau tight, even as tears streamed down her face. "Stay. It's okay. We love you. I'll come to Jamaica. I will. We'll go to the beach and talk and play and I'll come."

Beau absently stroked her hair as he stared between his two daughters, then he pushed Ariana away. "I can't do this."

"Beau," Laurel began, but he shook his head and started walking. Ariana rushed after him, grabbing his arm.

"Daddy, no! Daddy, stay. You have to stay. I love you. Daddy, I love you."

He shook her off and disappeared into the bright sunlight. Ariana began to sob. She pointed at her sister.

"You did this. You made him leave. You said you hated him and he left."

Laurel hurried over and picked her up. Ariana wrapped her arms around her and gave in to heartbreak. Jagger stood with her head hanging down.

"You're not in trouble," Laurel told her, trying not to give in to the hopelessness of the situation.

Jagger rushed over and wrapped her arms around her waist.

"You're not in trouble," Laurel repeated. "And you didn't make your dad go away. Not either of you."

"He doesn't love us," Jagger said.

Ariana cried harder. "He does, he does."

Laurel sank down onto the concrete floor, bringing both her girls with her. They huddled there, hanging on, dealing with the pain that Beau had once again inflicted on their small family.

"You didn't make him go away," she repeated.

Jagger brushed away her tears and stared at her with a wisdom far beyond her twelve years. "I know, Mom," she said quietly. "He doesn't need an excuse to leave us."

fifteen

Cassie finished dressing for work and grabbed her book. She had about an hour before she had to get to the wine bar and thought she would finish *The Endearment*. She was enjoying the story and found that while the writing style was different from what she was used to reading, the book was still compelling. Karl and Anna were caught in an impossible situation. While Karl blamed Anna, Cassie could see both sides.

She stepped onto the side porch, only to find Jagger sitting on the steps, face in her hands, shoulders shaking as if her heart were breaking. Cassie sank down next to her and pulled her close.

"I'm here," she said quietly. "I'm right here."

Jagger buried her face in her shoulder. Her skin was blotchy, her eyes swollen from crying.

Cassie rubbed the preteen's back and murmured for her to breathe. After a few minutes Jagger sniffed, then raised her head.

"I hate my dad."

Cassie didn't react to the raw statement, instead pulling her close again. "Tell me what happened."

"He was here. We haven't seen him in forever and he just

showed up." Another sob shook her body. "Like he thought it
was all fine, that we'd be happy to see him."

She shifted back so she could see Cassie. "Ariana doesn't care.
She'll forgive him anything and I don't get it. He left us and
never called. I doubt he even thought about us."

Her pain was palpable. Cassie struggled to find something to
say but the situation was so far from anything she'd experienced.
Her grief had come from her parents dying. Jagger's agony was
the father she loved had abandoned her.

"I don't know why she's so willing to forgive him, but I'm
not. I don't care about him at all."

Cassie lightly touched her arm. "If you didn't care, you
wouldn't hurt so much."

Jagger nodded, tears slipping down her cheeks. "He said he
wants to take us to Jamaica. Like on a vacation. Mom said he
couldn't because we don't know him anymore and she's right.
I don't want to go anywhere with him."

Cassie wondered if Laurel's main concern was her daughters'
comfort or her worry about what her ex would do.

"Is he gone?" she asked.

"He left after I told him I hated him and never wanted to see
him again." Her voice was sad yet defiant. "I meant it."

Cassie doubted either was true, but didn't say that. She hugged
the preteen. "You've had a really tough morning. I'm sorry you
had to go through that."

Jagger hugged her back. "Ariana only thinks about what she
wants, but it's not only about her. I matter and we have to look
out for Mom. When Dad left, she said we would be fine and she
was really brave and pretended everything was okay, but I heard
her crying every night." She looked up at Cassie. "I know he took
all the money. I heard Mom talking to Marcy. She was scared
and she never said anything to us because she wouldn't want us
to worry. She takes care of us. Dad never did."

Cassie hung on to Jagger, wishing for wisdom, but there was

nothing. She was still holding her when Laurel walked around the side of the house.

"That's where you've gotten to," she said lightly.

Jagger immediately jumped up and ran to her. Laurel gathered her close.

"You okay?" she asked.

"No."

"I think we should go inside, wash our faces, then go for a walk on the beach. We won't talk about what happened until you and your sister are ready, but I want us to get away, breathe a little salt air and clear our heads. How does that sound?"

"Good."

Laurel glanced at Cassie. "Thank you for being there for her."

"I didn't do anything but hug her."

"Sometimes that's enough."

Cassie got home close to five and found a sticky note on her front door.

The girls decided to go to friends' for sleepovers. I'm going to order Thai. Let me know if you'd like to join me for dinner and hard liquor.

Cassie pulled out her phone. Give me ten minutes to change my clothes.

Seven minutes later she knocked on Laurel's front door, then let herself in.

"It's me."

Laurel walked out from the kitchen. "I just ordered. I should have waited for you, but I skipped lunch and I'm starving." She shook her head. "This is my day of reacting badly to every situation."

"I love all Thai, so whatever you ordered is my favorite and from what I heard, you're the best mom ever."

"I wish. Margaritas?"

"I'm in."

In the kitchen, Cassie got ice while Laurel measured out the ingredients. As she'd already juiced the limes, it only took a few minutes to get everything into the blender. They took the drinks to the family room.

"Delicious," Cassie said after her first sip. They were perfect—not too sweet, with a touch of smoky tequila flavor.

"Paris and I spent the summer we turned twenty-one coming up with the recipe." Laurel leaned back against the sofa. "What a horrible day."

"Are the girls feeling better?"

"Yes. We walked on the beach for an hour before either of them said anything, then we sat on the sand and discussed what happened." She looked at Cassie. "Jagger told you their father showed up?"

"She did and I assume no one was expecting him."

"I haven't heard from him in months. He's supposed to text the girls every week, but that rarely happens." She picked up her drink. "Beau's never been good at follow-through and it's so hard on both of them."

Cassie thought about what Jagger had said. "It's a lot for a couple of kids to deal with."

"I know. Ariana will forgive him anything, but Jagger gets mad."

"It hides the pain. Anger's easier to deal with than hurt or sadness."

"You're right. Jagger's always been more about action than wallowing. Sitting around missing her father would be too hard, so it's easier to say she hates him."

"I admire her fearlessness," Cassie admitted. "I'm a wallower."

"I think you're more proactive than you think. You've settled in here. You have a place to live and a job. New friends."

Cassie smiled. "Which sounds great, but what about the past

ten years when I basically went through the motions of having a life?"

"Water under the bridge."

"How come it's so easy to rationalize what I've done and so hard for you to forgive yourself for what Beau's doing to the girls? You know his behavior isn't your fault."

Laurel flinched. "That was very blunt."

"It was."

Laurel sipped her drink. "I don't blame myself, exactly. I'm so pissed at Beau for being a crappy father. I got over him a long time ago, so I don't have any of my own pain, but I ache for them." She angled toward Cassie. "Did Jagger tell you he mentioned taking them to Jamaica? There is no way he's taking my daughters out of the country. I wouldn't trust him to take care of them. The man can't even text when he's supposed to."

"Plus, you'd be worried he wouldn't bring them back."

"Yes, that, too. Fortunately the parenting plan says the visitation has to be within the state. He said something about talking to a lawyer, but again that would require follow-through. He never bothered during the divorce—he signed what I sent him."

"So you could have totally screwed him when it came to seeing the girls."

"Yes, but I didn't. Once he sees them regularly on the schedule we agreed to, he can ask for more time. But honestly, I don't see that happening. I wish he didn't hurt them."

Cassie agreed. She didn't understand how a father could simply walk away from his children. She knew her parents would have done anything to get back to her.

"They have you," she said.

"I wish that was enough. Jagger's got her thing about hating men and who knows what Ariana is going to be dealing with as she approaches puberty. I just want them to be happy."

"You must be doubly grateful you've got Colton."

Laurel shifted as if she were uncomfortable. "I don't *have* him.

We're friends. Or we're going to be friends. But you're right—
he'll be a good male role model for both of them."

"Plus, the sex was great."

Laurel grinned. "We're not going to talk about that."

"Oh, I don't know. I'm certainly not getting any. I have to live
vicariously through you."

"It was a onetime thing," Laurel said primly.

"Uh-huh. Like I said before, no one believes that." She let her
smile fade. "They're going to be okay."

"I wish that were true."

"They know you'll always be there for them. That's what
matters."

"Thank you for trying to make me feel better."

"Is it helping?"

"Maybe a little. Everything you said also makes me more determined to help Jagger get over the man-hating thing. I should
have recognized what was going on myself."

"You know now. We all get caught up in patterns."

Laurel laughed. "Now you sound like Paris."

"That's sweet. Thank you. I admire her."

"Me, too." She held up her glass. "To Paris, who always does
the right thing."

Paris had an entire list of things to do with Danny the day
of his grandmother's surgery. The normal morning fog hadn't
materialized so the day would be hot, even by the water, which
meant outdoor activities should be done in the morning.

She got to Natalie's house at six forty-five, so Jonah could get
his mother to the surgery center by seven fifteen. Danny was
eating breakfast. He ran to her and threw his arms around her.

"You came! We're going to have the best day."

"We are," she said, glancing at Jonah over his head. "He'll be
fine."

"Thank you for doing this." He gave her a faint smile. "He's promised to be on his best behavior."

"I'm sure he will be," Paris said, telling herself not to react to seeing Jonah so early in the morning. He'd showered, shaved and dressed, so there was nothing intimate about the encounter, but she couldn't help feeling like there was.

Maybe she was remembering all the times she'd been late to the fruit stand because Jonah had pulled her back to bed. Gaming hadn't been his only passion—he'd wanted her with a fierceness that had taken her breath away.

Natalie limped into the kitchen.

"I'm ready," she told Jonah, then offered Paris a wan smile. "Sorry for the early start."

"I'm always up at this time. Did you sleep?"

"Not a bit."

Paris wasn't surprised. She'd probably spent the night worrying.

"Go," she said, pointing to the door. "I've got this one. I'm thinking I'll tie him to the roof and speed through town."

Danny laughed. "I know you're kidding, but that sounds fun."

"Not happening, kid."

Danny hugged his grandmother, then his dad. The two of them left. Once Danny had eaten, Paris cleaned up, then faced her charge.

His expectant expression had her stomach flipping over a couple of times. The day stretched out endlessly and she wondered if she'd planned the right activities.

"So, ah, I thought we'd pick up Bandit and hang out at the farm stand for a couple of hours. You can help with deliveries. Then we'll play Frisbee at the dog park. After that, we'll give him a bath."

Danny laughed. "Bandit takes baths? Does he like them?"

"Not really, but he cooperates because he's a good guy."

There was more to her plan, but she didn't want to over-whelm him.

"Ready?" she asked.

He nodded. "Let's go."

Once they'd collected Bandit, they drove to the farm stand. She was relieved to see two delivery trucks parked on the side.

"I think we have first cherries," she said. "Not sure what's in the other truck."

"I love cherries."

"Then we'll have to taste them and make sure they're good enough for my customers."

"Do they get mad if they're not good?"

"Not so much mad as disappointed. If my customers aren't happy, they won't come back and that would be bad."

Tim, her general manager, introduced himself to Danny, then handed him a LoLo's baseball cap.

"Kid size," he told the boy.

"Wow. Thanks!" Danny put on the cap and grinned. "Can I help with the delivery?"

"Sure." Tim winked. "We'll do all the work while Paris handles the invoices." He lowered his voice. "The boring business part." He looked at her. "Cherries and corn."

She brightened. "The first corn of the season?"

"Yep and it looks good."

"I need to post something up on social media. We'll be swamped by noon and sold out by five."

"I think so, too. We'll get another delivery for the weekend." He put his hand on Danny's shoulder. "Danny and I will take care of the hard stuff. Go do your thing."

She looked at Danny. "You okay hanging with Tim? Bandit will be right there with you."

"I'm fine, Paris. We've got real work to do."

She grinned. "Then you'd better get to it. Once I've finished with the invoices and social media, we'll taste the cherries."

"Yay."

Paris confirmed the order, then posted online. Once that was done, she helped get the cherries and corn up front, where customers could find them easily. She and Danny tasted the cherries and pronounced them perfect. Around ten thirty, they left for the dog park.

Danny and Bandit chased each other, then Danny threw the Frisbee. Her dog jumped and spun to catch the toy in midair. When everyone was exhausted, she drove them to the dog wash.

As always she had to lift a recalcitrant Bandit into the tub. She clipped him into place and together she and Danny scrubbed him with the doggie shampoo. Once he was rinsed off, she told Danny to run, but they were both too slow and got soaked when the dog shook.

"I'm wet," Danny said, laughing as he pulled his spattered T-shirt away from his chest.

"He's a good shaker. Okay, now we towel him dry."

She and Danny dried Bandit as best they could with the big, fluffy towels, then walked him outside in the sun. Danny controlled the leash. He was a good kid, she thought. Cooperative and friendly. She liked his sweet spirit and how gentle he was with her dog.

The next stop was lunch at Treats N Eats by the pier. Bandit waited patiently while they ordered at the to-go window, then followed them to a table in the shade. He stretched out by their feet, knowing he would get a little snack when they were done.

The temperature had warmed, but they were comfortable under the umbrella. The scents of salt water, french fries and churros mingled.

"I need to think of my fruit of the month," she said, taking a fry. "I was thinking of cherries, but they're small and I don't know how to feature them."

"You mean like the strawberry concert?"

"Yes, I pick a fruit or vegetable every month and I like to

make it fun. I don't know what cherries could be doing. I thought about mountain climbing, but I don't know how to make a mountain and I'm not sure everyone would get what they were doing."

Danny scrunched up his face, as if he were thinking really hard. "Maybe you could buy a toy mountain," he said, sounding doubtful. "It would be for something else, like a soldier or maybe a game, but you could use it for the cherries."

"Maybe. I don't love the mountain climbing." She hadn't figured out how to make rigging look authentic. Without rigging and gear, it would just look like fruit stuck to the side of the mountain.

"What about a racetrack?" He looked at her. "A cherry race. I have a couple of really cool race car sets and the cherries would fit on top of the cars."

Paris stared at him, impressed by his creativity. "I like that. Cherries racing. I could get a track and we could do a different race every day, so different cars win."

"I can help," he offered.

"That would be great. Thank you so much. It's a terrific idea. Do you like cars?"

"You mean playing with them? I do. I like computer games more, but Dad limits my time. He says I have to be doing other things."

"That makes sense. What else do you like to do?"

"Take things apart." He grinned. "I'm better at that than putting them back together, but Dad doesn't mind. He says I need to let myself be creative." He put down his burger. "I used to play violin."

Paris went on alert. She wasn't sure which way the conversation was going, but she was concerned about saying the wrong thing.

"I never played an instrument," she admitted, hoping that was a neutral enough statement.

"My mom played the violin. She was excellent and in an orchestra. She wanted me to learn, so I took lessons and stuff." He looked past her to stare out at the ocean. "She liked when we would play together, but it wasn't my favorite so I didn't do it very often." His voice was quiet, his eyes sad.

"But you did it sometimes," Paris said. "You'll always have those memories."

"I know. I didn't like the lessons very much, but she said it was important and Dad agreed." He turned to her. "She died. I was really sad and that's when I wished I'd played more."

"You loved her very much."

"I did. I don't play anymore. Dad says I don't have to if I don't want to. Sometimes I think about it, but there's so much practice. Do you think she minds that I don't take lessons?"

"I think she loves you and wants you to be happy."

"That's what Dad says. That she's watching from heaven and is proud of me."

"I believe that, too."

She figured she couldn't go wrong agreeing with Jonah. He was a great father who had been there for Danny through the worst.

"I'm sorry you lost your mom," she said. "That's really hard."

He nodded. "It made me grow up faster. Sometimes at school I wanted to cry, but I waited until I got home."

Because if he'd cried in class, he would have been picked on, she thought sadly.

"I don't mind if you ever want to cry," she said. "It's healthy to deal with emotions when we feel them, but I understand why you waited."

He nodded. "I'm better now. I miss her, but it doesn't hurt so much."

Her phone buzzed. She pulled it out of her pocket and glanced at the screen, then smiled and showed the text to Danny.

"Your grandmother is out of surgery and did great."

He grinned as he read the words. "She's in recovery. That's where you go after surgery. They help you wake up. Grandma is going to stay in the hospital tonight. That's a good thing, not a scary thing. The nurses will take care of her. Dad said getting your knee replaced can hurt a lot."

"I'll bet. Let's text your dad back."

Danny typed in a few sentences about his morning. Paris added an offer to pick up dinner for him and his dad on her way to dropping him off.

Get enough for three and join us, Jonah answered.

"Say yes!" Danny grinned. "You and Bandit can have dinner with us and then we can watch a movie. Say yes, please?"

His enthusiasm warmed her. "I'd like that. Do we like Mexican food?"

"We love it!"

After lunch, she took Danny to meet Laurel and the girls. Jagger and Ariana showed him the barn and explained thrifting while Laurel filled Paris in on the "Beau incident."

"That man," Paris muttered.

"I know." Laurel sounded more resigned than upset. "If it were up to me, I'd never see him again, but with the girls…"

"You don't have a choice."

"Exactly. On a more cheerful topic, did you get Cassie's text?"

Paris nodded. "She's done with *The Endearment* and ready to talk whenever we are. She also picked the next book." She pulled out her phone to remind herself of the title. "*Night into Day*. I haven't heard of it or the author. Sandra Canfield. But I'm sure it will be good."

"I couldn't find it in print," Laurel said. "I told Cassie I'd order three copies from eBay."

"Thanks for doing that. Speaking of books, I was thinking of swinging by the bookstore with Danny. Want me to take the girls? I can bring them back when we're done."

Laurel grinned. "They'd love that, but tell them only two books each. We have a budget."

"I'll remind them."

Paris took all three kids to *Books and Bottles*. After they'd picked out what they wanted to read, they'd bought cookies from Cassie. Because more sugar couldn't hurt.

Back at the farm stand, Danny helped restock, then learned the basics of the cash register and practiced his math by counting out change. When Jonah texted he was home, she and Danny swung by her place to feed Bandit before going to Bill's Mexican Food for takeout. Once they reached Natalie's house, Danny raced out of the truck, calling for his dad. Paris followed with Bandit and dinner.

"I learned how to do a fruit display," Danny was saying when she walked inside, "and we went to the dog park and we gave Bandit a bath! He didn't like that at all. And I met Jagger and Ariana and we went to the bookstore." He waved his books. "I know what carnival glass is and I counted money."

"That's a full day." Jonah looked at her. "Thank you so much for taking care of him."

"Anytime." She handed him the bags of food. "I might have gotten too much."

"That's okay," Danny told her. "Dad and me love leftovers."

After washing their hands, they set the table. Paris put out the food while Jonah poured milk for Danny and iced tea for the adults. They sat down and said grace.

"Your grandmother's doing well," Jonah said, serving Danny enchiladas, beans and rice. "She's a little groggy, but feels pretty good, considering. She should come home around noon."

"She must be relieved the surgery is over," she said. "Of course now your work begins." She turned to Danny. "Ready to help take care of your grandmother?"

"Yep! I'm a good helper."

"You are."

"She won't be able to do much at first," Jonah said. "Her knee will hurt and she'll have stitches and a bandage. You okay with that?"

Danny's eyes widened a little, but he nodded. "You said she's okay, Dad. I believe you." He glanced at Paris. "Dad tells me the truth. That's why I wasn't worried today. He said Grandma would be fine, and she is. He always told me what was happening with my mom, even when it was scary and she was really sick. He didn't treat me like a little kid. He knew I could handle it."

Jonah shrugged. "He was going to find out what was happening eventually. I thought if he knew what she was going through, he would deal with the situation better."

"Sounds like you made the right decision."

Once again she had the thought that he was a wonderful parent. Caring, honest, sensible. Regret gripped her as she thought about what could have been. Only she and Jonah would never have had a child like Danny because she would never have been like the boy's mother. Back then she would have been like her own—angry, unpredictable and possibly terrifying. She wouldn't have wanted to be that way, but ten years ago, acting out was all she knew. Wanting her past to be different was an exercise in futility.

Now she had skills and knew how to use them. Trusting herself was a different problem, but as no one was interested in having a kid with her, hardly an issue.

After dinner, Danny asked to be excused to watch a movie with Bandit, leaving Paris alone with her ex-husband.

"I doubt he'll make it halfway through," Jonah said with a grin. "He's exhausted. Did you see how his eyes were drooping during dinner?"

"I thought the day would go better if I planned a lot of activities. I'm glad it worked out."

His dark gaze met hers. "Thanks again for taking him. It was a relief not to have to worry about him."

"He's easy to be with."

"I'm glad you think so." He leaned back in his chair. "It's nice you're still friends with Laurel."

"Always. Since the first grade. I can't imagine life without her."

"I always admired your loyalty."

Interesting. That wasn't how she'd ever thought about herself, but she understood his point.

"We've always been there for each other. She was with me when you left and I was with her when Beau left. She's helped me use social media to grow the business." And when Beau had cleaned out their bank accounts, Paris had covered Laurel's expenses. Not that Jonah needed to know that.

"We don't do everything together," she continued with a smile. "But we do a lot. Right now we have our sad little book club."

"Why is it sad?"

She explained how almost no one was coming to their summer version. "I think it's because people are busy traveling and the kids are out of school. Cassie joined, so it's just the three of us."

"I'll be part of your book club. I like to read."

The offer surprised her. "We're doing romances this summer. I'm not sure that's your jam."

He grinned. "I've never read a romance novel. Maybe it would be good for me." He pulled out his phone. "Give me the title. I'll download the book."

She laughed. "Jonah, this is going to shock you, but the next book we're reading isn't available digitally. You'd have to read an actual book."

He feigned surprise. "People do that?"

"Apparently."

"Huh. Old-school. Then I'll find a copy and read it. Like I said, maybe I'll learn something."

"I sort of doubt you have trouble with women." She paused, thinking of his late wife. "Not that you'd be dating or anything, what with having lost Traci. Unless you are, then it's perfectly fine." She groaned. "I'm saying this all wrong."

"I know what you mean. It's been nearly a year. Danny and I are both healing."

Healing how? Healing as in not being as sad or healing as in he was dating someone? Was he dating? Crap! Had he left a girl-friend in DC? All questions that wouldn't be answered because there was absolutely no way she would ask. Jonah's personal life wasn't her business. They were friends. Exes. Friendly exes and nothing more.

"What are you thinking?" he asked.

No way she could tell him the truth so she searched franti-cally for something to say.

"Laurel's having a barbecue," she blurted. "You and Danny are invited."

"Sounds like fun. When is it?"

"Saturday. I'll text you the time." She rose. "Speaking of the time, let's clear the table so I can head home. You've had a long day."

They made quick work of the cleanup. As Jonah had suspected, Danny was asleep on the sofa, Bandit curled up next to him. Her dog jumped up when he saw her.

"Don't wake Danny," she said softly. "Just tell him I had a great time."

"I will." Jonah walked her to the front porch. "Thanks again."

"Anytime."

Before she could say more, he leaned in and lightly kissed her cheek. Like she was his grandmother!

"Night," she said, hurrying to her truck.

"See you at the barbecue," he called.

She waved and opened the door for Bandit, then got in and drove away.

If she'd wanted absolute proof that Jonah had zero interest in her, she had it. No surprise. How could he after what she'd put him through? But being logical and telling herself to get over it didn't stop her from feeling a little ache of disappointment. Because while he'd moved on and fallen in love with someone else, she'd only ever loved him. And now that she'd spent time with him, she was more than a little concerned that she'd never fully put him behind her.

sixteen

If you never hear from me again, my body's in a cave.

Cassie saw three dots on her screen followed by, I doubt a tenured professor would be a serial killer.

He's an archaeologist. Who better to hide a body?

So you're excited about the cave paintings but wary about the hunky man who'll be accompanying you?

Yes.

Faith answered with a laughing until crying emoji. That's twisted. Have fun. Send me a picture of this hunky guy.

Cassie wasn't sure how she was supposed to casually take a picture of Raphael, but answered, I'll do my best, then slipped her phone into her pocket.

She'd arrived at her property with time to spare. After a quick walk through the orchards, she found Raphael at the mouth of the cave, looking tall and buff in his cargo shorts and tight fit-ting T-shirt. He had muscles for days and big blue eyes and a mouth that...

"You made it." He sounded delighted.

No, she mentally amended. Not delighted. Excited about cave paintings. There was a difference. She was a means to an end.

"You can go into the cave by yourself," she told him. "I don't mind."

He grinned. "It's more fun with a partner."

Uh-huh. He was still talking about the cave painting, wasn't he?

She pointed to the opening. "They're not that far inside. I didn't want to explore much because I didn't have a flashlight with me and you know...snakes."

"Not a snake fan?" he asked, handing her a very large, very manly flashlight.

"No. It's the whole slither, fangs, poison thing. I'm sure you're fine with snakes." He seemed the type.

Raphael clicked on his flashlight. "I keep a respectful distance from rattlers. Otherwise, most of the snakes around here are no big deal."

"You haven't heard me shriek."

He chuckled. "Then I'd better lead the way."

She turned on her light and followed him into the cave. Behind Raphael, the space seemed smaller, but much less scary. The flashlights illuminated every corner and from what she could see, the air was cool and dry. Nothing slithered or rattled.

"They're just up here." She pointed left.

Raphael came to a stop so suddenly, she ran into his back.

"Sorry," she murmured. "You forgot your turn signal."

He glanced at her, his expression intense. "What?"

She waved her hand. "Nothing. It's fine." So much for him thinking she was funny, she thought with a sigh.

He turned his attention back to the wall. Cassie used her flashlight to help illuminate the cave paintings.

"These are them," she said unnecessarily, only to get caught up in the pictures. Now that she knew they weren't from Uncle Nelson, she found them a lot more interesting.

"Don't cave paintings tell a story?" she asked, peering at the woman and children, wondering who they were and how long ago they'd lived.

"Yes, and these are stunning," he breathed. "Look at the detail and how well they're preserved. They're close to the opening, so there could have been a lot of degradation, but they're in excellent condition. This stretch of land doesn't get the heavy fog, and the outcropping protected them from rain. The wind comes from the other direction."

He slipped off his backpack and set up several freestanding lights. After he turned them on, the cave was completely illuminated.

"I can't do this for long," he told her. "I don't want to risk damage. But I need to get some pictures." He flashed her a smile. "This could be a real find."

"I hope so." She liked the idea of adding to the body of knowledge about the past. It wasn't exactly the same as having purpose, but it was very cool.

She watched him work for a few minutes, then slipped past him. "I'm going to see if there's anything else in here." Well, anything other than snakes, she thought grimly.

"It's me," she called softly as she walked deeper into the cave. "A very unassuming human who doesn't want to scare you. Go back to sleep."

The walls were rougher here. No cave paintings—in fact, not much of anything. The temperature dropped noticeably, and she shivered in her light T-shirt. She rounded a corner and stumbled to a stop. What on earth?

Big barrels were stacked on top of each other—the kind wineries used. There had to be at least a dozen, maybe more. She carefully checked for snakes, then moved closer to study the wooden containers. They looked old and worn, but she didn't see any leaking. Maybe they were empty.

She tried to move one on top. Nothing happened, so probably not empty. The writing on the side was all in… She frowned, studying the words and numbers. French? Italian? Those would be the two main languages on barrels because the whole French and Italian wine thing. But why would someone store wine out here?

She scanned another barrel and her breath caught as she recognized a single word. Cognac. Not wine. Something that would age much, much better.

She stared at the—she counted quickly—nineteen barrels, and tried to remember how many bottles each contained. She'd been studying California wines for her day job, but couldn't recall the exact proportion of bottles to a barrel. She knew it was a lot, so if this was good cognac, was this a windfall?

"Cassie?"

Raphael's voice came from farther back in the cave.

"Over here. Keep walking." She illuminated the way.

He rounded the corner and smiled. "Thought I'd lost you."

"I was exploring. Look." She swung the light back to the barrels. "I think these are French cognac, which is crazy. How would that end up here? On my land. Well, I guess on Uncle Nelson's land."

Raphael studied the writing on the barrels. "French isn't my strong suit. These are from a little town in the Cognac region."

Genuine French cognac? "It has to be really old. I can't see Uncle Nelson buying them and leaving them here." She pointed to the numbers. "If these are right, the barrels predate the second world war." Some of her excitement faded. "They could be stolen. I've been reading for my job. Winemakers brought clippings when Germany invaded, before the war, to ensure different lineages of grapes survived. Barrels were shipped out to protect wine from the Germans, but it was a hectic time and a lot was stolen."

She looked at her barrels. "If these were taken, they'd have to be returned." Assuming she could find the owner and figure out a way to get the barrels back to France.

"Nelson could have bought them."

"Maybe, but then I'm back to my original question which is how on earth did he get them here and why would he have bothered?"

Raphael peered around the back of the stack.

"What?" she asked.

"I'm looking for documentation. A packing slip, anything that would tell us how these got here."

"Maybe a barcode of some kind?" she asked, her voice teasing.

"A barcode would be amazing."

Cassie joined him in the search, shining her light between the barrels. She was careful not to put her hand in any dark spaces because, you know, snakes, but she was willing to look.

"Over here!"

Raphael was struggling to reach behind one of the barrels, but his thick forearm wouldn't fit.

"Let me try."

He showed her a corner of fabric. "Oilcloth protects paper from the elements. I can't quite reach it."

She slid her hand between the last barrel and the rough rock, as far as her elbow. Her fingers brushed the oilcloth.

"I've got a corner of it."

She tugged. Nothing happened. She pulled harder and it slowly slipped loose.

"It's moving." She tugged out enough to get a good grip, then drew it free.

The package was about seven-by-six inches and two inches thick, secured with twine and covered in dust.

"This will be easier to see outside," he said.

They made their way into the sunlight. Cassie squinted for a few seconds until her eyes adjusted. At her SUV, Raphael opened the package. Inside the oilcloth was an envelope, sealed with wax, and several sheets of what looked like inventory, or possibly a bill of sale, all in French. The only words she recognized were *cognac* and her uncle's name.

"Provenance," Raphael said happily. "The barrels weren't stolen."

"What's provenance?"

"Proof of ownership. It's something we look for all the time with antiquities. Once you get those papers translated, you'll find that your uncle left you what could be a small fortune in French cognac."

She stared at the writing, not sure what to think. "In the will, he said the land and all that's on it and the contents of the cave. I didn't think I'd find anything valuable." She frowned. "Should I put up a gate or something? Are they safe?"

"They've probably been here since the 1960s, according to the date on the inventory. They should be okay while you decide what to do." He paused, then frowned. "Unless you're worried about me. I'd never take anything from a site without permission."

She stared at him. "Raphael, you're not the issue. Seriously. It feels strange to find these and then leave them. But you're right. They've been sitting there for sixty years. They'll be fine."

She glanced back at the opening to the cave. "Cognac. I wasn't expecting that." She turned back to him. "How are your cave paintings? As good as you hoped?"

The slow, sexy smile returned. "Better. As I thought when I saw your pictures, they're done by women. I can tell by the subject matter. With your permission, I'll bring better lights and cameras to document them for study."

"Have at it."

"I'll do the work myself so no one else is in the cave."

He was surprisingly sweet, she thought wistfully. He could have been just a pretty face, but he was so much more.

"This has been a very interesting afternoon," she said as she waved the paperwork. "Now I have to figure out how to translate these."

"Would you like to have dinner?"

She frowned. "To discuss the translations?"

He chuckled. "No. To have dinner."

She didn't understand. "As in we go out to eat together?"

"Yes."

But why would he want to do that? Dinner with her? She was letting him have access to the cave paintings so they didn't need to talk about that. He didn't speak French so the invitation wasn't about the provenance.

His smile returned. "I'm asking you out on a date. I want us to get to know each other better."

A man with seven degrees, the face of an angel and the body of a god wanted to go out with her? Cassie burst out laughing.

"You can't be serious," she said, patting his arms. "That is just so funny. You're sweet, but that is so unrealistic. A date? With me?"

She was still laughing when she got in her SUV and drove away.

The morning of the supposedly casual let's-meet-Mommy's-new-friend barbecue, Laurel woke with a stomachache that came from guilt, worry and nerves. Her daughters were still dealing with the fallout from Beau's unexpected and disastrous visit. Not only had he showed up with no warning, he hadn't been in touch since bolting. Jagger was defiant, but Ariana was back to crying herself to sleep every night. Having a nice, normal man in their life seemed more essential than ever and Colton was her best hope.

She had a plan and good friends to help execute it. She would take the girls to the fruit stand later that morning where the three of them would oh, so casually run into Colton and invite him for dinner. Cassie was coming, as were Marcy and Darcy and Paris. Surprisingly, her BFF had invited Jonah and Danny, so there would be plenty of people around to lessen the potential awkward factor. Even better, the girls had already met Danny and liked him, so that was easy, plus Jonah was a good guy, so yet another happy male role model.

She managed to get through the Saturday breakfast routine without anyone asking if she was okay—something she considered a win. About ten, Cassie came by the barn to ask what she could bring to the barbecue.

"I think I have everything," Laurel told her, hoping her words sounded natural rather than practiced. "We're heading to the farm stand to pick up some corn on the cob and fruit. Want to come?"

Ariana rushed over and grabbed Cassie's hand. "Say yes. You're always so fun."

"That's sweet. I'll come, but I have to take my own car because I have to go to work afterward." She looked at Laurel. "But I'll be home at four fifteen and at your place by four thirty to help with setup."

Cassie was turning out to be the kind of friend who had your back, Laurel thought gratefully. "Thanks."

They made their way to the farm stand—a busy place on a Saturday morning. Jagger got a shopping cart and then they discussed how much corn to buy.

"Two dozen ears at least," Laurel said, thinking Jonah and Colton might want more than one and Marcy had said something about maybe bringing someone. Darcy's last romantic relationship had been with Laurel's dad but Marcy was forever searching for the next Mr. Right.

Cassie helped the girls with the corn selection. Laurel spotted Paris with a customer, then felt someone tap her on the shoulder. Jonah.

"You really are here!" She impulsively hugged him and was grateful when he hugged her back. "It's been forever."

They stepped back and smiled at each other.

"Over ten years," he said. "It's good to see you." He pointed to her girls. "Jagger and Ariana?"

"That's them. You were here when Jagger was born, but I was pregnant with Ariana when you, um, when…"

Paris breezed up and grinned. "You can say 'left.' Or more accurately, ran. Possibly bolted. You know, I think I like *bolted* best."

Jonah groaned. "I'm a solid no on *bolted*. It makes me sound like a frightened horse."

They all laughed. Paris excused herself to help customers.

"How's your mom?" Laurel asked. "Home from surgery?"

"Yes, and she's getting around. Watching her move is uncomfortable for me, but she swears she's doing great. We set up a bedroom with a hospital bed downstairs, but her physical therapist told her she would be back in her regular room in a few weeks."

"Modern medicine. Always a miracle." Laurel glanced over to make sure the girls were doing all right, then turned her attention back to Jonah. "I heard you won a couple of tournaments. Congratulations."

"Thanks. It was exciting. Now I leave that sort of thing to kids."

"But you're rich, right?" She laughed. "I still put on the annual garage sale at the end of summer. Bring your wallet."

"I wouldn't miss it."

Cassie and the girls joined them. Laurel made introductions. Jagger studied Jonah.

"Did I know you when I was a baby?"

"You did. You can't remember me, though."

"No, but I did the math and I would have been about two when you moved away."

"Bolted," Laurel said softly. Jonah groaned.

"Did you know my dad?" Ariana asked hopefully.

Jonah's smile faded as he seemed to struggle with what to say.

"I did. When Paris and I were married, the four of us would double-date."

Laurel held her breath, afraid what Ariana would ask next, but that answer seemed to have satisfied her. Danny ran over, Bandit at his heels.

"Dad says we're coming to your place tonight for dinner," the boy said happily. "Bandit, too."

"It's a party," Laurel said lightly, grateful for her friends' support. If only there was—

"Hello, Laurel."

She didn't have to turn around to put a face to that voice, but the real surprise was the unexpected melting sensation low in her belly. Yes, the last time she'd seen Colton they'd been naked, but still. Shouldn't she have more control?

She faced him, prepared to force a smile, but it came naturally when she saw him grinning at her.

"I thought that was you," he said, sounding so casual, yet friendly. As if they really were friends running into each other. "Saturday morning at the farm stand is the place to be. I plan on lingering until the bake sale."

She was aware of her children, Danny and Jonah all watching her. Cassie had left for work, and Paris was helping a customer pick out a watermelon.

"You haven't met my girls, have you?" she said lightly. "Jagger, Ariana, this is my friend Colton. He works at the recording studio. He's helped me out with the Miles Davis record."

"That one went for a lot," Jagger said, swinging her attention between the two of them, her expression suspicious. "You're friends with my mom?"

"I am."

"Because you're dating?"

Laurel sensed danger, but before she could figure out what to say, Colton offered a disarming smile. "Nope. Just friends. I think she's funny. She's talked about how you help out with the business."

"I know stuff." Jagger seemed to relax. "What do you do?"

"I'm a sound engineer. I balance the songs. If the background music is too loud, you can't hear the singer. Plus, if the drums are off you have a big, loud mess."

Ariana smiled at him. "This is our friend Danny and Bandit." She paused. "And Danny's dad."

"I know my place," Jonah said easily, holding out his hand. "Jonah Towne."

"Colton Berger."

"Jonah was married to our friend Paris," Jagger said.

Paris walked over and was introduced. She pointed to the cart. "Is that enough corn? The parking lot is filling up and if my morning delivery doesn't get here soon, I'll sell out by noon."

Colton winked at Jagger. "You really like corn."

She laughed. "We're having a barbecue tonight with all our friends."

"Sounds like fun."

"It will be." Jagger looked at Laurel. "Did you want Colton to come?"

The unexpected statement was a little gift from heaven. "I think I would." She turned to him. "If you're available."

"I am. What can I bring?"

"How about a couple of six-packs? We don't usually have beer drinkers in the house and I'm not sure what to buy. Say at five?"

"I'll be there."

seventeen

Laurel spent the afternoon getting ready for her guests. Jonah had taken Jagger and Ariana to the pier with him and Danny to ride the Ferris wheel. The girls had begged to go with them—a positive situation all around. While she was sure Danny and the rides were the main attraction, Jonah definitely qualified as a male role model.

After making potato salad for twenty—literally—she made coleslaw. Darcy showed up at about three to help her carry the large folding tables to the backyard. They had plenty of mismatched chairs, gathered at various yard and estate sales. She always kept a couple of dozen around for events like this.

"Marcy's bringing someone," Darcy said, carrying out a box of plastic dishes.

"Like a man?" Laurel asked, following her with plastic flatware.

"Not like a man. An actual one." Darcy's tone was derisive. "My sister's always been a fool for love. She expects happily-ever-after no matter how unlikely."

"She can be a dreamer."

"She's too old," Darcy grumbled.

"Oh, I don't know. These days sixties aren't old. You could live thirty more years. Why not have someone in your life?"

Darcy raised her eyebrows. "You telling me how to handle my love life? Let's talk about where you are in the love department."

"Oh, let's not."

They began unfolding big tablecloths. Each corner would be secured to the legs so they wouldn't blow away.

"You're the one who's too young to give up on romance," Darcy told her.

"And yet I'm happily single."

"I'm not so sure about the happily part. Seems to me you're scared."

Laurel so didn't want to be having this conversation. "We were talking about you."

She expected a sharp comeback, but Darcy surprised her by slumping into one of the chairs. "Your father ruined me for love. I gave that man everything and he cheated on me. It broke my heart and I've never recovered."

Laurel moved next to her. "I'm sorry."

"It wasn't your fault. It's his. And hers."

She knew the "hers" in question referred to Marcy. Laurel's father hadn't just cheated, he'd slept with, then married, his wife's sister. The whole family had been shocked, and the sisters hadn't spoken for years. But then her father had dumped Marcy as well, and had moved on to another woman in another state. Eventually, the sisters had made up, but Laurel had often wondered at what cost. She thought maybe they'd never quite found their way back to being as close as they had been.

"Love sucks," Laurel muttered.

"Most of the time, but every now and then someone gets it right. I think that person should be you."

"I don't think I get a choice."

"Not if you don't try. Beau was a mistake. You're free of him. Don't waste your youth on bitterness."

"I'm thirty-seven. There's no more youth to be had."

"It's all relative, girly girl."

Laurel smiled. "You haven't called me that in years."

"Maybe not, but I think it all the time. I want better for you, the way you want better for Jagger and Ariana."

Laurel thought about her plan with Colton. "I'm doing the best I can."

"You're a good mom. I'm proud of you. But sometimes it's easy to get lost in worrying about everyone but yourself." Darcy squeezed her hand. "Just think about it."

"I will."

They returned to setting the tables. Paris showed up around three thirty, bringing wine and a tray of brownies. Jonah, Danny and the girls arrived twenty minutes later. The volume level went from conversational to loud in five seconds and that was before Laurel plugged in the speakers.

Marcy showed up on the back of a motorcycle, holding on to two bags of ice. Introductions were made, although Darcy didn't seem interested in meeting her sister's new friend. Laurel poured drinks and lemonade for the kids and tried not to watch for Colton.

Jagger spotted him first, shouting his name and rushing to greet him. Laurel fought the urge to do the same, ignoring that stupid melty thing in her belly.

"I didn't make this," he said, handing her a bakery box. "I only say that because I could, but I didn't."

She looked inside and grinned when she saw a Bundt cake. "You couldn't make a cake."

"My mom taught me and she'll vouch for my abilities." He held up the shopping bag in his other hand. "A local IPA."

"I don't know what that means, but thank you."

While he put the beer on ice, she took the cake into the kitchen then returned to her guests in time to see Jagger dragging Colton toward the barn.

"Hold on there," she said, hurrying to catch up to them. "No torturing company."

"He said he's interested in the business," Jagger said. "I'm going to show him what we do."

"I really asked," Colton said with a grin. "I'm curious."

Laurel went along with them. She flipped on lights in the barn. Colton gave a low whistle.

"This is huge. Look at all the shelves." He glanced around. "All of this is for resale?"

"It is. The office and shipping space are on that side." She pointed. "The rest is inventory. We separate it by category. When I buy something, we enter it into the computer with a description, a picture and purchase price. Once the items are ready to list on eBay, we have to decide between auction or a buy-it-now price. I have a booth in an antique mall a few miles away, so I also buy for that."

"Mom shops at thrift stores like Goodwill, and at estate sales. Sometimes she buys stuff from auctions, but that's more risky because you're basing your purchase on a few pictures and a description." Jagger spoke confidently. "But sometimes there's a find."

"How long have you been doing this?" he asked the twelve-year-old.

"Mom took me with her when I was a baby. I know a lot."

"She does. She can spot a glassybaby from three aisles away." Colton looked confused. "Is that a doll?"

"It's a candle holder," Laurel said with a laugh. "Handblown and very beautiful. They're made in Seattle and they've become a thing."

Jagger moved close and lowered her voice. "If I see something really good and someone else is looking at it, I start to cry so they let me buy it."

Laurel winced. "Yes, well, we try not to do that very often. It's getting a little too close to being a grifter."

Jagger rolled her eyes. "Mom worries about my moral compass."

"That's a real mom thing to worry about," Colton said solemnly. He pointed toward the far end of the building. "Are those shelves different?"

"Good eye. I host a big yard sale at the end of the summer. It's out at the fairgrounds and has become an event. Locals can sell things, crafters set up booths. I have a pretty big area for resale."

"It's Mom's Christmas," Jagger said. "Like in retail how the stores sell the most at the holidays? For us it's the garage sale."

"You've got a lot already," he said.

"I need about three times what we have," she told him. "The problem isn't finding things to sell, it's setting up. We only have a day to get everything loaded. We can price in advance, get the inventory handled, but the physical part is exhausting."

And it was followed by the long weekend sale. After which, all Laurel wanted to do was sleep for a week. Unfortunately, the girls would start school the next day and that was always fun, but stressful. Her life was full, she thought. No time for a man.

Her gaze drifted to Colton. Okay, she might make an exception for him, she thought, trying not to smile. Not that they needed to be each other's BFFs, but now that she'd gotten to know him better, she wouldn't say no to a repeat of their hot and heavy encounter.

"Are you really not dating my mom?" Jagger asked, dragging Laurel back to the present.

Colton gave her an easy smile. "I'm really not. We're friends."

"Men and women can't be friends."

Laurel cringed, thinking she'd said the same thing.

"Why not?" Colton asked.

Jagger pressed her lips together. "They can't. It's okay when you're little, but then everyone separates into teams. There's boys and there's girls. They can't be friends."

Colton winked at her. "Tell you what. When you can give me a better reason than 'because I said so' we'll talk about it."

Jagger grinned. "Deal!"

★ ★ ★

Paris could see Laurel, Colton and Jagger talking just inside the barn. As always, her friend impressed the hell out of her. Laurel was worried about her kids, so she was taking charge of the situation. Or at least trying to. She loved her children. It was a pretty universal emotion. Unless it wasn't.

Maybe it was hormones, maybe it was being around Jonah and Danny or maybe it was just fate having fun with her, but she'd been thinking about her mom today. It had started with an early-morning delivery when the driver, an old guy pushing seventy, said he remembered her mother. He said she was beautiful and fiery. Paris had assumed the latter description was about her temper. She'd found herself remembering different incidents from her childhood. Like the time her mother had threatened to move and leave her behind. Or when she'd pushed her down the stairs and Paris's arm had broken.

The beatings had always come without warning. She didn't have to mess up for her mother to turn on her. Sometimes she did something she shouldn't, but mostly the triggers were invisible—at least to the child she'd been. She'd learned early to run, to hide, to deflect. But when she'd turned sixteen, she'd figured out how to fight back.

She still remembered the first time her mother had raised her hand to hit her and Paris had turned on her, just as furious, just as willing to take her on.

"Don't you ever do that again."

Paris had growled the words, feeling an inner power that told her this time she would win. She hadn't known what to expect, but her mother had backed away, fear obvious in her eyes. The moment had taught her to stand strong, and it wasn't a big leap to becoming the aggressor.

What she hadn't seen at the time was she'd learned the wrong lesson. *She* became the bully, the one who terrorized. She'd been so excited to go to college, yet she'd dragged her bad habits and poor social skills with her. The temper she'd hated in her mother had cost her more than one friendship.

Paris told everyone she'd come back to Los Lobos because her mother had died and she had responsibilities here, but the truth was more complicated. She'd also come back because she'd run out of people willing to work with her.

"So many mistakes," Paris murmured to herself, walking to the drinks table and debating whether or not she wanted a glass of wine. She could manage her emotions now, but there was no erasing the past.

She looked out at the group of friends laughing and talking. She'd made a good life for herself, she thought. She had friends, a business she loved, she was a good, kind person and wasn't that enough?

Jagger came running over and flung herself at her. "I haven't seen you in forever."

Paris laughed as she hugged her back. "I think that's probably closer to three days, but it does feel like it's been a long time." She sank onto the grass and patted the space next to her. "What's going on? Did you invent something better than sticky notes?"

"I wish." Jagger flopped back on the lawn. "My dad showed up."

"I heard. That was tough for everyone." And Beau was a total loser asshole who didn't deserve the family he'd walked away from, but she wasn't going to say that.

"I was so mad." Jagger sat up. "I wanted to hit him."

"Sure," Paris said calmly. "You were processing a lot of negative emotions. A lot of times we use something physical to distract ourselves from how icky we feel inside. It's not a good solution because it only makes the problem worse, but it's not a surprise that you were tempted."

"You're saying I wasn't mad at him?" She didn't sound convinced.

"Oh, you were mad. You were also really hurt. You want

your dad to hold you tight, tell you he loves you and that he'll never leave again."

Jagger sank onto the grass again and closed her eyes. "He's too selfish to ever think about me or Ariana."

"That doesn't change what you want. And you know what? You're right to want that. Being around your dad should make you feel safe."

Jagger looked at her. "It doesn't. It makes me feel like I'm going to throw up. I'm never going to trust him. Not ever!"

"That's a long time. You're right to be careful, but sometimes people change."

"My dad hasn't."

"Not yet, but maybe one day he will." Paris had her doubts, but this wasn't about her. "The way to stay safe is to be open to the possibility. But after all that's happened, your dad would have to prove himself. You'd need to see actions, not just words."

Jagger sat up again. "I get that. I can't believe the words, but maybe I can believe what he does." She groaned. "You know the worst part? Right now, while we're talking about it, I miss him. I want to hate him all the time, but I can't."

"That's because you're a warm, loving person. That's a good thing, Jagger. It means you can be happy and you care about others."

"I'd rather be mad all the time."

"No, you wouldn't. Angry people live in a dark place. No one wants to be friends with them. From the outside looking in, it seems like it would be safe and powerful, but it's really sad and lonely. Angry people are scared all the time. That's why they lash out."

Jagger's eyes widened. "I didn't know that."

"Hey, I take my grown-up responsibilities very seriously. If I taught you something, I can rest easy tonight."

Jagger grinned as she scrambled to her feet. "I love you, Paris."

"I love you, too, kid."

Jagger waved and walked away. Paris glanced again at the drinks table, thinking a glass of wine sounded even better than it had. But before she could summon the energy to stand up, Jonah moved toward her, a glass in each hand.

He settled next to her, taking Jagger's place, but her reaction to the two of them was completely different. He handed her the white wine.

"I heard part of that."

"Beau's a jerk."

"Not a surprise. He was a jerk before." Jonah looked at her. "You gave her good advice."

"When it comes to being pissed off, I'm kind of an expert."

She spoke lightly because she really wasn't in the mood to do another round of mea culpas only to blurt out, "I've been thinking about my mom today. How she acted, what I learned from her. My childhood was a mess. I wish she'd been different or I'd been stronger."

"Hey." He touched her arm. "You were the kid. It's not your job to be stronger. You survived a horrible situation the only way you knew how."

"How can you defend me?"

"I was in love with you. I married you."

Words that made her ache inside. "And I pushed you away. That's what I regret most."

They looked at each other. She wanted to read regret in his eyes, or a hint that he still had feelings. She knew she had a chance with the former, but not the latter. He'd married someone else. For all she knew, he was still mourning the loss.

"I'm reading the book you told me about. The one for book club."

She laughed. "Actually reading it? Word by word."

"That's generally how I read. It's interesting. Different. She changes viewpoint a lot—like in the same sentence—but I think that's more about the time in which the book was written."

"You're really joining book club."

"Why not? I can impress you with my intellectual prowess."

She laughed. "When did I think you weren't smart?"

"It could happen."

Cassie felt left out. Everywhere she turned, people were talking and having fun. Laurel was hanging with her kids and Colton, Paris was with Danny and Jonah. They all belonged together and while she was happy for her friends, she was feeling a little like she didn't have anyone in the world.

"Pity much?" she asked herself, careful to keep her voice down. Besides, she wasn't alone. She had family. All right— maybe they'd thrown her out, but they'd said it was for her own good and she was starting to believe them.

Paris walked over and linked arms with her. "So I did something you might not approve of."

"How is that possible?"

She turned and pointed. Cassie gaped as Raphael walked toward them. He moved with the grace of a natural athlete who absolutely knew his place in the world. And he was smiling. At her.

"He came by LoLo's this afternoon," Paris said. "Somehow I mentioned the barbecue and invited him."

"Why?"

"You'd make a cute couple."

"He's not interested in me. Why would you think that?" Despite the whole asking-her-out thing, he couldn't want her. "He doesn't need fixing. That's all I know how to do in a relationship."

"Then maybe it's time you learned some new skills." Paris stepped back and gave her a little push in his direction. "Go say hi. Run your hands all over his body. Something. The poor man doesn't know anyone here."

"He knows everyone." She had more to say, but Raphael was probably within earshot, so she gave Paris a pointed stare before turning back to smile at the very handsome man in front of her.

"Hi. You're here."

"I am. Paris invited me. I'm glad because we have some unfinished business."

"About the cave? I told you that you can do whatever you want there. Study, take pictures. I'm excited about what you're going to discover."

"No, about going out with me."

She stared at him. "Are you seriously asking me out on a date?"

"Yes."

"Why?"

One corner of his full, kissable mouth turned up. "Is this a West Coast–East Coast thing? Don't people date in Maine?"

"You're asking me out on a date?"

"Yes."

"Why?" She held up her hand. "I'm not playing a game here, I genuinely don't understand why you'd want to go out with me."

Perhaps not the most sophisticated thing she could have said, but the truth. She didn't get it at all.

"I mean, look at you," she said.

"I don't have a mirror."

She groaned. "You are very aware that you're in a whole different band when it comes to looks. You're super educated, you have a body like, well, a superhero. I'm some ordinary person with no special skills and an uncertain future." She thought about what she'd said to Paris. "I fix people. More specifically men. In relationships, I fix them and they move on. From what I can tell, you don't need fixing."

He smiled. "Have dinner with me."

"Didn't you hear anything I said?"

"Every word. Have dinner with me. Tuesday. I'll pick you up at six thirty."

She didn't want to ask "why" yet again but nothing else came to mind. Which could be the reason she found herself whispering, "Yes."

★ ★ ★

In her quest to have a man friend, Laurel made arrangements for Colton to fix a leaking faucet. She wouldn't admit to her daughters that she'd loosened the fittings in the first place. Colton obliged and as per their plan, she suggested an impromptu dinner at Bill's Mexican Food.

Halfway through the meal, she realized that despite the machinations involved with the evening, she and her girls were having a great time. Colton was relaxed and funny. Nothing seemed to faze him—not even Jagger and Ariana fighting over the last taco.

Laurel insisted they split it, which annoyed both of them.

"When I have kids I'm going to let them do whatever they want," Jagger muttered, finishing her half.

"You say that now," Colton told her. "But I doubt that's really true. It's not healthy to let kids do whatever they want. What if your three-year-old wants to play with fire?"

"That's different."

"Is it really?"

Jagger sighed. "You're talking like a grown-up. You know what I meant."

"I did."

She laughed. "So you're being annoying on purpose."

"A little. It's fun."

Laurel smiled at her daughter. "Don't forget, Colton has four sisters. He's wise to your games." She paused. "I guess to all our games."

"Four sisters is a lot." Ariana reached for a chip. "I only have one and that's enough."

"At least I'm older," Jagger said. "I get to be bossy while you're just annoying."

"Am not."

"Are, too!"

Laurel looked at Colton. "Was it like this at your house?"

"Times three or four." He chuckled. "Don't forget, I was the youngest, so they all found me annoying. When I was a baby, they thought I was fun, but by the time I was five, they were ready to be done with me and play with their friends."

"Were you sad?" Jagger asked.

"For a while, but then I made friends of my own. Plus, my dad was always there for me. We would do things—just the two of us—like camping."

Laurel saw the exact second Colton realized he shouldn't have mentioned his father. He looked at her, his expression stricken. Before she could reassure him, Jagger spoke.

"Our dad left us." Her voice was flat.

"He didn't *mean* to go away," Ariana said quietly. "But he did."

"Of course he meant it," Jagger snapped. "If he hadn't meant it, he wouldn't have done it."

"That's hard," Colton said. "For both of you."

"It is." Ariana glanced at her sister. "Jagger's mad all the time."

"Not all the time." Jagger pressed her lips together. "Paris told me that I'm using anger to hide what I really feel." She turned to Laurel. "I don't want to be sad all the time."

"You don't have to be and sometimes it's okay to be angry."

"I wish he didn't go," Ariana whispered. "Maybe he'll come back."

Jagger rolled her eyes. "Dads leave. It's what they do. Men leave."

"Not all of them." Colton smiled at her. "My parents have been married for over forty years."

Both girls stared at him.

"For real?" Jagger asked.

Ariana seemed equally impressed. "That's a long time. Nearly forever."

"It is, and they're still in love." He smiled at them. "It's nice. Oh, they fight every now and then, but it's over quickly. They're each other's best friend. That's how marriage should be."

Laurel heard something in his voice. A tone maybe, or a sense of loss. Divorce wasn't easy. She knew that herself.

"I want to be married for forty years and still be in love," Ariana murmured. "It sounds nice."

"Not me." Jagger's voice was determined. "I wouldn't ever trust a man that much."

The words nearly echoed what Laurel had been thinking for months now, she thought sadly. She really had taught her daughters the wrong lesson. Hopefully, Colton would help her reverse that, because without him, she was out of options.

eighteen

On her day off, Cassie decided to visit her land. She'd scanned the documents she and Raphael had found and sent them for translation. Once they came back, she would figure out what to do. In the meantime, she felt an odd need to hang with her trees.

She parked by the orchard and walked through the grove. Maybe she could take a few pictures and find out what they were. As she walked, she tried counting them but quickly got lost and had to move to the edge of the orchard to figure out where she was and start over.

Between ninety-seven and ninety-eight, someone called out a loud "Hello!"

She spun and saw an old man walking toward her. She wasn't great with ages of anyone over forty, but if she had to guess, she would say he was maybe seventy. He had on a big straw hat and loose overalls, with a chambray shirt underneath. She waited as he got closer.

"I was hoping you'd come back."

The words surprised her, causing her to blurt, "That's creepy in a very stalkerish way."

The old man grinned. "Didn't mean it that way. I saw your

car parked here before. Thought you might be a troublemaker. But you're the new owner, aren't you?" He stuck out his hand. "Westin Bernheim."

"Cassie Hayden."

"I knew your uncle," Westin told her. "He was an adventurer, but he didn't have the time or the patience to be an orchardist. Shame. This is good land."

"Orchardist? Not farmer?"

"You farming here?"

"I genuinely have no idea." She pointed at the trees. "What are they? There's more than one type? I mean, they look different."

"You've got your Washington naval oranges and Hass avocados."

She groaned. "Avocado trees?"

"Don't you like avocados?"

"Not as much as everyone else in California." She looked around. "Why aren't they growing?"

"They are, best as they can. They need a little help. Pruning, fertilizer. Some of them need to be cut down. The irrigation system's turned off, so that's a problem. We don't get enough rain to support them. But it's all recoverable. The land's good and you have water rights."

"I do?"

"Yep. They're in the deed. You haven't read it?"

"The deed? Um, no." Did anyone read a deed?

"Water's king and you have your share." He pointed to the orchard. "With a little backbone, some knowledge and a couple of years, this could be productive again. Getting labor's easy. I'd be happy to consult. All you need is money." He eyed her. "You have a good-sized savings account?"

"I wish." Although she did have nineteen barrels of what she hoped was prime cognac.

"Come with me."

He led her through the trees, pointing out problems.

"Bad drainage there. Those half dozen need to come down and the area needs to be graded. Then you plant new. Those need to be cut way back." He kicked at the high grass and weeds. "This all needs cleaning up. You can do it mechanically or you could get in some goats. You've got the time and they'd do a better job."

"Goats? I don't want to own goats."

He grinned at her. "You rent them."

"Oh, sure. We did that all the time back home."

He kept moving, overwhelming her with information and his expertise. A half hour later, her head was spinning.

"This is more than I want to take on," she admitted.

"We'd go step-by-step," Westin told her. "Think about what you have here, Cassie. This is more than land, it's your heritage. The history of Los Lobos lives in the land. Plus, growing things is a noble calling."

His lips thinned. "If you don't get the orchard up and running, then you're not going to want to keep the land. You know who's going to buy it?"

Based on his tone, she half expected him to say *the devil himself.* "Who?"

"Developers." Disgust thickened his voice. "They'll tear this all down and put up town houses. Ticky tacky places that will be falling down in five years. You could be feeding the world."

"I'd need a lot more trees to do that."

Westin laughed. "You know what I mean."

"I do. It's a lot to think about."

"Have you seen the house?"

She glanced in the direction of the old place. "No. The lawyer is still trying to get the keys so I can see inside. Unless you have a set."

"Nope, but I've been in the old place. It's solid. You'll say it's old-fashioned, but it's all you need. The roof is in good shape and the foundation is sound. The rest can be fixed."

With money she didn't have, she thought. Sure the cognac,

but between the orchard and the potential remodel, she felt as if she'd already spent it three times over. Even more significant, she wasn't staying. In six months, she was out of here, so why bother starting something?

Only she couldn't seem to say that to Westin and when she thought about developers tearing down her trees, she got a lump in her throat.

"You've given me a lot to think about."

"Good. There aren't enough people willing to take on something like this," he said. "I have three boys. Only one of them is working with me. The other two work in tech." He practically spat the word.

"We all love our internet," she told him.

"We all have to eat. You've been given a gift, Cassie. A rare one. Land matters. Land is forever." He fished a card out of his pocket. "That's my number and email address."

"I thought you hated tech."

He flashed her a smile. "I do, but a man has to keep up with the times. Call me with any questions or if you want me to walk the orchard with you. I can also get you in touch with an arborist who specializes in what you're growing here."

"Oranges and avocados. I remember."

"Washington naval oranges and Hass avocados. Names matter."

"You're a weird old man."

He smiled again. "Yes, I am. We'll talk soon."

Paris arrived home to find Danny and Jonah sitting on her front porch, a pink cake box between them. At the sight of them, well, mostly of Jonah, her heart gave a little shimmy.

"Don't go getting ideas," she murmured quietly as she pulled into her driveway. Bandit gave her a quizzical look.

"I'll explain later," she told the dog.

They got out. Bandit raced over to greet first Danny, then Jonah, his tailing swishing back and forth as he danced his excitement.

Paris felt somewhat the same, but kept her emotions a little more in check.

"Hi. I wasn't expecting you," she said, walking toward them.

Danny scrambled to his feet. "We brought cake. It's really good."

"Then you probably want a taste."

Jonah rose and gave her a lazy smile. "We were driving by the bakery, and it occurred to me I hadn't thanked you for looking after him while my mom had her surgery."

"You thanked me about ten times, but I'll take cake."

She led the way inside. Bandit made a beeline for the kitchen where he sat by the cabinet, his tail wagging against the floor, his gaze intense.

"You can put the cake on the island. First this guy needs to be fed."

"Can you show me how?" Danny asked eagerly.

"I can."

She measured a portion of his ridiculously expensive dog food into a bowl. Danny watched intently while Bandit whined.

"I give him a little kibble, as well," she said. "Use the measuring cup. Uh-huh. Just like that."

She stirred it for a couple of seconds, then walked over to the pet place mat. Bandit immediately sat, licking his lips.

She set down the bowl, mentally did a slow count to three, then told him, "Okay."

He began to devour his food. She washed his water bowl, then refilled it. Once that was done, she washed her hands.

"Who wants cake?"

"That's for later," Jonah told her. "You're not expected to share."

"I can't eat a whole cake by myself."

She had a feeling she was missing the point of the visit. Was it really just to drop off a thank-you cake? Did Jonah want her to invite him and Danny to dinner? As she didn't have much of anything in the refrigerator, should she suggest they go out or something?

Bandit finished his meal. Paris let him and Danny out back to play. Jonah watched through the window.

"You're patient with him."

"I assume we're talking about Danny and if so, he's easy to be with."

He looked at her. "I owe you for your help."

She waved away the comment. "We've been over that and no. I was happy to do it. How's your mom doing?"

"Better every day." He glanced around. "You remodeled."

"A few years ago. It was past time. Obviously the kitchen, but also the hall bath. It was all original fixtures and tile." She grinned. "Some lady drove in from San Francisco to chip out the two-tone pink tile from that bathroom. She resold it for big money and we split the profit. I'm shocked to say that tile sale covered the bathroom remodel."

"Nice."

"I was happy. My contractor blew out the back wall on the main bedroom, giving the space a decent closet and doubling the size of the attached bath. The rest of the house needed paint and new flooring."

He rubbed his hand along the front of the cabinets. "Are these the originals?"

"Yes. They're real wood and were in good shape. I had them stripped and painted."

"You made good choices."

"Thanks."

"I always liked this house."

She stared at him. "Why?"

"Because this is where we lived when we were married. We made memories here."

She tried not to wince. "Bad ones."

"That's not true. I liked being married to you." He studied her. "You only focus on the bad stuff. We had great times together.

You were always so full of life. You forced me out of my shell and made me laugh."

"Then I screamed and threatened you."

He waved that comment away. "Good happened here, too," he said firmly. "I was happy here."

Until he wasn't, she thought.

"I wish I could have been different," she admitted. "Nicer. More understanding and less angry. It took me a long time to find my way. I'm not sure I would have done the work if I hadn't lost you, but without me doing the work, you were going to walk away regardless. I guess what I'm saying is we were doomed and that's mostly on me and I regret that."

"Doomed sounds so tragic. Like I said, I have happy memories."

She had trouble accepting that, but she chose to believe him. "I'm glad. Me, too."

"The barbecue was fun," he said. "Laurel hasn't changed. She's done great with her thrifting."

"She has. It's such an interesting business model. One that wouldn't have existed twenty years ago. I go with her on thrifting trips when I can." She grinned. "It turns out I have a good eye for milk glass."

"That's a thing?"

"It is."

They were facing each other across the island. Paris liked being close to him with a safe, solid barrier between them to keep her from doing something stupid. Because she could feel herself wanting to lean in and… What? Kiss him? Ask him to hold her? Tell him she had feelings for him?

All really dumb ideas she needed out of her head.

She looked at the clock over the stove and feigned surprise. "Look at the time. Natalie's going to wonder where her family is." She reached for the pink box. "Let me give you part of the cake. I hear it's excellent."

Jonah watched her without moving. "You're throwing me out."

"I am." Safer for everyone…or at the very least, for her.

"Then Danny and I will leave you be. But we'll see you soon."

"I look forward to it," she murmured, knowing she meant every word.

"I read about this online," Jagger said as Laurel pulled her van into the recording studio parking lot. "When you meet somebody famous, you have to act casual. Like it's no big deal. We can't shriek or try to touch him or anything. He's really a regular person."

"You're assuming he knows that," Laurel teased. "What if he expects us to scream? Then he'll be disappointed."

Jagger sighed heavily. "I'm being serious. This is important. We want Micah Ruiz to like us."

"I don't even know who that is," Ariana grumbled.

"Yes, you do. He sings that old song, 'Moonlight for Christmas,' plus he wrote and sings 'When the Snow Falls,' which is, like, your favorite Christmas song ever."

Ariana stared at her sister. "We're going to meet him?"

"Yes."

"Is he going to sing that song?"

Laurel glanced at her in the rearview mirror. "He is. It's for a Christmas album that—"

The rest of her words were drowned out by Ariana's high-pitched screams.

"You didn't tell me that. Micah Ruiz! I can't stand it." She rocked back and forth in her seat, continuing to scream.

Jagger looked at her mom. "This is what I was talking about. She has to be controlled."

"Oh, like you're not excited."

"I am, but I'm being mature."

Laurel got out of the van and opened the rear door, then pointed at her youngest. "Stop."

Ariana went silent.

"Don't do that again. It's terrifying. Colton invited us to a re-cording session because he thought we'd enjoy it. We're not going to embarrass him or act like groupies. We're going to be pleas-ant, friendly and watch without any high-pitched noises. Do I make myself clear?"

Jagger stood next to her. "She means you, Ariana."

"Both of you. It's easy to be all cool and disinterested out here, but once we're in the studio, you're going to want to react."

"I won't," Ariana grumbled as she got out of the minivan. "Mom, I'm not a kid."

Because ten was so grown-up? But Laurel knew better than to say anything.

"This is the first session in the studio," she said, locking the van, then leading the way to the building. "Colton said they'd do a run-through of the song a couple of times, then start lay-ing down tracks."

Both girls looked at her blankly.

"From what I read online and what Colton told me, a song is recorded in layers or what they call bed tracks. First the drums and maybe a guitar. Because if the beat's not right, the song will be off."

"Drums rule," Jagger said confidently. "Everybody knows that."

Ariana sighed heavily. "Mom, she's acting like she's the queen of everything."

"We're all a little excited." Laurel held open the door to the building. "Let's be on our best behavior."

She was beginning to rethink accepting Colton's very gener-ous invitation. What if she and the girls got in the way of Micah Ruiz recording his song? It would almost be as bad as ruining Christmas.

Every time she'd been inside the recording studio, it had been nearly deserted, but this afternoon it was a busy place. Groups of people stood talking in the open area by the stairs. There was a receptionist up front, but instead of her friend Victoria, a young woman with several facial piercings and a tattoo of fairy wings on her cheek stood by the desk. She totally carried off the look, but Laurel couldn't help thinking that years from now, the twentysomething was going to regret the wings.

"Can I help you?" Fairy Wings asked, eyeing the girls the way some people eyed ants at a picnic. "We're not open to the public."

"Colton invited us," Jagger said coolly. "We're on the list."

"There's no list," the receptionist told her. "This isn't a party."

Laurel got between them. "We're guests of Colton. If you'd check with him, please. Or I can text him."

The receptionist sighed heavily. "Name?"

"Laurel Richards."

"I'm Ariana," her youngest offered with a hesitant smile. Jagger simply glared.

Fairy Wings picked up a phone and pressed a couple of buttons. "Some woman is here with her two kids and I—" She paused while she listened. "Oh. All right."

She hung up and seemed to gather herself, then offered a bright smile. "Let me show you back."

"Colton said we were his special guests, didn't he," Jagger said loudly. "I told you we were on the list."

"Enough," Laurel told her.

Jagger sighed heavily.

They went down a long hallway toward the recording studios where Laurel had first met Colton. Several of the studios were in use. While she could see people singing or playing instruments, she couldn't hear anything.

They went to the end of the hall to what looked like a stadium-sized area. The panel with the computer monitors and the dials was twice as long as in the other studios. Behind the glassed-in area was a small stage with a full drum set, several chairs and a half-dozen people standing around and talking. Colton sat with two other guys, looking at something on a computer screen.

"Wait here," Fairy Wings said forcefully, before stepping inside. She went through two sets of doors to get to the control room. Colton glanced up at her, then turned and looked out the glass window.

The second he saw her, he smiled. Laurel appreciated the welcome, but found herself a little more concerned about the weird fluttering sensation in her stomach. What was up with that? She and Colton were just friends. She loved Paris like a sister, but had never once *fluttered* in her presence. Was it because Colton was a man and her body couldn't help reacting? Was it because they'd had amazing sex and her hormones were all about a repeat performance? Or was it something less easily defined?

He came out into the hallway. "You made it."

Both Jagger and Ariana raced toward him, arms outstretched. He crouched down to hug them, looking at Laurel over their heads.

"This is nice," he told her with a grin. "I haven't been greeted like this in a long time. I'll have to invite you here more often."

"I'll bet *she* wouldn't like that," Jagger grumbled, pointing at the retreating receptionist. "She didn't believe us when we said we knew you."

He rose and put his hand on Jagger's shoulder. "Don't worry about her. She just broke up with her boyfriend, so she's in a mood. Come in, let me show you what we do."

They went into the studio. Colton pointed out the speakers, the microphones and explained how they'd lay down the bed tracks.

"We're recording 'When the Snow Falls' a couple of different ways. First we'll do a traditional rock version with drums and guitars, along with a few other instruments. Later this week, we're bringing in a full orchestra."

Jagger looked around. "Will they fit?"

"They will. It'll be crowded, but Quinn designed this studio to handle it. We've already done a couple of different tracks with the drums, bass and rhythm guitar. Micah will sing with each of them, then he and Quinn will decide which version they prefer."

Ariana looked up at him. "What do you do?"

"I make sure everything records correctly, and some quick cleanup work and editing." He pointed to the drum set. "Let's say the drummer messes up three seconds. He can redo that part and I can replace the bad section instead of recording the whole song again."

"But isn't that cheating?"

Colton grinned. "More like if you're taking a test and you realize you answered one question wrong. You don't retake the whole test, you change the one answer."

She beamed at him. "I get it. Are we going to see Micah sing?"

"We are."

Ariana leaned against him. "Mom says we have to behave."

"No screaming," Jagger said, pointing at her sister. "No shriek-ing."

"I would never do that." Ariana's voice was prim.

"What if I want a little screaming?"

They all turned. Laurel blinked twice, unable to believe Micah Ruiz was standing right there, looking like his album covers. Jagger seemed immobilized as she stared, but Ariana had to slap her hand over her mouth to keep from shrieking.

Colton chuckled. "Micah, this is my friend Laurel, and her daughters, Jagger and Ariana."

"Nice to meet you." He looked at Ariana. "You should prob-ably let it out before you explode."

She dropped her hand, then began jumping in place shout-ing, "It's really you! I love you so much. You're going to sing my favorite song ever."

"She only likes the Christmas songs," Jagger said with a long-suffering sigh. "Sorry about her. She's still really young."

Micah's mouth twitched, as if he were trying not to smile. "Being the older sister is a lot of responsibility."

"You have no idea."

He laughed. "You're right. I don't. But I do have a little girl who's about two and a half and we have another baby on the way, so she's going to be a big sister, too. Maybe you can be her role model."

"I could tell her what to look out for."

Laurel was about to tell her daughters to leave Micah alone when he looked at her. "I'm playing guitar on the next track. Mind if your two sit with me while I warm up?"

"They'd love that."

He led the girls to a couple of chairs. Once they were seated, he dragged over a stool and sat, then showed them how to tune the guitar.

"Want to ask if you can sit on his lap?" Colton asked, his voice teasing.

She grinned. "I'm happy over here. He's great with kids."

"He has that reputation. He lives up in Washington State, in a little town called Wishing Tree, but he does charity events for children all over the country."

"He sounds like a good guy."

"He is. I've worked with him before. He's one of the more normal artists. No crazy demands, no tantrums. He does the work, then he goes home to his family."

There was something in his tone, Laurel thought. A wistfulness, maybe. Because Colton's marriage had failed, just like hers, only he didn't have the benefit of a couple of kids to be part of his family.

"Do you regret not having children with your wife?" she asked before she could stop herself. She immediately held up her hand. "I'm sorry. That was not an appropriate question."

He looked surprised but not upset. "We were going to start a family, but didn't feel there was any reason to hurry. Then things started going south. I still want a family, but I'm glad it didn't happen then." He looked at her. "Let's just say I don't think I'd have your grace."

"What does that mean? My grace?"

"You're great at being a single mom. Honestly, I don't think I could handle being a single parent. Everyone says we do what we have to, but there's so much, every second of every day. I want to be an involved dad for sure, but having a partner would make things a lot easier."

"The right partner," Laurel said, thinking about all the times Beau had let her down. "The wrong one makes it worse. Although I guess my ex not being around much was good training for when he left."

"You make it look easy."

The fluttering returned, but she ignored it. Colton was turning out to be a good friend to her and the girls and that was far more important than any silly physical reaction on her part.

nineteen

"You seem nervous," Raphael said quietly, looking at Cassie over his menu.

They were seated in the fine dining restaurant in the Los Lobos Hotel, with a view of the sloping lawn and the Pacific Ocean. A white awning and the careful placement of trees kept the setting sun from being a problem.

"Nervous?" she repeated, her voice at an uncomfortably high pitch. She cleared her throat. "I'm fine."

Raphael's blue eyes remained locked on her face. "I don't believe you."

And wasn't that just like a man, she thought with a sigh. "This isn't my thing. I don't date."

His perfectly arched eyebrows drew together in a way that made him even more handsome. "I thought you had recently broken up with someone."

"Oh, I didn't mean I didn't have relationships, I meant I don't date. I tend to just, you know, get involved." Perhaps more quickly than she should, she thought unexpectedly. Was that part of her problem? Jumping in before she was ready?

"If you don't date, how do you get involved?" he asked.

"It kind of happens. I meet someone and right away I know he needs something. By that I mean fixing," she clarified. "Maybe he doesn't have a good job or any job. Maybe he has a crappy roommate or a difficult ex. Maybe he needs to learn confidence or help painting his house."

"You've painted your boyfriends' houses?"

"Just the one and not by myself." This subject wasn't especially flattering, but she didn't know how to change it. "I'm sort of a relationship handyman. Handyperson. I fix men."

"And then they leave you."

She winced. "Not always. Sometimes I leave. Sometimes the relationship just sort of ends." She told herself to stop talking—she was making herself sound pathetic. "I can be fun, though."

He smiled. "I happen to know that's true."

How could he? They'd been at the table fifteen minutes. She needed a little more time to figure out the fun.

"The fixing thing is interesting," he said. "Do you do it because you're the only one who can?"

"I don't know. Maybe because it's what the other person obviously needs. I don't think I'm especially better than anyone else at it." And she'd been wrong about her brother and sister needing her. They'd insisted they would have been fine. "Maybe it's a story I tell myself."

"Life is all about telling stories," he said. "There's an old saying. 'To the winner go the spoils.' I think of it as more to the winner goes the history." He leaned toward her. "Take China."

"The country?"

His smile returned. "Yes. As each dynasty fell and a new one took its place, history was rewritten. The victor gets to tell the story. We have an idea of Chinese history, but so much was lost because the winner wanted that."

"But I'm not China."

"No, you're the youngest of three. How much of your memory is true and how much were you told because that's the story your older siblings tell themselves? We all remember things differently, based on our perspective. Truth can be subjective."

She struggled to understand. "When my parents died, we all suffered. But Faith had her husband and Garth had his friends' support. I didn't have anyone." At fourteen, none of her friends had been equipped to deal with her grief.

"I was alone and so scared. I didn't know what to do. I felt like a different person."

"You didn't know how to make the pain go away," he said. "It would have felt like a living creature, following you around."

She supposed he was right. "But when I took care of things, I felt better. Maybe helping out was a distraction or maybe it was real, but it's the lesson I learned."

"To live for someone else?"

"Not exactly." She paused. "I don't think of it that way. It's more that I'm needed. I'm essential." She stared at him. "Wait, is that my story? I have to be the only one who can do it because then I'll always be needed. And if I'm always needed, I don't have to take any risks because that would be irresponsible?"

She felt like an important truth was there in front of her, if only she would see it.

"With the guys—I made sure they needed me. At least that was what I told myself. Because if they needed me, then I mattered. Only that's not a real relationship, is it? There's no meeting of equals. They needed me, but I didn't need them, so when they were quote-unquote fixed, they moved on."

She drew in a breath. "This is a lot to think about and we haven't even ordered cocktails."

Raphael laughed. "Good point." He motioned to their server. After describing the specials, she took their drink orders and stepped away.

"How were you different before you lost your parents?" he asked.

"That was a long time ago. Fourteen years." Half her life, she thought in surprise. "I guess I was more outgoing. Everything was easy. I had that confidence you get from being totally loved and supported. It never occurred to me to be afraid of trying. Of course everything would be all right."

"And a single phone call shattered that. You're incredibly strong."

"Excuse me?"

"You're willing to look inside yourself and figure out if you like where you are. Most people aren't. They go on doing what they do, never considering it might not make them happy."

He was making her sound a whole lot braver than she was. "I'm only here because my brother and sister threw me out."

"I don't buy that. You could have told them no. They didn't physically force you to leave. They made their point and a part of you recognized it as truth. That's why you left."

"You're giving me more credit than I deserve."

His smile was easy. "I don't think so."

"I thought you spent your life digging in the dirt. How do you know so much about people?"

"It's my job to study other cultures and figure out how they function. I spend a lot of time coming up with theories that may never be proven to be correct."

"But that also means no one can prove you wrong."

He grinned. "That's the part I like."

Their server returned with their drinks and took their dinner order. Cassie waited until they were alone to say, "All right, we've psychoanalyzed me enough for one evening. It's only fair that you share something personal and not very flattering. I'll let you pick the topic."

He studied her for several heartbeats before saying, "Women either assume I'm incapable of having genuine feelings or decide I couldn't possibly like them."

She hadn't been expecting that. "Because you're so gorgeous?" She felt herself flush, but forged ahead. "I'm stating the obvious."

He looked down at the table before raising his head. "Yes, the looks are a problem."

"Oh, I doubt that," she murmured, then laughed. "Okay, I guess intellectually I can understand they would be, but speaking as one of the regular people, you have doors opened to you that no one else gets to walk through. You have opportunities and better service and perks because you're possibly the best-looking man on the planet. It's kind of hard to feel sorry for you."

"I'm not looking for pity. You asked me to share something intimate that wasn't flattering." His mouth curved up. "No pun intended."

Would it be difficult to be that attractive? She thought there might be issues, but wouldn't the good outweigh the bad?

"You can have anyone you want," she pointed out.

"Not if they don't believe I like them."

She hadn't thought about that. "That really happens?"

"You laughed when I asked you out."

"Oh. But that was different."

One eyebrow rose. "Explain to me how."

"It just is." Hmm, that didn't sound especially scientific or even reasonable. "Okay, I laughed because you're you. Not just the good looks, but the whole package. You have, like, seven degrees. I couldn't get out of my own way enough to go to community college. You have a career you're passionate about. I have no idea what I want to do with my life."

"Life's a journey."

"If that's true, I haven't even figured out where to buy a ticket. So that's why I laughed. Why would someone like you ask me out to dinner?"

"So I was playing with you? Asking you out to amuse myself?"

"No. That sounds mean and I didn't think you were being…" What? Cruel? From what she could tell, he was a nice guy, which only added one more item to the forty-seven-reasons-he-was-amazing list. But she *had* laughed and he really had been asking her out.

"I assumed you didn't have feelings," she blurted, then stared at him. "That's not good. I was flip because I couldn't believe you'd want to go out with me, so I reacted in a way that protected myself but wasn't very nice to you. I'm sorry. I'm usually more careful."

"You usually take care of the world."

"I try, but you're a little too together to be in my comfort zone. So you really wanted to ask me out?"

"I believe us sitting here together for dinner illustrates that point."

"Because you like me?" OMG! She couldn't believe she was asking that question.

"Yes."

"As friends?"

He laughed then, a deep male laugh that made her toes curl a little. "I'm interested in you romantically, Cassie. Friends first, because that always makes sense, but make no mistake—my intentions go way beyond that."

Was he talking about sex? "So you're going to try to seduce me?"

"Not anytime soon. We need to get to know each other. Rushed intimacy can get in the way of a relationship."

"You've put some thought into this."

His dark blue gaze locked with hers. "I have."

So he liked her and wanted to take things slow because that gave them a better chance at a future? No one she'd ever been involved with had showed up with a plan. The best she'd seen with a guy was a great smile and a six-pack of beer.

"You like me," she repeated, more to herself than him. "I'm going to have to sit with that for a while."

"Take as long as you need. I'll be right here."

"The whole virgin thing is annoying," Cassie said from the back seat. "I mean, come on. She was practically raped. It's not her fault."

"It was a different time." As always, Paris's tone was calm and reasonable. "Karl got over it."

"Plus, she lied." Not that Laurel blamed Anna, given the circumstances, but she hadn't been honest with the man she'd married. Not about anything.

"You're taking his side?" Cassie asked, her voice nearly a shriek. "How could you?"

"I'm not." Laurel grinned at her in the rearview mirror. "You have energy."

"I can relate to Anna."

"You're a good book club member," Paris said. "You make this more fun."

"Thanks." Cassie held up her e-reader. "I've never done book club in the car before. Or in a minivan. I think I like it."

Laurel laughed with them as drove south on I-5, heading for the Santa Monica Goodwill. She always went to the southernmost store and worked her way north, stopping at five stores, finishing in the San Fernando Valley. With luck, she would head home with a full van.

"That's all the questions," Paris said. "Next up is Cassie's choice. *Night into Day.* I'm looking forward to it." She paused. "I told you Jonah's going to read it, right?"

"You did." Laurel glanced at her. "An interesting turn of events."

"Oh, please. It doesn't mean anything." She pointed out the windshield. "We're getting close to the 405 turnoff."

Laurel held in a smile. Paris was trying to distract her from the fact that she'd asked her ex-husband to join book club.

"This is exciting," Cassie said. "I've never been thrifting before. Not professionally."

"It can be challenging." Paris turned to face her. "I always feel as if I know nothing. I finally decided to focus on three things I'm good at."

Cassie moaned. "I didn't get the homework assignment? It's like that nightmare of not being prepared for the final exam."

"No homework." Laurel slowed with the traffic. She would take 405 down to I-10, then fight her way to the store. "You're here to hang out, nothing more. Oh, wait. Paris can show you how glassybabies are marked. Those are always fun to find."

"I don't know what those are."

"Votive candle holders," Paris said. "I'm also pretty good at finding Fenton Art Glass. Sometimes those are signed or have a sticker. Laurel will be on a mission to find the good stuff, so you can shop slower with me."

"Or you can just enjoy yourself." Laurel smiled into the rearview mirror. "No work required."

She'd planned to take the quick trip down south by herself. Only Paris had asked to tag along, then Cassie had gotten the day off to join them.

This felt good, she thought happily. It had been too long since she'd gotten away with her friends, even for the day. The girls had spent the night with Marcy, who would take them to and from camp and keep them until Laurel got home. She had an empty van, a hopeful attitude and plenty of cash for treasures.

"Still avoiding sex with Colton?" Paris asked.

Laurel's insides clenched at the reminder of that glorious morning. "No sex," she said firmly. "We're friends for the greater good."

"Bummer," Paris said and they all laughed.

"It's been fun," Laurel admitted. "I'm kind of surprised. I thought I'd feel awkward around him and that pretending to be friends would be a chore, but he's great and the girls enjoy spending time with him."

"What started out as a lie turned real." Cassie sighed. "It's like the perfect ending."

"No ending." Paris turned to shake her finger. "The beginning. The girls need the whole guys-are-great thing to be ongoing."

"It will take time," Laurel said as she changed lanes. Traffic had eased. With luck they would reach Santa Monica in half an hour.

She glanced at Paris. "They liked Jonah. You should bring him around more."

"He's not mine to bring."

"Are you sure?" Cassie asked with a grin. "You two were pretty tight at the barbecue."

"We're exes who happened to not hate each other." Paris sighed. "Which is really good for me. He could have avoided me. It's nice that he didn't."

"I wish you'd let the past go." Laurel's tone was gentle. "You're not who you were."

"But I was that person. I have to own it."

"There's a difference between taking responsibility and beating yourself up all the time. Self-forgiveness can be a good thing."

"She doesn't think she deserves it," Cassie announced.

Laurel glanced at her in the mirror. Cassie shrugged.

"Paris isn't the only one who can be insightful. We all have our moments and I just had mine for the month." She grinned. "We should take a second and enjoy it."

"Ignoring the whole past-you-regret thing," Laurel said, "is it nice having Jonah and Danny around?"

"It is. Danny's so much fun. He's not just a nice kid, he's funny and sweet, and he adores Bandit. Jonah's who he's always been, a good guy with a big heart."

"But you won't kiss him."

"What?" Paris's voice was a yelp. "No. Jeez. We're friendly and nothing more. The man left me. I'm not going to kiss him."

"He's back now. That could mean something."

"It means his mother had to have knee replacement surgery and she lives in the same town as me. Trust me. Jonah has no ulterior motive."

"I want to say you're wrong, but I actually don't know if he does or doesn't."

"He doesn't."

"So you say."

Cassie grinned. "It's kind of fun when you two fight, because I know it's going to be okay. It's like you're both trying to make a point, but we can all still feel the love."

Paris looked at Laurel. "You're annoying as shit sometimes."

"Back at you. And I do love you."

"Me, too." Paris turned in her seat. "All right. We've recapped Laurel's relationship with Colton and we're going to pretend to believe her when she says they're not having sex."

"We're not doing that."

Paris waved her comment away. "Obviously Jonah and I are just friends, so it's your turn, Cassie. How was dinner with the world's most handsome man?"

Cassie slumped down and covered her face with her hands. "Awful."

Laurel looked at Paris, who appeared as confused as she felt.

"How is that possible?" Paris asked. "I would think sitting across from him, drooling, would be its own reward."

Cassie straightened and dropped her hands to her lap. "We talked about how messed up I am—never my favorite topic— although I think I made some progress in understanding where I've gone wrong. Anyway, that's not the point." She paused dramatically. "He said he likes me and wants to go out with me. Romantically."

"Isn't that good?" Laurel asked. "Dating someone who doesn't like you never works."

"But I don't know why he's interested. He's so smart and educated and nice and funny. He has a plan for us. He said we should get to know each other first, that rushed intimacy messes things up." She waved her hand. "Or something like that. I can't remember exactly."

"You don't think you're good enough," Paris said.

"I'm not!" Cassie voice was practically a shriek. "In the regular world I'm relatively attractive but next to him, I'm a troll."

Laurel laughed. "You're not a troll."

"Almost, and what about education? I couldn't get through a quarter at community college. He has all the degrees. He's a college professor. Shouldn't he be dating a doctor or an astronomer?"

"Do we have an observatory?" Paris asked thoughtfully. "I don't think we do. It's the fog so close to the ocean."

Cassie slumped back in her seat. "You're missing the point. Raphael doesn't need fixing and that's the only thing I know how to do."

"Maybe it's time to step out of your comfort zone," Laurel told her. "Come on. You like the guy, he's very pretty and he likes you. Plus, you said he was nice. So go forth and have a little fun. What's the worst that could happen?"

Cassie considered the question. Her expression brightened. "You're right. The worst is he leaves me. Guys leave me all the time and I always get over them. It's no big deal."

Paris sighed. "You realize now she's going to go out with him assuming he'll dump her."

"I know," Laurel said with a laugh. "And when he doesn't, then we'll have a real crisis."

"I can hear you," Cassie grumbled.

"This wouldn't be fun if you couldn't."

twenty

Cassie had no idea what to expect at the first Goodwill. Laurel and Paris each took a cart. Cassie wasn't sure whether she needed one.

"Stick with me," Paris told her. "We'll run all our purchases by Laurel, so we're unlikely to fill a cart for a while."

"I'm looking for things to sell on eBay and for items for the big, annual garage sale," Laurel told them. "Anything for eBay needs to be shippable. Nothing too delicate, heavy or big. I don't usually buy a lot of art, but with the garage sale coming up, I'm in the market for it. Small furniture is okay, as long as we have room in the van."

"Remember when we had to rent a truck?" Paris said with a grin.

"I do." Laurel turned to Cassie. "It was a couple of summers ago. Paris and I came down here and someone had donated their entire house's worth of furniture to one of the Goodwills. We rented a small moving truck to get it all home."

"I don't want to make a mistake," Cassie said.

"You'll be fine." Laurel patted her arm. "I'll go over everything before I pay, so don't worry. If it looks interesting, run it by me."

They went inside. The store was huge, with lots of overhead

lights. There were racks of clothing to one side and rows and rows of open shelving everywhere else. Big signs identified the various departments.

"Oh, look." Paris pointed to shelving up by the cash registers. "A Christmas in July sale. We'll have to check that out."

Laurel nodded. "Let them unload the carts first."

Their first stop was by the figurines. Laurel picked up a pretty blown-glass sitting cat and showed it to Cassie.

"This is very salable. It's appealing, it will ship easily." She held it up. "First look for obvious damage. Cracks, chips and previous repairs. Unless it's a spectacular piece, any of those mean we put it back. Second, check the bottom. We're looking for a marking, label or signature. A ceramic pitcher from a big box store won't make me any money. A ceramic pitcher from Italy is worth looking at."

She showed them the bottom of the figurine. It was a little rough with several chips and a lot of scratching.

"See how this isn't smooth," Laurel continued. "I'm not talking about the damage, but the actual workmanship. A good quality piece is going to be finished well."

She put the cat back and reached for a pretty basket made of pink glass. There were white flowers on the side and a fluted opening with a twisted handle.

"Fenton Art Glass," Laurel said. "Huge seller. But the handle's been broken off and glued on. Always check the handle."

Cassie looked more closely and saw the jagged line where the handle had been clumsily reattached.

"Laurel, look at this." Paris picked up a small round dish made of delicately woven porcelain. "My heart's beating really fast. Is this what I think it is?"

The container was maybe six inches across, with tiny pink, white and yellow flowers and green leaves on the scalloped top.

Laurel flipped it over and her breath caught. "Belleek," she breathed, showing Cassie the underside. "See how it has the name and how it's a numbered piece?"

"That makes it easier. I can find those."

Laurel smiled. "I'm not sure how many there will be. These can be tough to find and they sell fast." She turned it upright. "Now we check for damage. Belleek makes exquisite pieces, but if someone's careless, they can have broken leaves and flowers."

She studied the dish, then ran her fingers over a few flowers. "This is in great shape. It's ten dollars, which is perfect. I can sell it for several times that." She put the Belleek in her cart.

Laurel went on to the dishware while Cassie and Paris stayed to check for crystal vases.

"The high-end stuff is easy to pick out," Paris said. "Clear. Heavy for its size. We want Waterford or Baccarat. They etch their name into all their crystal."

They didn't find anything noteworthy.

Cassie was surprised at how busy the store was. It took them a couple of minutes to work their way through the customer-filled aisles to their next stop, glasses and mugs.

"Ignore the thin glass," Paris told her. "We're looking for crystal. Just pick up anything that looks interesting and turn it—"

Paris's phone buzzed. She pulled it out of her pocket and frowned at the screen.

"Laurel wants us in dishware right now." Paris grinned. "She found something great and needs our help."

They worked their way around other carts, shoppers and children. Laurel was waiting, practically hopping from foot to foot.

"They have Courtly Check," she said quietly, sounding a little breathless. She pointed to several black-and-white dishes stacked in her cart. "It's from MacKenzie-Childs."

She showed them the marking on the back of a plate. "I think someone donated an entire collection. This is huge. This stuff sells like crazy. We're talking serious money."

She scrolled through her phone and showed them pictures of canisters, bowls and even a candle pillar.

"If you see anything like this, pick it up. We'll look for other things later."

Cassie and Paris hurried away to look for anything with a black-and-white-check pattern.

"My heart's racing," Cassie said with a laugh. "And I'm not even the one we're shopping for."

"The hunt is contagious."

Cassie spotted a small canister while Paris grabbed a teapot. They found two larger canisters, three bowls and a pet mat in the shape of a dog bone.

"There," Paris whispered, pointing through the shelves. "On the other side. Can you run around and get that pitcher?"

Cassie took off at a fast walk. She wove through the maze of carts and shoppers, ducked around a spinning little girl and claimed the pitcher.

She held it close as she walked back to their cart, feeling like she'd declared victory in a life-or-death battle.

"I've never been much of a shopper," she told Paris. "But this is different. I like the challenge and the thrill of finding what we're looking for."

"I know, but it's not always a sure thing. During the school year, Laurel does a thrift store run every week. She shops auctions online, drives hours to estate sales, constantly replenishing inventory. She does well, but it's not an easy business."

"She loves it, though," Cassie said, wishing she had a job she loved. But for that to happen, she would have to figure out her passion.

"She does. She knew as soon as she came up with the business plan for one of her college courses that she'd found her path."

"What about you?" Cassie asked. "Was running the farm stand always the plan?"

Paris's expression turned rueful. "No. I wanted to be a costume designer for the movies. I went to college in Los Angeles and then got a job. But then my mom died and I came home." She shrugged. "I planned on selling, but after a while I realized I was happier in Los Lobos. I met Jonah and we got married. You know—it was a life thing."

Cassie nodded because it was the expected response, but in truth, she had no experience with dreams or taking a chance or even moving out. Excluding where she was living now, the apartment above the family bar was the only home she'd ever known.

"Let's go by the Christmas in July section," Paris said. "There might be holiday serving pieces that were part of the collection."

At the front of the store they discovered several Courtly Check pieces, including two sleighs. Paris picked up a white bowl with large red flowers and green leaves. What made it unusual were the four red shoes that were the base.

"There's something about this," she murmured. She texted a picture to Laurel, who answered immediately.

On my way!

Laurel raced toward them, her cart nearly filled with black-and-white-checked dishware.

"It's Patience Brewster," she said as she approached. "I can't believe it. Look for anything whimsical. A bird flying with rings, an alligator ornament."

Cassie found several ornaments in a cocktail and wine design, with characters wearing the drinks like clothing.

"Are these them?"

Laurel pressed a hand to her chest. "Yes! Grab them all."

They found nine of the Twelve Days of Christmas ornaments, several Santas and six camels. Laurel began jumping in place when she found two baggies filled with Christopher Radko ornaments and three sets of delicate vintage glass decorations in their original boxes.

An hour and $450 later, they were back in the van. The pur-chases were secure, carefully wrapped in paper and tucked in the boxes they'd brought.

Laurel laughed as she buckled her seat belt. "I'm so happy." She started the engine. "All right, my friends. We just paid my mortgage for the next six months. Now let's go find more trea-sures so I can meet payroll through the end of the year."

"Don't run," Paris said calmly as twin boys, around ten or eleven, raced through the farm stand. The permanent displays could handle a run-in with a kid, but the stacks of crates could easily go tumbling.

Neither boy glanced at her or slowed down. She wished the parents would watch their kids more closely. Or take them to the half acre out back, she thought, telling herself to breathe as annoyance built up inside of her.

She pushed away the feelings and turned back to Fred, who held out boxes of luscious, ripe, picked at perfection raspberries.

"I saved the best for you," he said in a low voice.

"You're a good man." Paris put one of the raspberries in her mouth. There was a summer-worthy explosion of flavor and sweetness on her tongue. She smiled.

"Fred, you are brilliant. These are incredible. I'll need more as soon as you can get them."

He grinned. "I'll see what I can do."

The two boys raced by again. Paris quickly stepped in front of them, forcing them to a stop. They both glared at her.

"What?" the one on the left demanded.

"Don't run in the farm stand. Go out back and run. Not in here."

"Hey, my nanny's a customer and you don't get to talk to us that way. We'll report you."

"To who?"

"Your boss." The one on the right smirked. "We could say you hit us. Then you'd get fired." He offered a casual shrug. "We've done it before."

Her mild annoyance blossomed into something closer to actual anger. She could feel her heart rate increasing and a prickling sensation on her skin. As much as she wanted to twist their ears until they whimpered and said they were sorry, that wasn't an option.

"There's a minor problem with the hitting thing," Fred said in his deep voice. "I'm a witness."

"Naw. You're just some old guy. No one will believe you."

"You know who they will believe?" Paris offered a faint smile. "My security cameras. They're everywhere. That fruit you stole a few minutes ago? It's on video. I go over it every evening, then report criminals to the police."

Okay, that was a stretch. There were cameras and the recordings were saved for seven days, but Paris hardly had the time or the interest to watch all that happened in a day. Still, the self-entitled duo in front of her didn't know that.

The boys looked at each other then bolted toward the back area. Seconds later they were running out on the grass, away from her produce.

"How'd you know they stole fruit?" Fred asked.

"I didn't, but they seemed the type."

He chuckled. "That's why you get the good raspberries. I'll be back tomorrow."

"See you then."

Paris got a couple of her guys to set up a raspberry display. If they sold well the next couple of hours, she wouldn't bother notifying her Facebook followers. If not, she would start taking orders and putting flats aside to be picked up after work.

Blueberries were next, she thought happily. They would complete the summer berries and keep her customers happy well into August.

She walked to her office. The heirloom tomatoes were selling like crazy and if she could get more delivered she could move them fast. She'd taken a seat in front of her computer when she heard a few shouts, followed by a crash.

Paris ran out and saw the crates of raspberries lying on their side, the squashed fruit on the concrete. The boys stood off to the side, looking both guilty and defiant.

Tim pointed at them. "They were running in the store. I don't know if it was an accident or on purpose, but they knocked over that stack."

A woman hurried over. She was in her late twenties and didn't look anything like the boys. She put her hands on her hips and shrieked, "What did you do?" then spun to face Paris. "Oh, no. I'm sorry. They're awful. So hard to control. You should see what they did to their hotel room last night."

She glared at the boys. "Get in the car right now. I mean it!"

The boys reluctantly headed for the parking lot. The woman sighed heavily. "Just tell me how much the damage is. I have a separate credit card to take care of it. The bill at the hotel was nearly five thousand dollars. They used ketchup to paint the walls."

Paris was confused. "You're their...mother?"

"What? God, no. I'm the temporary nanny, hired to drive them to their father's house. They usually take his private jet, but it has maintenance issues. The boys refused to fly commercial so the parents hired me to drive them." Her shoulders sagged. "We just spent four days at Disneyland. It was so horrible. This has been one of the worst experiences of my life. I'm a child development major. You'd think I could handle this, but I can't. I miss normal people."

She held out the credit card. "Whatever it will take to make you whole."

Under other circumstances, like hey, a real accident, Paris would have simply absorbed the cost. But after listening to the nanny, she was fairly sure the boys had dumped the fruit on purpose. She calculated the exact cost of it and rang it up on the card.

"What she said puts my kids' tantrums in perspective," Tim said as she closed out the transaction and the nanny and the devil spawn drove away.

"Oh, don't say that. It's not their fault. Their private jet has mechanical difficulties. That would upset anyone."

Tim grinned. "You handled them real well, Paris. Fred said you were as cool as a cucumber." His humor faded. "You've come a long way. I know it's not my place, but I'm proud of what you've done and I'm proud to work with you."

The words brought unexpected tears to her eyes. "Thank you. I'm proud to work with you, as well. You're my rock. Without you, this place would slowly crumble to dust."

"Naw. You'd find someone else."

"But I don't want to."

"Good. I don't want that, either." He shook his head. "All right. Let's see what's salvageable."

An hour later, cleanup was done. They'd managed to rescue a few flats of raspberries, but had lost over half of the delivery. She placed an order for more and thought how she was glad she'd waited on sending the social media post.

Her phone buzzed. She pulled it out of her pocket and smiled.

We're going to throw something on the barbecue. Want to join us for dinner?

The text from Jonah was unexpected but welcome. Sure, for the sake of her mental health, she should probably stay away from him, but she couldn't seem to help herself.

I can be there at 6.

We'll see you then. Bandit's welcome, of course.

Thanks. He'll be excited to see everyone.

She left work at five thirty, made a quick stop at her place to feed her dog, then drove them both to Natalie's house. She'd barely parked when Danny burst through the front door and raced toward her.

"Paris! Paris! You came!"

Danny threw himself at her, hugging her tightly before turning to wrestle with Bandit on the grass. Jonah stepped out onto the porch.

"Saying hello seems anticlimactic after that," he said. "But hello."

"Hi." She grinned. "Did you want to wrestle with Bandit, too?"

"I'll wait on that, if it's okay with you."

"He's always up for a romp."

She got the flat of blackberries out of the back of her truck. "Fresh today. I've sampled and they're delicious."

"It's that time of year."

Jonah held open the door. She, Danny and Bandit went inside. Natalie was limping from the kitchen counter to the island.

"Good to see you, Paris. Oh, blackberries. My favorite."

Paris hugged her gently. "How are you feeling?"

"Still recovering. The pain's much better and my physical therapist is pleased with my progress. Some days I'm grumpy." Natalie laughed. "You know, the usual ups and downs."

Paris washed her hands. "Tell me how I can help."

"It's mostly done." Natalie sank onto a stool at the island. "Jonah's handling the chicken."

"I'm about to put it on the barbecue."

"I can help!" Danny told him.

"You can stand at a safe distance and watch," his father said. "You'll learn how to barbecue when you're ten."

Danny signed heavily. "Dad, I'm old enough now."

"So you say, but I get the final vote in that." He softened his tone. "Why don't you take Bandit outside to wear him out?

Weren't you just telling me that border collies are high energy dogs?"

Danny grinned and called for Bandit, who happily joined him as they went into the backyard.

Paris raised her eyebrows. "Someone's been reading up on border collies."

"Not just them. Most breeds. I've been hearing a lot about how we should get our own dog."

"Bandit's a good guy. He'd be hard to replace."

"I'm sure that's true." He returned his gaze to his mother. "You okay, Mom? What can I do for you?"

"Just cook the chicken. Paris will take care of everything else."

He hesitated a second before nodding and going out back. Paris looked at Natalie.

"He seemed concerned." Very Jonah-like, she thought. He paid attention and followed through. Qualities she'd appreciated when they'd been married.

"Oh, I overdid it and my knee is swollen. I get impatient to be better now and healing doesn't work that way. I'll be fine, just not today."

Paris eyed the stool. "Is that the most comfortable seat? Do you want to settle in one of the chairs? You could prop up your leg and maybe ice your knee."

Natalie slowly pushed herself to her feet. "You know what? That sounds wonderful. Thank you, Paris. There's a gel ice pack in the freezer. Could you bring it to me, please?"

Paris watched anxiously as Natalie limped to the kitchen table. Once she was seated, Paris moved a second chair into place, then helped the other woman raise her leg. She put on the ice pack.

"Perfect," Natalie breathed, her eyes sinking closed. "Ice really is a miracle cure, isn't it? At least in the moment."

"I'm glad it's helping. So what's left to do?"

"If you could be a dear and set the table. I made the macaroni salad that Jonah likes." Natalie smiled at her. "The green salad needs fixing, if you don't mind."

"Of course."

She knew her way around Natalie's kitchen. She quickly made her ex's favorite vinaigrette. Jonah, Danny and Bandit returned with a platter of cooked chicken and they sat down to dinner.

After the meal, Danny pulled Uno cards from a cabinet in the dining room. Paris hadn't played since she was a kid, so had to read the directions.

She sat across from Jonah as Danny dealt them each seven cards, then turned over the top card to start the discard pile. A red seven.

"You go first," he told Paris.

She played her red two. They went around the table. Conversation was easy, with everyone telling jokes and stories. Paris made them laugh with an only slightly exaggerated version of the entitled twins who had ruined most of her raspberry delivery.

This, she thought longingly, glancing at Jonah out of the corner of her eye. This was what she missed most about being married to him. Hanging out, having fun—him around, them together. She supposed, except for the fighting, she missed all of it.

Jonah loved playing games of all kinds. Yes, video games were his superpower, but they'd often played board games, too, until her temper got in the way.

How many times had she yelled that she hated him? How many times had she seen the hurt in his eyes? Too many, she told herself, once again wishing she could have been different.

"You can't play that card," Danny told her.

Paris glanced at the discard pile and saw she'd put a blue seven on a green five. The price of not paying attention, she thought, then hid her smile as she pretended to be confused.

"But that's a green card."

Danny shook his head. "It's not, Paris. It's blue."

"It looks green to me."

Danny's eyebrows drew together as he glanced from her to the card and back. Then he caught her smiling and giggled.

"You know it's wrong!"

"I do." She picked up the card and tucked it back in her hand. "Sorry. I wasn't paying attention." She put down a green three. "Better?"

"Yes."

Jonah watched her quizzically, no doubt remembering, as she had, all the times game night hadn't ended well.

He could be kind and charming and trusted her with his son, at least for the day, but he would never forget who she'd been, she thought sadly. Not that she blamed him, but still…

After the game, Natalie and Danny went into the family room to watch a movie. Paris collected Bandit and called out her goodnights.

"I'll walk you out," Jonah said, joining her. They stepped into the quiet night.

"He's doing great," she said. "Despite being in a new environment and dealing with his grandmother's surgery, he's thriving."

"I know. It's a relief. I'd worried that moving here for the summer would upset him, but now I'm thinking getting away from the memories has been good for him. It makes me more determined to move when we get back home."

She wanted to point out his mother wasn't getting any younger and wouldn't it be nice if he were close. Only she was afraid he would read the real meaning behind that message and know she wanted him to consider Los Lobos for more selfish reasons.

"If you meet someone, she might have some thoughts of where the three of you live," she said instead, trying to inject a little teasing tone into her voice.

"That's true. So I shouldn't date someone from a place I don't want to live."

"Probably for the best."

"That could be a limiter."

"True love will always win," she told him. "If you love her, you won't mind moving."

His gaze settled on her. "That's true."

She wanted to read significance into his words, but honestly couldn't find any. Just to prove the point, she said, "So you'd get married again?"

"I would. Not just because Danny needs a mom but because I really liked being married. I enjoy having someone in my life, someone I can love and be there for. I like being the one my partner turns to first."

Her throat got a little tight and she had to clear it before she could talk.

"Speaking as a former spouse, I can vouch for the fact that you are a very good husband. If you need a reference."

He grinned. "That would be an interesting conversation starter. Hi, I'm Jonah. If you want to know if I'm a good guy or not, I have references from my ex-wife."

"In the right circumstances, that could work."

"You're an optimist. I see it as a crash and burn moment."

They both laughed. He held open the passenger door of her truck for Bandit before walking her around to her side.

"Thanks for coming over," he said, making absolutely no move to kiss her.

Paris slid onto the seat. "I appreciate the invitation. And Uno was fun. Say good-night to Danny and your mom for me."

"I will."

He closed the door and stepped back. Paris drove away. When she got home, she walked into the dark house and sat on the sofa without bothering with a light. Bandit joined her, whining softly as if asking what was wrong. She put her arms around him, pressing her face against his silky coat. Only then did she allow herself to give in to the tears.

Jonah couldn't have made it clearer that he wanted nothing but friendship from her. He was being nice and sweet and that was all there was. She would wish-think all she wanted, but it didn't change the truth. Nor did her still being in love with him. And the sooner she accepted that cold hard truth, the better off she would be.

twenty-one

Cassie watched as Westin hammered a slim metal tool under the top two hoops on the cognac barrel. She'd borrowed the tools she would need to open the barrel, but hadn't had the sheer brute force necessary to do the job. On a whim, she'd texted Westin. The old man had showed up immediately, ready for the adventure.

She'd set up several lanterns to light the cave. All the barrels were on their side, as they should be, per her research, but one had been left upright, as if inviting inspection. The risk of leaving a barrel in that position was the top and bottom were the places most likely to leak, but the ground around the upright barrel was dry, so either it was reinforced or the evidence of a leak had long since drained away.

Excitement tightened her chest, but she told herself not to expect too much. In a few minutes a lot of questions would be answered.

"You think these will be worth anything?" he asked as if he'd read her thoughts.

"If it's eighty-year-old French cognac, like the paperwork says, then it's probably worth a lot." She pointed to the rest of the barrels. "Each of those is about three hundred wine bottles, times nineteen barrels and it starts to add up."

He slid around to the next section of the barrel. "So you'd have money to fix up the orchard."

"I haven't thought that far ahead," she said. Probably because she didn't know enough about an orchard to know *what* to think.

She was starting to like the land. She'd come out here a few times before her shift. On her last day off, she'd brought a blanket and her lunch and had sat in the shade of one of her trees, just enjoying the quiet and the beauty of the place. Knowing all of this was hers had been a heady realization. She'd never owned anything significant before.

"Are you afraid to dream?"

She glared at the old man. "No." She paused. "All this is new to me. It's hard to think about a future when I don't have enough information. You talked about having to replace trees and fix drainage. How long would all that take?"

"Until they were producing? Two to three years."

"Years?" Her voice was a yelp.

"We're not repairing a barn door, Cassie. Nature takes time to heal."

Three years? "So there'd be no crop between now and then? No income? Who can afford that?"

"You have a job. You'll be fine."

"It doesn't pay much. Plus, don't I need a degree in agriculture?"

He grinned at her. "Like I said, hire me as a consultant."

"I'm not sure I could afford you."

"You can. I can evaluate the orchard. You'd probably get some fruit in the second year. In the meantime, I'll teach you everything you need to know. By the time the orchard is flourishing, you'll be an expert."

She liked the sound of that. Yes, it would be a lot of work, but how satisfying to actually have something so tangible and important to show for her labor. No offense to her current and previous jobs, but sending a shipment of oranges or avocados off to market felt a lot more meaningful than pouring someone a glass of wine.

"Getting the orchard in shape is an exciting thought," she said, "but I worry about having enough money. You're right—I'll have enough to survive on and if I can sell the cognac for a decent price, then that would help, but is it enough?"

Westin looked at her. "Honestly, no. You'd have to sell some of your land."

"What? No. Not the land. You said a developer would be interested and I don't want that any more than you do."

"There's that land behind this cave," he said. "That strip between here and the road. It's, what? A couple of acres? Sell that to one of the local developers. It's in a good location and they can put up their townhomes without bothering you. Between that and the cognac, you'd have enough money to revive the orchard and have a little left over."

She wasn't sure what land he meant. She'd been spending most of her time in the orchard itself. "I'll check it out. If I move forward with restoring the orchard, that would be a good suggestion. Thanks for the idea."

"I've got a million of them."

Westin returned his attention to the hoops. The one second from the top loosened and he slid it off.

"Careful of the nails on the inside," he said, handing it to her. "They're still sharp."

She leaned the hoop against the cave wall. He passed over the top hoop as well, then reached for the chisel to loosen the top. It wasn't elegant, but given the limitations of location and equipment, it was the simplest way to find out what was inside. Once she'd taken a few samples, Westin would reseal the barrel and she would figure out what to do next.

After several minutes he worked the top free. Cassie waited anxiously as he pulled it off.

She stared at the clear, deep golden brown liquid. Seconds later, the glorious aroma swirled around them. Fruity and rich, with a hint of oak. Westin inhaled deeply.

"Now, there's a smell a man could get used to."

"We never carried any special cognacs at the bar," she said, dipping the ladle she had brought into the barrel and pouring the contents into a mason jar. "I haven't tasted anything older than a VSOP."

When the jar was about a quarter full, she held it up to the light. The liquid was clear, the color uniform. Westin reached for the container.

"I'll do the honors."

She winced. "No. It could be poison or something."

"We both know it's not. Besides, I've lived a good life."

He took a sip, held the liquid in his mouth for a second before swallowing. His smile was slow and satisfied.

"Amazing. It's balanced on the tongue, the finish is excellent. I'm sold."

She eyed him. "You're a wine guy."

"I've been known to enjoy a glass or two."

He handed her the mason jar. She inhaled and closed her eyes, letting the warm aroma delight her senses, then she took a taste.

The smooth flavor went down easy. She tasted hints of the fruit she'd smelled, along with a bit of spice. As Westin had promised, the finish made her want more.

"I love it," she breathed.

"Fill your jars, then let's seal this back up. We don't want the exposure to air to ruin it."

She filled three mason jars, then lowered the top in place. He removed the old nails from the hoops, before hammering them into place with new ones. When that was done, they collected the lanterns and headed for the entrance.

"Now what?" he asked when they stepped into the sunlight.

"Now I find an expert to help me get the barrels to market."

"You won't bottle the cognac first?"

"Not if I don't have to. I'm hoping someone will want to buy the whole lot and put it out under their label as a once-in-a-lifetime product."

"You've been studying up."

She smiled. "Someone has to pay for the orchards." She handed him one of the jars. "I suggest you wait a few days before drinking this again. Just to make sure neither of us die in our sleep."

"Thank you. I'll text you in a couple of days and let you know how I'm feeling, but I think we're both going to be fine and you're going to be rich."

Not rich exactly, she thought as she walked to her SUV. But maybe she would have enough to start nursing the trees back to health.

Laurel glanced back toward her living room where everyone was gathered for book club, then down at her list.

"I agree," she said into her phone. "We can't have too many food trucks. As long as they all know that there's a little competition."

"That's what I thought," Marcy said, rustling paper. "I need to get this all onto my spreadsheet. I'll say yes to the falafel truck. And we've agreed to the ten extra porta-potties."

"We have."

"Then that's it. Get back to your book club."

"Thanks, Marcy. See you tomorrow."

She returned to her guests.

"Sorry," she said, taking her seat. "We're finalizing details for the big garage sale. The two food trucks we had last year were overwhelmed and ran out of supplies before one in the afternoon, so we're getting in a few more."

"Plus the porta-potties, right?" Paris wrinkled her nose. "Last year the line for the women's bathrooms was endless."

"Ten are on order." Laurel looked at the five people all staring at her—Cassie and Paris, of course, plus Colton, Jonah and, surprisingly, Raphael. "So I'm starting this?"

"Who's usually in charge?" Colton asked.

"Laurel."

"Paris."

The two women spoke at the same time, then laughed.

"You go," Laurel told her friend. "You have the questions."

Paris picked up her battered copy of *Night into Day*. "Everyone's read it?"

Five heads bobbed.

"So let's talk about our impressions before we get to the book club questions Laurel and I prepared."

"I liked the book a lot." Cassie was curled up on an oversize wingback chair. Every few seconds her gaze drifted over to where Raphael sat, as if she couldn't believe he was there.

Laurel was with her on that. Colton and Jonah had offered to join the book club. Paris had mentioned it to Raphael a couple of weeks ago, but neither of them had said anything to anyone else, so his knock on the door had been unexpected.

Cassie motioned to Laurel and Paris. "The parts about rheumatoid arthritis were heartbreaking. I didn't know much about RA, but I guess if you have a really bad case of it, the results can be devastating."

"I think the drugs are better now," Paris said. "At least I hope so. So maybe there's more control." She looked at Jonah. "What did you think?"

"It's a good story, but come on. Patrick isn't a real guy."

Colton and Raphael nodded.

"No guy thinks like that," Colton added. "He was too emotional and worried about the wrong stuff. Plus, he bought her bath oil. I get why for the story, but in real life, guys don't do that."

"I liked Patrick," Cassie said. "He took care of her. You knew no matter what, he was going to be there with her."

"They were apart for weeks." Raphael shook his head. "If he was as crazy about her as he claimed, he would have flown in to see her."

"He was getting the ranch ready."

"He has staff. It's not just him. He could have spared a weekend."

Laurel found the male point of view interesting. Wrong, she thought with a smile, but interesting.

"Some of how the book is structured probably has to do with the fact that storytelling has evolved," she said. "Paris and I have seen that the past couple of summers when we've read older science fiction and mysteries."

"I don't get why she didn't trust him," Jonah said. "He told her how he felt and she didn't want that."

"She was scared." Cassie shifted, putting her feet on the floor. "Her reluctance wasn't about him, it was about her."

"What about the love-at-first-sight part?" Laurel asked, expecting the guys to all say that wasn't realistic. "Basically he sees her and is interested, then spends the book pursuing her. She doesn't go after him."

"It could happen," Colton said. The other two nodded.

"You believe in love at first sight?" Paris asked, sounding disbelieving. "Isn't that kind of reaction simply chemistry?"

"Without chemistry, what is there?" Jonah asked mildly.

"You mean without sex, what is there?"

"Yes." Jonah shrugged. "Without sex, you're just roommates."

"Without love, then what's the point of a relationship?" Cassie shook her head. "I don't think people instantly fall in love. I think there's attraction that draws people together but the real part, the important part, requires us to get to know each other."

Laurel put down her copy of the book. "So have any of you experienced instant attraction?"

Raphael looked at her. "Attraction, yes. Love, no."

"I've come close," Jonah admitted.

Laurel immediately wondered if he was talking about Paris, but didn't want to embarrass her friend by asking. If the answer was yes, it made their divorce even sadder. If the answer was no, then Paris would feel awkward.

"It's never happened to me," Cassie said flatly.

"Given the guys you've dated in the past," Paris teased. "Are you surprised?"

Cassie laughed. "Not really."

"I was a goner the second I met Beau," Laurel admitted. "There was something about him."

"Dumbass chemistry," Paris said flatly.

"Maybe. But it took me years to be strong enough to tell him no. Now I look back and wonder what I saw in him." She looked at Colton. "What about you? Love at first sight believer?"

"No." He smiled at her. "Attraction and interest at first sight? Absolutely. But the kind of true love that lasts a lifetime? That takes time to develop. I'm more of the slow and steady type."

"No lightning strikes for you?" Cassie asked. "We can be on the same team, then."

Paris asked a question about Patrick's football career and conversation shifted. Laurel followed along, but part of her was still caught up in what the men had said when they talked about love. All of them were open to the possibility. She knew for a fact both Colton and Jonah had loved deeply before. Something she'd never fully internalized. She realized that between Beau's indifference to his children and her father marrying and divorcing regularly, she'd assumed men didn't have the same level of feelings as women. But she was wrong about that.

Not that the information changed anything, she told herself. She wasn't giving her heart to anyone ever again. Love turned people into idiots and she intended to avoid the process. Even with a guy as tempting as Colton.

★ ★ ★

Now that she'd gotten over the shock of Raphael sitting across from her, Cassie found herself enjoying the book club meeting. Having the male point of view was interesting.

"You know what surprised me," Jonah said. "Alex was brave about her disease and how she planned those trips, but she made her own life small."

"She was afraid," Raphael said. "She'd been hurt, but she was also dealing with her disease. She didn't have any more bandwidth. Small was safe."

Cassie carefully studied her book, afraid if she looked up she would see everyone staring at her. While she didn't have Alex's experience with a difficult disease, she had been hurt and until now, her life had been very, very small.

"She should have recognized he was the right guy for her," Raphael continued.

Cassie's head shot up. "You said you didn't believe in love at first sight."

"Finding the right one isn't the same thing."

Paris turned to him. "Are you saying there's only one person for each of us?"

Raphael smiled. "No. I'm saying there are people who will make us happy and people who won't. Recognizing the difference makes things a lot easier. She could trust Patrick, but she was afraid to believe."

"But he was determined. He wasn't going anywhere." Laurel waved her copy. "He questions himself and his ability to be what she needs, but not how he feels."

"If she'd kept pushing him away, he would have gotten tired," Raphael said. "Eventually a guy accepts there's no chance. Only a fool won't give up."

"Or a stalker," Colton said cheerfully.

They all laughed.

Later, when the discussion was over, Cassie and Raphael

walked out together. He pulled her around the side of the house, then faced her.

"When can I see you again?" he asked, his gaze intense.

She was still caught up in how the book discussion had made her think about how she had made her own life so very small.

"I'm so confused," she admitted.

"About me?"

"Some. Why are you here?"

"Paris invited me to book club. The team and I stop by the farm stand every morning we're heading to the dig. We talk. She mentioned the book and I said I was in."

"Because old romance novels are your thing?"

"I thought it would be interesting to read the story and then to discuss it with you."

As easy as that? The man was so out there with what he was thinking and feeling. She couldn't imagine being that brave. Of course, from his perspective, maybe he wasn't being brave at all. Maybe he didn't think he had anything at risk.

"I still don't know what you see in me."

"Do you want a list?"

"Maybe."

But instead of giving her a list, he leaned in and brushed his mouth against hers. Heat immediately flared, igniting desire and the urge to lean in for a whole lot more of that. Unfortunately, Raphael stepped back.

"I like your smile," he said, his gaze still locked with hers. "You're beautiful, you're funny, and when you look at me I get a warm, happy feeling in the pit of my stomach. Like I don't know what will happen next, but I'm sure it will be great."

She stared at him. Was that how he saw her? But that sounded amazing and she knew she was ordinary at best.

"I, ah… I'm, ah, so dinner?"

"I'll text you when I get home and we'll set up a date and time."

He kissed her again, lingering, then walked to his truck. She was opening her front door when she heard him drive away.

Once inside, she sank on the sofa and tried to make sense of his words. His view of her had nothing in common with reality. She didn't think he was playing some twisted game—he was too nice for that. Then what?

She texted her sister.

Raphael wants to see me again.

That's terrific. You said he's totally hot and you like him.

Yes, but where is this going? I'm only here for six months and he's got all those degrees. I'm not his type.

He obviously disagrees. Cassie the point of going to California was to live your life, not hide from it.

Which was another way of saying she was living too small, she thought, trying to ignore the jab of pain the words caused. Like Alex in the book, she was afraid to put herself out there. But to act otherwise required more bravery than she had.

You still there? Faith asked.

Yes. I'm thinking about what you said. Anyway, enough about me. How are you doing? How are the kids?

Three dots appeared as Faith typed her answer. Cassie leaned back against the sofa. She knew her sister was right about putting herself out there. It was just Raphael was way too evolved for the likes of her. A relationship with him could be amazing, but she could also end up totally destroyed. After all, every guy she'd ever dated had left her. That had been hard enough, but they'd been losers, and in the end, she'd been okay. Raphael was on a totally different level—so his dumping her would be ten times worse. She wasn't sure she could survive it.

The obvious solution was to end the relationship first, or at the very least mess up what they had. If she was the one breaking up, then she would be fine. The only question was how.

Paris felt a little weird wrapping beautiful peaches in tiny blankets, but her social media posts had been getting so much attention, she didn't want to stop. The cherry race cars had been a huge hit and now she was going to photograph a peach baby nursery. She'd spent the evening gluing lace onto small squares of fabric and she'd figured out a way to reconstruct a pint-sized fruit carton into an almost bassinette. A quick trip to the craft store had yielded black eyes with a vicious-looking pointy back. The eyes were generally used in amigurumi and had a safety washer to hold them in place, but Paris planned to plunge hers into the peaches, giving the little babies a hint of a face.

She'd sorted through the morning's peach delivery, finding the most "photogenic" of the group. She grabbed two extra small peaches, to make a set of twins.

Once the project was complete, she took dozens of pictures with her digital camera, adding and removing light, trying different backgrounds. When she'd finished, she placed the peach babies onto the display shelf under a sign reading *Congratulations! It's a Peach!*

"Is it just me or is that a little strange?"

Paris smiled as Jonah walked up to her. "This display? I thought it was brilliant. A peach nursery. You're not going to see that at every farm stand up and down the highway."

"You're not." He tapped her camera. "You have plenty to post on social media?"

"Yes. It's good to have content. Coming up with something new and different day after day is exhausting. I'm happy if I post something every other day. But it does bring in customers."

It was warm and sunny. She wore her usual jeans and a T-shirt with sturdy boots because she was on her feet all day. A ponytail kept her hair out of her way. She wasn't the least bit glamorous.

For a brief moment she allowed herself the fantasy of being in a cute sundress with strappy sandals and her hair all fluffy with beachy waves. But to what end, she asked herself. The man had zero interest in her romantically. Zip. Nada. Not happening. She should be grateful for the closure he'd given her and the fact that they'd both moved on. That she couldn't help noticing how sexy he looked when he pushed up his glasses was her problem and no one else's.

"Where's Danny?" she asked as Bandit sprinted over to greet Jonah.

He bent down to rub the dog's ears. "Still at camp." He straightened. "I wanted to ask you to have dinner with me."

She waited for him to finish his sentence, or at least clarify, but he was silent.

"At your mom's, with her and Danny?"

The smile returned. "Ouch. No. I'm asking you out to dinner. Just the two of us. I really am out of practice."

Her mind went blank as her brain tried to process the words. Cassie had mentioned her shock when Raphael had asked her out. Paris could suddenly relate.

"So a date?" she asked to confirm.

His lips twitched, as if he were holding in a smile. "Yes, Paris. I'm asking you out to dinner, as in a date. Just the two of us. I'll be driving."

"That makes no sense. You're not interested in me romantically. You've made that clear." She held up her hand. "I'm not saying you should be, because of our past and everything, but you're so neutral when you're around me. Why would you ask me out?"

"I'm not neutral. I'm curious, but given our past, I wanted to be sure first. I have Danny to consider."

Curious? Like he couldn't wait to hear the new Pantone color of the year?

"You're not making any sense."

He smiled at her. "You don't date much, do you?"

"You mean since the divorce? No. I don't date at all. At first I was too much of a mess, but once I started figuring out how to change, I was focused on healing. Then a lot of time had passed and, well, I wasn't sure if I could trust myself. So no, I don't date. It seems easier not to."

His brown eyes widened slightly. "I've been gone over a decade."

"I'm aware of the passage of time."

"There hasn't been anyone special?"

"No." How could there be? She worried about how she would act in different circumstances—if somehow she could be pushed into anger. So she was careful. Maybe too careful, now that she thought about it, but it was hard to look for someone else when she was still in love with her ex.

"Have dinner with me," he repeated, then added, "It's just dinner."

Maybe to him, but not to her. The whole "still in love with" put a different spin on the request from her perspective. While the thought of sitting across from him for a whole evening sounded delightful, especially with the possibility of a little kissing thrown into the mix, she knew there would be a price to pay. Her heart would yearn for so much more and then he would leave and she would shatter.

"I appreciate the invitation," she told him. "Thank you, but no."

He studied her for several heartbeats. "You're afraid."

"More than you know."

"I'd never hurt you."

"You can't possibly know that." Because he'd hurt her before—so very much. It hadn't been his fault, but the pain had been real.

She expected him to reply, but instead he lightly stroked her cheek, then he turned and walked away. She forced herself to go into her office and upload the peach pictures onto the stand's social media accounts. There was work to be done—regret was for later.

twenty-two

Cassie wasn't proud of her decision, but she didn't see any alternatives. Raphael liked her—he'd made that clear. He planned to move things in a certain direction and he was a man who got what he wanted. She, on the other hand, had no experience with anyone like him. Things would end—the only question was when and how badly she would get hurt. As far as she could tell, her only hope for survival was to take control and finish things now, while she still could.

Oh, she wasn't going to break up with Raphael. He was too yummy for her to walk away. But she could sabotage the whole thing and create a dumpster fire right in the middle of what they had going on. Not trying her hardest to please went against her nature, but hadn't everyone told her she needed to break the pattern? Deliberately screwing up her relationship would certainly be a first for her.

She arrived right on time, walked up to the front door of his small but well cared for house, and rang the bell. She had condoms in her bag, was wearing nothing under her short halter dress and carried with her an attitude of determination.

"Cassie."

Raphael smiled as he opened the door, then stepped back to let her in. She followed, nearly tripping over the threshold. She might be determined to sabotage this relationship, but she wasn't very practiced. Nor was she especially good at seducing a man. She was already having thirty-seventh thoughts and was telling herself to flee for safety.

Instead, she set her small bag on the sofa table and turned to Raphael.

Getting a full look at him made her mouth go dry. The man was gorgeous with his curly blond hair and big blue eyes. And that body, those shoulders. He stretched out his T-shirt and the jeans fitted perfectly. Could she really follow through on her plan? It required a level of self-confidence and courage beyond her. Still, for the greater good and all.

"I thought we'd—" he began, but she walked up to him put her hands on his shoulders, raised herself up on tiptoe and kissed him.

He immediately wrapped his arms around her and settled his mouth on hers. As she'd hoped, the kiss quickly deepened and within a minute she felt the telltale pressure of his erection against her belly.

Relief allowed her to relax enough to feel a little wanting of her own and when his hands moved up and down her back, she wiggled closer. At the same time she tugged up her skirt so the next time his fingers did a downward stroke, they encountered bare skin.

He drew back and stared at her. His eyes were slightly closed with obvious passion and his breathing was deep.

"You're wearing a thong."

The sentence was more statement than question. Cassie ignored her nerves as she drew up her skirt again, showing him the curve of her butt.

"Not really."

She watched him process her words, as if trying to make sense of them and knew the exact second he got that she was naked under her dress. He took a step toward her, then stopped.

"We're moving too fast," he said. "I like you."

She smiled. "I like you, too. I brought condoms." She turned her back to him, then drew her hair over one shoulder and pointed to the button at the top of the dress. "If you could get that, please. It's kind of all that's holding this up."

The room went silent, except for the sound of his breathing. She glanced at him, not sure what he would do. She couldn't read his expression anymore and unease started to settle in her belly. Had she made a mistake? Was he going to reject her?

Raphael ripped off his T-shirt in one quick, smooth movement. She had a brief impression of living perfection, then he pulled her close and kissed her as if he would never stop.

Less than ten minutes later, she was on her back, her heart still racing as the world slowly stopped spinning. She'd showed up with a plan to seduce Raphael, but she hadn't expected to have her world rocked. Sex wasn't new to her, nor had this been her first orgasm, but there was something different about the experience. Maybe it was the way he'd touched her everywhere with an almost reverence that had left her shaking and vulnerable. Maybe it was how he'd looked so deeply into her eyes as he'd entered her. Maybe it was simply emotional exhaustion for all she'd been through lately.

Whatever the reason, instead of feeling pleased that her plan had worked, she felt vulnerable and shattered. As much as she tried to gather herself together, she kept falling apart, then shocked herself and most likely him by starting to cry.

The tears began slowly, then quickly escalated into sobs. Instead of running like any normal man, Raphael gathered her against his very impressive, bare chest and held her.

"I'm right here," he murmured, stroking her back. "Right here."

She refused to relax, telling herself to get a grip so she could escape. She was fairly sure her dress was somewhere down the short hallway. As that was the only item of clothing she had to worry about, along with her sandals, her getaway should be easy. Only she couldn't seem to make herself move.

When the tears stopped as quickly as they'd begun, she drew back and took the tissue he handed her.

"I don't know what that was," she admitted, feeling embarrassed and stupid. "Sorry. Crying wasn't part of the plan."

"But seducing me was."

She looked around, desperate for something to cover herself. Raphael's T-shirt was even farther away than her dress and his jeans were on his side of the bed—not that they would fit her. She didn't think she had the strength to pull the top sheet free to wrap around her and there was absolutely no way she was walking across the room naked.

"Can I have a robe, please?"

He shot her a look that seemed to be a fifty-fifty combination of exasperation and affection, got to his feet and walked barefoot into what she assumed was the bathroom-closet area. He returned with a white terry cloth robe. She slipped it on and prepared to slip away, only he caught her wrist before she could run.

"We have to talk," he said, his voice low and gravelly.

"No, we don't."

"Cassie, you did this on purpose. I'm not saying I wasn't a willing participant. You're hard to resist. But you came here wanting us to have sex and I need to know why."

She tightened the belt on the robe. The soft fabric was heavy and smelled like him. "You're a guy. You like sex. What's the problem?"

He frowned. "You know you matter to me. We talked about taking it slow."

She got up and stood by the side of the bed. "No, *you* talked about taking it slow. I was in the mood to do it and you said yes. Where's the bad?"

Only she knew where the bad was. What had seemed such a good idea an hour ago suddenly felt impulsive and immature. Had she really showed up at his house naked, hoping to convince him to have sex with her as a way to ruin everything?

"Did you think I was telling you what to do?" he asked. "I'm sorry. That was never my intention. I was trying to show you that you matter to me and I want to respect you and us."

His words should have made her want to fly—instead, she felt stupid and small. He was offering her everything she'd ever thought she wanted in a relationship and she'd blown it because she was incapable of being a normal, mature, rational partner. She'd assumed pain was coming and had wanted to avoid it. No, that was wrong. She'd *known* the pain was inevitable and had tried to control how and when it happened. Either way, she'd been a fool.

"You're right," she said quietly, the tears returning. "You made it very clear how you felt and I couldn't deal with it. I still can't. You frighten me because I don't understand the rules. When the other guys left, it hurt, but it didn't really touch me, if that makes sense. It was one more thing that went wrong. But when you leave, it won't be because I've helped you grow so much you don't need me anymore. It will be because you've figured out I'm not good enough."

He started to speak, but she shook her head. "I can't face that. I just can't. Please. I have to go."

She ran out of the bedroom and found her dress at the end of the hall. She struggled to step into it, but her fingers were shaking too much to fasten the button. Large hands pushed hers away as Raphael took care of the button for her. He turned her to face him.

"Don't run."

"I have to. It's all I know."

He stepped back then, giving her the space she needed. She took in his perfect, still naked body, the concern in his eyes, and knew that she would regret her actions for a very long time. Then she grabbed her sandals and her bag and hurried for the door.

Laurel watched Colton pace in her living room. He'd texted to ask to meet her privately. She'd suggested her place after she'd dropped off her daughters at camp. Colton had showed up on time, looking worried.

Her stomach sank a little with each step he took. She didn't know what the problem was, but it was obviously bad. Was he no longer interested in being her friend? Was it too much work or too tedious or...

"I can't stand this," she blurted. "Just say it. You're breaking up with me."

He turned to face her with such surprise that she relaxed.

"No," he said walking toward her. "Not even close. I like being friends with you and the girls."

"Then what? Spit it out. You have a tumor. You've been drafted." A horrifying thought made her breath catch. "You've met someone and you think I should invite her over to dinner."

Because she and Colton were "just friends," despite that one-time sex thing. They weren't dating or falling in love or anything like that, and a man had needs. It made sense that he would date. At least that was what she tried to tell herself.

"My parents are coming to visit."

Laurel sank onto the sectional sofa. "That's why you needed to talk? You've told me about your parents, and they sound really nice."

He sat at the other end of the sofa and hung his head. "This is so embarrassing."

"Tell me!"

He nodded slowly and looked at her. "It's mostly my mom. She loves me and wants me to be happy."

Which sounded great, but didn't explain the problem. "And?"

"My parents worry about me." He looked at her, his expression pleading, as if he really wanted her to understand. "They think I'm lonely. My mom was threatening to find local single women online for me."

"Couldn't you do that yourself?"

"Yes, but it's not my thing. I tried to explain that, but she wouldn't listen. So I told her about you."

Laurel hadn't been expecting that.

"I told her we were dating."

There was something about the way he said the words. Something...

"You told her I'm your girlfriend?" Laurel was pleased that her voice was only slightly raised and didn't come close to shrieky.

"Yes," he said, looking directly at her. "Which wouldn't be a problem except they're coming to visit for two weeks. Obviously they're expecting us to be together."

She was trying to grasp all he was saying. "That's the crisis?"

"Yes."

"You're not dating someone?"

She immediately wanted to claw back the words. His mouth twitched.

"If I was seeing someone else, I wouldn't have to ask you to be my fake girlfriend."

Oh, right. Good point. "So that's what you want? Me to be your fake girlfriend for two weeks?"

"Yes. I could easily tell them as far as the girls are concerned, we're just friends, so nothing would have to change." He paused, then shifted uneasily. "Okay, that's not true. My mom's really good at asking probing questions. Before you know what's happening, you spill everything."

Laurel grinned. "I think I'm going to like her. That's a talent I can respect."

"So you'll do it?"

He sounded so hopeful, she thought. Because he loved his family. She understood why he'd lied—it made his parents happy and was nearly the truth. What he hadn't expected was the in-person visit.

"You have to talk to them about Jagger and Ariana. The girls can't know about the fake girlfriend thing. They both like you and it's good for them to see you as a friend in our lives. I don't want that to change."

"Me, either. I'll warn them. I suspect they'll be impressed that you're such a good mom."

She hoped so. "Then I'm in." Her smile returned. "I've never been a fake girlfriend before. This will be fun."

Too bad there wasn't real sex to go with it, she thought wistfully, before telling herself that she needed Colton as her friend a whole lot more than she needed him for sex. This was about her daughters, not the fact that she wasn't getting any.

"Thank you," he said as he stood. "I'm sorry to involve you in this. I've learned my lesson. Next time I'll suck it up and tell my mom I'm single. That way I won't have to drag you into my problems."

"I totally get what happened and I'm fine with it." She rose and tried to keep a straight face. "Although a really good boyfriend would apologize with flowers."

He chuckled. "Point taken. Thanks, Laurel. You're the best."

Paris sat with her feet up on Laurel's back porch railing. Bandit was inside with the girls, watching a movie. Or in his case, sleeping through one. The sun had nearly set, putting the big barn in silhouette. The warm day was cooling, there was the promise of stars later, and if she ignored the fact that her ex-husband had asked her out, she was in a really good place.

"Why did I say Ariana could invite ten friends to her birthday party?" Laurel said, staring at her tablet. "What was I thinking?"

"You weren't," Paris said cheerfully. "You were worried about her having a great birthday and she asked for ten and you said yes before you could stop yourself."

Laurel sighed. "You're right. That's exactly what happened."

"You'll be fine," Cassie told her from the porch sofa. "You've already decided to order pizza and you're getting those cute custom cupcakes, so all that's left is what's in the goody bags and some games. Let's brainstorm."

"*You* can brainstorm," Paris said. "Except for Jagger's party, I have no eleven-year-old girl birthday experience and I'm pretty sure we want to do something different so Ariana doesn't feel we didn't put any effort into her day."

"Karaoke is always fun." Cassie leaned back in the seat. "I'm pretty sure you can rent a system somewhere. Colton probably knows about stuff like that. Oh, and because it plays music, we can have a dance party out here in the backyard. We can get those glow sticks and it will be great."

Laurel typed on her tablet. "I love that idea."

"Me, too." Paris picked up her lemonade. "Want me to find a few lawn games?"

"Would you? That would be great." Laurel scrolled through her list. "I like this. I'll run our ideas past Ariana, but I'm pretty sure she'll be happy. She can help me figure out what to put in the goody bags."

"Problem solved," Paris said, her gaze sliding to Cassie. Despite the other woman's great ideas for the party, she'd been quiet most of the evening. "You okay?"

Cassie offered a faint smile. "I'm a little tired. I'm not sleeping. That happens to me sometimes."

For some reason, that explanation didn't sound like the whole story, but Paris didn't want to push too hard.

"If you need anything," she began.

Cassie cut her off with a quick shake of her head. "Hopefully tonight will be better."

"We're on a roll here." Paris kept her voice teasing. "We've solved the birthday party crisis. Who knows what else we could accomplish."

"I'm good."

Laurel set her laptop on the faux rattan coffee table. "Do you miss your family?"

Cassie looked startled by the question. "I do. I've always been close to my sister and her kids. It's hard to be away from them. At the same time, I like being here." She smiled. "More than I thought I would. My job's great and learning about the land and the trees is interesting."

Paris watched Cassie as she spoke. From what she could observe, the other woman was telling the truth. She was settling into life in Los Lobos.

"I'm sure your family misses you, too," Laurel said.

"They do. We text all the time. Faith and I talk every now and then. I like that we're staying connected. You know—it's a family thing."

"It's nice that you're all close." Laurel looked at Paris. "We didn't have that luxury when we were growing up."

Paris thought about her strained relationship with her abusive mother. "That's one way of describing it. My mom liked to take out her frustrations on me, and Laurel's mom was always interested in being somewhere else. Your dad stuck around a little more, though."

"Yes, but he was busy marrying other women. Family is complicated."

There was something in her tone, Paris thought. "What's going on?"

Laurel surprised her by grinning. "Whatever you're thinking, it's not that."

Cassie sat up straight. "That sounds interesting. Come on. Now you have to tell us."

"Colton's parents are coming to visit." Laurel paused to glance around, then lowered her voice. "His mom's been threatening to find him someone local."

Paris stared at her. "Oh, no! He said you were his girlfriend."

Laurel laughed. "He did, which wouldn't be so bad, except his parents are coming to visit and they want to meet me."

Paris grinned. "Now he's in trouble. Are you going to pretend to be his girlfriend? What about the girls?"

"He's going to tell them that as far as my daughters are concerned, we're just friends."

Cassie leaned back against the sofa. "How good are your acting skills?"

"Not great, but I think I can pull this off."

Paris studied her friend. "You're doing it?"

"Sure. Colton's been so good with Jagger and Ariana. They adore him. From everything he's told me, his parents are amazing. They've been married forever and are still in love."

"You're thinking they'll be a good influence, as well."

Laurel nodded. "I want them to see that some relationships last. They've only ever seen relationships failing. Both my parents are multiply divorced, I am, Marcy and Darcy."

"Me," Paris added. "Although Jagger was too young to remember that, but we've talked about it. I know it's a little unconventional, but I think you're making the right decision."

"I've never been a fake girlfriend," Cassie admitted. "You'll have to tell us how it works out."

"Will you be having fake sex?" Paris asked, her voice teasing.

"I'd rather have real sex, but no, we're staying with the friends-only thing."

"Too bad."

"It is." Laurel sighed. "I wish someone was getting some."

Cassie's breath caught. They both turned to her.

"What?" Paris asked. "You're not okay, are you? Something's wrong."

"No. I'm great. Really. I, ah, I hiccupped. So any news with you and Jonah?"

At the mention of her ex, Paris felt herself blush, which was so dumb. There was nothing to talk about, let alone be embarrassed about.

Laurel slid forward on her seat and pointed at Paris. "If you could see your face. Something happened. What? He told you he's crazy about you and wants to get back together?"

"He did?" Cassie asked.

"No! Not even close." Paris pressed her palms to her cheeks. "Can we change the subject?"

"No." Laurel's stare was intense. "Spill."

Paris gave in. "Jonah asked me to dinner. He showed up at LoLo's and asked. No warning."

"He wants to sleep with you," Cassie said. "That's fun."

"It's not fun. It's confusing. And no on the sex thing. He's not giving me any hints that he's the least bit interested in me. I've been paying attention and there's nothing. Not a whisper. He treats me the same way he'd treat his grandmother, so I have no idea why he suggested dinner. It's ridiculous."

Laurel sighed. "You told him no."

Cassie looked back and forth, finally settling her gaze on Paris. "No! You didn't. Really? You told him no? But you're crazy about him, aren't you?"

Paris supposed that was as good a phrase as any to define her feelings. "Yes, and that's not the point. He's not looking for anything permanent. He doesn't even live on this coast. I confirmed it was a date, by the way. What's up with that?"

Laurel looked at her without speaking. Paris groaned.

"Fine. Yes, I'm afraid. I'm still in love with him and going out with him would make things worse, at least for me. I don't want to get involved." She paused. "No. I don't want to be hurt again."

"What about closure?" Laurel asked. "You never got that before. One second he was there and the next he was gone. Wouldn't it be nice to talk about what happened, to say the things you wished you'd said, and hear what he has to say?"

"I doubt it would be anything good," she grumbled, then sat

with the idea of closure. She understood the point. Her therapist had talked about it. After all she and Jonah had been through, maybe it was something to consider.

"You think he wants to rehash our former relationship."

"It's what you have in common," Cassie pointed out. "It's going to come up."

Laurel nodded. "She's right. And if he doesn't mention it, you can. I know going out with him is risky, but maybe it will be worth it. You know I'm only Team Paris, right?"

"I do and I appreciate the support."

"Plus, it would be practice," Cassie said. "You've said you haven't dated in forever. If you go out with Jonah, it's a twofer. You get closure and you get to remember what it's like to go out with a guy. For when you find someone you're interested in."

That sounded nice, she thought, because she *was* tired of being alone.

"I'll do it," she announced. "If Jonah asks me out again, I'll say yes."

twenty-three

Cassie walked through the old house. The inside was in better shape than she'd thought. Assuming the structure was as sound as Westin had claimed, all it needed was a thorough cleaning and maybe some fresh paint to be livable. The style was more farmhouse than Victorian, but in a way, it reminded her a little of Laurel's place. Maybe they'd been built by the same architect.

The kitchen hadn't been updated since the fifties or sixties. The tile was two-toned—light green with a darker green border. The refrigerator was newer, but the stove was practically an antique. Cassie didn't have a prayer of cooking on it and wondered if she could sell it and replace it with a cheap drop-in range. The cast-iron sink was still in good shape. Adding a microwave wouldn't be too expensive. The hideous yellowing floral print wallpaper had to go, but the hardwood floor was gorgeous.

If she decided to restore the orchard, she would have the house inspected, then renovate. Removing the wallpaper here, in the dining room and in the upstairs bedrooms would be a job, but she would save a lot if she did it herself. Patching the walls would require a professional. Then she could paint, get the new range and replace the two cracked windows. All that would probably take her to the end of her lease with Laurel, so perfect timing for her to relocate.

She'd walked the land Westin had mentioned her selling. It was, as he'd said, right by the road, giving future residents an easy way to town. If she was seriously considering staying in Los Lobos, she should find a real estate agent. Once she had an estimate, she could figure out a budget. A lot depended on how much she would get for the land and for the cognac.

Assuming she was staying.

The four large bedrooms upstairs had tall windows and high ceilings. The only closets were obvious add-ons and those weren't very big, but the shared bathroom was huge. In time she could look at combining the two largest bedrooms into a main suite with a walk-in closet and private bath.

If she was staying.

Because she didn't know what she wanted to do. Her mind was full of possibilities, but no answers. She missed her family and her old life, but Los Lobos was so much more than she'd thought. She liked her job, she had friends. The land was a pull she hadn't expected—it called to her in a way she'd never experienced before. She could feel herself growing and changing. Well, except for how she'd behaved with Raphael. That had been a disaster and now she was ghosting him, which made her cringe, but she didn't know what else to do. She couldn't figure out how to apologize and even if she did, why would he want to keep seeing her? She'd made a mess of everything and didn't know how to fix things now. Ironic considering the whole point had been sabotage.

Worse, she couldn't bring herself to talk about what had happened. She'd stopped herself from confessing to Paris and Laurel the other night. She hadn't wanted to disappoint them.

Her cell phone rang. She glanced at the screen, then sighed in relief when she saw it was her sister and not the hunky archeologist she'd run out on.

"Hey, you," she said, walking into the smallest bedroom and sitting on the built-in window seat. "What's going on?"

"Nothing much. I miss your voice."

Cassie immediately felt a tightness in her chest. "I miss you, too. It's hard being away."

"For me, too."

"Is this where I remind you that you're the one who kicked me out?"

"If you want, but I stand by my decision. You needed to get out of your rut and you have. So what's going on there? Did you hear back from the cognac guy?"

"He said he'd let me know his schedule by tomorrow."

She'd found a cognac expert online, a little surprised that such a person existed. They'd agreed she would fly him out to sample her cognac and review the paperwork. If he liked what he found, he would arrange for the barrels to be sold, either at auction or privately.

"He's really insisting on flying first-class?"

"Yes, and I fainted at the ticket price. I'm also putting him up in a very nice suite at the Los Lobos Hotel. He graciously offered to pay for his own meals."

"I guess that's something." Faith sounded doubtful. "You sure this isn't some guy trying to get a free vacation?"

"He has excellent credentials and yes, I called his references and did a very thorough search online." She'd even paid one of those services that allowed her to check out his credit history and criminal record. "He's legit."

"I can't believe Uncle Nelson left you cognac. That's so crazy. Why didn't he say anything? You would have gone out sooner if you'd known."

Cassie was less sure about that. She wasn't sure anything less than what her siblings had done would have forced her out of her stuckness.

"So what's going on with you?" she asked.

Faith hesitated long enough for Cassie's body to go on alert. "Something's happened. Tell me. Is anyone hurt?"

"We're all fine. Don't freak. I've met someone."

If Cassie hadn't already been sitting, she might have fallen over from the shock. "You mean like a guy?"

Faith laughed. "Yes, I mean exactly like that. We've gone out a couple of times and I think I like him."

"You didn't say anything."

"I didn't want to mention it until I knew there was potential. You know how J.J. dying nearly destroyed me. If you hadn't been there, I'm not sure what would have happened."

"You would have found a way," Cassie said loyally. "You wouldn't have let down your kids."

"I hope that's true. Anyway, his name is Garek and he's a landscape architect. He's divorced and his two kids are nearly the same age as mine. Not that they've met or anything. We're getting to know each other, but it's nice. I'm hopeful."

"I can't wait to meet him. I wish I was home."

"No, you don't. No one's meeting anyone for a while. Not unless and until this gets serious."

"I don't know what to say. That's great. I'm happy for you." And she was. Mostly. Her only complaint was that now she felt even more separated from her family.

"What else am I missing?" she asked, expecting Faith to laugh and say, "Nothing," only once again her sister was silent.

"There's something else?"

"Nothing bad," her sister said quickly. "Holli got her learner's permit. She's learning to drive."

"Are you kidding?" Cassie's voice was a shriek. She sprang to her feet, prepared to... Well, she wasn't sure what, but something.

"She has her learner's permit and I'm all the way across the country? I should come home. I need to be there to help teach her to drive. When did this happen? I've been texting with her and she never said a word."

"I asked her not to tell you because I knew you'd react this way. Cassie, it's fine."

"It's not fine." She pressed a hand to her chest, even as she blinked away tears. "I can't believe I'm missing this."

"This is why I didn't want to say anything. I knew you'd take it wrong."

"Oh, so you keeping this from me is my fault?"

Faith sighed. "It's no one's fault. I love you and I miss you, but I know you. Cassie, please. You're doing so great in Los Lobos. Please don't be mad or upset. Yes, you're not a part of everything that's happening, but you're not telling me everything, either."

An instant wave of guilt rushed through Cassie. Faith was right—she was keeping secrets. Big, Raphael-sized ones. She hadn't told anyone how she'd seduced him in a boneheaded move that had ruined all chance of a real relationship with a great guy, nor how she was now basically hiding from him.

"You're keeping me from being a part of my family."

"That's a little harsh."

She heard the hurt in her sister's voice and the guilt level increased. "I'm sorry. I don't mean to upset you, but Holli learning to drive is huge. And you're dating and all this is happening without me."

"Do you want to come home?"

The unexpected question surprised her, and her answer was automatic. "Of course. I'll leave right now."

Faith didn't say anything, leaving Cassie alone with her swirling thoughts as she considered what she'd just said. Yes, a lot was happening back home and she desperately wanted to be a part of it all, but...

But what about the cognac guy and her land? She had an orchard to learn about. Oh, and Ariana's birthday was coming up and the big garage sale. She had to read the next book for book club and she and Paris were going hiking. And Raphael—was she going to walk away without saying goodbye?

"It's not so easy, is it?" Faith asked softly. "We miss you so much, but this is better. You need to grow and change away from us and we need to figure out how to let you do that without screwing up your life."

"But I belong there."

"I'm less sure about that and I think maybe you are, too."

Cassie didn't know what to say. Part of her knew Faith was right, but the rest of her couldn't believe what she was missing.

She sank back on the window seat. "Tell me what's happening in town."

"It's summer, so tourists are everywhere. The B and B is full and I have a waiting list in case of cancellations. Dick Wolf had a huge Hollywood-type party up at his place. Garth swears he saw Taylor Swift driving there."

"Why would Taylor Swift go to a party with the guy who created *Law and Order*?"

"That's what I said."

They talked for a few more minutes. Cassie tucked her phone in her pocket and walked downstairs to lock up the house. It still had a lot of potential, but her initial pleasure at seeing the place had faded. Instead of hopeful, she felt unsettled and more than a little uneasy. Where did she belong? What would make her happy? She was missing so much back home—she was missing her family. Yes, she'd made a life for herself here, but it was temporary. What if when she went back home, she didn't fit anymore? What if she changed too much? What if they did? What if she never belonged again?

Jagger and Ariana were uncharacteristically quiet as Laurel rang the doorbell.

"This is exciting," she said with a big smile to conceal her own apprehension. While the girls were a little nervous about meeting Colton's parents, she had to deal with the whole "fake girl-friend" plan.

"Hi," he said as he opened the door. "You made it."

Laurel wanted to ask how things were going or possibly request a delay of the meeting, but when they stepped inside, she immediately saw an older couple smiling and waiting.

They were probably in their late sixties or early seventies, but looked much younger. The man was about five-ten, with gray hair and a smile exactly like Colton's. His wife was a little shorter and rounder, with pretty brown hair and eyes and a welcoming demeanor.

"Mom, Dad, this is Laurel and her daughters, Jagger and Ariana. Everyone, these are my parents. Val and Stan."

"Nice to meet you," Stan said, walking toward them, his hand outstretched. "Colton's told us all about you." He winked. "At least the good stuff."

"Why would there be anything else?" Laurel asked with a laugh. "Welcome to Los Lobos."

Val surprised Laurel with a hug.

"You are so lovely," the older woman said. "I knew you would be. And your girls are so pretty." She pulled her phone out of her pocket and clicked it open, then showed the girls. "Look. I have eleven grandchildren and some of them are your age. Isn't that something?"

"Eleven?" Jagger's eyes were huge. "That's a lot."

"Do you have trouble remembering their names?" Ariana asked.

"No. I have a good memory, but even if my mind did forget, my heart would always know." She lowered her voice to a conspiratorial whisper. "Did you know that every time a child is born into a family, everyone's heart grows just enough to hold all the love?"

Jagger glanced at Laurel, then back at Val. "I don't think hearts really grow."

"They do where it matters. Now, are you hungry for lunch?"

They went past the formal living room into the open-concept family room, dining area and kitchen. Colton had promised an easy meal of burgers and salads. Laurel could see that Val had been hard at work on the latter.

"You should have had me bring something," Laurel said, before turning to Val. "You've done so much work. Please let me help."

Val waved. "This was nothing. There's only the six of us. When the whole family gets together, that's a crowd." She smiled at the girls. "I have five children. Four daughters and Colton, who's the youngest."

"Like me," Ariana said.

"Exactly like you.

"It's only a few salads," Val continued. "But you can help me with what's left. Stan, why don't you take the girls outside and play a little soccer to burn off energy?"

"You play soccer?" Jagger sounded doubtful.

"Yep, and I'm good, too." He pointed to the big window next to the table. "Your mom can keep an eye on you while we're playing and I'm winning."

Jagger headed for the back door. "You're so not winning. I'm really good at soccer."

"Maybe I'm better."

The three of them went outside. Laurel and Val washed their hands, then Val showed her the bowl of fruit to be cut up.

Colton stayed close. "What can I do?"

"Stop hovering." Val waved toward the yard. "Hang out with your father and the girls. You spend your day trapped in a recording studio. You could use a little outdoor time."

"I don't think so. If I leave, you'll grill Laurel."

"Would I do that?"

"Yes, and I told her she would like you."

Val laughed. "Of course she will. What's not to like? Now go on. We'll be fine."

He looked at Laurel, seeking confirmation. To be honest, she wasn't thrilled about the alone time with Val—she barely knew the woman. But there was no gracious way to say that. Better to accept the inevitable and remind herself that she didn't have to confess anything she didn't want to.

"It's fine," she said with a smile.

Colton nodded. "Wave if you need anything."

When he'd closed the door behind him, Val said, "Stan and I miss having him close. I know why he felt he had to move away, but it's not the same without him. I've been blessed. Until Colton came here, all my children were close. We have monthly family dinners, we share all the holidays. As my daughters have gotten married and had children, we've had to buy a bigger table."

"That sounds nice," Laurel admitted as she rinsed grapes and strawberries. "I'm an only child."

"Your celebrations are probably quieter. At ours, you can't hear yourself think." Val mixed a vinaigrette.

"But you love it."

"I do." Val glanced up. "How long have you and Colton been dating?"

A reasonable question, Laurel told herself. Only she and Colton hadn't discussed the "fake girlfriend" logistics.

"Not long," she hedged. "But he's great and the girls adore him. Did he tell you we met by literally running into each other several times?"

"Maybe fate was telling you something."

"Maybe."

"He told you about his divorce?" Val asked. "They tried, but I don't think they were ever meant for each other. Colton would have kept trying, but she left. It's sad. I wish they could have found what Stan and I have. We're more in love than ever after nearly forty-five years of marriage. There's nothing like finding the right person. No matter what, we know we'll be there for each other." She paused. "You were married before."

Laurel reached for a pineapple. "Yes. Beau and I have been divorced about a year. It's been hard on the girls. Beau and I hadn't been happy for a while, but I never expected him to take off to Jamaica."

Val's expression turned sad. "Colton mentioned that. I take it he doesn't see his daughters much."

"No, which breaks their hearts. He's their father and they miss him." Laurel found herself fighting emotion. "I knew he wasn't the most stable guy when I married him, but I didn't think he'd leave. When my parents divorced, they both stuck around until I graduated. I want my daughters to have two parents to lean on, but he doesn't see it that way."

She looked at Val. "Well, that was more than I planned on saying."

"I can be a good listener and the problem has obviously been on your mind. I hope he comes around. If not, your daughters can depend on you."

"They can, but they also know their dad isn't who he should be. I used to feel bad about that, but now I think this is all on Beau. I'd never talk trash about him, but I won't defend him, either."

"He doesn't deserve it. Besides, you don't want to give them false hope." Val put the dressing in the refrigerator. "About done with that salad?"

"Yes."

"Good. Let's go see who's winning at soccer."

But outside, Stan was pointing at some flowers and talking. Her daughters listened attentively while Colton watched.

"Oh, no." Val shook her head. "He's lecturing them on the plants. That man!" She sped up. "Stan, stop. No one cares if it's a lily or a rose. If the girls are interested, they'll ask."

Stan didn't look the least bit chagrined. "I was furthering their education. It's important to know about nature."

Jagger turned to her. "Stan knows everything about flowers and vegetables, Mom. He and Val have a big garden back home. They grow things and can them. Only it's not cans, it's jars, which means it should be called jarring, but it's not."

"You grow your own vegetables?" Laurel asked, thinking she had neither the patience nor the time.

"Dad's always grown things," Colton said easily. "He's gotten more serious about it since retirement."

"I like the challenge. We take the excess to the food bank." He turned to the girls. "If you two come visit us, you can help me in the garden. Don't let Colton talk you out of it. Gardening is more fun than he thinks."

"I never said it wasn't fun."

"You implied it." Stan's tone was affectionate.

Laurel could tell they were a close family—they'd have to be to survive monthly dinners. But even as she wondered if that was a little too much togetherness, she envied the traditions, the rituals. She'd never had much of either growing up. She tried to create memories with her daughters and give them a stable, dependable childhood, but she wasn't sure if she was successful.

"How old are you?" Ariana asked Stan.

"Very old," he said with a grin. "We're grandparents."

"I wish we had grandparents."

"You do." Laurel looked at her youngest. "My mom and dad are your grandparents."

"We know, but we never see them." Jagger sounded wistful. "And they don't have a garden."

"What do you say to us being your temporary grandparents?" he offered.

"Dad!" Colton stepped between his father and the girls. "Aren't you rushing things?"

Val seemed equally surprised. "Stan, you're presuming." She turned to Laurel. "He didn't mean anything by that."

"What would I mean?" he asked. "I'm talking about while we're visiting. Just for the next two weeks."

Laurel didn't know what to say. She thought she understood what Stan was saying, but the statement had been a little off-putting. Still, she didn't want to assume the worst about Colton's parents.

"What do grandparents do?" Jagger asked cautiously.

"Fun stuff. Like hiking."

"Old people don't hike."

"Jagger." Laurel pointed at her oldest. "Let's start thinking before we speak."

"I didn't mean anything bad. Hiking is hard."

"Bet we can keep up," Stan told her. "We can do some baking, go to the movies. There's not enough time to teach you about gardening." He paused as if considering options. "You know, I'm good at fixing things. Would that interest you?"

Jagger nodded. "I'd like that. Sometimes we find stuff when we go thrifting. It could sell but there's something wrong like a broken hinge. If I could fix stuff I could help more."

Because Jagger felt she had to take care of her family, Laurel thought, wishing things were different.

"Then we'll do that," Stan said. "Two-week grandparents. If it's okay with your mom."

She looked at Colton.

"He means well." He shrugged. "I've got nothing."

"Oh, Stan." Val sounded dismayed. "Let's wash for lunch. We'll pretend this never happened."

"What did I do?"

"Mom." Jagger moved in front of her. "I want to learn how to fix things from Stan. He's a real grandfather. We'll be fine."

Laurel trusted Colton and he trusted his parents. They had plenty of experience with children and her gut said she liked them.

"Sounds like fun," she said. "I'm sure the girls would love to hang out with you both, but remember you're on vacation. Enjoying your time with Colton comes first."

"Why can't we do both?" Stan asked, putting a hand on each girl's shoulder. "After lunch, let's sit down with our calendars. Hiking for sure, just to prove we can. Then I'm thinking some quality time in the workshop. Hinges are easy. You're both smart. You can learn how to fix them in no time."

twenty-four

Cassie couldn't shake the feeling of missing out on her former life, while at the same time she knew she was where she needed to be to grow as a person. The conflicting emotions didn't make for restful nights, but even as she drank extra coffee at work, she thought she was making progress on her life plan.

With one notable exception, and two days later that notable exception walked into the bookstore.

He crossed to the wine bar. Part of her wanted to run and hide, but the rest of her said to stand her ground. Scurrying away didn't feel right. He would talk, she would listen and possibly learn. It might not be pleasant, but it was time to deal with the consequences.

Raphael stopped in front of her, looking all tall and sexy in his rugged archeologist clothes. She remembered how his skin had felt and the way he'd touched her as if he couldn't get enough.

"You're ghosting me."

The quiet statement cut through the mental fantasy and a little of her happy at seeing him deflated as she remembered she'd been wrong and then she'd run like a scared little girl.

She forced herself to hold his gaze as she said, "I am. I'm sorry."

"We need to talk. What time do you get off work?"

"Four. I'll come by your place."

She expected him to ask if she really would, or try to pin her down. Instead, he nodded and left without saying anything else. She wasn't sure if that was good or bad. Not that it mattered. Time to do the right thing.

To that end she clocked out and drove directly to his house. Without seduction and sabotage on her mind, she could appreciate his quiet neighborhood. The houses were older and smaller, but well cared for, close enough to the ocean to get the cool breeze, but not so close that one had to pay for the view.

She knocked once. Raphael opened the door immediately, then stepped out onto the porch, motioning to the steps.

He didn't let her inside, she thought, not sure what, if anything, that meant. She dutifully settled next to him, careful to keep her shoulder from brushing his. Neither spoke for a few minutes.

Finally, Cassie said, "I know I messed up. It's hard to explain."

"You wanted to end things, but didn't know how."

"What?" She spun toward him. "No! I was just... Okay, maybe that's true, but you know..."

"I don't know. I don't understand. I thought we were going somewhere."

"We were and I got scared. You probably can't relate."

His dark gaze was steady. "You don't think I'm afraid?"

"Not of me."

"You're like quicksilver. Just when I think I understand you, you prove me wrong. I messed up and I'm sorry."

What was he talking about? "Don't you dare apologize for us having sex. That was on me. You liked me and wanted a relationship and that terrified me. I was tempted enough not to walk away, so I tried to sabotage it all. You wanted to take things slow, but my fear was greater than my common sense."

She paused as another truth occurred to her. "And possibly my willingness to respect your position."

Wow. She had never been so honest about her emotions. The feeling was exhilarating and terrifying.

"Do you want this?" he asked, his gaze intense. "Us?"

Every fiber of her being said to make a joke, then change the subject. Only she couldn't think of anything funny and despite Raphael being unlike any man she'd ever known, she liked him. A lot.

"Yes."

The word came out as a whisper and she practically cringed as she sat on his porch step. But instead of laughing and pointing, he smiled.

"Good. Me, too. So let's do this right, get to know each other."

"No sex."

His brows drew together. "I wouldn't say no sex ever. Just not until we're in a better place. I want this to be solid, Cassie. Sex changes everything."

She knew he was making the mature decision. She mostly agreed. Only two things held her back. The first was what if he was disappointed by the real her? What if he realized that, compared to him, she didn't have a lot to offer? And second, having experienced sex with Raphael, she didn't want to wait for more.

"What about kissing?" she asked. "Does kissing change everything?"

The smile returned as he leaned close and brushed her mouth with his.

"Kissing makes things better."

She wrapped her arms around his neck. "That's a very interesting theory that we should explore. Thoroughly."

"Hope I'm not interrupting."

Laurel looked up to see Stan standing in the middle of the barn. She smiled as she hurried toward Colton's father.

"Good morning. I dropped the girls off at day camp a few minutes ago."

"That's okay. I thought I'd learn about your business. If I'm not in the way."

Laurel would have expected Val to check her out, but maybe the older couple was splitting the duty.

"Want a tour?" she asked.

"Sure."

She showed Stan around the stations of the business, including where inventory was logged in.

"Once we know what we have, we prepare it to sell." She pointed to a large sink filled with soapy water. "Some items go out as is, but others need cleaning or tags removed. Hot water can do a lot."

She showed him the cleansers.

"Denture cleaning tablets?" He chuckled.

"You'd be amazed. But we have to be careful. I once used them on what I thought were glazed plates only to have the design dissolve."

She put a small Italian pitcher into a light box, then demonstrated how different shades of light—bright white, warm white, yellow white—changed how the pitcher photographed.

"I want the light that photographs as true to life as possible," she explained. "Buyers should get what they're expecting." She pointed to the sink. "Washing items is one thing, but repairs are trickier."

"So you're willing to add a screw to a hinge, but not glue something back together."

"Exactly. Plugging a piggy bank or putting batteries in a clock is fair."

"Speaking of hinges, show me your stash of broken things."

"Over here." She led the way, then stopped. "It's great you want to teach Jagger, but I don't want her feeling more responsible for me than she already does."

"She's the oldest, second in line to be mom. That's how nature and families work, Laurel."

An interesting perspective, she thought. "Her worldview is skewed because her dad left."

"And she's having a hard time forgiving him."

"She said that?"

He raised a shoulder. "She mentioned it while we were looking at the garden. She both loves and resents him. That's a lot for her to carry."

"Plus protecting me and her sister. She's only twelve. I want her to be a kid."

"She is and she knows you love her. Helping you makes her proud of herself. As long as it's only now and then, it's fine."

"Giving me advice?" she asked. "You barely know me."

"I know enough. Besides, a man learns a thing or two when he watches four daughters become women."

He was right, she thought. Colton often mentioned his sisters. "Colton's the youngest."

"Yes, and we spoiled him, but he was our baby."

"He talks about how you and he used to do things together."

"That was important for us both. The usual stuff. Camping, hiking. Colton was interested in music from the time he was young. For a while he played in a band."

"Really?" She smiled at the thought. "He never said."

"Not much came of it, but that was when he got into recording. He started finding old equipment at garage sales. I helped him repair it. Soon everyone came to him to record a single."

"I'll have to ask him about his wild past."

"Make him tell you about his first band," Stan said with a grin. "He really likes to talk about it."

"You're trying to embarrass him."

"Only a little. You don't seem like the type to be scared away by bad drumming and a geeky haircut."

"I'm not."

Other things frightened her, she thought. Worrying about her kids growing up happy or never having a relationship with their father. But even with Colton's divorce she didn't see any red flags.

"Want to photograph some carnival glass?" she asked.

"Sounds like fun."

Paris sped up as she started up the trail. The early morning was still cool, although the clear sky promised a hot afternoon. Bandit kept pace easily, stopping to sniff every now and then. As they rounded a curve, her dog raised his head, barked once, then raced off. Paris didn't bother calling him back—he knew better than to tangle with an animal larger than himself so he'd probably caught a familiar scent.

Sure enough, when the trail straightened she saw him dancing around Jonah, delighted. She, on the other hand, felt more ambivalent. They hadn't spoken since she'd turned down his invitation. Not that her refusal meant she didn't love him, but seeing him was a bit uncomfortable. Or maybe any awkwardness was in her head. Jonah knew Bandit and hadn't bolted, and when he saw her, he grinned.

"He is one happy guy."

"He knows what's important in life." She caught up. "Getting your run in before it gets hot?"

"That and before I get some sleep. Last night my meetings were on Singapore's time zone."

"You haven't been to bed?"

"No."

What she thought was *You could use mine*, although then she would want to be in it and weren't things complicated enough without sex? What she said instead was, "Maybe sleep is a better use of your time than running."

"I was trying to decide, but I'm taking your arrival as a message from the universe."

"That's too much pressure."

He laughed. "I get that. I'm pretty wiped. Mind taking it slow today?"

The implication being they were going to run together.

"Slow it is, although I might have to mock you a little."

"Fair enough."

They began at a slow jog. Bandit ran ahead, circling back to check on them regularly.

"When's the tournament?" she asked.

"Eight months."

He would be long gone by then. Back to his regular life.

"You'll be there for the whole thing?"

"At least three weeks. A long time to leave Danny."

She thought asking who would take care of his son was too personal. If Danny was in school, Natalie would probably fly out to be with her grandson.

"He understands you have a job," she said instead of offering. "And, come on. It's a video game tournament. You're practically Santa Claus."

He grinned. "Red isn't my color. Want to go out to dinner?"

She stumbled to a stop. He slowed more elegantly and watched her.

"You're asking me out again."

"I am."

She wanted to demand he tell her why only to remember how she'd promised herself if he mentioned the date again, she would say yes.

"On a date," she confirmed.

"Yes."

"Okay."

The happy grin returned. "I'm glad, but what changed your mind?"

"To give us both closure."

The smile faded. "I never meant to hurt you."

"I know and you didn't. Not in the way you mean."

"I left, Paris. I walked away without saying anything."

"I know why."

He shook his head. "No, let me say this. I was wrong to run. I was happy in our marriage, except when we were fighting."

"Which was all the time."

"No, it was some of the time and I didn't know how to handle you or your temper. Rather than try, I retreated. I should have confronted you."

"That wouldn't have gone well." He was a regular kind of guy with a regular kind of temper. She would have chewed him up and spit him out. "When we were married, I couldn't have heard you. We aren't born knowing how to cope with emotion and conflict—we have to learn. I never did and you paid the price."

"I still shouldn't have walked out. It wasn't because I didn't love you."

Silly words, but she treasured them all the same. "I know."

"So dinner?"

"Yes."

She knew him hurting her was inevitable. Regardless, she now had the tools to manage the pain and the support to survive.

They started running again.

"I have a personal question," he said. "You said you haven't dated much."

An understatement, she thought. "No."

"Have you had sex?"

She laughed. "Of course."

"With anyone but yourself?"

She laughed again, then let the humor fade. "Yes. A few times. They weren't great. Casual sex was never my thing and my caution about getting involved creates a challenge."

"You have a lot of rules."

"I always have." But now the rules were more about her behavior than the other person's.

Maybe it was time to let a few of them go, she thought. She

wanted someone in her life, which meant she had to learn to trust herself enough to give her heart. Maybe dinner with Jonah was a start. Not because they might get together, but because letting go of her past might be the first step in moving forward.

twenty-five

"If you don't stop staring at me, I'm going to ground you."

Laurel's voice was light, so it took Cassie a minute to realize she was serious.

"Was I staring? I'm sorry."

They were in Laurel's barn, getting items ready for the big garage sale in a few weeks. Cassie had spent two hours washing glass items. Now she was helping Laurel photograph some interesting finds for an online catalog.

"I was admiring you," Cassie admitted, feeling a little foolish.

Laurel's surprise was almost comical. "But I'm a mess."

"I'd like to be that big a mess." Cassie shifted the Waterford vase in the light box. "You run a business, you're managing a huge event, you're a single mom with great kids and a sexy faux boyfriend. I, on the other hand, am a total disaster."

"You're a cognac heiress with an orchard, along with a hot, very sexy real boyfriend. You're no one's idea of a disaster." Laurel stared at her. "What's really wrong?"

Cassie thought about deflecting her friend with humor, but she'd taken the coward's way out too often.

"Wait." Laurel pulled out her phone. "Let's ask Paris to join us. After years of therapy, she's good at getting to the heart of the problem."

"I don't want to bother her. I'm being a baby."

"I'm ignoring you," Laurel said cheerfully as she texted. Seconds later she said, "She's on her way."

They took pictures for twenty minutes, until Paris breezed into the barn.

"I was summoned," she said.

They sat around the table with diet sodas in the small break room. Paris looked at Cassie.

"What's going on?"

"Nothing."

Paris waited. Cassie couldn't think of a good lie.

"I don't know how to be with a guy who doesn't need me to fix him. Raphael says he likes me, but why? Without the fixing, I have no value."

She hadn't meant to say that, but somehow she'd blurted out her greatest fear and now it hung in the silence as Laurel and Paris exchanged a glance.

"You were the youngest child, right?" Paris asked. "The one everyone spoiled."

Not the question Cassie had been expecting. "Yes. I know a lot of older siblings resent the baby, but Garth and Faith were always sweet to me."

"They would do what you asked?"

"Mostly."

Paris sipped her soda. "So from a child's perspective, you had power."

"I wouldn't think of it as power," Cassie began, only to stop and consider the statement. Had it been a form of power? She'd always felt special, as if she mattered to everyone.

"Like Ariana always knows that Jagger will take care of her," Laurel said, nodding. "I get it. They fight and God knows Jagger can be bossy and stubborn, but under that is a sister who will do anything to protect her." She sighed. "That must have felt good."

"It did."

"And then your parents died." Paris's tone was flat. "Without warning, your world upended. You were emotionally shattered. We've talked about how your brother and sister didn't help you process your grief."

"I was on my own," Cassie admitted.

"So you started fixing problems." Laurel smiled at her. "You took care of them because you were terrified you would lose them, too."

Was that true? Had helping been her way of keeping her brother and sister close and safe?

"I never articulated that," she said slowly. "Taking care of people justified my existence."

"You can't be loved for you," Paris told her. "By the way, I don't think the loser boyfriends were about helping as much as they were about relationships with an expiration date."

"What? That's not true."

Paris's gaze was steady. "You sure? Because with those guys, you knew it would never work out. You didn't have to protect your heart against surprises. Their leaving was a level of pain you could survive—it happened and you moved on. But with someone else…"

"Raphael?" Laurel asked, her voice innocent. "Is that who we're talking about now?"

"You can't predict with him. And he doesn't need saving, so you have no idea where it's going and that's terrifying."

She knew they weren't wrong.

"I miss my sister a lot more than I ever missed my boyfriend," she murmured. "Faith and I talked a couple of days ago and she broke my heart. She said her youngest is learning to drive and I'm not there to help. And Faith is seeing someone. I'm glad she's willing to let someone into her life. It's like their lives are going on without me." She blinked away tears. "I know that sounds stupid. The world doesn't revolve around me, but…"

"Sometimes it feels like it should?" Laurel asked sympathetically.

"Maybe. They're fine without me. I knew they would be, but to have it shoved in my face." She sniffed. "It hurt."

"Do you want to go back to Bar Harbor?" Laurel asked.

Cassie stared at her. "No. Of course not. I mean, I had the thought, but I have so much going on here. You two and the girls, the orchard. I just miss them and wish we weren't so far away."

"But you're happy for them?" Paris asked.

"Yes. I want Holli to drive and Faith to have a great guy. Losing her husband was horrible. She had two little kids and was all alone."

"She wasn't alone." Laurel smiled. "She had you."

"It wasn't the same. I did what I could, but I couldn't take away her grief. She had to heal on her own." Cassie stared at them. "Oh, no. Is that the lesson? That I've been so busy doing for everyone else that I haven't processed my grief?"

"I don't think your issues are still tied up in that so much as they are tied up in patterns." Paris shrugged one shoulder. "We all get stuck. We find something we think works and repeat it. A great idea if the behavior really is helpful, but kind of sucky when it isn't."

"Is there anything you don't know?" Cassie asked.

"Yes, I don't know how to trust myself."

The blunt statement surprised her. "You're smart and caring and grounded. Is it the anger thing? I've never seen it."

"That doesn't mean it's not there."

"It's not there," Laurel said flatly. "It hasn't been there in years. Could you get pissed? Yes. We all do. Will you ever hit anyone again? No. But you won't believe that. You keep telling yourself that if you pass one more test, you'll finally take an emotional risk.

Only it's never one test, is it? You never reach the end. It's never enough so you miss out on what matters."

Cassie wondered if Paris would snap back, but instead she simply nodded slowly.

"You're right."

"If only insight meant change," Laurel murmured.

"If only."

They smiled at each other, then Paris reached across the folding table and touched Cassie's hand.

"Enough about me. You, my friend, need to start testing your assumption that you bring nothing to the table. You're afraid to get to know a very nice man."

She was right, Cassie thought ruefully, then admitted, "It's worse than that. I tried to sabotage things with sex."

She had to give them credit. Neither of them outwardly reacted to her confession.

"And you say you don't know how to have a life," Laurel said with a smile. "Can we all assume the sex was amazing?"

Cassie grinned. "You can."

"And now?"

"We've agreed to take things slow."

"Colton and I have agreed not to have sex at all." Laurel picked up her soda, then looked at Paris. "No pressure, but apparently you're the only one of us with a chance of getting any."

"That is so not happening."

Laurel's smile turned knowing. "Oh, I wouldn't count Jonah out just yet. The man has always known how to push your buttons."

"Thank you for letting me tag along," Val said as they left the party store.

Laurel nodded toward the two big shopping bags the other woman carried. "I would have had to make two trips to the car without you."

They put the party supplies in the back of her minivan before Laurel checked her list.

"We have goody bags, a few things to put in them, lawn Twister and Hula-Hoops." She smiled at Val. "Great idea."

"I think the girls will love them."

"I'm sure of it." She shoved the list into her back pocket. "Okay, all that's left is the bakery."

"Once we get the cupcakes safely home," Val said as she slid into the passenger's seat, "I'd like to treat you to lunch. If you have time."

Laurel thought about all she had to get ready for the party to-morrow, not to mention work. Then she thought about how great Val and Stan had been and how much she enjoyed their company.

"I'd love that."

"Me, too." Val drew in a breath. "It's possible Stan and I went a little overboard with the presents. We couldn't help ourselves. Oh, and we might have bought a couple of things for Jagger so she doesn't feel left out."

Laurel felt her eyes burn. Tears? Over presents? Only they were for her kids and the most her parents did was send a card with ten dollars. The thought counted, but there wasn't much thought in sending cash in a card. Val and Stan barely knew her and her children, but they'd bought presents.

"You're going to make me cry," she admitted. "You didn't have to, but thank you for making the effort. The girls will be thrilled."

"It was fun. I'm not usually a big shopper except when it comes to the grandkids."

But they weren't her grandchildren, Laurel thought, glanc-ing at the older woman. They weren't anything to her. The gifts spoke to who she was as a person, who Stan was. The man had already bought Jagger tools and was showing her how to use them.

It wasn't just a good male role model her daughters had been missing, she thought. It was extended family. They had Paris and Marcy and Darcy, but what about grandparents and cousins and their father?

At the thought of Beau, all the warm feelings inside bled away.

"Oh, my." Val's voice was concerned. "What are you thinking?"

"What?" Laurel glanced at her as she drove toward the bakery. "Nothing. No, that's not true. I was thinking that I need to remind Beau about Ariana's birthday. She'll be getting a phone so he can text her directly."

"You're afraid he won't remember?"

"I know he won't."

"That has to be hard on all of you."

"More the girls than me. I don't need him, but they do. He's their father and most of the time he seems to forget that."

"I'm sorry."

"Me, too. The worst part is I picked him. I fell for him hard. But he wasn't interested in forever, so we kept breaking up. I had decided to let him go once and for all when he announced he didn't want to lose me."

"Meaning he was finally willing to marry you?"

Ugh, when she said it like that... "Sadly, yes. I should have seen him for what he was. I shouldn't have trusted him with my children's future."

"You were young and in love."

"So were you and you made a much better choice."

Val smiled. "I was very lucky when I found Stan."

Laurel had a feeling Stan would say he was the lucky one. They were good together, good for each other. They demonstrated how a relationship should look.

"You can't change Beau," Val said. "You can only do what you're doing—providing your girls with a loving home where they can feel safe and thrive."

"You're being very kind."

"It's true. You're a good mother. Colton was lucky to find you."

What? Why would she… Crap! The fake girlfriend thing. Laurel had nearly forgotten. "I'm lucky, too," she said, only to realize she was. He was a great, dependable friend. If she was ever looking for more, well, he would certainly be her number one choice.

Paris couldn't remember ever being so nervous. She'd changed her clothes three times only to end up in the simple fit and flare green dress she'd started with. Bandit watched from her bed as she, yet again, checked her reflection. He'd been fed and walked. They'd taken a long run that morning and he'd had a busy day at the farm stand, so he was more than ready to nap the evening away.

"Is this okay?" she asked him, not actually expecting an answer.

He yawned once, gave her a doggy grin, then stretched out on the bed and closed his eyes.

"This is you helping? You could at least give me a tail wag of approval."

The very tip of his tail rose half-heartedly before falling back to the bed.

"I'll remember this," she warned him.

He wasn't the least bit impressed by her threats.

She walked to the living room where she paced until she heard a car.

"He's here," she called. "I won't be late."

She was going out to dinner, nothing more. It was six forty-five. She would be back by, what? Eight? Maybe eight thirty?

She stepped outside and locked the front door, then started toward Jonah's car. He got out and came around to the passenger side.

"Hi," she said brightly. "How are you? Bandit's exhausted. We had a busy day. How's your mom? And Danny?"

Jonah stared at her. "I would have come to the door."

"What? Oh, right." On a date, guys knocked on the front door. Oops. "Sorry. I was nervous."

Some of which was him and some of which was the whole not-dating thing.

He opened the door and waited until she was seated to close it. When he was starting the engine he said, "You look beautiful."

"Oh, um, thank you." Beautiful? Hardly. "I don't wear dresses much. They're not really practical for what I do."

"Guess not."

They drove in silence to the restaurant. After Jonah parked, he walked around to open her door. As they went inside, he placed his hand on the small of her back. The light touch didn't mean anything but politeness. But she couldn't help the shiver that shot through her or the urge to step closer.

The host showed them to a quiet table in the corner.

"Your server will be right with you."

"Thanks." Jonah waited until he left to add, "I'm nervous, too." He gave a little laugh. "I've never been on a date with my ex-wife before."

"That makes two of us." She paused. "Not the ex-wife part."

He grinned. "I know what you meant. But this is nice."

Nice? "My stomach's churning and I'm afraid I'm going to pass out. Hardly anyone's definition of *nice*." She groaned. "Sorry. That came out wrong. I'm so confused. Why did you ask me out?"

"So we could get to know each other again. It's been a long time and we've both changed a lot."

"You haven't. Okay, you're a father now, but honestly, you're kind of the same guy you were."

"I'd like to think I've matured," he said, his voice teasing.

"There was never anything wrong with you."

She hadn't meant to say that, but didn't take it back. He'd been good to her, always supportive.

"I walked out. That was a flaw."

"Not to me. I'm happy you stayed as long as you did."

They ordered drinks and talked about Natalie's progress.

"Any new interesting shipments?" he asked. "Fruit you're going to turn into a rock band?"

She smiled. "Oh, I can't repeat my social media displays. Maybe I'll ask Danny. His idea about the cherries in race cars was perfect."

"Does the social media help with sales?"

"It does and just as important, it keeps people from phoning all the time to ask when a certain item will be in. Say we get a new batch of peaches. I can post about it and say that we have X number of flats available for preorder."

"You're successful."

"I am and that makes me happy. I have great employees, loyal customers and plenty of tourists stopping by. It's all good."

"I'm glad."

They looked at each other. Paris had no idea what he was feeling, but she felt a distinct connection between them. Unexpected wanting had her wishing he would kiss her or even suggest they skip dinner. Only that wasn't going to happen. Despite what he'd said, she genuinely had no idea why he'd asked her out. She was supposed to be getting closure, but her emotions seemed to want to go in another direction.

"Tell me about Traci," she said in a desperate effort to distract herself, then immediately thought better of that particular line of conversation. "Unless it's too hard to talk about her."

His gaze was steady. "What would you like to know?"

"I'm not sure." A lie—she wanted to hear all the bad stuff, but doubted he had any tales to tell. "She was so young when she died. You must have been in shock."

"I was. One day she was fine and the next the doctor was telling her she was dying. It was a tough time."

Great. Because of her Jonah was now thinking nostalgically about his late wife.

"She wasn't like you."

Paris looked at him blankly. When his words sank in, she

laughed. "Of course not. I would guess the opposite. Why would you want to be with someone else so emotionally volatile?"

"She was a very restful person."

"You're being polite. What you mean is she didn't throw plates at your head."

One corner of his mouth turned up. "That, too. She loved music and reading. She didn't like being outside very much. She had an ethereal quality. Very little upset her."

Paris told herself to stay in her head. Traci was gone—Jonah's past was his alone and shouldn't mean anything to her.

"That sounds nice," she murmured.

"She was passionate about her work, her training, her violin. But not so much about anything else. At first I liked how nothing fazed her, but eventually I realized that unless her music was involved, she didn't feel very much. She wasn't like you."

She tried not to wince. "Angry and unpredictable?"

"All in. You were always more than your temper. You throw yourself into life. You're not just Jagger and Ariana's mom's friend. You're *their* friend. They can depend on you. Bandit's not just your dog—he's a part of your life. You trained him from the time he was a puppy to be well-mannered so you could take him to work. He would never run off on the trail, not because he's instinctively going to stick close to you, but because you trained him. He's part border collie—he wants to work. You channeled that energy. You always have an opinion. Whether you loved a movie or hated it, you would stand up for what you believed. The longer I was with Traci, the more I missed your passion."

She had no idea what to say to that—to him. She liked how he saw her, but didn't know what to do with the information.

Their server returned with their drinks. When she left, Jonah added, "I realized a few months before she died that I wasn't in love with her. I was thinking about leaving her when she was diagnosed. I knew then I had to stay, so I did."

His gaze was on her as he spoke, showing her he meant the

words. Paris could barely absorb the meaning, let alone make sense of it. Then she reminded herself Jonah being or not being in love with Traci had nothing to do with her. He was sharing, not hinting.

"I'm sorry you had to go through that," she told him. "But I'm not surprised you stayed with her. That was a very Jonah thing to do."

twenty-six

They spent the rest of the meal talking about ordinary things. She brought him up-to-date on a few mutual friends, he told her funny stories about living in DC and what it was like to be married to a concert violinist.

"I got good at taking care of Danny by myself," he said as he drove her home. "Traci was gone five or six nights a week, so I gave him his dinner and bath, read him stories, and put him to bed. We had help while I was at work, but I raised him."

"You're a good dad."

"I wasn't at first. There were a lot of tears, mostly mine."

She laughed. "I doubt that. You have all these unexpected skills."

"I guess I am impressive."

He was, in ways she wouldn't admit. As they neared her house, she found herself fighting nerves again. The evening had gone well. She'd enjoyed his company and she thought maybe he'd had a good time, too. But to what end? Was he going to ask her out again or had this evening answered all his questions? And what did she want? When Natalie was better, Jonah would leave. Even if he did decide to move from DC, what were the odds he would settle in Los Lobos? The closest big fancy international airport was all the way down in Los Angeles.

She was still in a state of confusion when they reached her house. Her instinct was to run, leaving him alone in the car, but she'd already had the awkward start by not letting him pick her up at the door. This time she would play it cool.

She waited while he circled the car and opened her door, then stepped out into the warm night. Together, they walked to her front porch. Paris ignored the uneasy combination of anticipation and awkwardness, forcing herself to smile casually.

"I had a nice time," she began, not sure when she was supposed to unlock the door and escape inside. Saying thank-you seemed like the polite thing to do.

"Me, too."

They stared at each other. Now what? Did she say something else? Should she open the door and go inside? Was he expecting her to invite him in? This, she thought grimly. This uncertainty was why she didn't ever want to date again.

She started to pull her bag around so she could fish out her keys only to have him put his hands on her shoulders and draw her closer. Because it was Jonah, because she knew him and the once-in-love muscle memory kicked in, she stepped into his embrace with a practiced ease. His head lowered and his mouth brushed against hers.

The soft, gentle kiss promised nothing. It was a brief contact, a light touch. She told herself not to react, not to let him know the familiar Jonah-induced fire had ignited. Whatever problems they'd had, sex hadn't been one of them. They'd known how to turn each other on and had taken advantage of every opportunity.

A reality she would deal with later, she thought even as she told herself to step back and say good-night. Only before she could, he kissed her again, lingering this time. His hands moved from her shoulders to her waist where the familiar weight had her stepping even closer until they touched everywhere. She wrapped her arms around his neck and lost herself in the sweetness of his tongue against hers and the arousing heat his touch generated.

Wanting pooled inside of her. She'd been without this man for so many years, she thought wistfully, without his warmth, his sure, confident hands. She'd missed the taste of him, the scent of him, the way his breath caught when he entered her and how their eyes locked as he drove them both to ecstasy.

Even knowing how that time couldn't be replicated, she was still bereft when he drew back, his eyes bright with passion, but his expression unreadable.

"Good night, Paris."

Before she could say anything, he was gone, striding toward his car, leaving her alone on her porch. No, not alone, she thought as she let herself inside and greeted her dog. She had her regrets to keep her company and she always would.

Laurel sat on the edge of Ariana's bed and smiled. She still remembered when she'd brought her youngest home, had carefully carried her over the threshold. She'd been sore, exhausted, and wondering how to cope with a newborn and a twenty-month-old. Beau's parenting style had been erratic even then. She'd known she couldn't depend on him to actually look after her babies. He was always chasing some dream, and she had a business to run, and most days, a family to support.

But she shouldn't have worried, she thought, watching her beautiful eleven-year-old sleep. She shouldn't have doubted. Marcy and Darcy had come up with a schedule to take care of Jagger for the first couple of weeks and Paris had simply moved into their small house, sleeping on the sofa, getting up every two hours to bring baby Ariana into the bedroom for Laurel to nurse, then changing her and rocking her back to sleep.

Eleven years ago, Paris had been deep in her recovery—

seeing a therapist two times a week, attending anger management classes, working on getting her employees to first trust her, then return to work. But none of that had mattered. In Laurel's hour of need, Paris had been there.

Laurel brushed the hair off her daughter's face, remembering how Paris had been nervous about being so tired. She was careful about taking care of herself, keeping to her schedule, journaling any strong emotions. Laurel had known helping with the baby could shatter what she'd built for herself, so she'd told her friend she would be fine. But Paris had showed up anyway. Day after day, no matter what.

She thought about all the times she'd awakened to see her best friend gently rocking Ariana, soothing her, loving her. With Jagger, who was all about going and doing—as fast as she could—Paris would invent running games that an unsteady twenty-month-old could master. They played outside, shrieking and laughing. Paris wouldn't come in until Jagger was exhausted. Only then would she return her to a grateful Laurel, who could put her down for a nap and possibly squeeze in a five-minute shower.

She always thought of her best friend on her daughter's birthday. She thought of how Marcy and Darcy were there for her, too. And she wondered how Beau could choose to stay away from his own children.

But regrets were for later. Maybe tomorrow, maybe in a couple of weeks. Today was about Ariana.

She lightly stroked her daughter's cheek. "Morning, my love. Happy birthday."

Ariana's eyes fluttered open. "Mom? Is it really today?"

"It is. How does it feel to be eleven?"

She closed her eyes and scrunched up her face. "Not very different. I thought I'd be taller."

"You're still in bed. It's kind of hard to tell."

Laurel stretched out next to her, pulling her close. Ariana settled in the crook of her arm.

"You were late," she said quietly. "Everyone says first babies are late and second ones are early, but you were late."

"Was Jagger late, too?"

The same question every year, Laurel thought happily. "She was. I guess my babies had better things to do than to come out and meet me. But I was ready. I was so excited and so was your dad." A lie, she thought, but a worthy one. "Jagger was confused. Some days she wanted to play with you and some days she wanted you to stay in my tummy."

"That's because she's an older sister. She gets that way."

Laurel laughed and hugged her. "She does. But then you were born and I was so happy."

Ariana hugged her back. "Me, too, Mom. I'm glad I picked you."

Laurel sat up and handed her a small box. Ariana's breath caught.

"For real?"

"Yes. I've already programmed in my number and your sister's along with your dad's and Paris and Marcy and Darcy. We've been over the rules."

As she'd already put a copy of the phone rules on the back of Ariana's bedroom door, she didn't feel the need to repeat them.

Her daughter opened the box and took out her new phone. She held it lovingly against her chest. "It's perfect," she breathed. "Thank you."

"You're welcome."

"Did you give my number to Daddy?"

Laurel struggled to keep her good mood in place. "I texted it to him a couple of days ago."

She glanced at the screen. "Do you think he's going to call me?"

"It's early, kiddo. He probably thinks you're asleep."

"Can I call him? Please, Mom. I know it's international, but it's my birthday."

Her daughters were allowed to text Beau, but calls had to be cleared by her. Phoning Jamaica wasn't cheap.

"Sure, but keep it short."

Ariana expertly turned on the phone, then scrolled through the handful of numbers. She frowned. "Mom, we need to put Colton's number in here. And Val and Stan."

Laurel didn't show her surprise. Colton almost made sense, but Val and Stan? Had they all gotten that close? "We can talk about that later." She didn't want her girls bugging them when they went back to Tennessee. Especially given the fact that she and Colton weren't actually dating.

Ariana nodded, then tapped her father's name. She waited patiently through five rings, her smile fading a little with each one. Finally, his voice mail came on.

"Daddy, it's me. Ariana. It's my birthday and I got a phone. You're my very first call. I love you so much. Please call me later. I want to talk to you on my birthday. I love you, Daddy."

She hung up. "He'll call."

Little shards of pain cut into Laurel's heart. She didn't care about Beau's crap for herself, but when it came to their kids, she wanted to beat some sense into him. He only had the two. How hard could it be to make a thirty-second call? She'd already reminded him twice, but she would send a third text later that morning. Anything to keep him from letting his daughter down.

Laurel stared at the impressive stack of presents from family and friends. Ariana would get even more from her friends at the party. Ah, to be young enough to want one of everything. At this point in her life, Laurel's birthday fantasy included a quiet day and possibly a certain man in her bed. Not that her birthday was for several months, but still, a woman could dream.

And speaking of dreamy, Colton walked into the kitchen with

bags of chips, boxes of cookies, enough soda to float a ship, and the flavored waters that were suddenly all the rage.

"I got everything on the list," he told her. "Nothing more."

She laughed as she helped him unload. "Thank you. We're going to have so much food. I know tween girls can eat like locusts, but I suspect we'll have junk food in the house for weeks."

"If you really want to get rid of the leftovers, I'll take them to the studio. We have a big recording session tomorrow. The food won't go to waste."

"Sold!"

She checked her master list. "I think we're ready. And to be clear, you aren't expected to stay after dinner. That's when all rational adults should flee. Once the fun begins for the girls, the sound level climbs to shrill and shrieky. You don't want to be here for this."

"I'm going to be your backup."

Something he'd already offered. Twice.

"But you have a life. It's a Saturday night."

His posture was relaxed, his smile easy. "You can't scare me away."

Before she could try to read something he didn't mean into that very nice sentence, Ariana ran into the kitchen, her new phone clutched tightly in her hand.

"He called! Daddy called. He wished me happy birthday and said he missed me."

Laurel's relief was instant. She'd been so concerned that Beau wouldn't get in touch with his youngest. He hadn't bothered with Jagger, despite the messages Laurel had left for him. Jagger had claimed she didn't care, but Laurel knew otherwise.

"I'm glad you heard from him," she said, hugging her daughter. "Your friends should be here in an hour. Maybe try to rest a little between now and then. It's going to be a long night."

Ariana practically rolled her eyes—something new for the

now eleven-year-old. "Oh, Mom, I'm too old for naps. I'm going to tell Val that Daddy called."

She raced out of the kitchen, screaming for Val. Laurel watched her go.

"I'm glad he called," she said quietly. "Now she can stop worrying and enjoy her birthday."

"How many times did you remind him?" Colton asked quietly.

She looked at him. "Three."

He put his arm around her. "You're a good mom."

"She's my daughter and I love her. I wish Beau would step up. But responsibility was never his style."

"I wish I could fix that."

"Me, too, but that's on him." She looked around the kitchen. "I haven't seen Jagger for a while."

"She's probably with my mom, filling the goody bags. Let's go check."

But she wasn't in the dining room. Laurel left Colton with his mom and walked outside. Now that she thought about it, she hadn't seen Stan in a while, either. No doubt the two of them were hanging out in the barn, repairing the items that needed small fixes.

She walked the short distance from the house and went in through the main door. Sure enough voices came from the far side of the building and she walked toward them. She was about to announce herself when she heard Jagger say, "He called her on her birthday, but he didn't call me."

"That's not right." Stan's voice held outrage. "He should have called you. I'm sorry he didn't."

"I don't care."

"If you really didn't care, him not calling wouldn't hurt so much. But you do care. He's your father. That means something."

Laurel came to a stop so she could listen. Tacky, but possibly important. She thought maybe Jagger would say things to Stan she wouldn't say to anyone else.

"I don't care," Jagger said defiantly. "I hate him."

Laurel flinched at the harsh words. She knew her daughter didn't mean them, but her heart still ached for her.

"You're angry and hurt," Stan corrected. "There's a difference."

Jagger sighed. "Mom tells him it's our birthday and to call. I heard her once, leaving a voice mail. She probably texts him, too. She does it because she doesn't want to disappoint us and she knows he won't remember."

Her oldest's voice thickened. "She does everything for us and he doesn't do anything. We're his daughters, too. Dads suck."

Laurel was about to step forward and join the conversation when Jagger added, "Maybe not all dads. You're great. And Jonah's good with Danny. Some of my friends have great dads."

"Everyone is different," Stan said. "Everyone has their own strengths and weaknesses. I don't know your father so I can't make a judgment, but I do know a man who ignores his own daughters is a fool and someone I pity. He's missing out on two wonderful relationships."

"Ariana wants him to come back and live with us. She still talks about it, but I don't want that. It was hard when he left, real hard. Even if he wanted to come back, he wouldn't stay."

"Plus, your mother might want a say in that decision."

"She wouldn't let him back. She knows he's bad for all of us. But Ariana can't help wishing. She doesn't see him the way he is. I don't get that. He's so selfish, but she loves him the best."

"I think it's more that the hope makes her happy and you feel safest hiding behind your anger. Being angry can make a person feel powerful. But it's also tiring to be angry all the time. And you end up missing out on a lot."

Laurel wanted to hug them both. Her daughter to offer comfort and Stan because he was the most thoughtful, kind, insightful man she'd ever met. Instead, she stayed where she was, hoping he would get through to Jagger in a way she couldn't.

"You're going to be a teenager soon," he said. "You're old enough to make some decisions for yourself. You need a father in your life."

"But I don't have one."

"I know, so you find one or three. Twenty is better. Take advantage of the good men in your life. Use me. Use Colton. Watch what we do and learn. Ask questions. You said you liked Danny's dad. What can he teach you? What about Raphael? He seems like a decent guy and he's pretty smart. Let us all into your life, then hold us to account. Don't settle for less than you deserve."

"What if my dad comes back?"

They'd finally reached the point where Stan couldn't answer the question. Laurel walked toward them, then smiled as she stepped out from behind one of the shelving units.

"There you two are."

"We were fixing the woven box," Jagger said. "And talking about Dad."

"I heard that part of it." She sat across from her daughter. "Your father won't ever be coming to live with us again. I know it's what Ariana wants, but it will never happen. Not only does he have a new life in Jamaica, but our marriage is long over." She reached across the table and took Jagger's hands in hers.

"But maybe it would be nice if you saw him a little more regularly."

"That would require him to show up, Mom. We both know he won't."

"People change."

Jagger pulled her hands back. "Why do you always do that? Why do you always defend him? Why don't you hate him? He hurt you. I heard you crying. You tried to hide it, but I heard."

Laurel glanced at Stan, who nodded encouragingly. The truth, she thought. Jagger was old enough to handle it.

"I wasn't happy that my marriage ended," she said slowly. "Even though it was the right thing for your dad and me. We hadn't been happy for a long time. Marriage requires two people who want to work toward the same things on the same time frame. Your dad and I wanted different things."

Which sounded so much better than saying Beau was never willing to do the mundane things required to keep a family going. He was only interested in himself and his dreams.

"But even when I realized that and we decided to divorce, I still had a long past with your father. I was sad to lose that, even though it was the right decision."

"He took all the money, Mom. I know that, too." Jagger grimaced. "I heard you talking to Paris. I couldn't sleep and I started to come downstairs and then you said he cleaned out the bank accounts and took everything. You were so scared and then I got scared."

Laurel rose and circled the table. She pulled her daughter to her feet and hugged her tight.

"I'm sorry," she whispered. "I'm so sorry. You were never meant to know that. You weren't supposed to worry. No matter what, I'll always take care of you." She drew back enough to look into Jagger's face. "We're okay now. You know that, right? The business is doing great and there's money in the bank. We're fine."

Jagger nodded. "Plus the money from Cassie's rent. I knew you'd get us through, but how could he do that?" Her mouth twisted. "I never told Ariana, even when I got mad. She's too young. That's why she still thinks he's great. She doesn't know the truth."

"You're so strong." Laurel smiled at her. "And grown-up. I didn't realize what was happening." No wonder Jagger had mixed feelings about men in general and her father in particular.

"Stan's right," she added, glancing at the man. "About many things but especially about holding people to account. Your dad's doing better now, but that doesn't mean he's going to get it all right. Stan was also right about finding other men to teach you the dad stuff. Maybe we can do that together."

Jagger nodded slowly. "I thought I didn't need a dad, but maybe I do. And Ariana does, too. The dad we have isn't enough."

A hard lesson, but a good one to learn, Laurel thought, hugging her daughter. Stan joined them, his strong arms holding them both so tight, Laurel wished he would never let go.

Three days after the fact, Paris was still as confused about her date with Jonah as she had been when he'd asked and when he'd dropped her off at home. She'd tried to consider the why of it from every angle and honestly had no idea what he wanted from her or why he'd bothered.

During her third sleepless night, she'd come up with what seemed like the most obvious answer to all her questions. Maybe Jonah hadn't been looking for closure at all. Maybe he'd been looking for something a little more basic.

With that in mind, she texted him, asking him to stop by LoLo's when he had a chance. He replied that he would come by in a couple of hours, which immediately got her heart racing and made it impossible to concentrate.

Fortunately, she had plenty of mindless busywork. She refilled bins with fresh sweet corn, helped two shoppers pick out watermelons, explaining that a yellow cast was better than a white one and round was sweeter than oblong. She'd started replenishing the Roma tomatoes when the back of her neck prickled. She turned around and saw Jonah walking toward her.

For a second she allowed herself to believe that everything would be fine—that he was as much in love with her as she was with him. That he would move here and they'd remarry and live happily ever after. Only that wasn't reality and the sooner she truly believed that, the sooner she would be able to put the past behind her and get on with her life.

But it was impossible for her to do anything but love him. A true pickle, she thought ruefully, even as she smiled at him.

"Hi," she said as cheerfully as she could in a pathetic attempt to conceal her real feelings. "Thanks for stopping by."

"Anytime." He smiled at her. "I've been thinking about you and was going to call you later."

"Yeah? Then this is perfect. We can talk about my thing, then your thing." Although she had a feeling her thing was going to solve any "Paris issues" he might have.

They went into her small office. She shut the door behind him and escaped to the safety of her desk, thinking a physical barrier between them might make her feel a little safer, or less vulnerable. Regardless, she was going to say it.

"You have an unrealistic view of our marriage," she began.

His eyebrows rose, but he didn't speak.

"We did have some good times, but I wasn't good for you. Back then I wasn't good for anyone."

She raised her chin. "I'm not saying I have it all together now, but I've developed skills that make me better than I was."

She paused to see if he was going to disagree, but he only nodded as if encouraging her to go on.

"But I'm still not in a place where I trust myself completely. I'm not sure I'm ready to be in a relationship, especially when there's a child to consider."

"You mean with me."

She told herself to stand strong. "Yes, with you."

"For what it's worth, I trust you."

"You don't know me."

"I know you better than you think."

She ignored that. "My point is that after the other night, it's obvious we still have a lot of chemistry, so if you want to have sex while you're in town, I'm open to that."

She expected him to smile at her and move closer or, at the very least, look intrigued by her suggestion. Instead, he frowned and stepped back.

"Is that the plan? We'll screw each other until I go back to DC?"

He didn't sound happy about her suggestion and she didn't love the way he'd phrased it.

"I wouldn't have put it that way, but yes."

"And then what?"

"I don't understand the question."

He looked at her, his dark eyes unreadable. "Then what happens, Paris? We have sex for a couple of months, and never see each other again?"

Well, sure. She wasn't going to expect anything more.

Jonah shook his head in obvious disgust. "You don't know me at all," he said, before turning and walking out.

Paris stared at the open door, not sure what had gone wrong. She could guess he was mad and had no idea why. She would have thought she had offered him everything he could possibly want.

twenty-seven

Earlier that morning, Ariana had flung her arms around Val and begged her not to leave. Now faced with the fact that the older couple would be heading to the airport in a few hours, Laurel found herself wanting to do the same. They were spending a few days in San Diego before returning to Nashville.

"We've enjoyed ourselves so much," Val said as she touched a milk glass vase on a shelf. "Meeting you and the girls has been so special. To be honest, I had my doubts when Colton said he'd met someone. Romantically, he's pretty much kept to himself since the divorce." She laughed. "I wasn't completely convinced you were even real. But you are and you're obviously so happy together."

Guilt hit Laurel like a flatbed truck, but she ignored the instinctive need to confess and instead went with a different truth.

"I've loved getting to know you. The time has gone so quickly. I wish you weren't leaving. I know you love your daughters and your grandchildren, but you should think about visiting here more."

"Stan and I have been talking about that." Val tilted her head. "We were hoping Colton would bring you and the girls home for Christmas. They're off from school for two weeks. Or are we asking for too much?"

Nashville for Christmas? She'd never not been home for the holiday, but seeing Colton's parents again was tempting.

"I'm not sure about the two weeks, but we could certainly discuss a visit. It's complicated with all the orders we get out for the holidays, but if I had enough inventory and hired a part-time person to help Darcy with the shipping, I might be able to get away around then. I know the girls would love to see where you live and meet your daughters and grandchildren."

"It would be quite the party," Val assured her. "You think about it and I'll mention the idea to Colton. Maybe you two will surprise us all with some happy news."

Laurel stared at her blankly. Happy news? What did that mean? Happy as in…

"You mean an engagement announcement? But we're not—"

She managed to stop herself before she blurted out that she and Colton weren't even dating. They were friends, nothing more, and the pretense of them as a couple had simply been for his parents' benefit. Which meant if they did go visit Val and Stan over the holidays, there was a very good chance she and Colton would be expected to share a bedroom and more importantly, a bed.

"If you're talking about us getting married, we're nowhere near ready to think about that," she said instead. "The girls are still dealing with the divorce. Besides, Colton and I haven't known each other that long."

Val's expression turned knowing. "It's all right, my dear. I'm not trying to pressure you. It was just a thought. For what it's worth, you might not have been dating very long, but you and Colton have figured out what's important about each other and sometimes that makes all the difference in the world."

What did that even mean? Not that she was going to ask.

"Whether or not you have a relationship status change, we

very much want to see the three of you at the holidays. We're all smart people. We can figure out the details."

"I'd like that."

Val hugged her. "I have to get back to finish packing. Meeting you was such a joy. You're lovely."

"So are you and Stan. You've been wonderful to my girls."

"They're in our hearts. If you ever need anything, please reach out to us." She cupped Laurel's cheeks. "A woman can never have too much support."

Laurel's eyes filled with tears and she hugged Val again, wanting to hold on forever. Her mother had loved her, in her way, but she'd never offered this kind of unconditional caring.

"Thank you," she whispered. "For everything."

She walked Val to her car and watched her drive away. Back in the barn, she told herself to be happy that the visit had gone so well. The girls had loved being with Stan and Val, Colton had convinced his parents he was in a relationship, and she'd made new friends. It was a win-win.

If things were different... No, if *she* was different, she might allow herself to play the what-if game. What if her relationship with Colton was real? What if there was a possibility of them taking the next step and being part of his family? Only she knew better than that. To have that happen, she would have to fall in love with him and she would never let that happen.

She went back to work, focusing on photographing the items she would list for sale or put in the garage sale inventory. But about an hour later, she had the thought that Stan and Val had been in love with each other nearly their entire lives and they weren't fools. On the contrary, they were the wisest people she knew. So who was right about love? Them or her?

Raphael lit several citronella candles. Cassie watched him as he put them on the smaller tables surrounding the larger one he'd brought for them to dine on. Yes, there were just camp chairs and paper plates for their dinner in her orchard, but somehow the evening felt special—romantic, even.

They'd gotten takeout from Bill's Mexican Food. Bottles of beer were on ice and the avocado trees around them provided shade from the setting sun.

He held out one of the camp chairs. When she was seated, he opened two beers and handed her one, then settled across from her.

"This is nice," he said, touching his bottle to hers.

"It is." She looked around, then grinned. "Okay, maybe this is weird, but I'm feeling a prideful ownership about the orchard. Like 'Hey, trees. It's me, your new mom.'" She frowned. "Hmm, that sounds strange. Do trees have parents?"

"They understand."

"You think the trees speak English?"

"I think they feel energy. All living things do. They recognize your positive intent."

She eyed him over her beer. "Now you're freaking me out a little. I thought you were into the long past, not the supernatural."

"The long past, as you put it, is about connection. Connection requires attraction. Not all of it sexual, by the way. We're drawn to certain people, places, activities. That's a form of energy. I'm saying the trees are happy you're happy."

"Still freaking me out," she admitted with a grin.

"I can live with that."

She looked around at the rows of trees. Westin was putting together a plan for refurbishing the orchards, or whatever it was called, prioritizing certain sections to get them fruit-bearing as fast as possible. Every couple of days he sent her articles on everything from soil health to the futures markets. He'd also ordered a couple of agricultural textbooks for her. She'd found them waiting on the bar when she'd gone in for her shift.

"I'm getting excited about the orchard," she admitted. "I have a lot to learn, but I trust Westin to be a good teacher. I do feel hopeful about the land."

"What about the house?"

She glanced in that direction. "I've been inside a couple of times. It's in decent shape. I have a home inspection scheduled, so I can be sure all the big systems work. It will take some scrubbing and wallpaper removal followed by paint to get it livable, but I think I can get it done by the time my lease with Laurel is up. The alternative is to fix it up and lease it out for income and stay at Laurel's. I haven't decided. Either way, it needs to be updated."

"I'm available as labor. Wallpaper removal is one of my specialties."

"I appreciate the offer, but no one likes removing wallpaper. It's a horrible job."

"I've done it before." He smiled. "I mean it. I'd like to help."

"I won't say no."

Not only could she use the help, but watching Raphael do physical stuff would be fun. Even though she'd seen him naked, she still couldn't get over how gorgeous he was. And smart and nice. The whole package, she thought, ignoring the doubting voice that once again asked why he would be interested in her.

"I want to get the downstairs in shape before I move in," she continued. "And one of the bedrooms upstairs. Assuming all goes well with my plan, then I want to save up and convert two of the bedrooms into a main suite with a big bathroom and walk-in closet."

"So you're serious about staying?"

She looked at him. "I'm not a for-sure yes, but I'm leaning in that direction."

"You're making a lot of plans that will take time."

She couldn't tell what he was thinking as he watched her. "Is that a problem?"

"Not for me. I want you to stay."

She put down her beer. "How do you do that? How do you say something so…"

"Honest?"

"I was thinking more along the lines of belly baring."

He glanced down and lightly brushed his fingers against his shirtfront. "I don't see any belly."

"Very funny. You know what I mean. You're so confident, you can say stuff like that."

"Like what?"

She looked into his dark blue eyes and wondered if he was testing her or genuinely confused.

"You saying you like me."

"I do like you. Don't you like me?"

"Of course, but I'm not running around saying it."

"Why not? It's something I'd like to hear."

"Yes," she said, trying not to shriek. "Of course you want to hear it, but that's not the problem. It's me saying it. Words like that make a person vulnerable."

"But that's how we connect. Through our vulnerabilities. We earn trust, we show the hurt parts and our partner offers understanding and protection. We do the same with them. Back and forth until we reach a point when we realize this is someone worth having in our lives. This relationship is important."

Wow. Just wow. "You should have been a psych major."

"Naw. Too much talking."

She laughed and they changed the subject, but she couldn't stop thinking about his openness with his feelings. Showing that much of herself meant being vulnerable in a way she couldn't imagine. Even the thought of it terrified her.

"Your cognac expert comes next week?"

"Yes, he confirmed. I'm nervous."

"The cognac is great."

Once she and Westin had survived their tasting with no ill

effects, she'd offered samples to her friends. "We think so, but what do any of us know about cognac that old?"

"It's going to be good and you'll make a lot of money." His gaze settled on her face. "Still planning to put it into the orchards?"

She frowned. "We were just talking about that."

"I know, but I want to be sure. When you got here you were determined to stay for only six months. You mention you're fairly sure you're staying, but that's not all in." He smiled briefly. "I want to know your intentions."

"The direct question," she said, shifting in her seat. She looked at him, then away. "I've made a life for myself here and much faster than I would have thought. I have friends, the orchard, my job." She swallowed hard and broke through the fear enough to add, "You."

Some of his tension eased. "So you want to stay."

"Mostly. I also miss my family. My sister's dating for the first time since her husband died and I've never met the guy. My niece is learning to drive. Their lives go on without me."

"Did you think they wouldn't?"

"It would be easier for me if they were suspended in time."

She'd meant the comment to be funny, but Raphael didn't smile. "You're not that person. You're struggling with what you see as missing out, but you'd never not want your family to grow and be happy."

"You're right, but it's still hard. And I keep wondering what else I'm missing. At the same time, I'm really loving Los Lobos. Plus—" she waved to her left "—I own a house now. Me. I've never lived in a house. Technically, I've never lived on my own before. I've always lived in that apartment above the bar. I've never had a yard."

"Or an orchard."

She grinned. "That, too. It's nice."

"Great place to raise kids."

She nearly fell off her chair. "You didn't just say that."

"Why not? I'm stating the obvious. This is a great place to raise kids."

"I know, but don't you think our, what, seventh date, is too soon to be talking about children?"

He raised one eyebrow. "Is it? I'd like a family. A big one. I was an only child and I didn't like it. What do you want?"

For him to stop talking about things like this, she thought. Yes, the man was totally in touch with his feelings and he always said stuff that made her feel good, but kids?

Even as she started down Freak-out Road, she found herself asking why it bothered her that he brought up the subject? He was into her—he'd made that clear. The probing questions about whether or not she was staying hadn't bothered her. Asking about children was simply more of the same. He was judging how serious she was and finding out if they wanted the same thing.

"Talking about family in that way implies a long-term deal," she said slowly, thinking out loud. "Commitment and permanency. No guy has ever hinted at a future before, because none of my previous relationships were going anywhere."

One corner of his mouth turned up. "You dated a lot of really stupid men."

"I did."

"So kids?"

She grabbed hold of her courage and nodded. "I would like children. More than one."

"Good to know."

"Hey."

Laurel, focused on listing items on eBay, jumped, then spun in her seat to find out who was sneaking into her barn. The last person she expected to see was Beau.

She got up and stared at him. "What are you doing here?"

His smile faded. "I stopped by to see the girls."

"Without calling? Without any warning? We talked about

this the last time you dropped in. You don't get to do that, Beau. It's not right."

"They're my kids, too."

"They are and that's why this isn't fair. You obviously knew you were coming. You had to make an airline reservation, then pack and fly out. In all that time you never thought to text me that you'd like to visit? Why is giving us warning so difficult?"

"Why are you so grumpy? Got your period?"

She ignored the bait, saying, "You're trying to piss me off so I'll get distracted. Showing up without warning isn't acceptable. You're supposed to let me know you're coming. This isn't fair to me or the girls."

He avoided her gaze. "They'll be happy to see me," he said, his tone implying he'd noticed she wasn't.

"Happy or not, this isn't right and you know it. Come on, Beau. It's what? A four- or five-hour flight to LA then the drive to Los Lobos. You could have called."

"Fine." He glared at her. "I could have called, but I didn't and I'm here and I'd like to see my daughters."

She wasn't going to keep him from them, but why did he have to keep doing this to them? She glanced at her watch. "I'll get them from camp. You can keep them for the afternoon." She paused. "Assuming you're going to be around that long."

His expression turned guilty. "I thought I'd, you know, take them to lunch."

"Really? You blow into town to spend, what? Two hours with them?"

"I have a meeting in LA."

At night? Laurel wanted to ask if the meeting was with a blonde or a brunette, then realized she honestly didn't care. The only thing that mattered was how Beau treated his daughters.

"I'll go get them," she repeated. "You can wait here."

"Or up at the house." He flashed her his best smile. "I still have a key."

"I changed the locks."

He shook his head. "That's cold, even for you, Laurel."

"It's practical. You don't live here anymore, Beau. There's no reason for you to have a key to my house."

She drove to the park and waited her turn in line. Her girls came running toward her. Jagger climbed into the front seat—a perk of being the oldest—while Ariana sat in back. After greeting her, they both launched into a description of their morning. She half listened as she drove to a shaded area on the large parking lot and pulled into a space. Instantly, the girls went silent.

"What's wrong, Mommy?" Ariana asked. "Aren't we going home?"

Laurel unfastened her seat belt so she could angle toward them. "Your dad showed up. He's here for a couple of hours and wants to take you to lunch."

"Daddy's here?" Ariana clapped her hands together. "Yes, yes! I want to go to lunch with him. Is he really only staying two hours? Can't he stay longer? Let's go. We have to hurry!"

Laurel turned to Jagger, who watched her with a wary expression. "What does he want?"

Her flat tone made Laurel's heart ache. "From what he said, lunch. He has a meeting in LA he's going back to after that."

"Why didn't he tell us he was coming? He had to know. He didn't just wake up on the road to Los Lobos." Her tone was bitter. "I guess texting was too much trouble."

Ariana watched her sister. "It's okay, Jag. He's our dad. We want to see him."

Laurel touched Jagger's arm. "What do you want to do?"

Jagger sighed. "I don't know. Stan said I should listen and then decide. That reacting means I'm not thinking things through. I'm older now—almost a teenager. I need to make more responsible decisions."

If Stan had been there, Laurel would have hugged him so

tight, he wouldn't have been able to breathe. He'd given them all so much.

Jagger turned to Ariana. "I know he's our dad and you love him, but you're wrong to always go running to him. He's back for a couple of hours and then he's going to disappear again. You always forgive him without making him say he's sorry for hurting us. You never expect anything from him."

Ariana's eyes filled with tears. "But he's our dad."

"The word isn't magic. It's the actions that make a person a father. He needs to act like our dad. Every time you run to him and tell him how much you love him and miss him, you're saying it's okay for him to act the way he does."

Ariana wiped her face. "I know," she whispered, surprising Laurel. "Stan told me that, too. He said if I want more, I have to expect more. I want to be strong, but I'm so happy he's here."

The sisters shared a look, then Jagger said, "We'll see him and have lunch, but we want to talk to him first."

"I don't," Ariana said. "I can't say that stuff. But you can."

"You two are amazing and I'm so proud to be your mom." Laurel shifted in her seat and started her van. "Let's go."

The drive home was quick. When she parked by the house, the girls got out. Beau walked out of the barn, moving toward them. Ariana immediately took off.

"Daddy! Daddy!"

But halfway to Beau, she slowed, as if remembering she was going to be strong. She came to a stop and looked at her sister. Jagger joined her and they reached for each other's hand.

"Hey, girls." Beau closed the distance, his smile welcoming. "How are my best girls?"

He held open his arms, as if expecting them to hug him, but they stood their ground. He looked from them to Laurel, his expression hardening.

"What did you say to them?"

"That you were here and wanted to have lunch with them."

"It had to be more than that."

"It wasn't," Jagger said flatly. "This isn't about Mom, it's about you."

Laurel started for the porch. "Let's go inside and talk."

She figured there was a fifty-fifty chance that Beau would get pissed off and leave, but instead he put on his "fun dad" face.

"How was your birthday, Ariana? I wish I could have been here. I was thinking about you all day."

"You were? I miss you so much." Ariana stopped talking and looked at her sister.

"It's okay," Jagger told her.

"What's okay?" Beau asked.

Laurel ignored the question and led the way into the family room.

"What's going on?" Beau glanced between the three of them. "There's something."

Laurel looked at Jagger who drew in a breath before speaking.

"We have expectations," Jagger said, meeting Beau's gaze. "From you. Dads don't show up when it's convenient and then run off two hours later. They show up when they're supposed to. You're not acting like you care about us at all. You never call or text. It's like you forget about us for weeks at a time, then suddenly remember you have daughters. That's not okay. You're hurting us by the way you're acting." She raised her chin. "You should be our dad for real or you should go away."

The words hung in the room. Beau looked stunned and Ariana started to cry. Laurel moved behind them so she could put a hand on each of their shoulders. She'd never been more proud of her oldest. Jagger was defining the problem and demanding a solution. It was impressive and a little intimidating.

Beau looked out the window. "I can't believe you said that."

"It's true," Laurel told him. "We all know it."

Ariana rushed toward him, tears running down her face. "No, Daddy, don't be mad. We're sorry. Don't go. We love you."

Laurel squeezed Jagger's shoulder, then said, "Ariana, your sister's being honest. It was hard to say and hard to hear, but denying it doesn't help." She looked at Beau. "They love you and they deserve more than you're giving them."

"You're attacking me." Beau sounded more surprised than hurt. "But I'm here."

"Here isn't good enough," Laurel told him. "They want more."

She could see him trying to process the information. "My business makes scheduling hard," he said. "And the time difference, not to mention the distance." He looked at his girls. "I didn't mean to hurt you. I thought you'd be happy to see me."

Ariana threw herself into his arms. "We are, Daddy. I am. I miss you so much."

He hugged her tight. "I miss you, too." He looked at Jagger. "Both of you." He smiled. "I didn't know the scheduling thing was such a big deal, but if that's what you want, then I'll let you know ahead of time. How's that?"

"It's good," Ariana told him.

"Jagger?"

"Sure, Dad. That would be great."

His good humor returned. "Excellent. All right, we have a plan. So lunch?"

When the girls were back, Jagger came to find Laurel.

"Did you have a good time?"

Jagger leaned against her. "You know Dad. He was funny and listened to everything we had to say. Ariana totally believed him, but I know better."

Laurel hugged her. "Maybe it's okay to believe him. He showed up."

Jagger stepped back and shook her head. "That's not enough, Mom. You don't just show up. Val said if we let people win by just showing up, we take away their opportunity to grow and change. She's right. We have to make Dad understand he needs to be more."

Laurel touched her cheek. "You are wise."

"Not me. Val."

"I agree that she's amazing, but you're pretty impressive yourself. It wasn't easy to stand up to your father, but you were right and you did it. I'm so proud of you."

"Ariana caved."

"She has to make her own decisions, like you've made yours."

"I want to see him." Jagger leaned against her again. "I don't want him to disappear, but it's too hard when he shows up for a couple of hours, then leaves."

"You told him what you want and why it's important. Now it's up to him to be what he should be."

"Do you think he will?"

Laurel desperately wanted to lie and say of course Beau would change. Only she didn't think Jagger would believe her.

"I guess we have to wait and see."

twenty-eight

Paris hadn't heard from Jonah since she had offered sex. She didn't know what his absence meant, but she knew it wasn't good. The most frustrating part wasn't even how much she missed him—which she did. It was not knowing why he was upset. She had logic on her side, so why was he being so weird?

Fortunately summer was busy season so she was able to distract herself with work. Deliveries were frequent and customers plentiful. The Saturday bake sales had people lining up to the parking lot.

Late morning she was busy unloading crates of sweet corn when Tim swung by, flats of blackberries on his hand truck.

"Maybe I'm being paranoid," he said, not quite meeting her gaze, "but there's some guy playing with Bandit out back. He's got to be thirty, so it seems strange he's throwing a ball for your dog." He paused and looked at her. "Usually it's kids, you know. Not grown men. But maybe I'm reading the whole thing wrong."

Paris immediately started for the rear of the store. Tim fell into step with her.

"You have good instincts," she said, even as she told herself not to assume the worst. Anxiety and fear immediately turned off the logical front part of her brain, causing her to react with a fight-or-flight response. Or in her case, rage.

But she trusted Tim. They'd worked together for years and she knew he looked out for her.

Sure enough, some skinny guy in dirty jeans and a torn T-shirt was out with Bandit just beyond the picnic area, throwing a tennis ball. Bandit raced after it and brought it back, his tail wagging as he enjoyed the game. The guy squatted down and hugged him, then stood and threw the ball again.

Her dog had always been friendly, she told herself, and she'd worked with him to get him to the place where he assumed every stranger was a friend. It was a good quality in a dog— especially one that interacted with the public, including lots of kids. But right this second, she wished Bandit was a little more standoffish.

She couldn't say why. Sure, the guy looked like he was experiencing hard times, but that didn't matter. Tim's gut instincts were part of her unease. She would guess part of her reaction came from the way the guy hung on to Bandit a little longer after each throw.

She gave a sharp whistle. Her dog immediately abandoned the ball and ran toward her. The whistle was his recall signal. No matter where he was or what he was doing, when he heard the sound, he found her.

The guy turned and spotted her and Tim. For a second she would swear she saw fury in his expression, but it was gone so quickly, she figured she had to have imagined it.

"Hey," he said, waving to them then collecting the ball and walking toward them. "That your dog?"

"It is." She smiled. "He's great, isn't he?"

"Sure is. I had a dog just like him until about a year ago. His name was Oscar." His mouth turned down. "Cancer. He went fast." He stopped in front of her. "I was just playing with him. I didn't mean nothing."

He was standing too close and she immediately wanted to

back up. Wariness had her on alert and she had no idea why. Technically nothing bad had happened.

"It's fine. He likes to make new friends. Were you shopping for anything in particular? We just got in a new shipment of sweet corn. It's the peak of the season. Oh, and the blackberries are especially good right now."

His gaze shifted from her to Tim, as if trying to figure out the other man's place in their conversation. But when Tim didn't speak, the guy turned away.

"I stopped to look around," he said. "I'll be going now."

Paris smiled at him. "Then you have a good day."

She and Tim returned to the store. As he'd promised, the man drove away in a battered SUV.

Tim sighed. "I probably shouldn't have said anything. He was just throwing a tennis ball."

"I'm glad you told me. There was something about that guy."

"You felt it, too?"

She put her hand on Bandit's head. "I'm going to keep my man here close today. I doubt that guy will come back, but let's watch out for him, just in case."

She returned to work. Bandit was happy to stay within arm's reach—there were still plenty of customers for him to greet. About an hour later, she was surprised to see Jonah and Danny. When the boy spotted her, he ran toward her, arms outstretched.

"Paris!"

"Hey, you." She hugged him tight. "I didn't know you were stopping by."

She kept her attention on him to avoid looking at his father, unsure how much awkwardness there would be after their last conversation.

Jonah joined them and gave her a friendly smile. "He's been missing you and Bandit. I said we could visit."

"I'm happy to see you both."

"Can I take Bandit out back and play?" Danny asked, already starting in that direction. "We won't go near the road."

Paris started to mention that maybe it wasn't a good idea, but then told herself that the guy from earlier was long gone.

"You've got ten minutes," Jonah called out.

"Oh, Dad. I know."

"You have to be somewhere?" she asked, more for something to say than because she was prying. So far there hadn't been any tension or any anything. It was like he'd never turned down her offer to have a summer affair.

"I have a conference call in half an hour."

"You can leave him here if you want and I'll drop him off later this afternoon."

He frowned. "You're busy at work."

"It's not like I'm a surgeon. Danny usually has fun when he's here and everyone looks out for him. Besides, I enjoy his company. I'm good if you want to leave him."

"You sure?"

"Yes." She smiled. "Go do your mogul thing." She glanced at her watch. "I'll take him to lunch and bring him back around two."

Something flashed across Jonah's eyes—an emotion maybe. She couldn't tell.

"Thanks, Paris. I know he'll enjoy being with you a lot more than being stuck at home, having to be quiet."

He hesitated a second, then walked away. She refused to watch him go, so headed out back to tell Danny about the change in plan. He whooped with excitement then raced to her office to get one of Bandit's Frisbees.

"Stay where we can see you," she told him as he ran back to her dog.

"I know what to do, Paris. I'm not a baby."

"No, but you're my responsibility and I take that very seriously."

He waved in response and started throwing the Frisbee. She

told Tim that Danny was out with Bandit, so he would spread the word and everyone would be aware of where he was.

"No sign of that guy," Tim told her. "I've been watching."

"Me, too. I guess it was just one of those things."

She relieved one of the cashiers so she could go take a break. Once Paris was free to leave the register, she grabbed a couple of cold drinks from the machine in the break room and walked toward the back. She couldn't see Danny or Bandit, but the grassy area was big and there were plenty of—

She heard Danny scream. She dropped the drinks and ran toward the sound. When she barreled out of the rear door, she saw Danny racing down the feeder road that paralleled the freeway. He was running hard, not looking back. She could hear him calling out something.

Fear clutched her as she debated running after him on foot or getting her truck. She shouted his name, but he didn't look back, so she ran for her truck. Once she was inside, she went down the road and pulled in front of Danny, forcing him to stop.

"What were you thinking?" She demanded as she jumped out. "You don't take off like that. You don't—" It was only then she realized Danny was sobbing as if his heart was breaking.

"He took Bandit," he gasped, wiping away tears. "There was a man. He said he was your friend and Bandit knew him. Then he grabbed him." More tears flowed as he pointed down the road. "We have to get him, Paris! We have to!"

Terror kicked her in the gut. She knew exactly who the boy was talking about. The guy from this morning hadn't gone away at all—he'd waited for the right moment to steal her dog.

She hustled Danny into her truck. "I'm taking you back to the farm stand, then I'll go after him."

"No! That'll take too long. Just go, Paris. We have to get Bandit back."

She knew if she went back she would lose any chance of finding the SUV, but what about Danny?

"Please," he begged. "Just go."

She jumped into the driver's side and waited while Danny fastened his seat belt, then took off. As her truck raced forward, she called for help.

"Nine-one-one. What is your emergency?"

"Who am I talking to?"

"What? My name is Clarice. What's your emergency?"

Paris felt a rush of relief. At least she knew the operator. "Clarice, it's Paris. Some guy came to the farm stand and stole Bandit. I think he's heading north on the feeder road. He's in a red Ford Explorer. It's pretty beat-up and maybe ten or fifteen years old. I didn't get the license."

She paused, wondering if Clarice was going to tell her to knock it off. That 911 wasn't for dognapping calls.

But the other woman immediately said, "What a jerk. I've got a couple of units in the area. Let me call them and we'll see if we can find this guy. I can't believe he took Bandit. Hang on. I'll be right back."

Paris continued to speed along the feeder road, passing cars and searching for the SUV. Her heart pounded. Next to her, Danny shouted, pointing. "I see him. The car's up there."

She followed his direction and thought she caught sight of the SUV. Seconds later, Clarice was back on the line.

"They're headed in your direction."

"We think we see the guy," Paris told her. "Oh, he just turned onto Third."

"Keep your distance. I'd tell you not to follow him, but I know you won't listen. Just stay back, Paris. I mean it. Someone crazy enough to steal your dog is crazy enough to do other things."

"I know. I'll be careful. I just want to keep him in sight so I can tell the police where he is."

Only, when the SUV entered a residential neighborhood, she had to get closer to keep up with him. She rounded a corner to find the SUV had pulled across the road and come to a stop, as if trying to block her. Paris slammed on the brakes.

"Get down," she told Danny as she unfastened his seat belt. She pointed to the footwell. "Crouch down in there."

Danny did as she asked. She called 911 and told Clarice where they were, then studied the vehicle, not sure what to do. Staying where she was seemed like the safest option. Only then the guy got out of his SUV. He held his hands up by his shoulders, as if showing her he wasn't armed, but he started walking toward her truck.

"Stay here," she told Danny. "Don't move. He doesn't know you're with me, so you'll be safe down there."

The boy nodded, his eyes huge.

Paris got out and circled around to the rear of her truck where she pulled a tire iron out of the toolbox bolted there. She could hear Bandit barking from the SUV. Her heart was pounding as fear flooded her, but she told herself to be strong. Bandit and, more importantly, Danny were depending on her.

"Hey, what's that?" the guy asked, his tone startled. "I'm not going to hurt you."

"Stay back," she told him.

"I wanted to know why you're following me. I didn't do anything."

"You stole my dog."

His eyes clouded with confusion. "What are you talking about? I didn't take anything."

What? Paris stared at him. "You're saying you don't have a black-and-white dog in your SUV?"

"Sure I do, but that's my dog. Oscar."

Was he kidding? "You said your dog died of cancer a year ago."

"That never happened. Oscar's fine. Hey, what's wrong with you?"

Now Paris didn't know what to think. She looked from the

man to the SUV, then whistled loudly. From inside the vehicle she heard even more frantic barking.

"That's my dog," she said. "I can prove it. He's wearing a collar with a tag and he's got a microchip."

The guy's expression seemed to crumple. "No. He's Oscar. He's mine."

He took a step toward her. She raised the tire iron. At the same time she carefully slowed her breathing. She needed to stay focused on what was happening and not give in to anger or fear. She had to stay in control.

"Keep back."

He paused, as if confused. The longer she talked to him the more Paris wondered if the guy was having some kind of mental breakdown. She wasn't sure if he actually believed Bandit was his dog or if it was a game, nor was she convinced he wasn't dangerous. With every desperate bark from the SUV, she felt a flash of fear and concern, but she kept her attention on the guy.

"I'm going to leave now," he said, inching back toward the SUV.

"That's not a good idea." She thought about mentioning the police, but decided that might spook him into driving off. "At least let me see Oscar. If he's not wearing the tag I gave him then I'll apologize for the mistake."

Before the man could answer, a police car turned onto the street in front of his SUV. Another one pulled behind her truck. Two officers got out, guns drawn. Paris immediately put down her tire iron and raised her hands.

"Hey, Paris," Brett, the first officer, said as he walked over. "Clarice told us what was happening. Where's Bandit?"

"In the SUV. He says he thinks it's his dog."

"That puts a spin on things."

Danny popped out of her truck. "Are you the police? I heard everything." He pointed to where the second officer was talking to the guy. "He's not right in the head."

Brett hid a smile. "We're going to have to figure out if he is or if he isn't. Let's go make sure Bandit's the one barking in there. If it's him, we'll take the guy back to the station and figure out what's going on."

They circled around the guy and the other officer and walked to the SUV. Paris immediately saw Bandit tied up in the back, his rear legs bound as he thrashed on the seat, trying to get free. She jerked open the back door and reached inside to unfasten the ropes. Bandit barked and whined as she worked.

"It's okay," she told him, fighting anger and worry. "I'm right here."

The knots were tight and she broke a couple of nails tugging at them, but they finally loosened enough for her to get him out of the constraints. He bounded forward, running into her as if he couldn't get close enough. She hugged him.

"It's okay, baby. It's okay. You're with us now."

He gave her frantic kisses before jumping out to run up to Danny and circle him as if making sure his boy was all right. Brett patted him a couple of times before reaching for the tag on the collar.

"I mean, I know," the officer said with a grin, "but I'm going to cross all the *t*'s and dot all the *i*'s."

Once he'd confirmed Bandit was who Paris claimed, he asked what had happened. On the opposite side of the street, the skinny, raggedly dressed man was sitting on the curb, sobbing into his hands. It seemed the other officer had explained that Bandit wasn't his and he didn't take the news well.

"What happens now?" Paris asked.

"We take him back to the station and figure out who he is."

"You're going to arrest him, aren't you?" Danny asked. "Stealing a dog is against the law."

"Yes, it is, young man."

Danny glared at the dognapper. "I hope you put him away for a long time."

★ ★ ★

Niles Masters–Smythe's English accent matched his dapper appearance. He was tall and slim, with short hair and what Cassie would guess was permanently tanned skin. Despite the nearly eight-five degree temperature, he wore a sports jacket over a button-down shirt. His trousers were freshly pressed, his shoes perfectly shined and he carried some kind of hat—maybe a fedora?—in one hand. He should have looked ridiculous and out of place in her cave, but instead he seemed perfectly at home as he studied each of the barrels, knocking on them, testing the strength of the hoops. He'd already spent over an hour going over the paperwork, despite the fact that she'd scanned it all and had emailed it to him weeks ago.

Niles circled the barrels one last time, then smiled at her. "Excellent. Once I confirm the sample I took today matches the one you sent to me, we'll be ready to move forward. Interesting that there are only nineteen barrels. I would have thought twenty. Although there's no reason it should be an even number."

"I thought about that, too," she admitted. "I wonder if Uncle Nelson kept a barrel for himself."

Niles winked at her. "That's what I would have done if I were him. Although a barrel is three hundred bottles, assuming the standard seven hundred and fifty milliliters. That's a lot of cognac to get through." The smile returned. "I think I would have liked your uncle Nelson."

They made their way into the bright sunlight. Niles put on his hat. He slipped the sample he'd taken into his pocket.

"I fly out late tonight so I'll get this to the lab tomorrow first thing. Once we have confirmation that it's as wonderful as we think, I'll get you a contract for the sale."

Cassie's head was spinning. Niles had only arrived last night. Were things really going to happen that quickly?

"You think the cognac will sell?"

Niles laughed. "Oh, my dear, you have no idea what a fuss

your little find is going to make. I have a few contacts I'll reach out to just to get the buzz going. I'm thinking we'll offer the barrels in nine sets of two. Unless someone comes forward with a ridiculous price, we'll take it all to auction. There will be about ten thousand dollars in expenses, plus my fee. If all goes according to plan, you should clear over two hundred thousand dollars."

He'd mentioned that number before and she'd nearly fainted. How could it be that much? But he'd been very convincing and now she almost found herself believing him.

"In the meantime, I'll make arrangements to bottle the last barrel. You'll keep as many as you want and we'll sell whatever's left at the auction, as well. Agreed?"

She thought about her orchard and the time and money it would take to get it producing again, plus the changes she wanted to make on the house. Although it made more financial sense to fix up the house and turn it into a rental, she couldn't bring herself to do it. She wanted to live here, on her land, and the cognac money was going to make that possible.

She was nervous, excited and also determined. This was a once-in-a-lifetime opportunity and for the first time ever, she was going to take a chance on something that made her happy.

She held out her hand to Niles and smiled. "Agreed!"

Paris called Jonah to tell him what was going on, only to have him say he was on his way. Clarice had called his mother to share what was happening and she'd told him. Less than five minutes later, he drove onto the street. Brett looked up at him.

"The father?"

"That's him."

Paris waited while Jonah ran toward them. Danny grinned when he saw him.

"Dad! We caught a bad guy. He tried to steal Bandit, and Paris and I chased after him. Paris told him to give us back Bandit. It was so cool!"

Jonah hugged his son tight, looking from her to Brett over Danny's head.

"Someone tried to kidnap Bandit?"

Brett glanced where the other officer was putting the man into the back of the car. "I need to call for a tow truck. You got this?"

Paris nodded.

"I'll be back in a few to answer any questions."

When he'd walked away, Jonah pulled Paris close. "Are you all right? What happened?"

She felt the tension in his body and heard the concern in his voice. Now that the danger was passed, she wondered how long it would be until her own emotions hit her.

She explained about the guy who'd showed a strange interest in her dog. As she spoke, some of her calm drained away, leaving her a little light-headed. No doubt a result of the adrenaline easing.

"He came back while I was playing with Bandit," Danny said eagerly. "He started talking to me and Bandit. It was like he knew him, so I thought he was a friend of Paris's." His face fell as he turned to her. "Is it my fault he took 'im?"

"No," Paris said quickly. "Of course not. How could it be your fault? He stole a dog, Danny. None of that is on you. In fact, you were really brave." She glanced at Jonah. "He screamed for me when the guy took Bandit." She hesitated, not wanting to get Danny in trouble, but Jonah had to know. "He, ah, took off down the street after them."

"What?"

Jonah's voice was practically a yelp, but Danny stood his ground. "I had to, Dad. I love Bandit and I was responsible for him. The man just grabbed him and ran. At first Bandit didn't do anything. I guess he thought the man was a friend, but then he started to struggle and bark. I screamed and ran after them."

"Down the road."

Danny dropped his head. "I know I'm not supposed to do that." He looked up. "But this was an emergency."

"You could have been hit by a car."

"He could have gotten away."

"I went after him," Paris said quickly. "In my truck. I got Danny inside." Now it was her turn to feel uncomfortable. "I should have brought him back to the farm stand. I'm sorry."

"I told her no." Danny stared at his dad. "We had to go after the bad guy."

"I didn't plan to do anything," Paris said. "I called 911 and thankfully got Clarice, who sent the police. I stayed back, but I did follow him. I wanted to know where he was going. When he drove into a residential neighborhood, I told her the location."

Danny took over the story, explaining how the guy stopped and got out and Paris made him hide.

"It was like being in a movie," his son said eagerly. "Paris was the hero."

She explained about not wanting to confront the man, but added, "I knew I had to protect Danny. And then the man said the dog was really his and the police showed up."

She felt herself starting to shake. Bandit must have sensed what was happening because he moved close and pressed against her leg. The rush of emotion nearly overwhelmed her. She told herself to stay present. She would deal with what had happened later.

Jonah glanced at the street. "Is that yours?" he asked, pointing to the tire iron.

"Oh, I'd forgotten about that." She picked it up. "I keep it in the truck in case I get a flat."

He moved toward her and hugged her close. "You could have been killed."

"I'd never let anything happen to Danny. Jonah, you have to know that. I would absolutely stand between anyone and—"

He grabbed her shoulders and looked into her eyes. "You

could have been killed or hurt. I know you were protecting my son. I'm talking about you."

Oh. That made her feel better. "I was fine. I know how to take care of myself."

"You shouldn't have to."

She had no idea what that meant, but hey, the man was hugging her as if he would never let go and she kind of liked that. Only eventually, he did step back, leaving her feeling cold and alone.

Brett returned to them and answered Jonah's questions. Paris promised to be available should they need her. Before she was ready, they were all in the separate vehicles and driving away, Danny with his dad.

She sat in her truck, Bandit next to her. She leaned over and hugged her dog. "You're one popular guy," she whispered into his silky coat. "I could never stand to lose you."

Bandit nuzzled her hair before swiping his tongue across her cheek. She started the engine, but before she put the truck in gear, she thought about what had happened. Yes, the situation had been terrifying, but she'd managed to stay in her head rather than reacting. She'd faced down a man who scared her, but she'd done it in a normal, controlled way. Despite the fact that she'd been holding a tire iron, she'd never once thought about going after him. She'd been prepared to protect Danny and herself, but nothing more.

Twelve years ago, she probably would have swung that tire iron, she thought grimly. And once she hit him, there was a better than even chance that she wouldn't have been able to stop. She might have even killed him. Despite her fear and frantic worry for her dog and Danny, she'd been okay. She'd been strong, able to think rationally. All these years later, she'd been tested, she thought as she drove back to the farm stand, and she'd passed. She wasn't who she had been and she had a feeling she never would be again.

twenty-nine

Laurel watched Paris anxiously. Her friend waved her half-empty glass of wine.

"Stop monitoring me. I'm fine."

Paris had stopped by to tell her what had happened with Bandit and stayed for dinner. The girls were out having dinner at friends' houses and Cassie was working an evening shift.

"I'm fine," Paris repeated, even as she put her hand on her dog's back.

Bandit barely raised his head before stretching and going back to sleep.

"Obviously, he's been able to put it out of his mind," Laurel said, thinking it would be a long time until she could forget. "I can't believe some guy tried to kidnap your dog. And that you chased after him."

"Me, either. It's all very surreal. But he's in jail and that's what matters. Brett says he'll give me a full report in a couple of days, once everything's sorted out."

"You really threatened him with a tire iron?"

Paris grimaced. "Not threatening him. Protecting myself. And Danny."

"Hey, no judgment. You're my hero. I'm not sure what I would have done."

"For your girls, you would have done ten times as much."

"I'm glad you're feeling all right. You were so brave."

"I'm more happy about staying in control. That's a big step for me."

Laurel was glad she saw that. "You're not who you were. The good stuff is the same, but everything that made you so unhappy has been healed."

She thought Paris might protest, but her friend surprised her by nodding slowly. "I kind of agree with you, which feels very strange. I've spent so much time atoning for my actions and the things I said. Once I realized I was missing a lot of adulting skills I should have learned as a kid, I had a direction. I knew what I had to learn and my therapist helped me develop those skills in controlled situations. I got better at dealing with stress and annoyances. But I was never sure."

She looked at Laurel. "I wasn't willing to trust myself and now I think I might be ready to consider the possibility."

A huge step, she thought as she smiled. "Does that trust include a certain man?"

"I always trusted Jonah. He wasn't the problem."

"And now you aren't, either. Even if things don't work out with him, it sounds like you're finally ready to take a chance on a relationship. That makes me happy."

"I don't think *ready* is the right word. I'm still scared."

"But you know you're okay."

"I said I'm willing to consider I might be okay."

Laurel waved that comment away. "You are so there. And speaking of there, I can't believe how amazing my girls are."

Paris groaned. "Oh, no. You were going to tell me about Beau dropping in. I'm sorry. I should have asked what happened."

"You had a little dognapping on your mind. I get it." Laurel filled her in on the details of Beau's visit.

"I literally turned around and there he was," she said, starting her second rant of the evening. "I couldn't believe it. Just like last time. The man knew he was coming. He sat in an airport, for heaven's sake. He couldn't take thirty seconds and text me? He's such a jerk."

Paris waited patiently. Finally, Laurel wound down enough to add, "Jagger totally took him on, telling him he has to act right to be a dad and even Ariana tried to be strong. She held out for a few minutes before caving, but at least she made the effort. I'm so proud of them."

"You should be. They're growing up."

Laurel nodded. "More important, they're getting wise. They see what's happening and are dealing with reality rather than wishes. Having Stan and Val hang out with them was the best thing for them. And for me."

Paris smiled. "So your family's getting a little bigger. That's nice."

What? Laurel shook her head. "What do you mean? They're Colton's parents, not mine."

"You said you might visit them for Christmas."

"Well, yes, but that's different."

Paris stared at her without blinking.

"You're saying you think it's strange that I'd take the girls to spend the holidays with someone they don't really know. It would be after Christmas, by the way. I wouldn't run out on you or Marcy and Darcy. Plus the business. So really the week after Christmas. That's hardly the holidays."

"Close enough." Paris smiled. "Why are you resisting admitting Stan and Val are the parents you wish you'd had? I know I wish I'd had them in my life. They're so warm and caring. They know just what to say and how to act. Maybe with them around, I wouldn't have been so messed up."

Laurel reached out and grabbed her hand. "You're not messed up. You're my best friend and I'll love you forever."

"I'll love you, too, and hey, now I'm an even better friend. Isn't that nice?"

"You were always a good friend."

Paris laughed. "That's because when we were seven and I yelled at you, you punched me in the mouth."

"I was establishing boundaries."

"It worked."

They smiled at each other.

"We're in a good place," Laurel said happily. "I want to stay here forever."

"Sorry, kid. Life doesn't work that way."

"Well, it should."

Cassie was already regretting not ordering the pancakes. She'd gone sensible, with an egg white omelet and fruit while Jagger and Ariana had each ordered blueberry pancakes with bacon. Just the thought made her mouth water.

It was relatively early on a Saturday morning. Laurel had been up past midnight to work on next weekend's garage sale, so Cassie had offered to take the girls to breakfast. She'd thought she'd might have to wake them, but they'd both been up and dressed at exactly 7:05. They'd gotten to the diner before the weekend crowd.

As they waited for their order, she sipped coffee while the girls blew on their hot chocolate.

"Are you going to keep working at the bookstore?" Jagger asked. "I don't know how long it takes to fix an orchard."

"Westin thinks I can keep my regular job while we're working on the orchard," she said. "He thinks we'll get some fruit next year and have it mostly back to full production by the following year."

"I'll be fourteen then," Jagger said with a grin. "Nearly fifteen."

"I'll be a teenager!" Ariana sounded delighted. "I can't wait to be a teenager."

"It's a pretty fun time," Cassie told them, giving in to the inevitable and flagging their server. "Can I change my order?"

The fiftysomething woman laughed. "Blueberry pancakes and bacon?"

"Yes, please."

"I'll tell the kitchen."

When she'd left, Jagger asked, "When can we see your house? We want to know where you'll be living."

Her kind question filled Cassie's heart with affection. "We can go whenever you like. It's not much to look at, but it's a good house and I think I'll be happy there."

Ariana's brows drew together. "But we'll miss having you live with us."

"I'll miss that, too, but it's not for a few months and I'll still be close."

"It's not the same," Jagger told her, then sighed. "It's always like that. People change and move on."

"You're wise," Cassie said, thinking she should tell herself that same thing. Her family was changing and moving on— something that made her long to return home. Only she was doing the same, right here in Los Lobos. And somehow being here felt...right.

"Do you have a new kitchen at your house?" Ariana asked with a grin. "Mom says your apartment is much nicer than where we live, but I like our house. It's very us."

"Mom wants a new kitchen, but we have to save the money." Jagger sounded older than her years. "It's important to have a budget. If the garage sale does well, we'll be back on track with our savings."

Ariana's good humor faded. "It's because Daddy took all the money." She looked at Cassie. "We're not supposed to know, but we do."

Jagger looked surprised. "You're not supposed to know. You're too young."

"I'm the same age you were when he left, Jagger. I'm not a
baby. I'm part of the family and you shouldn't keep secrets."
She looked at Cassie. "I heard her talking to Mom about it."
Her voice lowered. "I'm glad I didn't know when it happened.
I would have been scared, but we're fine now."

Cassie was staggered by their maturity. At eleven or twelve,
she hadn't been aware of anything like money or stressors in her
family. She'd been too busy being the adored youngest child.
Her parents and older siblings had protected her from the real
world. Something she now appreciated.

"Are you going to marry Raphael?" Ariana asked.

Cassie nearly fell off her chair. "What? No. Marry him? We're
barely dating."

Jagger sighed heavily. "I told you not to ask the question.
People don't like to talk about that kind of stuff."

Ariana seemed undeterred. "But you're going out with him
and you like him a lot, don't you?"

"I, well, yes, we're dating and he's very nice." Which was
light-years away from marriage. "But we're, you know, not that
involved."

"But I've seen you kissing," Ariana said.

"People can kiss without being in love," Jagger told her.
"Persephone Wilson has kissed lots of boys and she doesn't care
about any of them. She says kissing a boy means power, but I
don't think anyone can give you power—you have to find it inside yourself."

Cassie was still caught up in the part about her marrying Raphael. But she told herself to put that aside and keep up with
the conversation.

"You're right, Jagger. Power and confidence do come from
within. They're about how we see ourselves and whose opinion
matters. Sometimes boys are confusing and they act like they
know everything, but they really don't. I'm sorry Persephone
is so willing to kiss a lot of boys. It sounds like she's desperate

to be liked, but going about it all wrong. She needs to respect herself. It's not wrong to kiss a boy—it's just important to do it when you're ready and for the right reason."

She'd had similar talks with her nieces. There was so much pressure for girls to grow up quickly and become sexualized. Cassie didn't want that for either Jagger or Ariana. She made a mental note to talk to Laurel about what they'd discussed.

Fortunately, the pancakes and bacon arrived just then, allowing her to change to a safer topic.

After breakfast, Cassie drove home. The girls hurried to the barn to help their aunts with all the prep work. She'd just made it inside to get ready for work when her phone rang. She glanced down at the screen and was surprised to see Faith's picture.

"Hey, you," she said. "Calling on a Saturday? Aren't you busy with your B and B guests?"

"Oh, Cassie." Faith's voice was thick with tears.

She instantly went on alert. "What's wrong? You're crying. Tell me." Her stomach clenched as she regretted her heavy breakfast. "Is someone sick? Are you guys okay?"

"Yes. We're fine. It's just, I miss you so much. I thought it would be easier having you gone. I thought it was no big deal—that you just needed some space to figure it all out. But nothing's been the same."

Cassie clutched her phone. "I miss you, too. Faith, there's something. Tell me."

"Holli was in a car accident."

"What?" Cassie's chest tightened as fear filled her. "What happened? Is she all right?"

"She's fine now. She spun out in the rain and hit a tree. She was a little banged up, but they released her from the hospital after keeping her for observation."

"Holli was in the hospital and you didn't tell me?" She practically shouted the question. "Did she get a concussion?"

"They don't think so. Like I said, she has bruises and broke her right arm."

"She broke her arm!" It was difficult not to sound frantic. "Why didn't you tell me?"

"It just happened a couple of days ago and I knew you'd worry. Once we knew she was all right, there didn't seem to be any point in upsetting you."

"I'm your sister! You're my family. If something happens I want to know."

Faith started crying again. "It's not just that. Garek dumped me. I thought things were going great, but he texted me the morning of Holli's accident and said he didn't want to see me anymore. No chemistry, he said."

The tears turned into sobs. "I thought we really liked each other. I slept with him, Cassie. Now I think that was all he was interested in. Just getting me into bed. Two days later, he walked away. I can't do this. There's too much and I'm all on my own. I have the B and B and the girls, then I get my heart broken and you're not here. I need you. Please come home. Please."

The words were a blow to the gut. Cassie nearly doubled over from the pain in her sister's voice. The need to be there, to fix things, was overwhelming.

"Yes," she said quickly. "Yes. I need to do a few things here first, but I can leave on Monday. I'll be there. I'll come home."

"You will?"

"Yes." There was a lot to do, she thought frantically. She had the orchard to deal with. Niles was taking care of the cognac, but she had so many people to tell.

"I'll quit my job and pack up. You're what matters. You and your kids and Garth. I need to be home."

"And we need you. It was dumb to make you leave. I don't know what we were thinking."

Words Cassie had been longing to hear. Words she needed to hear. Los Lobos was great, but she belonged back in Bar Harbor.

She understood that world. Her family was there. Living here had never been about forever, she told herself. It was a means to an end. She had always planned to serve out her six months and then go back.

Except even as the thoughts formed, a voice in her head whispered that she hadn't been planning on going back. And that the life she wanted was here.

She pushed the words away. Her family needed her and she was going home.

Cassie showed up at Raphael's house after work. She'd given notice, finished up her shift and walked away, ignoring the emotions swirling inside of her. Guilt for leaving, she thought, but also regret. She'd grown to like the quirky little town. She'd made friends, had started to belong, but none of that mattered. Family came first.

Telling her boss had been hard enough, but telling everyone else was going to be so much worse. She had connected with people here and she was going to miss them.

Raphael opened his door and smiled at her. "Did we have a date?"

"No, but I—"

She'd been planning on telling him she was leaving town, but before she could speak, he drew her into his arms and kissed her. Really kissed her. She felt the need and passion in his kiss and instantly responded.

"I know what I said," he murmured, kissing his way along her jaw to her neck. "I know we should wait, but I want you, Cassie. You're all I think about."

Her head arched back as he nibbled his way down her collarbone. Her body was on fire and she didn't want to deny him anything. Yes, she had to tell him she was leaving, but first she had to touch him and kiss him and...

Twenty minutes later, she was trying to catch her breath after the most incredible sex ever. Raphael stretched out next to her, his hand making a lazy exploration of her breasts.

"You're so beautiful," he whispered before kissing her again. "I can't get you out of my mind."

Contentment turned to pain as she thought about what she had to say.

He picked up her hand and kissed her palm. "Want to go get dinner?"

"Raphael, I'm leaving."

He sat up and stared at her. "What did you say?"

She pulled up the sheet to cover herself, then forced herself to look at him. "I'm going home to Bar Harbor. Faith needs me."

He went still. The warmth left his eyes as he shifted away from her, then stood beside the bed.

"You said you were staying, that you belonged here. I thought we meant something to each other."

All true, she thought, sitting up. "We do. I care about you."

"But you're leaving." He waved toward the bed. "You didn't think to mention that before we made love?"

"I wanted to, but I was a little swept away."

She meant the words to be light, but even as she said them, she realized how ridiculous they were. He was right—she should have stopped him, should have said something.

He pulled on his jeans before facing her again. "So we're done."

"What? No. I don't want to end things."

"Then what did you see happening? I live here, Cassie. This is where I teach and I work."

"I know, but..."

"But what? We have a long-distance relationship? We Face-Time and fly back and forth?"

"I don't know. I hadn't thought that part through. Faith just asked me to come home."

His expression darkened. "Let me make sure I understand this.

You're saying the sister who insisted you leave, who basically tossed you out of the only home you've ever known now wants you to come back and you're going? I thought the purpose of leaving was to figure out what you want, not what Faith wants."

She knew he was both reacting out of emotion and a hundred percent right.

"She needs me."

"Today. What happens when she gets herself together in a couple of weeks and doesn't need you? When are you going to think about what you want and what's best for you?"

"She's my sister."

"She's using you."

Cassie glared at him. "You don't get to say that. She's not. She's all I have. She needs me and I have to go home."

"If that's true, then I guess we have nothing else to talk about."

Laurel tried to understand what her friend was saying. "You're leaving?"

Cassie stood in front of her, looking miserable. "Faith needs me. I have to go."

"I understand being there for family, but why not just fly back for a few days? Why are you upending your whole life for her? I thought you wanted to stay here. I thought you were excited about the orchard."

"I am." Cassie twisted her hands together. "You don't understand. Faith is my sister."

"I'm actually pretty clear on the relationship. What I don't understand is your reaction to what she said. Her daughter was in a car accident, but she's fine. Faith's new boyfriend dumped her and that's hard, but what are you going to do when you get there that you can't do from here?"

Laurel held up her hand. "I'm sorry. This isn't my business. This is your family and you have to make your own decisions. I just feel bad because I thought we were your family, too."

She also thought Cassie was making exactly the wrong decision, but she knew better than to say that. Pushing her friend away wouldn't help.

"You are my family," Cassie said softly. "I feel awful. I don't want to go. It's just, she needs me."

"Are you sure that's it? Are you sure you're not running away because you're scared about all the possibilities you have here?"

Cassie stepped back. "What do you mean?"

"All your life you've done what you had to because you were 'needed.' You've told me and told me how you weren't living your life, you were living *their* lives. You helped. That was your role. For the first time ever, you're doing what you want to do. Yes, it's a little scary, but it will be worth it. Change is hard and this is a huge change. So maybe it's not a surprise that when Faith tells you to come back, it doesn't occur to you to say anything but yes."

"You're saying I'm a coward."

"I'm saying you love your sister and you want to be there for her, but again I ask, why can't you just go back for a couple of weeks, then come home?"

Cassie glared at her. "Maybe you'd understand this a little more if you had a sister, but you don't."

"I have a sister."

They both turned as Jagger walked into the barn. "Are you fighting? I could hear you yelling at each other."

"We're not fighting," Laurel said automatically. "I'm a little upset because Cassie's leaving."

Jagger immediately swung her gaze to the other woman. "Where are you going?"

Cassie seemed to shrink a little. "I have to go back to Bar Harbor. My sister needs me."

"So for a visit? Will you miss the garage sale?"

"Not for a visit," Cassie told her. "I'm moving back home."

Jagger looked stricken. "For good? But why? You live here now. If you go, you'll miss everything."

"I'm sorry. This is important."

Jagger's eyes filled with tears. "You're walking away, like my dad. We should never have trusted you."

She ran off. Laurel knew she should probably tell her daughter not to talk to Cassie like that, only she kind of didn't blame her. Jagger was saying exactly what she felt. Emotions swirled. Not only disappointment, but something else. Something bigger.

"You're making a mistake," Laurel said quietly. "This isn't the lesson you're supposed to learn."

"I have to go back. I don't have a choice."

Laurel hugged Cassie. "You make me sad."

"Because I won't stay?"

"Because you're still living for them and not for yourself."

thirty

Laurel was torn between guilt about how she'd talked to Cassie and belief the other woman was making a mistake. Not that she could convince her of that. In fact, a case could be made that Cassie's life choices weren't her business. Only her kids were upset she was leaving and Laurel would miss her, too. She wanted to blame Faith for asking Cassie to come home, but knew the real fault lay with Cassie herself. She'd reverted to old patterns. She wasn't ready to stand up for herself—something Laurel could totally relate to. How many times had she given in to one of Beau's crazy plans? How many times had she said yes when she meant "hell, no!" Loving someone, loving family, was always a complication. Sometimes a good one and sometimes not.

A topic she would come back to, she told herself as she surveyed the overstocked shelves, boxes and bins that represented all she had to take over to the fairgrounds starting Friday. She'd rented a cargo van, and Paris and Colton were taking the day off. Marcy and Darcy would help, as well. They only had a short time to get their extra-large corner booth set up before the sale started Saturday morning. The girls would spend the long weekend with friends, dropping by to see her a few times. The fairgrounds' recently upgraded secure Wi-Fi would make running charges easier. She was about as ready as she could be. Well, ignoring the pricing she still had to do, not to mention packing up.

She was knee-deep in packing paper when Colton walked into the barn a little before five. Her heart immediately flip-flopped in her chest and her girly bits sighed.

"I wasn't expecting you," she said, walking toward him. "You get stood up by a band or something?"

Jagger and Ariana abandoned their pricing chores and raced toward him. Jagger got there first and flung her arms around him.

"Colton, you're here."

He put down the grocery bags he'd been carrying and hugged her tight, then pulled Ariana close.

"You two working?"

"We're helping Mom," Ariana told him. "She's packing and we're pricing. It's called teamwork."

"I've heard about that." He smiled at her over her daughter's head. "I can help, too." He nodded at the bags. "I'll make dinner, then help pack."

Laurel stared at him as if he'd started speaking German. "I'm sorry, what did you say?"

"I'm going to make dinner then help you pack. Unless you want me to do something else. Whatever you need, I'm here."

Jagger looked at her, seeming just as confused. "It's the dinner part," she said.

Laurel nodded. "Yes, that's the puzzling bit. You're cooking?"

Now it was Colton's turn to frown. "Just burgers and a couple of salads. I made the pasta salad this morning before work. It's my mom's recipe. The other one is a simple green salad. So not really cooking in the traditional sense."

"You can't make dinner," Ariana told him. "Men don't know how."

"Some men do."

"Daddy doesn't."

And he'd never helped in the kitchen, or anywhere, Laurel thought, still surprised. "You brought us dinner?"

He sighed. "Yes. It shouldn't be this big a deal."

"Because you knew I was scrambling and you thought it would help."

"Yes."

Now it was her turn to fling herself at him. She wrapped her arms around him and told herself there was absolutely no way she was going to cry. "That's the nicest thing anyone's ever done for me."

His strong arms held her against him. "It's just burgers."

"It's thoughtful and you got up early to make pasta salad." She looked into his smiling eyes. "You are a good, good man and I'm so grateful."

He grinned. "This is kind of nice. I can't wait to see how you three react when I make spaghetti." He stepped back. "I'll start the grill. You three keep working. I'll yell when dinner's ready."

"What about setting the table?" Jagger asked, sounding scandalized.

"I'll figure it out."

"Mom, is he for real?"

Laurel smiled at him. "I think he might be."

Less than an hour later, Colton called them in to dinner. As promised, the table was set, the milk for the girls poured. There was a glass of red wine at her place and at Colton's. Two salads, one pasta, one green, were in serving bowls and four juicy burgers sat on plates.

"You're amazing," Laurel told him. "Thank you so much."

"Anytime. Don't pass out, but after dinner, I'm going to clean up."

The girls gasped in mock shock, but Laurel's surprise was real. "I can do it."

"Yes, but you don't have to."

They washed their hands and sat down. As they passed the condiments and salads, Ariana leaned close and whispered, "Daddy would never have cooked us dinner."

"It's a nice surprise," Laurel whispered back, opting for the neutral response.

Once they were munching on their burgers, Jagger said, "I heard from Stan and Val today. We're going to FaceTime after the garage sale. They want to hear all about it."

Ariana nodded vigorously. "We have a texting group—just the four of us. They ask us about camp and stuff. I wish they could have stayed longer."

"Me, too." Jagger ate some of her salad. "I hope we get to go see them this fall."

Colton looked at Laurel as if asking what the girls knew about the holiday visit. As the details hadn't been worked out and she didn't want to disappoint them, she said, "Me, too. When the garage sale is over, we can all sit down with our calendars."

"I like that they want a specific date," Jagger said. "It's good to know when things are going to happen. We can have fun just thinking about seeing them again." She turned to Colton. "Our dad never tells us when he's going to see us. And we don't hear from him much. I wish he was more like your mom and dad."

Laurel touched her arm. "I know you do, sweetie. I wish that, too. But you set ground rules and now it's up to your dad to respect them."

"What if he doesn't?"

Ariana put down her fork. "I think about that, too, Mom. We told Dad he has to act right and stay in touch. We said he had to let us know ahead of time when he's coming to see us, but what if he doesn't?"

"Let's give him a chance to surprise us in a good way with his behavior," she told them. "If he doesn't then we'll sit down as a family and make a plan."

"If he can't bother to call us and stuff, I don't want to see him," Jagger said flatly. She looked at her sister. "But you'll still want to forgive him."

Ariana nodded slowly. "I know you're right, but I'm not strong like you. He's our dad and I need to see him."

"Whatever happens, Beau will always be your father," Colton told them. "Nothing will ever take that away. You have good memories and hopefully you'll make more."

Ariana nodded, but Jagger glared at her plate. "I don't know why he's such a selfish jerk all the time. He would never make us dinner like you did, Colton." Jagger turned to her. "Mom, do you regret falling in love with him?"

After all they'd been through, it was hard to remember why she had. "Our lives were different back then," she said instead. "We were both young and your dad was charming."

"Is it different being in love with Colton?" Ariana asked.

The question stunned her. "Why would you ask that? We're not in love, honey. We're friends."

Good friends. Great friends. He'd become a part of their lives and had shared his parents and was always around and so fun and funny, and yes, sexy, but they couldn't go there so she rarely thought about it, or what had happened that morning in his bed.

Jagger gave her a surprisingly knowing look. "Come on, Mom. We're not babies. Maybe you were friends before, but you're not now. You're together. Everybody knows."

Laurel felt her cheeks flush and she had no idea why. She glanced at Colton, who was watching her with an intensity she found unnerving.

"Tell them," she said helplessly.

"We're friends." He smiled at her daughters. "Men and women can be friends. It's kind of nice to be that way, but if anything changes, you'll be the first to know."

Jagger glanced between them, as if unsure she believed the explanation. "I heard Val and Stan talking and they think you're in love. They said you were good for each other and they were happy Colton had found someone so great."

Oh, crap! Of course Stan and Val thought they were a couple—that was what Colton had told them. Now what? She couldn't explain the whole fake girlfriend thing.

"That's very sweet of them to say," she murmured instead. "I like them a lot, too."

Ariana leaned toward Colton. "If you marry Mom, I want to be in the wedding. I've never been in a wedding before and I think I'd like it a lot."

"No wedding," he said easily. "But thanks for letting us know where you stand. Did I mention I bought ice cream for dessert?"

"What flavor?" Jagger asked.

"Sweet vanilla chocolate chip."

"You went to the fancy ice cream store!" Ariana's voice was its typical "I'm excited" shriek. "We never get to go there because it's too expensive. Oh, Colton, you're the best."

And just like that, the subject was changed. Laurel told herself to relax, that her daughters were naturally curious about Colton. Val and Stan's comments hadn't helped. But with a little time, everything would get back to normal.

Only she couldn't forget Ariana's question about being in love. After dinner—and Colton really did the dishes—she sent the girls into the family room to watch TV while she retreated to the barn to continue packing. A half hour later, Colton joined her.

"The dishwasher is doing its thing," he said as he approached. "The counters are wiped down and the girls are watching something age appropriate." He stopped in front of her. "Are you going to let me help, or did we just hit a speed bump we have to deal with?"

She looked away and gave what she hoped was a casual laugh. "I have no idea what you're talking about."

He grabbed her wrist. "Yes, you do."

Somehow, she found herself looking into his dark eyes. "I'm

sorry about what Ariana said or asked or whatever. It was awkward."

"I'm okay with the question."

"Oh, good."

Only as she said the words, she suddenly wondered if he meant he wasn't bothered by the topic as in it didn't matter, or he didn't mind what she'd asked because he wanted to hear the answer?

"We're friends," she added brightly. "Good friends. You're a really good friend and I like that. And you. As a friend. Being friends is the best."

She silently screamed at herself to shut up, only to add, "I'm glad we got past being fake friends to actually being real ones and—"

He got her to stop babbling by leaning in and pressing his mouth to hers. She immediately went still as all her senses focused on the warm, delicious feel of his kiss. When he drew back, she wanted to whimper.

"You kissed me."

One corner of his mouth turned up. "I did."

"Friends don't kiss on the mouth. I've been tight with Paris since we were seven and we've never done that."

"We're a different kind of friend." His gaze met hers. "I liked you from the first time I saw you at the UPS Store." His smile returned. "Which was, I believe, the first time we danced together. There was just something about your combination of determination and exasperation that sucked me in. The more I know you, the more I like you. Hanging out with my parents just solidified how I feel."

As he spoke, her skin got all prickly in a weird I'm-uncomfortable-and-don't-know-what-to-say kind of way. She wanted to run away. She wanted to cover her ears. She wanted him to kiss her again.

"I'm crazy about you and the girls," he continued. "I have been for a while and I think the three of you like me, too. I'm honest, steady and you can depend on me to be a whole lot more than your friend, Laurel."

Her mouth was dry, her mind blank. He wasn't making sense. She tried to speak, but there were no words.

"Just something for you to think about," he said, right before he lightly touched her cheek, then turned and walked away.

She watched him go. After a few minutes, her brain started working again, although it was torn between telling her to run after him and getting pissed. She went with the latter because it was safer and there was energy in anger.

What had all that been about? He was crazy about her? In what way? And they were only supposed to be friends, so what was up with the kissing? And why did he have to be so damned cryptic?

She turned back to her packing, careful not to take out her temper on the carnival glass punch bowl set. Stupid man. Did he or did he not understand the meaning of the word *friend*? Now he'd gone and ruined everything, just like a man.

Paris answered the unexpected knock on the door and was surprised to find Jonah on her front porch. It was nearly eight in the evening on a weeknight. Not that the date and time had anything to do with why the man was here. At least she didn't think so.

"Hi," she said, stepping back and letting him inside. Bandit rushed over. "Did I know you were stopping by?"

"Not unless you're telepathic."

That made her smile. "Unfortunately, no. I never developed the skill, although it would be an interesting one."

He didn't smile at her attempt at humor, which ignited worry. Was this not a friendly visit? "Is Danny all right? Is your mom?"

"Everyone is fine. I came by because I wanted to talk to you. Is now okay?"

That really depended on the topic, she thought cautiously. If he was here to tell her he and Danny were going back to DC, she could go the entire day and not hear that. But his leaving was inevitable and she was going to have to adult her way through it.

They settled on the sofa in the living room. Bandit curled up in a club chair and dropped off to sleep.

Jonah angled toward her. "You talked to the police?"

"Yes, the guy has warrants in three states so there's a fight about where he's going to be extradited first. Obviously, he has some mental health issues, but he's also a criminal, which makes what happened even more terrifying. But he'll be out of the state soon, facing what Brett assures me are serious charges." She offered a faint smile. "Worry about him coming back for Bandit won't be keeping me up at night."

"I'm glad." He rested his forearms on his thighs as he leaned toward her. "You were incredible. You kept Danny safe and rescued Bandit."

"I was lucky. The whole thing could have gone incredibly wrong. But we're okay now and that's what matters." She hesitated, then decided to tell him the whole truth. "I'm really happy about how I got through the situation. I stayed in my head. I was scared and angry, but I didn't react out of either emotion."

"You're strong," he said. "I'm admire you so much."

"Me?"

"Yes, you. Look at all the things you've done. You've dealt with your issues while still keeping the essence of who you are."

While she liked his praise, it also made her uncomfortable. "I think calling my frightening temper an 'issue' understates the obvious, but thank you for being generous."

His gaze locked on hers. "I'm still in love with you."

She felt her eyes widen as she struggled to understand what he'd just said. There was no way she'd heard him correctly, she thought frantically, although she couldn't string another meaning together that made sense.

"I'm still in love with you," he repeated. "I was in love with you when I left all those years ago, but I couldn't deal with the anger and uncertainty. But my leaving didn't change how I felt. I pretended it was over, so when I met Traci I thought I could care about her. We were well suited and she made it clear she was interested in taking things to the next level. I thought I'd forgotten you. But you were always there—between me and her. You were always the point of comparison. I missed your laugh, your intensity, the way you felt every feeling, even the bad ones. The longer Traci and I were together, the more I knew leaving you had been a mistake."

He paused, glanced at the floor, then returned his attention to her. "When she got sick, I knew I couldn't leave and when we lost her, I was devastated and confused. I wanted to reach out, but didn't know how. My mom didn't say much about you and I didn't want to ask. When she asked me to help during her knee surgery, I knew I'd been given a second chance. I was determined to get to know you again and see if what I was feeling was real or just in my head."

She wasn't sure she was breathing or if her heart was beating. She stayed upright so maybe both were happening. She couldn't believe what he was telling her. He still loved her? He'd loved her all this time?

"You're even better than I remember," he told her. "You're so beautiful and kind, generous and sexy. I can't figure out why you don't have ten guys lined up, demanding you go out with them, but you don't and I'm grateful. I know I screwed up before by leaving, but I was wondering if you'd give me another chance to prove myself."

The tears came without warning. One second she was staring at him in disbelief and the next she was sobbing as if her heart were breaking and she didn't know why.

"Paris?"

He stood and pulled her to her feet, then hugged her close. "What's wrong?"

"I don't know. I'm sorry. I can't believe what you told me."
She sniffed and tried to get control. "It doesn't make sense. How
could you love me? I'm awful."

"You're amazing."

"I screamed and threw plates and terrorized you."

"You've changed."

She wiped her face and stepped back. "You can't ask for another chance. You can't. You never did anything wrong. It was
me. All of it was me."

"It wasn't." His tone was gentle, his expression loving. "It
was both of us."

He was wrong about that and nearly everything else, she
thought, still stunned by his words. He loved her. No, he loved
her and wanted another chance?

"You can't ask for that," she repeated, more tears falling down
her cheeks. "Jonah, you get all the chances, forever. I'm the one
who doesn't deserve any of this. I'm the one who ruined things.
I know that. I've thought about it, talked about it, journaled
about it, taken so many classes, joined groups. Our past is not
on you, it's on me, and I'm sorry I destroyed what we had."

"You didn't destroy it. If you remember, I started this conversation by telling you that I'm still in love with you."

"I'm having a little trouble understanding how that's possible."

"You're kind of unforgettable." He smiled. "In a good way."

"So you want to start dating?"

His smile turned rueful. "I was hoping to start a little further
down the road, but sure, dating is good."

"When are you leaving Los Lobos?"

"I'm not."

She stared at him, her heart pounding in her chest. "You're
staying?"

He nodded. "I have to go back to DC and arrange for our
things to be moved here. Then there's the issue of where we'll
live. I was thinking that was a conversation you and I should

have, but maybe I'm rushing things." He moved closer. "I want what you want, Paris. I know I come with a son, which could be a complication, but I'm thinking you like Danny and I know he adores you, so maybe it's okay?"

"I love Danny. He's terrific and so not a problem."

Instead, the problem was her and the past. Getting involved with him and Danny meant every day there would be a thousand ways to mess up. What if she got mad? What if she forgot how to be a normal person? What if—

What if she stopped living in fear? What if she finally allowed herself to be happy? Those were the real questions, she told herself. She'd been waiting for this man for over ten years. Now he was standing in front of her, offering her everything she could possibly want. Her choices were a lifetime of happiness or one of regret. Was that even a question?

"Yes!" She flung herself at him. "Yes. I don't know what you're asking, but yes. I'm in. I love you, too."

"That's what I wanted to hear."

He held her so tight, she couldn't breathe, but that was okay. Just being next to him, feeling his familiar body against hers, made her happy. The rest would take care of itself.

"So we're dating," he said, after he'd kissed her about fourteen times, each kiss lingering just a little longer than the one before. "Exclusively. With the idea of getting to know each other and then getting married."

He'd said the *M* word—just like that. The man knew no fear. She told herself to answer in kind. "Yes, and having a couple of kids together."

"I'd like that."

"Me, too." She kissed him, then tilted her head. "If you're so in love with me, why did you turn down my offer of sex?"

He groaned. "I didn't want our time together to be about getting off. I want the whole thing and I was afraid if we started having sex without admitting how we felt, somehow everything would get messed up." He stared into her eyes. "Just to set the record straight, I absolutely wanted to make love with you that night and all the nights since and a bunch before."

"You must be having trouble sleeping."

He chuckled. "You have no idea."

She took his hand in hers. "What time is your mom expecting you back?"

"I told her that if things went well, I'd be home in time for breakfast."

"That's quite the assumption."

"It was more hopeful than assuming."

She glanced at her watch, then smiled at him. "That only gives us about ten hours. We'd better get busy."

thirty-one

"Colton's ruined everything," Laurel grumbled as she sat in her friend's office at the farm stand. She had a million things she should be doing and no will to do any of them. The entire "we're a different kind of friend" conversation, not to mention the kiss, had thrown her.

"Why did he have to talk like that? We're just friends. I like how things are. We had sex that one time and it was amazing, but we've moved on, like the grown-ups we are. I feel that we lied to his parents, but that's on him."

"You like his parents. You want to visit them over the holidays."

"Yes, but that doesn't mean I want to marry him. Did I tell you Ariana mentioned being in the wedding? The wedding! As if. We're not getting married. We're not getting anything. You know why?"

"Because you're friends?"

"Yes. I'm not stupid. Not anymore. I've learned my lesson. It took a long time and a lot of heartache. It took Beau buying that monstrosity with a mortgage we couldn't afford, then cleaning out our bank accounts and running away. Any thoughts I had of ever being in love with anyone died that day, and I have no interest in reviving them. There is no way on this planet or any other than I'm going to be a fool for love ever again."

She waved her arms. "We're all idiots. Look at Cassie who's about to race back home to be with her ungrateful family. I can't tell you how much I want to call her selfish sister and tell her how horrible she is. Cassie finally starts to get it all together, but they can't stand the thought of her being independent, so they summon her back and now everything is ruined. The girls are upset and I am, too. It's just a waste."

"Plus, Colton's in love with you."

"What?" Laurel sprang to her feet and pointed at her friend. "Take that back."

"No." Paris's expression was more smug than worried. "You know I'm right."

"I absolutely do not. There's no love. He never said that. And I don't love him. Just because things worked out between you and Jonah last night doesn't mean the rest of us want some kind of sappy, lovey-dovey crap messing up our hair."

"Why would it mess up your hair?"

"I don't know. I was making a point."

"Actually, you weren't even making sense. You want to sit down now?" Paris asked.

Laurel sank onto the chair and covered her face with her hands. "What's wrong with me?"

"Aside from not making sense, you're tired and confused."

That was true, Laurel thought. She'd tossed and turned all night, thinking about what Colton had said.

"Why did he have to ruin what we have? We were good as friends."

"You're still friends. That's not over."

"It feels different." She looked at Paris. "I really am happy for you and Jonah. You were always good together, and you love Danny, and Bandit will be thrilled." She'd always liked the whole Paris-and-Jonah connection. "Plus, he's moving here and selfishly, I don't have to worry about losing my best friend."

"You can never lose me," Paris told her. "If you try to run, I'll hunt you down and cling to you like an emotional burr."

"Not an attractive visual."

"I'm okay with that. So what's the real problem with Colton?"

Laurel groaned. "The man said he's crazy about me and the girls. Then he kissed me. Like a kiss-kiss. Not a 'let's have sex and forget it' kiss. There's a difference."

"So I've heard."

"I don't want a man in my life. I'm happy alone." She paused as she questioned her words. "Happy-ish." She paused again. "Mostly happy. Except for, you know, Jagger and how she hates men."

"Which she doesn't anymore," Paris pointed out. "It's been weeks since she made one of her comments. She adores Colton and Stan and Jonah. She's been incredibly mature and strong about her dad. She's thriving, Laurel, and not because you're afraid to fall in love. She's thriving because you invited someone good into your life."

"No, I didn't. Colton offered to be my friend. It's all on him." She sagged back in the chair. "And then he ruined it. Stupid man."

"Okay, that's enough." Paris stood and shifted onto the corner of the desk between them so she was looming. Her expression was stern, her voice determined. "I'm going to talk and you're going to listen."

"Maybe I am and maybe I'm not," Laurel said automatically. "Sorry. I have no idea where that came from."

"Your inner toddler. You're acting out because you're scared to hear what I'm going to say."

Absolutely, she thought, but what she said was, "Maybe."

Paris ignored her. "Brace yourself because I'm going to tell you a version of what you told me after Jonah left."

Laurel straightened. "How can you remember what I said then? I sure don't."

"Because the words are burned into me." She paused. "You have a problem and if you don't fix it, you're going to live a very unhappy life. Worse, you're going to take your daughters down with you, and you'll never forgive yourself."

She drew in a breath. "You're acting out of fear. Do what you've always done and you'll get what you've always gotten. A crappy personal life without the loving partner you deserve, because you can't accept that picking Beau doesn't mean every other man is bad and every relationship sucks."

"It's not just Beau," Laurel said, interrupting. "It's my parents marrying and divorcing over and over. It's Marcy and Darcy, who lost their close sisterhood over a man. It's everyone."

"It's not everyone. You've convinced yourself it's better to think that because then you don't have to try. You get to be unhappy and it's not your fault. It's fate, it's men, it's whatever, but it's never you, so you don't have to change, but it is you, Laurel. It's all you. These are your rules and your consequences and if you're unhappy, you're the reason."

Laurel did her best not to cry. She knew the tough love was exactly what the name implied. Hard things to hear that came from a full heart.

"Colton's a great guy," Paris told her. "He's in love with you and your girls, and that freaks you out. The irony is you're just as in love with him, only you can't admit it, because that's not the story you tell yourself. Beau was always going to be a disaster. In some ways I think part of the attraction was *because* he was a disaster. Beau was going to affirm all your ideas about love and marriage. It was never going to work with him and you found that comforting."

Laurel shrank back. "That's not true."

"I think we both know it is. Colton isn't Beau. He's not like anyone you've ever known before. He's caring, he's dependable, he's—"

"Steady," Laurel whispered.

He always did what he said, showed up on time, took care of business. He was a rock and so good for her and her girls.

"Being with Colton would be totally different than being with Beau," Paris told her.

"But I'm scared."

"So?"

Despite all her swirling emotions, Laurel laughed. "This is you being supportive?"

"This is me kicking you in the butt."

"It hurts."

"It's supposed to. Don't lose this guy. If you do, you'll regret it forever. You'll mess up yourself and you'll mess up your girls. Believe me, living with what-ifs sucks."

Leaving Los Lobos was taking longer than Cassie had anticipated. She'd met with her real estate agent and told her that instead of selling the strip of land by the highway, she was putting the whole thing on the market. She'd avoided Raphael and Westin, but had gotten stuck for two extra days while Niles made final arrangements to ship the barrels.

Not running into Laurel and her girls had been easier than she thought. Laurel was scrambling to prepare for the garage sale, and she hadn't seen Jagger or Ariana since she'd told them she was leaving.

She also hadn't been eating or sleeping. She felt sick to her stomach most of the time and was constantly questioning her decision. But every time she weakened, she got a text from Faith saying how grateful she was. Even Garth had called to gruffly tell her he missed her and that sending her away had been a mistake.

She was going home, she thought as she drove to the orchard for one last time. She'd had such big dreams, but that was all they were. Dreams. She didn't know anything about farming or trees or avocados. She was a city girl who'd always worked in a bar and a B and B. She didn't have talent or the skills. Running an orchard wasn't realistic. Not for someone like her.

She parked on the driveway next to the house. Morning fog lingered and the air was cool as she got out and looked around. The house stood tall and stately, a little old-fashioned, but solid, she thought. She'd been looking forward to fixing it up and moving. She'd been excited to finally have a place of her own. Only soon the house would be gone.

Once the local developers got wind of the huge parcel of land she was selling, she would get plenty of offers, her agent had assured. The house wouldn't be updated. It would be torn down, the trees razed, their roots dug out.

"You're really leaving."

Westin was walking toward her. The old man looked like someone close to him had died. He seemed more bent than ever, and his usually smiling face was closed.

"I have to go home. My family needs me."

"So you're running away."

"I'm not," she protested. "They're my family."

"Then take care of the problem and come back. We had a plan, you and me. This could have been your legacy."

She pressed her lips together. "Westin, be serious. I couldn't take care of all this. I don't know how."

"I was going to teach you. You're a smart one—you'd catch on fast."

"I grew up over a bar in Maine. I don't know anything about nature or trees. I'm not the right person."

"Your uncle thought you were. This is where you belong, Cassie. Why can't you see that?"

"They need me," she repeated. "I have to help."

"No convincing you?" he asked.

She shook her head.

Without a word, he turned and walked away.

She watched him go, ignoring the tears running down her

cheeks, refusing to acknowledge the pain in her chest. She'd told him the truth. Family mattered and it was time to stop pretending she could have a life here.

On her way out of town, she stopped by the farm stand. The fall fruits—pears, apples and grapes—spilled out of containers. Tourists mingled with locals, filling shopping baskets and talking to each other. She spotted Paris at a cash register. When the other woman saw her, she waved over an employee and walked toward her.

"Heading out?" she asked.

Cassie nodded. "Everything is done. I wanted to say goodbye. You can yell at me if you want to."

Paris shook her head. "I'm not going to pile on, kid. You're in enough pain."

"I'm just sad. I'll be fine. Once I'm home and back in my routine, everything will be great."

She tried to sound enthusiastic as she thought about her small life in Bar Harbor. She would work for Garth and help at the B and B, hang out with her nieces.

"With the money from the sale of the cognac, maybe I'll buy a condo. I could go to college."

Paris studied her. "Cassie, are you sure you want to leave or are you doing what you've always done?"

"Faith needs me," she said for the four hundredth time.

"Yes, and you're a good sister for rushing to her, but what happens when Faith doesn't need you anymore? If going home makes you happy, then great, but I'm worried that you're defining yourself by how you help, not who you are. You're thinking about what makes them happy, sacrificing yourself and your future. You were going to rebuild an orchard and have a good relationship with Raphael. What about all that?"

Cassie didn't want to think about it—it hurt too much. "I have to go home," she repeated. "It's where I belong."

Paris hugged her. "Like I said, I can feel your pain. I just wish

I could do something about it. If you're serious about leaving, then I wish you the best. If you change your mind, you'll always be welcome here. We're going to miss you."

Cassie hung on to her. "I'll miss you, too. So much." Paris was the strongest person she knew. She couldn't imagine not having her to run to when she was confused or had a question.

She pulled away before she weakened, then hurried to her car. She made it through town and was heading for the freeway when she started to cry. After a few seconds, she pulled over to get herself under control. She parked right in front of a large sign that said "Thanks for visiting Los Lobos. We can't wait to see you again!"

At the sight of the cheerful font, the colorful lettering, more tears spilled onto her cheeks. She gave in to sobs and covered her face, letting all her emotions jump to the surface. She was overwhelmed by feelings. Guilt, regret, determination and a whole bunch of déjà vu.

Paris was right. She was doing what she'd always done, she thought sadly. Helping, fixing, showing up when needed because that was her place in the family. That was what was expected and she needed to be needed. And Faith needed her.

Only hadn't her sister told her she wasn't really helping? That for years and years her "help" hadn't mattered? Garth had said the same thing. He'd told her he could handle the bar and his personal life and she was fooling herself by thinking she made a difference.

She stared out the windshield, her tears stopping as quickly as they'd started. She wiped her cheeks, then sniffed. So which was it? Either she was there for her family because they needed her or they didn't need her at all and she was fooling herself. Because it couldn't be both.

She called her sister.

"Hi," Faith said happily. "Are you on the road? I can't wait to see you."

"I have a question."

"Sure."

"When you and Garth had your intervention, you both said that I was wrong to think I was needed. That you were fine without me and that it was time for me to start my own life. You said I was hiding, that I was still that fourteen-year-old who lost her parents and couldn't cope. Some part of me must have believed you because I packed up and left. And you know what? I found a life here. I have friends and a guy I care about and dreams, Faith. I have dreams about the orchard. It's scary because I don't know anything, but Westin was going to teach me and I was excited."

She cleared her throat, telling herself to stay in control. This was information she needed. "Then out of the blue you want me back. So I rip my new life apart and pack up my car because that's what I've always done. I've sacrificed everything for my family. But if I wasn't helping before, how can you need me now? I love you. You're my sister and I'll always be there for you, but I can't help thinking how after telling me I never sacrificed anything for you, you're asking me to give up everything I've grown to care about."

Over the phone, she heard Faith start to cry. Her gut twisted and the guilt settled on her shoulders with the weight of an elephant. Nearly every part of her screamed to stop talking and start driving. She had to get home!

But there was a tiny voice whispering for her to be strong. She wasn't sure if it was Paris or Raphael or just some piece of herself, but it said she deserved to be happy. She deserved to have dreams and that what Faith asked of her was not only unreasonable, it was selfish and wrong.

"I want to stay," she said, surprising herself with the words, then feeling the rightness of them. "I want to see where I am in two years or five years. I love you so much and I'll be there for you, but I'm not moving back. I'll fly out and spend a couple of weeks, but then I have to come home."

"I'm sorry," Faith said, her voice thick with pain. "Oh, Cassie, I'm so sorry. You're right. I wasn't thinking. I was so hurt by getting dumped and it brought up all kinds of junk from when J.J. died. Then Holli was in the car accident and it was more than I could handle. I needed you with me to hold my hand and get me through the tough stuff. Because that's what you've always done. You've gotten me through it."

The tears returned. Cassie let them fall, knowing she needed to hear her sister's words and believe them.

"I want to help," she said.

"I know and I love you for it. I freaked out. I was lost and scared and you were gone and I wanted you back. I was only thinking of myself. I'm so ashamed of how selfish I was. I can't believe I was willing to wreck everything you've built. Don't come home. Stay there. You're happy." She gave a rueful laugh. "Maybe a little too happy. I think I've been jealous."

Her eyes widened. "Of me? How can you say that?"

"Because you're doing so great. You're excited about your future, you have friends and plans and dreams, not to mention Raphael. Sometimes I feel trapped and stuck. Don't get me wrong. I love the B and B, but it's a lot of work, plus the kids."

Her first instinct was to say she would be there in five days. Then she reminded herself that she wasn't going to do that anymore. She was going to be supportive and loving, but not toss away everything that made her happy simply to please her sister. Just as important, she had to believe that deep down, Faith didn't want that.

"I've missed you," her sister said. "So much. I've had you here since you were born." She gave a strangled cry-laugh. "You're a part of me and losing you has been hard."

"You haven't lost me."

"I know. I didn't mean it that way. It's just different now. Cassie, I'm so sorry. I've been awful and selfish and I'm really embarrassed to think I asked you to come back because I was having a bad day."

It had happened because that was what both of them had always done, she thought sadly. Faith had asked and she'd been there. No matter what. Yes, "helping" had been an excuse not to live, but both her siblings had taken advantage of what she wanted to give.

"I think we're all still dealing with the past," she said slowly. "With the patterns created after Mom and Dad died. I think it's time for us to find new ways to deal with our issues."

"You're right. So you're staying?"

"I am." She wasn't sure how she was going to put the pieces back together, but however it turned out, she belonged in Los Lobos. "But I can fly back for a few days."

"That would be nice, but I'm going to say no. Just hearing you were coming back made me feel better. Later this fall, the kids and I will visit you instead. I want to see everything you've been telling me about."

"I'd like that a lot."

"I love you, Cassie. Thank you for calling me on my crap. I'm so proud of you. Unfortunately, I still have a little growing of my own to do, but I'll get there."

They talked for a few more minutes, then hung up. Cassie turned the car back toward town. She felt as happy as the Grinch at the end—when he'd come down the mountain and was tossing presents to everyone. She didn't have presents, but she was coming home.

But as she crossed into the city limits—such as they were—she wondered how much her impulsiveness had cost her. She'd cut a lot of ties and now she was going to have to find out which ones had survived the trauma.

Her first stop was Westin's house. The old man opened the door, his expression grumpy and annoyed.

"What do you want?"

Despite his hostile tone, she grinned. "To say my stupidity has passed and I'm back for good. From here I'm going to the real estate office to say I've changed my mind about selling. I want to keep to our original plan, Westin, to rebuild the orchard with your help."

He continued to frown. "Why should I believe you?"

"I have no idea, but I mean what I said. I want to work with you, if you'll give me a second chance."

His face relaxed. "All right, all right. If you're sure. Be at the orchard bright and early tomorrow morning and we'll get started."

"Not tomorrow," she told him. "I have to help Laurel get ready for the big garage sale." Assuming her friend was still speaking to her. "But Monday. I'll be there."

"You'd better be."

Undoing the sales contract only took a few signatures. The real estate agent was understandably disappointed, but did as Cassie asked. And there was still the big strip of land to sell. The agent perked up at the reminder and said they might have an offer next week. Which sounded great to Cassie. She had a feeling Westin was going to enjoy spending her money.

From there she made her way to the big Victorian house. She parked in her usual spot then ran to the barn where she knew Laurel would be frantically getting ready for the big sale on Saturday. Sure enough, her friend was busy packing glassware. Jagger and Ariana were pricing and then handing her items. All three of them looked up when she hurried inside.

"Cassie." Laurel sounded more surprised than happy to see her. "I thought you were leaving."

Cassie told herself to keep being strong. It was the only way to undo what she'd done. She'd messed up and fixing it all was on her. Laurel was a warm, loving person. Surely she would understand.

"I was such a fool. I can't go back to Bar Harbor. I don't belong there. I overreacted. Yes, Faith was in trouble, but your point was a good one. Why didn't I just fly out for a few days? Why did I have to drop everything?" She held up both hands. "I guess I'm not done growing up."

Both girls stared at her. Ariana looked at her mom. "What is she talking about?"

Laurel smiled. "I think she's saying she's back."

"I am. Permanently. I made a mistake and I'm sorry. I'll try not to mess up like that again and if my beautiful apartment is still available, I'd love to have it back."

Jagger stared at her. "But you left."

"I did. I'm sorry. I was reacting rather than thinking."

Jagger shook her head. "I'm starting to think grown-ups don't know anything. It's a little scary that you're all in control of everything."

Laurel grinned. "Get used to it. Things don't make any more sense when you're older, either." She turned to Cassie. "I should raise your rent."

Some of Cassie's tension eased. "I'd rather you didn't, but that's up to you."

"I'm kidding. I wouldn't do that." She pulled a set of keys out of her pocket. "Welcome back."

Ariana rushed toward her. "You're staying! I'm so glad. Are you helping with the garage sale? We still have a lot to do."

Cassie hugged her. Jagger and Laurel joined them. The four of them stood there, holding on tight. Cassie felt the love and knew she'd made the right decision. Next time she would try not to make the wrong one to begin with, but hey, apparently that was what it took for her to learn.

When they'd all stepped back she said, "Let me get my stuff into the apartment, then I'll come back here to help."

"What will you do about your job?" Laurel asked.

"Ask if they'll take me back and if they will, be the best employee ever."

"Welcome home, Cassie."

"Yes," Jagger said, grinning. "Welcome home."

thirty-two

Cassie spent the day helping out Laurel. They got the rental van filled with boxes, then did the same with her minivan. Tomorrow they'd all be up early to get the first load in place before repeating the process a couple of more times. It was going to be a long weekend. But a good one, she thought.

She'd texted her boss and had an appointment to explain herself Monday afternoon. If she got her job back, great. If she didn't, she would find something else. Eventually, she would have cognac money and the proceeds from the sale of the land, but she was hoping to put that toward the house and the orchard. She'd also spoken with Paris, who was her normally understanding and accepting self.

They quit work a little after six. Cassie begged off dinner. She had one more person to talk to.

She drove to Raphael's house and parked on the far side of the driveway, then settled on his front porch. As she waited, she thought about what she wanted to say. First, that she was sorry. Then she would explain what she'd done wrong. But that part was easy. What was hard came after. She had a feeling he was going to ask her what she wanted and she needed to be ready with an answer.

He was such a great guy. Ignoring how incredibly handsome he was, she knew his real appeal was what was on the inside. He was caring, honest, kind, funny and smart. Her biggest problem was she still wasn't sure what he saw in her. But obviously there was something and maybe it was time to simply accept what he said as the truth.

She spotted his truck down the road and immediately felt her heartbeat increase. Nerves made her slightly nauseous and she wondered if she was making a mistake, assuming he would want to see her again. Running seemed to make the most sense, but she ignored the need. She was done reacting to outside influences. From this moment going forward, she was going to think clearly and decide the right thing for her. And that meant facing Raphael.

He pulled in next to her and got out of his truck. When he walked around the front, her breath caught. That man, she thought, coming to her feet.

His baseball cap was pulled low enough that she couldn't see his eyes or know what he was thinking, but that was okay. She knew what *she* was thinking and for now, that was enough.

"I thought you'd be halfway to Maine by now," he said.

"I didn't leave until this morning so technically I wouldn't be out of California yet. Besides, I didn't leave."

"I can see that."

He stopped in front of her and pulled off his cap. His blue eyes were filled with a lot of emotion, but she still wasn't sure about his reaction to her being here. Again, not her rock.

"I realized I'd made a mistake," she continued, and went on to explain what she'd learned about her reaction to Faith's call. "I told her I wasn't leaving. That if she needed me, I'd visit, but I wasn't leaving Los Lobos. This is where I belong."

"So what happens now?"

"I try to pick up the pieces of my life. Laurel let me have my apartment back. I start work with Westin on Monday. I don't know about my job yet, but I'm hopeful. And then there's you."

"What about me?"

Ugh. She'd been hoping for a little bit more from him, but given how she'd acted from the very beginning of their relationship, she could see how he was done meeting her halfway. So it was up to her. Did she want to be brave and ask for what she wanted or was she going to let the best man she'd ever known walk away?

She opened her mouth, then closed it, as she searched for the right words. She wanted to say something sincere and honest so she could tell him how much he mattered to her and how she wanted them to be together. Maybe if she explained about...

"I'm in love with you."

The words came without warning and once she'd said them, she nearly fainted. She'd never ever told a man she loved him, mostly because she never had. It wasn't so much that she wanted to call them back—she didn't—it was more the fact that she'd been that brave. However Raphael reacted, yay her.

For a second he didn't say anything. Then he gave her a slow, sexy smile that had her toes curling and her thighs trembling.

"Yeah?"

"I love you," she repeated. "You terrify me, but that's not something we need to discuss."

He moved closer. "Don't be afraid, Cassie. You're my love-at-first-sight person. I thought you knew."

His what? "You love me?"

"From the second I saw you, I knew. Something inside of me said you were the one." The smile returned. "Scared the shit out of me. I'm not that guy. I'm usually slow to commit. But I couldn't resist you and I didn't want to."

He loved her? She stared at him, trying to take it all in. Raphael the Perfect loved her?

She managed to avoid saying, *But why?* Only to realize there really weren't any words necessary. She wrapped her arms around him and raised herself on tiptoe.

"Then it's probably really good I came back," she murmured right before he kissed her.

Friday morning, Laurel was up at four thirty. She would be putting in long hours through the weekend, then sleep for two days. The weather was supposed to be perfect for the garage sale, the other vendors were excited about the promise of big crowds.

She dressed and went to the barn to work until it was time to wake the girls. They would help until early afternoon, then hang out with their friends. Everything was going according to plan—the only question she had was about Colton and their recent discussion about how he was *crazy about her and her girls*.

Her talk with Paris had been reassuring and disconcerting at the same time. She got what her friend was trying to tell her and part of her believed Paris. But was being afraid such a bad thing? Didn't fear keep people safe? Even as she thought the question she knew she was lying to herself. She wasn't being safe, she was being stunted. Like Cassie, she was reacting to her past and shouldn't she do something about that?

"Not today," she said aloud and she stepped out into the dark stillness of the predawn hours. "I'll deal with this next week."

She barely started packing the last of the boxes when she heard a car. Before she could investigate, Colton walked into the barn with mugs of coffee and a box of doughnuts.

She stared at him in surprise. "I don't mean to sound ungracious, but it's, like, five thirty in the morning. What are you doing here?"

He handed her the coffee. "I'm here to help with last-minute prep work."

"But you're already helping at the garage sale. This is too much."

He shook his head. "It's not. I want to be here."

"But it's so early."

"You're really focused on the time."

His voice was teasing, his body language relaxed. Obviously, he wasn't upset or concerned about their last conversation, which confused her.

"If you're here to show the girls you're going to show up when you say, they already know that."

"I'm not here for the girls." He sipped his coffee. "I'm here for you."

If she'd been the fainting kind, this would have been the moment. "I don't understand."

"They already believe in me. You're the tough one to convince. I'm here because I want to help and because I want you to get that I'm not the running kind."

She had no idea what she was supposed to say to that. "Thank you." She frowned. That sounded wrong. Or unresponsive or something.

He smiled again. "Don't worry about it. We'll have plenty of time to deal with all this later. Right now we have the garage sale to worry about."

He was as good as his word. He packed the rest of the items then drove her van over to the fairgrounds while she woke the girls and drove the rental truck. Marcy and Darcy were there, and Cassie and Raphael were also waiting to help them unload. From the looks the two of them kept giving each other, she had a feeling the reunion had gone well.

A stab of envy surprised her. She was happy for her friend—why wouldn't she be? But part of her wondered what it would be like to give her heart again. Only she knew the price of that and she wasn't willing to pay it.

Except with Colton, a relationship didn't seem so risky. She liked him and trusted him. His parents were great and they had showed her what forty-plus years with the right person could look like.

Something to think about later, she thought as they set up her large corner booth. By six that night it was done. Colton and Raphael would be on standby on Saturday and Sunday to deliver more merchandise as the current inventory sold down. She was ready for the weekend. Exhausted but ready.

Colton followed her to the rental place where she turned in the cargo van, then he drove back to her place. As they stood staring at each other she had the thought that she should invite him in to dinner or something. Only things weren't as easy as they had been and she didn't know what to say.

"What do you want from me?" she blurted.

"I can't answer that without terrifying you."

Not what she'd been expecting, she thought, looking at him.

"What do *you* want from me?" he asked.

An interesting question. Being friends was good, but was there something better? Was she willing to risk being a fool again? Or was Paris right and was that not what would happen?

"Did you want to date?"

He smiled. "Dating would be good. As long as we're exclusive. I don't want some guy stealing you away."

She laughed. "I'm not the date-two-guys type." She looked into his eyes. "Are you in love with me?"

"Yes."

Her breath caught. "Just like that?"

"It's the truth."

"But it's complicated."

"Not to me. You're a little like Alex in *Night into Day.* You're afraid to take what's offered because of the stories you tell yourself. Love doesn't make you less, it makes you strong. It makes you safe. Love gives you wings, Laurel, and I for one can't wait to see you fly."

She realized that the most surprising part about his words was the fact that she believed him. Totally and completely.

"Can we take it slow?" she asked.

He leaned in and kissed her. "We can take it any way you want."

He was as good as his word. Through the long weekend of the garage sale, he never left her side. Tuesday morning, he showed up early to see the girls off to their first day of school and he was the one shooing her back to bed to catch up on her rest.

By Friday, she was willing to consider that being afraid made her an idiot. No man on the planet was better than Colton and if she didn't admit how she was feeling, she was not only stunted emotionally, she was a bad example for her kids.

She dropped off the girls at school, then made her way to his place where she knocked on his door and waited until he answered.

His slow, sexy smile was the best welcome yet.

"You're unexpected," he said, stepping back. "Here for some coffee?"

"Actually, I'm here for sex. Then maybe coffee."

Without missing a beat, he pulled his phone out of his jeans pocket. "Let me text the studio that I'm taking the day off."

When he was done, she looked into his dark eyes and thought about how life with him was going to be great.

"I'm in love with you, too," she whispered, right before she kissed him. "I thought you'd want to know."

He pulled her close. "You know how to turn a man's head."

She laughed. "Only yours."

"You're the one I want, too. Laurel. I love you."

There were logistics to work out, she thought as he led her to his bedroom. Telling the girls they were in love. Figuring out when and where they were going to get married. Because she didn't doubt that was what he wanted and now that she was willing to believe love just might give her wings, she knew she could fly anywhere with him. As long as they were together.

★ ★ ★ ★ ★

SUMMER BOOK CLUB

Reader Discussion Guide

Suggested Menu
Orange-Avocado Salad (recipe follows)

questions for discussion

Please note: These questions contain spoilers. We recommend that you finish the book before you read the questions.

1. There are three "inciting incidents" in this book—that is, three moments that propel each heroine's storyline, the moment when each heroine realizes that something needs to change. What are the inciting incidents for Laurel's, Paris's and Cassie's stories?

2. With which heroine did you identify most closely? Why?

3. Laurel worried that her own post-divorce attitude toward men was negatively affecting her daughters. Do you think she was right to worry? Why or why not? If you have children, how do you think your beliefs influence theirs?

4. Should a single mom with no male relatives make sure her kids have positive male role models? If so, what strategies do you think would work? Explain. How did you feel about Laurel's plan to find a guy friend?

5. How did Colton show that he was different from Laurel's ex-husband? Did Colton's parents impact your feelings toward him? If yes, how so?

6. Paris, on the other hand, married a great guy but lost him due to her temper. How did learning this make you feel about her? Did your feelings change as you read the book?

7. Jonah told Paris that he was partially to blame for their divorce. What do you think he meant? Do you agree with him? Why or why not? Do you think divorce is ever just one person's fault? Share your thoughts.

8. Through years of therapy and hard work, Paris was able to change how she reacted to the world, but she was afraid to believe in herself. What finally convinced her that she could risk falling in love again?

9. Why did Cassie's siblings kick her out? Were they right to do so? Why or why not?

10. In the beginning, all Cassie wanted to do was return home to Maine, but by the end, she saw the future of her dreams in Los Lobos. What changed her mind?

11. Although none of the men in the story was a point-of-view character, we learned a lot about them through their interactions with Laurel, Paris and Cassie. Which guy appealed to you the most—Colton, Jonah or Raphael—and why? What did you think of their reactions to the romance novel they read for book club? Do you know any men who read romance novels?

12. How does the structure of the summer book club in *The Summer Book Club* differ from the structure of your book club? How does your book club choose which book to read

next? How do you *wish* your book club would choose? Does your book club continue to meet in the summer months, and if so, do you change the types of books you read during the summer?

13. Laurel and Paris both own unusual businesses—Laurel's Happy Finds and the Los Lobos Farm Stand, respectively. Which of these businesses appeals most to you? Why? (Note: Laurel's Happy Finds is inspired by a real-life business with a strong social media presence—someone Susan Mallery truly admires. If you'd like to know the name of the business, message Susan via Facebook or Instagram. She is @susanmallery in both places.)

14. In *The Summer Book Club*, the women read classic mysteries one summer, old-timey science fiction the next and '80s romances this summer. What should they read next year?

orange-avocado salad

4 cups salad greens
1 ripe avocado, diced
1 bunch green onions, sliced
3 oz crumbled feta cheese
¼ cup pecan halves and pieces
Segments of 1 orange, cut into chunks
¼ cup maple-balsamic-orange vinaigrette, recipe follows

Toss all ingredients together, then serve. Delicious without meat
or with cooked chicken, ham or shrimp.

maple-balsamic-orange vinaigrette

Juice and zest of 1 orange
2 Tbsp balsamic vinegar
2 Tbsp maple syrup
1 clove garlic, minced
¼ tsp salt
⅛ tsp black pepper
½ cup olive oil

Combine all ingredients except olive oil in a blender. Blend well, then add oil in a slow stream. Yield: about 1 cup.